SOMEBODY I USED TO KNOW

DAVID BELL

BERKLEY
New York

BERKLEY
An imprint of Penguin Random House LLC
1745 Broadway, New York, NY 10019

Copyright © 2015 by David J. Bell
Readers Guide copyright © 2015 by Penguin Random House LLC
Excerpt from *Somebody's Daughter* copyright © 2018 by David J. Bell
Penguin Random House supports copyright. Copyright fuels creativity, encourages
diverse voices, promotes free speech, and creates a vibrant culture. Thank you for buying
an authorized edition of this book and for complying with copyright laws by not
reproducing, scanning, or distributing any part of it in any form without permission.
You are supporting writers and allowing Penguin Random House to continue to
publish books for every reader.

BERKLEY and the BERKLEY & B colophon are registered trademarks of
Penguin Random House LLC.

ISBN: 9781984802637

New American Library trade paperback edition / July 2015
Berkley mass-market edition / December 2018

Printed in the United States of America
1   3   5   7   9   10   8   6   4   2

Cover photos: shadowed figure by Elisabeth Ansley/Arcangel Images;
farmhouse on fire © Sandra Cunningham/Trevillion Images
Cover design by Anthony Ramondo

Also by David Bell

For Molly

CHAPTER ONE

When I saw the girl in the grocery store, my heart stopped.

I had turned the corner into the dairy aisle, carrying a basket with just a few items in it. Cereal. Crackers. Spaghetti. Beer. I lived alone, worked a lot, and rarely cooked. I was checking a price when I almost ran into the girl. I stopped immediately and studied her in profile, her hand raised to her mouth while she examined products through the glass door of the dairy cooler.

I felt like I was seeing a ghost.

She looked exactly like my college girlfriend, Marissa Minor, the only woman I had ever really loved. Probably the only woman who had ever really loved me.

The girl didn't see me right away. She continued to examine the items in front of her, slowly walking away from me, her hand still raised to her mouth as though that helped her think.

The gesture really got me. It made my insides go cold.

Not with fear, but with shock. With feelings I hadn't felt in years.

Marissa used to do the very same thing. When she was thinking, she'd place her right hand on her lips, sometimes pinching them between her index finger and thumb. Marissa's lips were always bright red—without lipstick—and full, and that gesture, that lip-twisting, thoughtful gesture, drove me wild with love and, yes, desire.

I was eighteen when I met her. Desire was always close at hand.

But it wasn't just the gesture that this girl shared with Marissa. Her hair, thick and deep red, matched Marissa's exactly, even the length of it, just below her shoulders. From the side, the girl's nose came to a slightly rounded point, one that Marissa always said looked like a light-bulb. Both the girl and Marissa had brown eyes, and long, slender bodies. This girl, the one in the store, looked shorter than Marissa by a few inches, and she wore tight jeans and knee-high boots, clothes that weren't in style when I attended college.

But other than that, they could have been twins. They really could have been.

And as the girl walked away, making a left at the end of the aisle and leaving my sight, I remained rooted to my spot, my silly little grocery basket dangling from my right hand. The lights above were bright, painfully so, and other shoppers came past with their carts and their kids and their lives. It was close to dinnertime, and people had places to go. Families to feed.

But I stood there.

I felt tears rising in my eyes, my vision starting to blur.

She looked so much like Marissa. So much.

But Marissa had been dead for just over twenty years.

Finally, I snapped out of it.

I reached up with my free hand and wiped my eyes.

No one seemed to notice that I was having an emotional moment in the middle of the grocery store, in the milk aisle. I probably looked like a normal guy. Forty years old. Clean-cut. Professional. I had my problems. I was divorced. My ex-wife didn't let me see her son as much as I wanted. He wasn't my kid, but we'd grown close. My job as a caseworker for the housing authority in Eastland, Ohio, didn't pay enough, but who ever felt like they were paid enough? I enjoyed the work. I enjoyed helping people. I tended to pour myself into it.

Outside of work, I spent my life like a lot of single people do. I socialized with friends, even though most of them were married and had kids. I played in a recreational basketball league. When I had the time and motivation, I volunteered at our local animal shelter, walking dogs or making fund-raising calls.

Like I said, I probably looked like a regular guy.

I decided I needed to talk to that girl. I started down the aisle, my basket swinging at my side. I figured she had to be a relative of Marissa's, right? A cousin or something. I turned the corner in the direction she had gone, deftly dodging between my fellow shoppers.

I looked up the next aisle and didn't see her. Then I went to another one, the last aisle in the store. At first, I didn't see the girl there either. It was crowded, and a family of four—two parents, two kids—blocked my view. One of the kids was screaming because her mom wouldn't buy her the ice cream she wanted.

But then they moved, and I saw the girl. She was halfway down the aisle, opening the door of another cooler, but not removing anything. She lifted her hand to her mouth. That gesture. She looked just like Marissa.

I felt the tears again and fought back against them.

I walked up to her. She looked so small. And young. I guessed she was about twenty, probably a student at my alma mater, Eastland University. I felt ridiculous, but I had to ask who she was. I wiped at my eyes again and cleared my throat.

"Excuse me," I said.

She whipped her head around in my direction. She seemed startled that anyone had spoken to her.

"I'm sorry," I said.

But I really wasn't. In that moment, I saw her head-on instead of in profile, and the resemblance to Marissa became more pronounced. Her forehead was a little wider than Marissa's. And her chin came to a sharper point. But the spray of freckles, the shape of her eyes . . . all of it was Marissa.

If I believed in ghosts . . .

Ghosts from a happy time in my past . . .

"I'm sorry," I said again.

The girl just looked at me. Her eyes moved across my body, sizing me up. Taking me in. She looked guarded.

"I was wondering if you were related to the Minor family," I said. "They lived in Hanfort, Ohio. It's been about twenty years since I've seen them. I know it's a long shot—"

The girl had been holding a box of Cheerios and a carton of organic milk. When I said the name "Minor," she let them both go, and they fell to the floor at my feet. The milk was in a cardboard carton, but the force of it hitting the floor caused it to split open. Milk leaked onto the cruddy linoleum, flowing toward my shoes.

"Careful," I said, reaching out for her.

But the girl took off. She made an abrupt turn and started walking away briskly, her bootheels clacking against the linoleum. She didn't look back. And when she reached the far end of the aisle, the end closest to the cash registers, she started running.

I took one step in that direction, lifting my hand. I wanted to say something. Apologize. Call her back. Let her know that I hadn't meant any harm.

But she was gone.

Just like Marissa, she was gone.

Then the family of four, the one I had seen earlier with the child screaming for ice cream, came abreast of me. The child appeared to have calmed down. She clutched a carton of Rocky Road, the tears on her face drying. The father pointed to the mess on the floor, the leaking milk and the cereal.

"Something wrong with her?" he asked.

My hands were shaking. I felt off-balance. Above my head, the cloying Muzak played, indifferent to my little drama with the girl who looked so much like Marissa.

"I have no idea," I said. "I don't even know who she was."

CHAPTER TWO

I thought of Marissa all evening. It's safe to say I was feeling a little sorry for myself. Indulging in nostalgia, which can be enjoyable up to a point.

I drank beer on the couch in my apartment while a basketball game I didn't care about played on the TV. A pile of work waited in my briefcase, but I ignored it. I never did that, but after seeing the girl in the store, I did. I ate some cheese and crackers but gave up on my plan to cook the spaghetti I'd bought. My only company that night was Riley, the aging mutt I'd rescued from the local humane society shortly after my divorce two years earlier. I volunteered there to keep myself busy and to give something back. Eventually, they convinced me to take a dog home. He looked to be a mixture of German shepherd and retriever, and the humane society had estimated his age to be at least eight when I adopted him, maybe older.

The humane society didn't know much about Riley's

life before he was abandoned to their care, but they suspected he'd suffered some neglect or abuse, because he was so passive and skittish when I adopted him. He used to jump and cower at every noise, and he rarely if ever barked or growled. He'd grown slowly more comfortable and confident over the previous couple of years, and I'd grown used to having him around. As I lounged on the couch, brooding, he sat at my feet, hoping for cracker crumbs.

Marissa and I had met during our freshman year at Eastland University. When I thought of who I was when I arrived at college, I realized I was just an awkward man-boy who only dreamed of meeting his soul mate. Marissa was beautiful, confident, outgoing, determined. Meeting her unlocked things in me that might never have been unlocked otherwise. She got me like no one ever had. And no one has since. We understood each other without words. I felt my connection to her in the deepest core of my being. How many people meet someone like that in their lives? Not many, but I did. And then, two years later, she was taken away from me in a house fire on a warm fall weekend.

That was why seeing the girl in the grocery store shook me to the core. I had managed to get on with my life. I had managed to tell myself I'd gotten over losing Marissa.

But I hadn't.

I went into my bedroom and dug around in the bottom of my closet. I kept a shoebox there full of items from my time in college, mostly things from my relationship with Marissa. Letters, notes, ticket stubs. And the multiple-time-zone watch she gave me on my twentieth birthday.

We were supposed to travel after college, which explained the need for a multiple-time-zone watch. We never got to take those trips, and I never wore the watch again after Marissa died. But I kept it, and from time to time I'd take it out of the box. When the battery died every few years, I'd take the watch to the jewelry store and have it replaced. I liked to think about that watch being there, close by me, and always running like a beating heart.

I brought it back to the couch with me and slumped down into the cushions, opening another beer. I was supposed to play in my basketball league, but I just didn't feel like it. I never drank very much, never more than one a day, if that, but when I came home from the grocery store that night, I threw back three and then four and opened a fifth, staring at my watch and wondering who that girl was. And why she'd acted so damn spooked when I simply spoke to her.

I fell asleep on the couch, the TV still playing, the open but unfinished fifth beer on the coffee table before me. My neck felt like hell from sleeping at an odd angle, and a trail of drool ran down my chin.

I slept until something started beating against my apartment door.

Someone was there, pounding on the outside. Each heavy knock caused a miniature earthquake in my skull.

I winced. A hangover at my age. Pathetic. I vowed never to have more than one beer again. I vowed to stop thinking about Marissa.

I probably would have agreed to anything to get the pounding on the door to stop. But it didn't.

I turned my head to the right, looking at the watch Marissa gave me. 6:53 a.m. 12:53 a.m. the next day in New Zealand, as if I needed to know that.

I normally woke up around eight. Made it to the office by nine. But I felt like shit. I needed a shower. Coffee. Food. I stood up, feeling a little wobbly. I looked down at Riley. He hadn't barked despite the pounding on the door. He never barked.

"Nothing?" I said to him. "Not even a growl?"

His tail thumped against the floor, and he yawned.

"One of these days I'm really going to need your help," I said. "I hope you're ready."

Riley walked off toward the kitchen, which meant he was hungry.

I was still wearing my work clothes from the day before. My tie and my shoes were off, and I needed to pee. But whoever was outside the door really wanted to talk to me. The person beat on the door again, shaking my brain like dice in a cup.

"Stop," I said. "Jesus."

I thought about calling the apartment complex security guard and asking him to find out who was making the endless racket. But he was an elderly man, the owner's uncle, and he usually didn't arrive until late morning and was gone by five. The noise wasn't the knock of a friend or someone selling something. It sounded urgent, determined. But my desire to make it stop overwhelmed any fears I had about who was out there. I stumbled to the door and looked through the peephole.

It took a moment for the scene outside to make sense to me, but when it did, my heart started racing.

I understood immediately why the knock was so heavy.

Through the peephole I saw two uniformed police officers and a detective I already knew.

"Mr. Hansen," the detective said. "It's the Eastland Police. We know you're in there. Open up."

"Damn," I said.

An already rough morning became totally shitty.

CHAPTER THREE

The morning sun nearly killed me.

It poured in when I opened the door, its rays penetrating my eyeballs like knitting needles. I took a step back, feeling as if I were a man under siege.

"Can we come in?" the detective said.

I didn't have to answer. He was already stepping across the threshold with the two uniformed officers right behind him.

"You can do anything you want if it means you'll stop knocking," I said.

Detective Reece stood about five-nine, a few inches shorter than me, but he was powerfully and compactly built. I suspected he'd wrestled in high school. Or maybe played nose tackle at a small college. He looked like that kind of guy. He didn't offer to shake my hand, but I'd shaken it before, the last time he and I had encountered each other. I remembered he possessed a strong grip, and

I always pictured him sitting at his desk, endlessly squeezing one of those hand strengtheners.

Reece saw the beer cans on the coffee table, and he raised his eyebrows. He was probably a few years younger than me, and his hair was thinning. He wore it cropped close to his head, and his suit coat looked too small for him.

"It's recycling day," I said.

"Think green, right?"

"Exactly," I said.

He pointed at Riley. "Does the dog bite?"

"Only his food," I said, trying to keep the mood light.

But Reece wasn't smiling. He looked around the room, taking it all in. The TV still played with the sound down, showing highlights of a hockey game from the night before. There were dirty dishes in my sink, discarded gym clothes on the floor. I needed to pick up, and I would have if I'd only known the police were going to show up.

"Have you seen your ex-wife lately?" Reece asked.

"Not in six weeks," I said. "Not since . . . that night you and I met."

"The night of the late unpleasantness," Reece said.

"I wasn't stalking her."

Reece turned to one of the uniformed officers. "He says he wasn't stalking her. The ex-wife says he was. Who would you believe?"

The young uniformed cop didn't answer. He wasn't supposed to.

"I was trying to see Andrew," I said. "I told you that then."

"This is the ex-wife's son from a previous relationship," Reece said to the cop again. He stopped looking around and turned to face me. The two uniformed officers stayed near the front door, serving as Reece's audience. "Kid's not even his son."

"Gina and I were married for five years, and Andrew and I became close, and I just want to see him from time to time. It's not unusual. I just wanted to see the kid."

"But she didn't want you there, and you showed up anyway. You've been divorced almost two years. Maybe you need to move on." He turned to the uniformed cops again. "What do you guys think? Is it time to move on?"

"Is that what this is about?" I asked. "Is Gina pressing charges? That was six weeks ago. I thought it was over."

Reece gestured toward the cluttered dining room table. "Why don't we sit down and talk, Mr. Hansen?" He waited for me to move, and when I didn't, he spoke again. "Please?"

He was acting like we were in his apartment and I was the guest. He'd reversed the situation and taken over my turf. I couldn't say anything to stop him, so I sat down. Reece took the seat across from me, and after he did, he reached out with his hand and brushed some old crumbs off the table and onto the floor. Then he took out his phone and started scrolling through it. I waited. For all I knew, he was checking his Twitter feed or looking up movie times.

"Can I ask—"

"Where were you last night, Mr. Hansen?" Reece asked.

I looked over at the beer cans on the coffee table, the deep indentation in the couch where I'd slept without a pillow or a blanket.

"I was here," I said.

"All night?"

"All night."

"Were you alone?" he asked.

"Yes. I live alone. I work a lot. I'm single." Then I glanced at the dog. "Riley was here."

"What time did you get home from work?" Reece asked.

"About five thirty. I stopped at the grocery store first."

Reece nodded. He peeked at his phone, tapped it a few times, and then looked back up at me. "I'm going to show you a photograph of someone. I want you to tell me if you know this person, and if you do know them, I want you to tell me how you know them."

"Okay."

He turned the phone around so that I could see the photo. I should have guessed who it was going to be before he even handed it to me.

It was a photo of the girl from the grocery store.

CHAPTER FOUR

It looked like a driver's license photo. Not many people look good in those, but the girl did. Her hair was loosely piled on top of her head in a seductive way, and she wore a friendly smile, a far cry from the look of fear she'd flashed at me when I spoke to her the previous evening.

"Do you know her?" Reece asked.

A little of the emotion from the grocery store welled up in me again.

"I think I know what this is about," I said.

"You do?" Reece looked surprised.

"Yes," I said. "After what happened with Gina, and then the way this girl acted in the grocery store when I spoke to her, you're thinking I'm some kind of serious creep. Someone who stalks strangers now and not just my ex-wife."

"What happened in the grocery store?" Reece asked.

"If you just let me apologize to her, I will," I said. "I'll call her or write a note—"

Reece interrupted. "The grocery store. What happened?"

I took a deep breath. I told him I'd seen the girl in the store the night before and she reminded me very much of someone I once knew. When I told Detective Reece she reminded me of my college girlfriend, his eyebrows rose again, even higher than when he'd noticed the beer cans. I said I just wanted to talk to the girl, to ask if she might be related to Marissa or her family, but when I approached her, she took off, dropping her groceries at my feet.

Reece took this all in, and when I was finished, he asked, "Did she say anything?"

"Nothing."

"Not a word?"

"Not a word. She acted like I was Attila the Hun. She ran off. Maybe she'd had a bad experience with a man before. Maybe she's just really shy and gets skittish around strangers. I don't know."

"Who did you think this girl was related to? Your ex-girlfriend?"

"My girlfriend from college. I guess technically she was my ex-girlfriend. She did break up with me right before . . ." I couldn't bring myself to say it. I held the image of the girl in my mind, and I could see Marissa's face there as well, the two of them as vivid and three-dimensional as real life. A piercing stab of nostalgia traversed my chest, striking every major organ and even some minor ones along the way. I felt like I couldn't breathe.

"Before what?" Reece asked.

"Before she died," I said. "She died in a house fire

when we were twenty. Right here near campus. She and her three roommates were killed. But right before the fire, a couple of days before, I guess, she broke up with me."

"She broke your heart," Reece said. It wasn't a question. He must have read something on my face or in my voice. I knew I couldn't hide my feelings for Marissa, then or any other time.

"She did," I said. "Completely."

"And what was her last name?" Reece asked. "The ex-girlfriend or girlfriend. Whatever she was. What was her last name and where was she from?"

"Her name was Marissa Minor. Her family lived in Hanfort, Ohio. It's about an hour from here."

"I know it." Reece wrote something down in a little notebook he had pulled from his jacket pocket. His fingers were stubby, the nails bitten. "And you thought maybe this girl in the grocery store was related to your ex-girlfriend, and so you wanted to talk to her? But instead, you spooked her."

"It all sounds far-fetched and ridiculous, I know. At least, you're making it sound that way."

"I'm not making it sound any way. It sounds the way it sounds."

"Look, Detective, I have to get to work. I had a shitty, embarrassing night last night. And I'm sorry if I bothered that girl in the store. If you just give me her name or something, I'll apologize. I know you've checked my record, and you know I've never been arrested and never hurt anybody. I'd just like to make this go away if I can."

"And you think an apology will make it go away?" Reece asked.

"It seems like the gentlemanly thing to do," I said. "I apologized to Gina after she called you."

Reece put his notebook away. He looked around the apartment again, his eyes passing over the clutter, the beer cans, even the impassive officers who still stood by the door. One of their radios crackled, but the officer ignored it. He pressed a button, silencing the sound.

"You can't apologize to this girl," Reece said, staring at me with more intensity. "This girl from the grocery store."

"What do you want me to do, then?" I asked. "You can't charge me with anything. It's not a crime to talk to someone in a store."

Reece kept his eyes on me. "You can't apologize to her because she's dead. Her body was found in a shitty motel out on Highway Six last night."

I studied Reece's face, looking for some sign that he was joking, that he was trying to scare me by saying something so patently ridiculous and absurd. But he wasn't joking. I could tell by the stony, stolid expression on his face. And the news hit me like a blast of cold air. My body tensed, locked up. I felt a pain at the base of my skull and realized I was clenching my teeth as tightly as I could.

That girl, that beautiful young girl, couldn't just be gone. Extinguished like a snuffed candle.

"What happened to her?" I asked. The question

sounded dumb to my own ears, insufficient to the gravity of the situation. But there was nothing else I wanted to know. *What happened?*

Reece continued to study me, as though I were a specimen in his lab. He reached up and rubbed his chin, his thumb and forefinger easing over his freshly shaved skin. He seemed to have decided something.

"She was murdered," he said. "Most likely strangled, although we'll wait to hear from the medical examiner's office for the official word."

Then I felt cold inside, as though the bitter wind that had first buffeted me had been internalized. I shivered, my torso shaking involuntarily.

"Murdered?" I said, sounding dumb again.

Reece nodded. "Are you sure you don't know this girl? I mean, outside of chatting her up in the grocery store."

"I don't know her," I said. "I'd never seen her before yesterday. Never." But then some things started to come together in my mind. I *was* telling the truth—I had never seen the girl before. And when I spoke to her, I didn't say my name or identify myself in any way. So if I didn't know who she was, how had the police ended up at my apartment—

"You didn't know her," Reece said. "But she seemed to know you."

"What do you mean?" I asked. "Why are you here?"

"This young woman you talked to in the grocery store, this woman you say you didn't know? She had a slip of paper in her pocket when she died, a slip of paper with your name and address written on it."

CHAPTER FIVE

Detective Reece said he wanted me to come to the police station with him. He said it was simple—I could agree to give a DNA sample and be fingerprinted and then they'd let me go. He told me I could feed Riley before we left, and he also made sure to tell me I could call an attorney at any time if I wanted, and while we rode downtown—me sitting in the passenger seat of his dark sedan, him driving and not saying anything else while pulsating jazz played on the radio—I considered doing just that.

But I hadn't done anything to that girl, except try to speak to her in the grocery store. As I rode to the station, I tried to understand how anyone could hurt a girl like that. Who would want to violently end such a young life? And for what reason? A rape? A robbery? A lovers' quarrel?

Other things came back to me during the brief car ride as well, things having to do with Marissa. We met during our freshman year of college when the dorm I lived in threw a mixer. I went with a few of my friends, not intending to stay long, but then a girl walked in wearing jeans that fit her body perfectly, her red hair cascading over her shoulders like a ruby waterfall. I'd seen her on campus a couple of times—walking on the quad, standing in line in the cafeteria—but we'd never spoken. She always seemed to be laughing or gesturing, always seemed to have some inner glow spilling out of her as though her body couldn't contain it.

If my life had been a cartoon, the illustrator would have drawn my tongue hanging out until it reached the floor.

But the crowd swallowed her up. I caught occasional glimpses of her dancing, her body swinging to the music, her hair—that rich, wild hair—flipping across her face and then back as she moved. I remembered the song she danced to. "Seether" by Veruca Salt.

I was transfixed.

When my friends wanted to leave for another party, I told them to go on without me, that I'd catch up later. But I never did.

I circled the edges of the party, dancing sometimes, talking to other friends, but with one eye always looking for that wild redhead. I never came close, and eventually I lost sight of her altogether and assumed she'd moved on, like my friends had. Why wouldn't she? I couldn't imagine a girl like that would have only a lame freshman mixer to attend in a dorm on a Friday night. I imagined she had parties and invitations and adventures awaiting her, as many as she wanted.

I went down a short hallway, searching for the bathroom. The redhead emerged from the ladies' room right in front of me. I almost froze in my tracks. We made eye contact, and I managed to say, "Hey."

"Hey," she said, smiling.

But I didn't stop. I went right on into the men's room, where I stood alone in the middle of the floor, the sweat from the crowded room and dancing cooling on my back. I saw myself in the mirror. Thick brown hair. Bright blue eyes. Thin and fit. A young guy in all his glory. In his prime, right? Why not?

I turned around and went back out to the party. And there she stood at the end of the hallway. Her red hair was piled on top of her head now, and she fanned herself with her right hand. When I came closer, I saw hair plastered to the back of her neck by sweat, a spray of freckles across her skin.

She looked over at me. "It's fucking hot."

"It is."

"Do you know what would be funny?" she asked.

I hesitated just a moment, a heartbeat that changed the rest of my life. I said, "It would be funny if you and I ended up married and having children, and we could always tell them we met outside the men's room at a lame freshman mixer."

It was her turn to hesitate. Everything hung in the balance between us. I figured she'd call me a creep or a weirdo. I wouldn't have blamed her one bit. I didn't know where my statement had come from or why those words had tumbled out of my mouth. I simply felt bold.

I felt that only bold words could work for a girl like the one standing before me.

"I was going to say wouldn't it be funny if you were some super-Christian guy and within the first three words I ever spoke to you I dropped the f-bomb." She smiled. "But your answer kind of surprised me, I have to admit."

"No offense taken by the f-bomb," I said. "I kind of liked it."

That was Marissa. There was nothing predictable or conventional about her.

We left the mixer together and walked around campus that night. We told each other about our families, our lives in high school, our hopes and dreams. I was majoring in philosophy and thinking about grad school or maybe a job as some kind of social worker. Marissa wanted to travel, to take photographs and write, and maybe someday turn her experiences into a book.

I remembered our first kiss. Late that night, we walked beneath the falling leaves on the quad, and our hands found each other as though they possessed minds of their own. Once our bodies touched that way, it was over. At least for me, it was over. I belonged to her. And that scared me, as I was sure it scared her. Young guys always got nervous when the feelings grew that deep. I'd dated other girls, sure, but I always felt in control with them. I always believed I could come and go from the relationship if I wanted. No harm, no foul. I knew that wouldn't be the case with Marissa.

And on that fall night, we came together. We stopped

in a darkened patch between the gas lamps that lit the campus walkways. We turned to each other and kissed, and it was one of the few moments in my life when I completely lost myself. The world around us disappeared. The buildings, the students, the night sky.

When our lips parted, I ran my hand through her thick hair, my fingers disappearing in the deep red waves.

"Are you ready for this?" she asked.

"For what?" I asked. "For you?"

"For everything," she said. "For this great adventure."

I told the truth. I couldn't tell her anything else.

"Oh, yeah," I said. "I'm ready."

And I was. For two years, it was the greatest ride of my life.

And I also remembered what it felt like when she broke up with me, just two days before she died. She didn't just end our relationship. She told me she didn't want to be my friend either. She told me she wasn't sure she ever wanted to see me again.

She didn't just break my heart. She steamrolled it.

And then two days later, she was dead.

The fire swept through the house she shared with three other girls on a Friday night in October, killing them all. An accident. A candle left burning unattended, possibly because the four of them had been out drinking. It could have happened to any young, careless kids. In this case, it happened to my favorite person.

I tried to convince myself over the years that it was all for the best, that Marissa and I wouldn't have spent our lives together. We would have broken up late in college or shortly after, like most couples, and we both would have gone on to find other partners, other lives.

But I didn't really believe any of that.

Marissa and I often talked about life after college and our fears about ending up stumbling through the kind of conventional lives our parents lived. One night a few weeks after we started dating we hopped into her car and drove off to Columbus, an hour away, to eat at a dumpy little diner called Heywood's. Marissa was always hearing about places like Heywood's and insisting that we try them. After eating hamburgers and sharing a milk shake, we sat across from each other, letting the conversation go wherever we wanted.

"We should run off somewhere," she said.

"We just did. Heywood's."

"I mean after college," she said. "Someplace no one would expect."

"Disneyland?"

"A real place. Far away. New Zealand."

"New Zealand?" I asked. "Do you know anything about New Zealand?"

"No," she said. "That's why we should go. Are you in?"

"Okay," I said, humoring her but also appreciating her boldness. "After graduation, we're going to New Zealand."

"Don't say it if you don't mean it."

"I mean it," I said.

She poked at the ice cubes in her water glass with her straw. "I don't want to end up like my parents."

"Old? With kids? What?"

"It's not those things." She kept poking the ice. "I don't want to be . . . complacent. I don't want to just . . . exist. You know? Moving from one day to the other as though I was just running out the clock."

"Sure. My parents can seem the same way. They exist. They don't live."

"I don't even know if my parents love each other," she said. "My dad dictates everything. My mom goes along. I love them, but I don't want to be like them when I get married."

"I hear that," I said. "My parents . . . they don't even act like they like each other anymore. They can go days without really talking to each other."

"Okay," she said. "It's decided. We both want more. We won't settle. Ever."

In some ways, it felt weird to be making postgraduation plans when we were still freshmen and had been dating for only a few weeks. But I loved her already. I knew that. And I also knew I shouldn't be thinking about the future so much and assuming the two of us would be together. I didn't want to get married young. I didn't want to think too soon about settling down. Wasn't that why we wanted to run off somewhere and avoid the traps of a conventional life?

"You never know," Marissa said, as casual as could be. "Maybe the two of us will end up getting married someday."

I can't describe the feelings that raced through my body. Electricity. Electric charges sharp and pleasurable filled every cell. Was it possible this girl in front of me was really thinking about marrying me? About spending the rest of her life with me?

"Sure," I said, "but isn't that all a long way off? I mean, you don't want to rush into anything, do you?"

Marissa looked up at me. She held my gaze for a long, steady moment, and our eyes locked into place, joined together as if by a magnetic force. Then she shrugged. Casually. Almost too casually.

"Yeah," she said, looking away. "There's time for all of that in the future."

What I wouldn't give to have that moment back.

I never met anyone else like her. I hadn't loved anyone the same way since then, not even Gina, the woman I'd married seven years ago.

When Marissa died, it was like a giant steel door slammed shut on one part of my life, the part in which I could have been happy, truly happy sharing my life with someone else. For just a moment in the grocery store, I felt as if Marissa were alive again, that some piece of her was back.

Was it crazy to say that the death of that girl—the girl whose name I still didn't know—hit me with the same force that Marissa's death had? Was it crazy to say I felt like I'd lost Marissa all over again?

My fingerprints were already on file with the city. Not because of my previous run-in with the law, but because of my job as a caseworker. In order to make sure landlords didn't violate the rights of their tenants, I went into a lot of homes and apartments, so they fingerprinted me when I was hired and did an extensive background check.

When the fingerprint technician at the police station took my hand in hers and told me to just relax, I'd been through it before. I wasn't relaxed, but I knew the procedure, so I tried to make my mind a blank while she rolled my hand around on the ink pad and then the card stock.

The DNA test was similar to going to the doctor's office to get checked for strep. The same technician pulled out a giant Q-tip thing and ran it around the inside of my cheek. She was about as gentle as someone trying to scrape rust off a boat hull. When that was finished, she led me to Detective Reece's empty desk and told me to sit and wait.

No one seemed concerned about me running off. Sure, the room was full of cops, but none of them paid any attention to me. Phones rang, printers printed, radios crackled. I called work from my phone and told them I was running late. I didn't say why, and they didn't ask. I worked on my own a lot, out in the field, so things were pretty flexible.

My head felt better. Not normal, but better. The pain from my moderate hangover had subsided, but I was hungry, and I knew I wouldn't feel one hundred percent until I ate something substantial.

Reece came back twenty minutes later. He sat at his desk without looking at me and started shuffling through some papers. I knew enough to suspect it was a strategy, one designed to make me feel uncomfortable, nervous. I refused to give in, so I sat back in my chair and waited for him to speak.

Finally, he said, "Is there anything else you need to tell me, Mr. Hansen?"

"No," I said.

"You've had time to think. Maybe something else has crossed your mind. Maybe you remember something that is relevant to this investigation."

"I have a question," I said. "What is the girl's name? Can you at least tell me that?"

"Why do you want to know her name?" Reece asked. "Assuming you don't already know it."

"I don't know it. And I don't like calling her 'the girl' as though she's not a real person. And I'm wondering, still, if she might be related to my ex-girlfriend. I knew her family pretty well."

Reece considered me for a moment, and then he said, "I had a girlfriend in college who dumped me. You know what I did?" He waited a beat for a response, and when I didn't say anything he went on. "I said to myself, 'Easy come, easy go.' Why would I want to be with someone who doesn't want to be with me? Am I right? Too many fish in the sea and all that. Especially for young guys in their prime."

I had the feeling he was trying to help me, that he really believed he was sharing some piece of profound wisdom with me.

"I hear you," I said.

"I don't think you do." He shuffled some more papers around on his desk. "The victim's identity will be made public pending notification of her next of kin. It should be in the afternoon paper."

The victim. It sounded so cold. Her identity was slowly being stripped away.

"Can I go, then?" I asked.

Reece considered me again. "You don't have any plans to travel, do you?"

"No."

"Don't make any. I want to be able to find you anytime I want."

"You know where I live."

Reece looked at something behind me, tracking it with his eyes. I waited for a moment, assuming he'd turn back to me, but he didn't. He followed the progress of something—likely *someone*—who was moving through the room.

I turned in my chair and saw what he saw. A man and a woman, escorted by another detective, were led into a private room on the far side of the station. The couple's heads were bent low, so I couldn't see their faces, but they seemed to be carrying a heavy burden. The detective with them, a woman, gently placed her hand on each of their backs as they passed her and entered the room. The woman had reddish hair, but from a distance I couldn't tell if it was her natural color.

When the door closed, I turned to face Reece again, and he looked at me.

"Who was that?" I asked.

His mouth pressed into a tight line. "Them?" he said, his voice distant. "They're the parents of the murdered girl, the one with your address in her pocket. They just came back from the morgue, where they had to identify the body of their child."

I felt my heart drop, a heavy stone plummeting through my chest cavity.

"We'll see you soon, Mr. Hansen," Reece said. "We'll be in touch."

CHAPTER SIX

I tried to forget about it all.

For a short time, I almost convinced myself I could.

I spent a busy day at work, out in the field. I visited four different housing units and took reports on a variety of violations that ranged from the ridiculous—someone complaining that his landlord wouldn't go to the grocery store for him—to the poignant: an elderly woman who couldn't afford her heat. I ate lunch with a coworker around noon and resisted the impulse to go home and take out my old photos from college, the ones that showed Marissa and me together at a homecoming dance, an end-of-the-year party, a trip to a lake by her house during summer break. In that way, the day passed as so many days passed. Fast, almost blurred, a race to get to . . . what? Riley and the TV?

Then, on my way home, at the corner of Eleventh and Main, I saw the word through the cracked glass of a newspaper box. "Murder." Even from my car, I saw her face and a headline. "Murder." Eastland wasn't a big town, only about twenty-five thousand people, so a homicide commanded a lot of attention.

I pulled over, slipped some coins into the slot, and grabbed a copy of the *Eastland Daily News.* I stood on the street, staring at that face again. People walked past me, and jangly guitar music leaked out of a coffee shop up the block. Then I read the caption. It gave the girl a name. Emily Joy Russell. Age twenty.

Twenty. The same age Marissa was when she died.

I scanned the article, looking for more information.

It said Emily was a student at the University of Kentucky, several hours south, and no one—not even the girl's parents—knew what she was doing in Eastland, Ohio, an hour west of Columbus. She didn't have any family in Eastland, or any friends that anyone knew of. Her parents, the people I had seen at the police station earlier that day, lived in Richmond, Kentucky, where Emily grew up. She had a younger sister, too. The cause of death was being withheld. And, mercifully, the story did not mention me or the note found in Emily's pocket.

There was no obvious connection to Marissa or her family. At least none I could see.

I took the paper back to my car and read the article all over again. I wasn't sure what I expected to find the second time through. Or the third. I tossed it aside and took out my phone. I needed to talk to someone, someone who might understand what I was thinking and feeling. Someone who remembered the same things I remembered.

Someone who could answer some questions.

I sent a text, received the reply I wanted, and drove off.

Heather Aubrey and I dated briefly during our first year of college, right before I met Marissa. We split up mutually, and then when Marissa and I started dating, we all remained friends. We traveled in the same larger social circle, and there were times—notably during a couple of summers—when Marissa and Heather were very close. A few months after Marissa died, Heather and I dated again for about a month. But the relationship quickly grew weird for me. It felt like I was cheating on Marissa, even though she was dead, and it seemed awkward to be with someone who knew Marissa so well. I broke it off, which didn't make Heather happy, but I couldn't do anything else.

Heather and I kept in touch sporadically over the years. We both settled in Eastland after college. Heather married, had kids, divorced. When Gina and I split up, Heather and I dated briefly again. Very briefly. She seemed to want to move quickly toward something permanent: a solid commitment if not engagement and marriage, which didn't surprise me. Heather was practical, more practical than Marissa or I. Heather even told me once that Marissa and I had been dreamers with our heads in the clouds. Heather majored in business in college and worked briefly as a sales rep before getting married and having kids. She liked to set goals and move toward them, but her practicality masked a surprisingly emotional side. When those goals weren't met, or even weren't met quickly enough, Heather could become intensely unhappy.

When I sensed her desire for a stronger commitment from me during our postdivorce reunion and decided to break things off, she told me, forcefully, never to speak to her again. And for close to a year I didn't. She'd issued the same threat when we broke up after Marissa's death. Over time, she eased back into my life. An occasional text. A Facebook message. And then we were acting like there'd never been a problem between us.

So we'd been cool for a while lately and even got together for a platonic drink or coffee now and then. She lived in a newer subdivision with her two teenage children and seemed to work only when she felt like it. Her ex-husband had a lot of money—he was a dentist who had once given me a crown—and in the wake of their divorce, Heather focused as much of her energy as possible on raising her kids. She looked like an upper-middle-class suburban mom. Fit, tan, cheery.

The evening I saw the headline about Emily's murder, Heather greeted me at her door with a hug and a kiss on the cheek, and I won't lie and say it didn't feel good to have a woman in my arms again. Did anything feel better than that?

"Well, you look great, don't you?" she said.

"Are you kidding?" I asked. "I'm tired, slightly hungover, and sliding into middle age. You're just being nice."

"I'm not," she said, patting my cheek. "Have you seen what most men our age look like? You've got your hair.

You're trim." She rubbed my upper arm. "You always were handsome."

She led me into a bright, clean kitchen. I accepted her offer of a glass of water, and then we were sitting across from each other.

"The kids are off at soccer practice and chess club," she said. "Do you still see Andrew? How old is he now?"

"I don't see him as much as I'd like. And he's nine."

"That's too bad." Some of her cheer slipped, and she became a little guarded, cautious. It was always chancy opening communication with an ex. "I was pleasantly surprised when you texted today."

"How long has it been since we've seen each other?" I asked. "A couple of weeks?"

"More than that. We said we'd be friends, but you're not much of one."

"I'm sorry about that. I work a lot. And I started playing in a basketball league."

"Really? Basketball?"

"It's an over-forty league. It keeps me active. We go out for beers after the games. There are some good guys in the group." I wondered if I'd made a mistake calling her, but I wanted her opinion. She knew Marissa well. Very well. "I came over because I need your help with something."

I held the afternoon paper folded under my arm. Heather nodded toward it.

"Did you get a paper route?" she asked.

"I wanted to show you something."

"Is it something good?"

I unfolded the paper and placed it in front of her, smoothing out the centerfold so she could see Emily's picture. I didn't say anything or prompt her in any way.

Heather reached over and picked up a pair of reading glasses. She slipped them on and studied the paper.

"Mmmm," she said, shaking her head. "I heard about this on the radio, but I haven't seen a picture of the girl." She scanned the story, still shaking her head. "This is awful. Her parents . . . My Amanda is sixteen, not much younger than this girl."

"Is that it?" I asked.

"Is what it?"

"Is that your only reaction to the photo?"

Heather slipped her glasses off. "I don't understand what you're asking me."

I tapped the paper. "Does that girl look familiar?"

Without looking back at the paper, Heather said, "I've never seen her before. And I don't know her name. It says she's from Lexington or someplace like that."

"Doesn't she look just like Marissa?" I asked.

Heather's face changed even further. All the cheeriness left, slipping into a look I imagined she showed to her children when they begged for a pony or clung stubbornly to a belief in the Tooth Fairy. She pitied me. But she also humored me by putting the glasses back on and studying the picture one more time.

She heaved a sigh.

"Sure, I see a resemblance," she said.

"Thank you."

"A general resemblance. Lots of girls have red hair and . . . maybe she has brown eyes. It's hard to tell in the paper. But lots of young girls are this pretty. Amanda brings her friends around, and I feel like Grandma Moses, they're all so beautiful. It's easy to feel a little intoxicated around them."

"You didn't see this girl like I did," I said, tapping the paper. "I saw her gestures, her walk. I can't believe you're not seeing it in this photo."

"Saw her where?" she asked.

"In the grocery store. Last night, right before she died."

Heather slipped the glasses off again. She reached over and patted my hand.

"Oh, Nick. You never got over Marissa, did you? All these years later, you're still chasing her ghost."

CHAPTER SEVEN

Heather poured more water for me, and then she sat down at the table again.

"I understand why you feel that way about Marissa. Even among a group of young people, she stood out," she said. "Her energy. Her laugh. And she was kind, too. A good friend. She just had . . . something." She sounded a little resentful when she said, "Hell, everybody loved Marissa."

"And you two got pretty close," I said, "especially during that summer you were both living in Eastland."

Heather looked out the window at the backyard. The grass was slightly yellow, just starting to recover from the cold of winter. The trees were barren, leafless.

"She had closer friends than me, I suppose," Heather said. "I kind of felt a rivalry with her. You know how girls are. Always trying to outdress or outshine the one right next to them." Heather looked back over at me. "And she got you."

"Were you angry about that?" I asked.

Her features sharpened. "My life worked out well. Pretty well." She gestured into the air, perhaps indicating the house, the yard, her life. "I know Marissa hurt you right before she died."

"What do you know about that?" I asked. "About why she broke up with me?"

A look of disbelief crossed Heather's face. "My God. You *are* on a ghost hunt. Did seeing this girl really send you this far into the past?"

"Yes, it has me thinking about all of that stuff. Chasing ghosts, as you say. I just want to understand, and I've never really talked about it with our college friends. Not since then. You and I didn't even talk about it, and we started dating right after she died."

"We were helping each other grieve," she said. "It's normal for friends to do that."

"I suppose."

"What do you want to know?" Heather asked, her voice a little colder.

The sun slipped away outside, the horizon slowly turning orange. The furnace clicked on and pushed warm air through the vents.

"Did she say anything to you about why she wanted to split up with me?" I asked. I really was chasing a ghost, one that had long ago fled from our lives.

"I thought she told you everything you needed to know."

"She told me she was unworthy of me, and that I needed to be done with her," I said. "Not just as a boyfriend, but also as a friend. She said she was thinking of withdrawing from school, which seemed crazy. She was a great student."

"And she told a lot of us that her parents were having financial problems," Heather said.

"Yeah, she kind of hinted at that."

"She said they couldn't afford to send her to Eastland anymore, so she had to say good-bye to her life here. You probably just got folded into that." Her voice lowered. "And then . . . the fire . . ."

She stared straight ahead, her eyes a bit vacant. She must have been imagining the flames, the horror of the heat and smoke.

I gently asked another question. "Did you know her parents?"

"I met them a time or two when they came to visit. I didn't know them well."

"I did," I said. "They weren't the kind of people to have financial problems. Quite the opposite. They had a nice house, nice cars. They belonged to a country club."

"Look at all those bankers and Wall Street guys who lived the high life, and then, beneath the surface, nothing." Her hand fluttered in the air to punctuate her comment. "All built on lies. How do you know her dad wasn't like that? Living beyond his means?"

"I guess I don't really know," I said.

"I always figured her dad got in too deep with something," she said, "and Marissa would have to leave school and go back home to Hanfort for a while. Maybe work, save money, take classes at a community college, and then bounce back. She'd land on her feet. I believed that. She always did. Things didn't get her down or derail her for too long. She had a brightness that never dimmed."

"That's just it, though," I said. "When she broke up with me, she seemed so defeated. So down. It wasn't like her."

"How would you feel if you found out your parents weren't what you thought they were? That would throw you for a loop, wouldn't it? Make you reevaluate everything? Every relationship and event in your life?" Heather leaned closer to me, and up close I saw the gold flecks in her blue irises. "She was young, and she broke your heart. We've all been there. Besides, Marissa could be so . . . bold sometimes, you know? So tough and cut-and-dried when she needed to be. Sure, she was a dreamer, but she was a fearless dreamer. She knew her mind. She went for things if she wanted them. If it hadn't been for . . ." Her voice trailed off. She bit down on her lower lip with her top teeth. "I don't like to think about that fire. It's too awful."

"I know."

I reached over and pulled the paper toward me. I studied the girl's face again. *Emily Russell's face.* Even if she was related to Marissa's family, which it didn't appear she was, then what did that matter to me? Marissa's family had moved on with their lives long ago. I knew they moved away from Hanfort shortly after the funeral. I assumed it was just too painful to see all the places that reminded them of their daughter—playgrounds, schools, parks, friends. I couldn't blame them.

But then why did the girl have my name and address in her pocket? What was I supposed to do with that?

I doubted Heather could tell me.

"It's jealousy, too," Heather said.

"What is?"

"These feelings you have now. The fact that you're hung up on Marissa after all these years. She was just your college love, but you're stuck on her because she rejected you for someone else."

"What are you talking about?" I asked. "She didn't have—"

"My husband cheated on me," Heather said, her face growing somber. "A younger girl." She forced a laugh, and it sounded thin and brittle. "I know I've told you about this. What a stupid cliché he was. Some twenty-year-old who worked in his office, probably couldn't even walk and chew gum at the same time, the little brat. And he turned me into a cliché as well. The bitter, spurned middle-aged mom who is left taking care of the kids."

"I'm sorry, Heather. But what are you talking about with Marissa? She didn't have anyone else. She broke up with me, and then she died. That was it."

Yes, it had been twenty years, but I still felt a tangled knot of jealousy swelling in my gut. It felt like a living thing, a rapidly growing organism.

"I thought you knew," she said.

"Knew what?" I asked.

"Oh, Nick. I fear this is just going to rip you wide-open again—"

"What?"

"People saw her that night," Heather said. "The night of the fire. She was in a bar. Razer's? Remember that place? Out on Grant Street?"

"I thought that was a dive for locals."

"It was. But some of us went there sometimes. They didn't card, and we could get cheap drinks. And no college boys breathed on us there. The locals were actually pretty nice." Heather swallowed hard and pursed her lips. "Look, Nick, Marissa was there the night of the fire. And she was with an older man."

"Was it her dad?" I asked.

"Not her dad. And not a professor. They were having a real intimate conversation, like they were emotionally entangled with each other. Nick, we all thought she broke up with you because she was involved with this older man."

"You saw her?" I asked.

"Does it matter?"

I'd been kicked in the nuts once, during a high school soccer game, and Heather's words hit me with the same force. A lung-emptying, heart-stabbing pain.

"She wouldn't do that," I said. "I would have known."

"I guess people were protecting you after she died," Heather said. "What point would there be to telling you about this man if Marissa was already gone? What did it matter at that point?"

"But she—"

I stopped myself. I remembered how Marissa had acted in the days leading up to the breakup and the fire. She was distant, cold. She wouldn't talk to me or explain the sudden change in her mood. She always told me everything, but she'd suddenly gone silent. If she had been cheating on me, if her loyalties had been divided in some way, then isn't that exactly how she would have acted? Wouldn't she already have been pulling away and shutting me out?

"Don't you think it's better you know this now?" Heather asked. "Isn't it better to know the truth about Marissa, even after all this time?"

"It doesn't make me feel better," I said.

"You will. Trust me. You can make a fresh start now." She folded up the newspaper and handed it back to me. "You can stop seeing things that aren't there."

CHAPTER EIGHT

Gina didn't answer my texts. She almost always did, even when things were bad between us, which they kind of were since she'd called the police on me. Then, when I got to her house—the house she and I used to share— no one answered the door.

I should have left.

I knew to leave. But I didn't.

Sometimes Andrew played in the backyard, and sometimes he went next door to hang out with the neighbors' son. So I walked to the back of the house to look.

Andrew was nine and a great kid. He looked a lot like Gina. Dark hair, dark eyes. He was still small for his age, but I figured that would change soon enough. His father, Gina's ex-boyfriend Phil, was tall, so the kid would eventually get some of that. Still, Andrew and I shared many interests. He liked sports of all kinds, and so did I. He was into monster movies, and he was curious about history. So was I. His father traveled a lot, so there was time for me to play the dad role while Gina and I were married. I'd always wanted to see him more often in the wake of the divorce, but Gina wasn't ready to go along with that. She thought it would confuse Andrew, since Phil was back trying to play a larger role in his life. My brain told me she was right, at least in the short term. But I struggled to accept a logical argument when I cared so much about the kid.

The voices of children screaming and laughing reached me, and when I came to the back of the house, Andrew saw me.

"Nick!" he shouted.

"Hey, buddy," I said as he came running over to me. He gave me half of a hug. He was young enough to think it was okay to hug his . . . whatever I was. Father figure? Kind of. Stepdad? Sure.

"Is your mom around?" I asked. The other kids in the yard, four of them, kept up their game. They chased one another in circles and occasionally somebody threw a football.

"She's at the store." Andrew pointed behind him. "Candace is watching me."

"Who?"

I looked up. A teenage girl with long blond hair stood on the neighbors' deck. I knew the neighbors, the Yarrows. They had a son Andrew's age, and the two of them played together all the time. But I didn't know Candace.

"Candace," Andrew said. "She's the new babysitter."

I waved to her. "Hi. I'm Nick. I'm Andrew's . . . stepdad. I know Steve and Linda Yarrow. I used to live here."

But Candace looked nervous. Her eyes narrowed, and she twirled the ends of her blond hair with greater ferocity.

"I came by to see Gina," I said. "But she's not home."

Candace stepped back into the Yarrows' house. I hoped she just heard the teakettle starting to boil or something like that.

"Are you staying for dinner?" Andrew asked. "They're showing the Reds game on TV. It's just spring training, though."

"No, I can't stay," I said. "I just wanted to talk to your mom." Through the Yarrows' kitchen window, I saw Candace with a phone pressed to her ear. She was talking with a concerned look on her face, and her hair was being twirled within an inch of its life. "I should go if she's not here. I'm really not supposed to be—"

"Let me just show you one thing." Andrew reached up and took my hand. He started tugging me toward the Yarrows' yard, where his friend Donal Yarrow stood holding a football. "We worked out a cool trick play."

"I can't, buddy."

"It will only take a minute. Please? One minute."

His small body managed to pull me toward the neighbors' yard, and my feet followed along. I wanted to go. I wanted to lose myself in a silly trick play, the kind of thing that could only be dreamed up by a nine-year-old.

"You'll like it," Andrew said. "First you snap the ball. Then the quarterback fakes—"

I stopped. "I can't. I have to go."

"It's only a minute. You never come around."

"I know. But I will." I looked at the house. Candace

was off the phone, but she stood near the kitchen window, staring out at me. She'd stopped twirling her hair. "It's a little complicated right now with me and your mom. But we'll figure it out. That's what I wanted to talk to her about tonight. I had kind of a long day, and I thought—"

"Are you moving back?" Andrew asked.

"Oh, buddy." I sighed. "Jesus. I doubt it."

Andrew looked crushed, like I'd dropped a ton of emotional weight on top of his soul. Tears welled up in his eyes.

I pulled my hand away from his, and then bent down closer to him. I sighed again. "It's not about you. It's about your mom and me. But I can't just come here any-more whenever I want."

"Or you'll get arrested again?"

"I didn't get arrested. But, yes, I could get in trouble."

Andrew looked away from me, trying to hold back his tears. I remembered that feeling as a kid, those years be-tween being young enough to feel hurt but also feeling too old to cry. "I just want to see you," he said. "You and Mom don't care."

"Don't say that." My voice came out with a harshness I hadn't intended. Andrew looked up at me, his chin quivering. "It's not true," I said, lowering my voice. "It's not true of either of us. But I have to go."

I gave him a quick kiss on the top of his head, and then walked off toward the car. Candace stood at the window, so I gave her a friendly wave. I wanted to let her know I was leaving, that everything was okay. Back to normal. Nothing to see here.

But when I reached the front of the house, Gina pulled into the driveway. She came out of the car quickly and walked around the front, her big, dark eyes wild. I suddenly knew who Candace was talking to on the phone.

"What the fuck is going on, Nick?" she asked.

"I came to see you."

"And you tried to take Andrew?" she asked.

"What? No. He wanted to show me a football play. But I told him I couldn't stay. Did that babysitter say . . ."

Gina slumped back against her car, lifting her hand to rub her forehead. Her body was trim and sleek from her years as a college swimmer, and a strand of brown hair fell across her face. "She just said my ex-husband was here, and he had Andrew by the hand."

"Jesus, Gina. Do you trust me that little?" I asked.

"I was scared," she said. "I thought . . . Oh, Nick, I've been trying so hard to keep Andrew from getting confused and hurt. Phil's back, but he's not always reliable. You're reliable, but . . ."

"I'm not his dad."

"I overreacted. I don't know what I thought."

"I just wanted to talk to you about Andrew. About me seeing him again. I had a long day, and I wanted something good to focus on."

Then I heard the approaching sirens.

"Really, Gina? The police?"

I stared at her, raising my arms in disbelief. She turned away.

It looked like I was staying.

CHAPTER NINE

I waited in the back of a cop car for close to an hour while the police spoke to Gina and Candace and, yes, even Andrew. I gritted my teeth at the thought of him facing questions from a police officer. I knew it was my fault. I should have gone home. I shouldn't have taken his hand and walked farther into the yard.

But I wanted to heed Heather's advice. I wanted to get on with my life. Forget Marissa and Emily and be normal: enjoy my job, spend time with my friends, play a basketball game here and there. I wanted to erase Heather's story about Marissa and the man in the bar from my mind.

The car smelled like body odor and sweat socks. I saw Candace in the window of the neighbor's house, twirling her hair again, and I quietly wished most of it would fall out, although I couldn't really blame her either. Someone—Gina most likely, or maybe Linda and Steve—had told her to call if I came over unannounced. Candace followed directions well.

Finally a familiar face showed up outside the cruiser window. He wore an odd little smile, one that made his face seem tilted. Detective Reece then pulled the door open and leaned in.

"This is getting to be a habit," he said. "We don't like these kinds of habits in law enforcement, Mr. Hansen."

"I was just trying to—"

He held up his hand, silencing me. "I spoke to your ex-wife. And your stepson. We're all clear now. The kid, Andrew, really seems to like you." Reece laughed a little. "He asked me if I was going to throw you in jail, and I told him no. He's a bright kid."

I let out some air. "Thanks."

"It seems like your ex has a lot going on. I guess the boy's father is back on the scene, and she wants to make sure everyone knows their boundaries."

"Boundaries. Yes, I've heard that word before," I said.

"But you're not off the hook," Reece said. "Can I trust you to meet me at your apartment in about thirty minutes? I've got something to show you."

What could I say? Where would I go?

"I'll be waiting," I said.

Because of my trouble with the police I was later than usual, and Riley acted less happy to see me. He gave me a worried look when I walked in the door, something that said, *I don't know what you're up to, but it has me concerned*. He also had an iron bladder for a dog his age, so there were no accidents. I took him on a short walk, fed him when we returned to the apartment, and then waited.

Detective Reece showed up forty-five minutes later and turned down my offer of something to drink. He'd come alone, without the uniformed escort, and we sat at the table again in our same positions. I hoped his visits weren't becoming part of my daily routine.

"Do I need to apologize to Gina?" I asked. "I know I shouldn't have been over there."

"It's done," he said. "Do you know how hard it is to be a single parent? My mom was a single parent. It's stressful." He took his phone out and scrolled through it again. Then he looked up. "By now I'm sure you've seen the identification of the girl in the motel."

"Emily Russell," I said.

"She was strangled. Manual strangulation."

"It sounds awful."

"It takes a lot of effort to strangle someone, you know. It's not like the movies where they do it in, like, five seconds. You really have to hold someone down. You're face-to-face with them."

"So this was personal," I said.

"Maybe."

"Am I off the hook based on the fingerprints and the DNA?" I asked.

"You're not close to being off the hook," he said, looking down at the phone again, acting coy. "It takes time to get those results. And maybe the killer wore gloves. Or wiped the place down."

"So what's tonight's visit about?" I asked.

He looked up at me again. "We've checked Emily Russell out. Background, criminal record, school stuff.

All of that. The Lexington police are talking to her roommates and friends. I may take a trip down there in a few days to ask around. And you know what stands out about Emily Russell?"

"What?"

"Nothing," he said. "Nothing at all. Good grades. She was an honors student. Wanted to be a pharmacist. She'd never been in trouble with the police. Not even a traffic ticket. She went to church on Sundays, volunteered at a senior center, returned her library books on time. The model kid."

"Is she related to the Minors?" I asked.

So much for turning the page. But if Detective Reece was going to show up at my house asking questions about Emily Russell, I was going to ask questions of my own.

"Not that I can see," he said, "and that's not really relevant to me. But I do want to know this about her. Why does this perfect kid who's never done anything weird or crazy in her life suddenly decide to get in her car, drive one hundred and fifty miles north to a town where she doesn't know anybody, not tell anybody where she's going, check into a cheap hotel under another name and pay cash for the room, and then end up dead with your name and address in her pocket? Why does that happen?"

"What name did she register under?" I asked.

"Ann Smith. Not a very creative spy."

I leaned back in my chair. "I don't know why she'd do all those things, but it seems like she was looking for me."

"Does it, now?" Reece said, his voice full of sarcasm.

He turned the phone around toward me and tapped the screen. "Look at this."

I studied the little document on the small display. It was a photo of a piece of paper, and on the piece of paper were written my name and address.

"Do you recognize that handwriting?" he asked.

I studied the image. The penmanship looked feminine, full of large loops and swirls. "I don't."

"Are you sure?" he asked.

"Should I recognize it?"

"I don't know." Reece took the phone back and slipped it into his pocket. "But I do know one thing."

"What's that?"

"We showed this to Emily's parents, and it isn't the girl's handwriting," he said. "Someone *gave* her your address."

CHAPTER TEN

Reece left after thirty minutes, but not before repeating his request—*demand*?—that I not leave Eastland without checking with him. He also reminded me again that the DNA results would be coming back from the lab soon.

"Do I need a lawyer?" I asked him.

"You're entitled to one," he told me.

"Am I a suspect?"

"Let's just say we're keeping our options open."

When he was gone, I looked over at Riley, who thumped his tail against the floor and then yawned.

"Shit," I said.

I needed help.

Laurel Davidson went to Eastland with all of us, although she didn't know Marissa as well as I did. Laurel and I were both philosophy majors, so we took a lot of classes together, and then she stayed in town after college and began her career as a police officer before going to work in corporate security for a statewide chain of convenience stores based in Eastland. Every time an employee skimmed from the register or absconded with a bank deposit, Laurel drove to that location and had a sit-down with the pathetic thief. Something about her feminine toughness and lightning-fast intellect always got the perpetrator to confess.

Just before ten a.m., I met her at her office, which was off the square downtown. She kept her hair short and always wore two-piece gray business suits—jackets and pants, not skirts. I never asked, but I had the feeling she carried a gun with her everywhere she went.

When we sat down across from each other, I noticed lines at the corners of her eyes, which were a striking shade of light blue. Laurel ran at least one marathon a year, and spent vacations with her family—her husband, Tony, and two kids—hiking or camping or biking in some far-flung region of the country.

"It's been a month," she said. "We used to see you every week. Dinners. Drinks." She put on a mock frown. "You don't call. You don't write. We miss you, Nick."

"I'm working a lot."

"Aren't we all?" She rolled her eyes. "That's why we're both millionaires."

"Yeah," I said, "social work pays really well. And then the government cuts the budget, so we get spread thin. And there are more people struggling than ever."

"And you love every minute of it, don't you?" she asked.

"'Love' is a strong word," I said. "But I like helping people."

"I know. And I know you're good at it."

"I do see Tony at basketball," I said. "You should come to a game. Or come out for a drink afterward. It's all guys. They'd love to have a woman around."

"I bet. Or maybe I could just enjoy the time alone." She smiled. "Okay, what's up?"

"Have you been following this Emily Russell murder?" I asked.

Recognition spread across her face. "The girl who was murdered in the motel? Sure."

"You've seen her picture?"

"It was in the paper," she said.

"Did she look familiar to you?" I asked.

Laurel stood up. She went over to her desk and dug around in a stack until she pulled out a newspaper. She unfolded it and came back to her chair, studying something on the front page while she walked, her movements brisk and efficient.

"Mmm. I see it now. You think this girl looks like Marissa, right?"

Relief passed through me. "Exactly. I'm not crazy, am I?"

"No, there's a resemblance. Same coloring. Same face shape. Did someone say you were crazy for thinking they looked alike?"

"Heather Aubrey."

Laurel made a noise like *pffft*. "You can't trust her. She hated Marissa."

"Secretly she might have."

"Exactly. And she never got over you." Laurel tossed

the paper onto her desk. "Heather? Marissa? Are you here to go down memory lane, Nick?"

I told her about the encounter in the grocery store with Emily. And the note in her pocket. As I explained it all, Laurel's face grew more serious, and she tilted her head toward me. A couple of times she stopped me and asked me to back up and repeat things I'd already said. When I was finished, she leaned back in her chair, taking it all in for a moment.

"Crap," she said finally. "That's bizarre."

"I know."

"And you *let* them fingerprint you and take the cheek swab?" she asked.

I heard the disdain in her voice. It said I trusted the police too much. "I wasn't in that motel room, Laurel. There's nothing to find."

She raised her eyebrows. "What's that little three-word expression? 'Famous last words.'"

"It's not that bad," I said. "I told the cops everything I knew."

"You need a lawyer," she said. "No way you're going into this without help." She stood up and went over to her desk. She scrolled through her phone, then forwarded something to me, making my phone chime. "Call him when you leave," she said, coming back. "He's good. I trust him. You should too, or you'll be up a creek."

I read the name on the screen. *Mick Brosius.* I slid the phone back into my pocket. "Thanks."

Laurel thought things over some more. "I get that it's

weird, that seeing this girl who looks like Marissa threw you for a loop. Especially since you've always been so hung up on her. And then she ends up dead. *And* the girl has your name in her pocket."

"See? It's weird," I said.

"Weird, yes. But maybe she had your name for a perfectly benign reason," she said. "Maybe you helped her grandmother with housing, and she wanted to thank you. Did you ever think of that?"

"I did. I searched all my records, and her name didn't come up. There were people with the last name Russell, but how could I tell if they were related? And her family is from Richmond, Kentucky."

"And her grandmother or another relative wouldn't necessarily have the same name as Emily. Right? Maybe it's her great-aunt or just a family friend you helped. If that's even what's going on."

Neither one of us said anything for a moment. The phone on Laurel's desk rang, but she ignored it. I had to hand it to her—she'd always been a good friend. Loyal, supportive. When Marissa died, she sat with me for long hours. Talking. Listening.

"Why don't you let the police have a little more time on this?" she said. "They know what they're doing. Something will turn up."

"But what if . . ." I wasn't sure I could say it. I tried again. "I keep thinking about something."

"What?" she asked.

"What if that girl, Emily, what if she really is related to Marissa? What if she's Marissa's daughter?"

"Her daughter?" she asked, the look on her face telling me I sounded crazy.

"What if . . . what if . . ." I was floundering, trying to get my thoughts together.

Laurel reached over and picked up the newspaper again. She scanned the article while I continued to try to speak. "Nick," Laurel said. "Marissa died in October of 1993, right? And here we sit in March of 2014, right? And the article says Emily Russell was twenty. She's twenty now. Are you saying Marissa gave birth to a baby one year *after* she died?"

But I hadn't heard her. Or I hadn't entirely paid attention to her. Because I kept going. I kept saying things that I felt but that didn't really make any sense. I couldn't stop myself.

"I keep thinking . . . what if Marissa was pregnant when she broke up with me? And what if that baby . . . what if Emily is really mine? What if she's my daughter?"

CHAPTER ELEVEN

Laurel tried to keep the shock off her face, but despite her efforts, her jaw dropped. "Honey, what's going on with you and your stepson, Andrew?" she asked me.

"No progress," I said. "I can't really see him. But you haven't answered my question."

"I *am* answering your question." She sounded calm, teacherly, and her voice was soothing as she laid out the facts. "You have some holes in your life, holes that are crying out to be filled. You're single. You see a girl who reminds you of the love of your life, and you go a little crazy in the head."

"You really think Marissa was the love of my life?" I asked.

"Don't you?"

"I do. I guess I always have, even when I was married to Gina. But you know how that is. People think two twenty-year-olds couldn't possibly be in love or know they belong together. I've wondered that myself. Am I just hung up on that time in my life? The freshness. The freedom. How beautiful Marissa was. How hungry we were for each other."

"I believe it's possible for young people to fall in love that way, but only you can know for sure. Gina's great. I really liked her. But I didn't get the feeling the two of you were . . . meant for each other, I guess. It felt like a nice marriage between two good people. But nothing that was destined in the stars."

"That sounds about right." I sighed. "You met my dad a few times, didn't you?"

"Sure. Good old Henry."

"Indeed. When he was dying, I mean when he was really at the end, I went to see him in hospice. He could barely talk. I was married to Gina at the time, but it wasn't going great. No one knew that, only Gina and I. I sat there in hospice, holding the old man's hand, and he opened his eyes and he looked at me. He said, 'You know something, Nicky . . .' He hadn't called me Nicky since I was about six."

"Cute."

"Don't get any ideas." I felt sad at the memory of my dad. His hand in mine, his big, strong hand, the life fading away. "He said, 'You know how you can tell if you're meant to be with someone? If you don't know anyone better than the person you're with. Or if you can't even imagine anyone better than the person you're with.' Then he closed his eyes again. He and I never talked about marriage or women or love. We had never talked about anything personal. Never. He just came out with that out of the blue."

"It was on his mind," Laurel said.

"Yeah. It's funny. I never really thought my parents were in love, but I do know one thing. They know *us* better than we realize they do."

"True," Laurel said. "So how did you answer your dad's question? Who did you imagine?"

I didn't hesitate. "Marissa every time. Even when I was married to Gina. Even now."

"So there you go," Laurel said. "Maybe you *can* know when you're twenty. I met Tony when I was twenty-five. That's not much older, and I knew right away. Your dad was a wise man."

"He was."

"Look, you've been through a divorce," she said. "You're middle-aged. You've found yourself in the middle of your life, lost in a dark forest."

"You're really quoting Dante to me?" I asked.

"That's what college taught us. The humanities, remember?"

"Is this supposed to make me feel better?" I asked.

"It happens," she said. "We all lose our way sometimes."

"You don't seem to," I said. "Ever."

"Do you remember sophomore year of college when I had that perm?"

I pictured it. Laurel's hair had looked ridiculous, even though beneath the artificial curls she had remained pretty. We all were beautiful then. We were young.

"Okay," I said. "Fair enough."

"And you've lost that kid," she said. "Andrew. He was like a son to you. Hell, forget that. He *was* your son, right? You felt like he was your own?"

"I did. I don't know any other way to think of it."

"So you have this one chance encounter in a grocery store, and it brings all these memories back up. Beautiful memories. Painful memories. What if I *were* with Marissa? What if *we'd* had a kid together? It's brutal to think about it, Nick."

"This is turning into therapy," I said.

"Wait until you get my bill." Laurel looked at her watch. "Try to do something else with your life. Get outside yourself. Volunteer more. Try Internet dating. Get a dog."

"I have a dog."

"That's right," she said. "I forgot."

"He's kind of quiet, so that happens."

"You're still young," Laurel said. "You can still have a great future. You can even get married and have a family."

"You think?"

"Of course."

"That's nice to hear. You know, I do still want to get married again. And I'd love to have a kid with the right person. I guess I'd like to think that if it can happen once, maybe . . ." I scooted forward in my chair. "Thanks. I know you have work to do."

"I'm sure you do, too."

"I do." But I didn't stand up. I sat on the edge of the

chair, leaning forward just a bit. "I do want to know something else, though. Why did Marissa do it? Why did she break up with me out of the blue and leave school? I went and talked to Heather Aubrey about this, and do you know what she said to me?" I took a deep breath. I didn't know if I could give it voice.

"What did she say?" Laurel asked. She sounded skeptical.

"She said that on the night Marissa died people saw her out at a bar, Razer's, and she was with another man. An older man. Heather implied they were having some kind of romantic relationship, that they were dating. And that's why Marissa dumped me out of the blue, because she was involved with this other man. Some old guy."

While I spoke, I stared at the carpet, and when I looked up, Laurel was eyeing me and not saying anything. I watched her for a moment. She clearly knew something she wasn't saying.

"That story's bullshit, right?" I asked. "It's just Heather telling me something to make me feel bad. Isn't it, Laurel?"

"I agree that Heather probably just wanted to hurt you," she said. "Or, more accurately, she wanted to give you a bad impression of Marissa."

"But? You're acting like you know something."

She didn't say anything.

"What is it, Laurel? It's a lie, isn't it?"

Laurel looked unsteady. "It isn't. I know because I was in Razer's that night, late, and I saw Marissa with that man."

"Were you with Heather?" I asked.

"No, Heather wasn't there. Not with me. I was with some other friends. I liked Razer's because students rarely went there, but we walked in and we saw Marissa. My friends didn't know her, but I did."

"Well—"

"I'd met her parents when they visited once," Laurel said. "That man wasn't her dad. And Eastland is a small campus. I'd been the student representative to the faculty senate. I knew most of the professors, at least by sight. I didn't recognize this man. I don't think he was a faculty member, and even if he was, why would she be in a dive bar with him late at night?"

"But if they were trying to hide whatever they were doing, why go out in public?" I asked.

"Who says they wanted to hide it?" Laurel asked. "Look, did you ever go to Razer's?"

"Rarely. Maybe two or three times."

"Right. Most of us went to places where students hung out. It's a fluke I saw Marissa there. And we didn't stay long. There were bikers there. Townies. We didn't stay."

I tried to steady myself by placing my hands on the armrests of the chair. "So all of my friends knew about this, but no one told me?" I asked.

"Think about it, Nick," she said. "Marissa died that night. Why would any of us tell you something like that right after the fire? The two of you had broken up, and then she died. You were devastated. A lot of people were torn up over her death. Marissa had a lot of friends,

Nick—she was a wonderful, warm person. People were just trying to protect your feelings. I know it must really suck to hear about this now, but we were thinking of you."

"But what Heather said isn't true. She said they were acting . . . intimate. As though they were really involved with each other. That's not true, is it? If she wasn't there . . ."

Laurel pressed her lips together, and then she said, "I'm only telling you this so that everything is out in the open. You seem to want to know it all, and maybe that's for the best. But when I saw them, they were holding hands across the table. And it looked like Marissa had been crying. I don't know what it means. I didn't talk to them. Believe me, I may not have dated much in college, but I recognized the signs. Those two people were *involved* with each other."

CHAPTER TWELVE

I was at my desk, compiling a case report. A landlord in a building mostly occupied by residents on welfare "forgot" to pay the water bill, leaving seventy-five people high and dry for a day and a half. Despite the grim event, I'd lost myself in the problem solving, a good feeling. Then my cell phone rang.

"What are you doing right now?"

"Laurel?" I asked.

"You heard me," she said. "What are you doing?"

It was just before noon, and I'd spent the previous evening at home trying to forget everything I'd been told about Marissa over the past couple of days. No matter how hard I tried, I kept seeing her in Razer's, that dark, shadowy bar. I could see her in my mind's eye, sitting at a table, her hand entwined with that of an older man. Handsome. Graying. Distinguished.

Who the hell was he? And why was he haunting my imagination twenty years later?

"I'm working," I said.

"Are you hungry?" Laurel asked.

"Kind of. Do you want to go to lunch?"

"Meet me out front in ten."

She hung up.

Laurel drove away from downtown, and we headed east toward the interstate, passing restaurants on every block. Seventies music played on the car stereo, and Laurel hummed along with it, her head bobbing slightly. Then she entered an on-ramp.

"Do I get to know where we're going?" I asked.

"I've been thinking of you."

"Thanks."

"Seriously," she said, turning the music down. "We've been friends a long time. I hated to see the way you looked yesterday when we were talking about Marissa and that guy in the bar. I know it hurts, even after all these years."

"You were right to tell me."

"But I hated to do it." She reached over and patted my knee. "You're a good guy. You deserve good things. And I know what you need."

"Can you really tell me what I need?" I asked. "I've been trying to figure that out for years."

"By the way, did you call the lawyer? Mick Brosius?"

"I did," I said.

"What did he say?"

"He seemed like a nice guy," I said. "Kind of young. I met with him this morning, and he looked like he should be in high school."

She flicked the blinker on and changed lanes. "You're getting old. What did he tell you?"

"He said to keep my mouth shut and not speak to the police unless he was there," I said. "Then he told me not to worry. I always worry when people tell me not to worry."

"Just listen to him," she said. "Do what he says."

Traffic was light, the lanes ahead clear. "You said you were thinking of me? And you know what I need?"

"Yes," she said. "You need proof. Once and for all you need proof that the part of your life involving Marissa is over. That's what we're doing today."

"We're not going to a cemetery to dig her up, are we?" I asked.

Laurel turned her head a little, giving me a look that said she didn't share my sense of humor. So I remained quiet. I knew Laurel well enough to know that when she set her mind to something, she finished the task. She would have been an excellent life coach or drill instructor. So she made a dogged investigator, and I just sat back and let her drive me to whatever she had in mind.

We went two exits and ended up in a modest subdivision six miles from Eastland. The houses looked to be about twenty years old and smaller than the new ones being built even farther out. Laurel's GPS told her where to turn, and we parked in front of a home with white siding and black shutters. An Ohio State flag fluttered limply in the light breeze. The yard was immaculately cared for, even in late winter. So much so I wondered if someone came out and painted the grass green once a week.

Laurel turned the car off, but we didn't get out.

"Is my lunch inside?" I asked.

"I still have a lot of contacts with the police, as you know," she said.

"I remember your days as a cop."

"I got the name of the detective who investigated the fire. He's retired now, but he agreed to talk to us."

"I don't need to do this."

"If you have any questions, you can ask him. He's sharp."

"Look." I reached over and rested my hand on her arm. "I appreciate this. I really do. You've always been a good friend. But I don't need to do this." I saw a small coffee splash on my pants leg, and I scratched it off with my fingernail. "I know I said some crazy things yesterday. I implied that Emily might be my child. I don't really think that. I was sad and feeling sorry for myself. I don't need to rehash this. Can you just call this old guy and let him get back to his retirement? I'll buy you lunch."

Laurel shook her head. "It's sweet of you to say those nice things about me. But we're going in."

Nate Denning no longer looked like a cop, if he ever had. He resembled a good-natured math teacher, the kind of guy who was eager to help you understand the quadratic formula or story problems. He greeted us at the door wearing jeans, a polo shirt, and a kitchen apron tied over the top of his clothes. He apologized for being slow to answer the bell, saying he'd just put a cake in the oven.

"My wife still works," he said. "People think it's funny, but I've taken up baking in my spare time. And I have a lot of spare time."

We walked through an orderly living room and then sat at his kitchen table. Nate carried a little gut around his middle and wore a pair of glasses on a chain around his neck. I placed his age in the early sixties as he offered us coffee, which I accepted and Laurel turned down. The kitchen felt warm and smelled like a bakery, making it a strange place to discuss the deaths of four young people.

Once we were settled, I apologized to Nate for disturbing him. I said we really didn't need to pick his brain, that Laurel was just being an overly concerned friend. Nate told us he didn't mind, that he liked to think about old cases sometimes just to keep his brain active.

"It's more interesting than crossword puzzles." He sipped his coffee, and then his face grew serious, his brown eyes turning sad. "I understand your girlfriend died in that fire back in ninety-three."

"That's right," I said.

"I remember that case very well," he said. "I was the lead for the police, but, of course, a fire investigator from the state handled the bulk of the work." He shook his head. "Four kids that young. It happens every once in a while, especially on a campus. Kids die. Accidents. Fire. Drinking. It's no good." He looked at me, his face sincere. "I'm sorry for your loss."

"It was a long time ago," I said.

"Whoever said time heals was lying," Nate said.

"What do you remember about the investigation?" Laurel asked. She was sitting on my left, her legs crossed and one hand resting on the table.

"That four kids died," Nate said. "That we had to notify four sets of parents about the worst thing they could imagine. I've never felt like cops need to make a lot of money, but when you have to do one of those notifications, then you're really earning your pay."

"So you used dental records to prove who died?" I asked.

"Not exactly," Nate said. "It can be tough to identify remains found in a fire, especially back then. We didn't have DNA to rely on like we do now. Fires are messy things. Buildings fall in. Firefighters tramp through debris. The temperatures get too high. Things get burned or crushed beyond recognition."

I looked over at Laurel. Her face remained impassive.

I asked Nate, "So what did you do then?"

"As I recall . . . we were able to use dental records for two sets of remains. For the other two, well, you rely on different things. Who was supposed to be home and in what part of the house. If there were no missing-persons reports filed after the fire, then it's easy to assume the four kids who died were the four who were supposed to be there. No one else was reported missing from campus, so it was a safe bet we had our four victims."

I hated to hear those words, to hear Marissa referred to as a "victim" or her body described as "remains." It sounded dehumanizing, and I started to get a sick feeling in the pit of my stomach as Nate spoke. The coffee tasted bitter, and I pushed the mug away.

"What caused the fire?" Laurel asked.

"It was an accident," I said. "Wasn't it?"

"It was," Nate said. "It was right before Halloween."

"And someone left a candle burning," I said. "Right? A candle or a pumpkin, something like that caught on fire while everyone slept. That's what I remember hearing back then."

Nate still looked sympathetic. "You're right. We knew Halloween was a big party time on campus, so it's possible the residents of the house had been drinking. No way to really tell that either with the condition of the remains."

"Can you stop using that word, please?" I said without thinking. The words jumped out of my mouth, as though someone else controlled my vocal cords.

Nate looked over at me. "What word?"

"'Remains,'" I said. "It's so . . . clinical. So cold."

"It's an old habit," Nate said. He shrugged, as though trying to plead his own innocence. "We use certain terms on the police force."

"I think we're done," I said, looking at Nate. "I'm sorry we took up your time. I know you're just doing what we asked, but I've heard enough."

I pushed back my chair, but didn't stand. Something ticked on the other side of the room. Ticking and ticking. I recognized it as the sound of a kitchen timer, counting down the minutes until Nate's cake was ready.

I held out my hand to Nate. "Thank you," I said. "I see the whole picture. I really do."

"Can I throw out one more question?" Laurel asked Nate.

"Come on, Laurel," I said, my voice low. She lifted an eyebrow, a modest admonishment, so I relented. She was there for me, trying to help. "Fine. Go ahead."

"Was there anything else unusual about the case?" she asked. "Anything that just jumped out at you? Unanswered questions? Any dangling threads?"

Nate considered the question. He lifted his hand to his chin and gave it a thoughtful rub. Despite my anger at Laurel and my desire to get out of Nate's house, I found myself anticipating his response.

"I've been thinking about that question all morning, ever since you called," he said. "To be honest, it was all pretty cut-and-dried. There were witnesses who saw these kids at the party. It was a huge one, hundreds of kids. It's hard to say who was with who and who left with who. You've seen the streets on a weekend night. Flocks of kids going every which way. The cops just try to maintain some semblance of order." He raised his index finger in the air. "One of these roommates got sick at the party. I can't remember which one. Drank too much, a witness said, and the other roommates were taking her home early to put her to bed. No surprise, the way these kids drink sometimes."

"Thanks," I said quickly, still wanting to get out of there.

But then Nate went on. "And the only other thing

that ever really stuck out to me was the nine-one-one call," he said.

"What about it?" Laurel asked.

Nate looked at me, as if asking for my permission to continue. He didn't need it. He was a free person, and so was Laurel. They could talk about it all they wanted. Clinically. Objectively. Like Marissa wasn't a real person, a person I loved. They could talk about these events as though they had happened far away, to people we didn't know, like a plane crash in Africa or a flood in Europe. So I nodded my head, encouraging him to speak. I *did* want to hear it. My curiosity—my painful curiosity— controlled me.

"It was a young woman who placed the call. It came in around one thirty or so. She said she was just walking by the house on her way home when she saw the fire. No cell phones back then, of course. She had to get to a pay phone. That's where the call was traced to. A pay phone half a block away. I'm sure it's gone now. You can't find those things anywhere. But this girl made the call, and she reported the fire to the dispatcher."

"And?" I said. "What was so unusual about that?"

"It was a gut thing for me. Nothing I could point to." Nate's hand rested on his coffee mug, which was deco- rated with some seagulls and read, THE OUTER BANKS IS FOR LOVERS. He turned it one way and then the other. "But the way she phrased things in the call. She said, 'They're in there. Oh my God, they're in there.'"

There was a pause, and Laurel filled it by asking the

question that had already crossed my mind. "Why was that strange?"

"It sounded personal, as though she knew the people inside."

"Maybe she did," I said.

"We put a call out for the person to come forward." He looked at me then. "Do you remember that?"

"I don't," I said.

"I do," Laurel said. "I figured it was just standard practice."

"It is," Nate said. "We like to learn as much as we can about the caller. We're never sure if it's going to shed light on an investigation to know who made the call, but we try. In the immediate aftermath of the fire, we didn't know what we were dealing with exactly. Everything was on the table. Arson. Accident. But the person—the girl who made that call—never came forward. Maybe she thought she was in trouble. Maybe she wanted to stay out of it. Maybe it was a kid who never heard we were looking for her. Some people aren't tuned in. Back then no Facebook. No e-mail. No Twitter."

"So maybe this person knew the people in the fire," I said. "It's a college town. Lots of people know other people. What does it matter if the person who made the call knew the kids in the house?"

"It might not matter," Nate said. "It just stuck with me. 'They're in there.' Why not 'There are people in there'? Or 'There's someone in there'? '*They're* in there.' Like she knew them . . . in some way. And that witness said they left the party earlier than they might have otherwise. You know college kids . . . those parties go until three or four in the morning usually."

"I'm about to ask a crazy question," Laurel said.

Nate answered before she said anything else, reading her mind. "The nine-one-one tapes from back then have all been erased. They don't keep those things forever, especially if the case is closed."

"Did anyone else share your opinion about the nine-one-one call?" Laurel asked.

"No. I mentioned it to the fire investigator. He listened, but, in the end, what could anyone do about it? This was just a hunch that the person who made that call knew the kids in the house somehow. Even saying it to you now, it seems . . . kind of odd. It's a college town, so maybe they did know them. But then why not stay at the scene and talk to us, right? I ran it by my boss, but he didn't want a turf war. I was told to follow the fire investigator. He died about five years ago." He played with the North Carolina mug some more. "The case is long closed. Life goes on."

"Right," I said. "It does."

At the door, we all shook hands, Laurel and I thanking Nate for his time.

"If you stayed longer, you could have some cake."

"That's okay. Laurel's buying me lunch," I said, even though talk of the fire had dampened my appetite. We stepped onto the porch, but I turned back. "I'm curious about something. You said two of the . . . people were identified with the dental records. Do you happen to remember which two?"

Nate's forehead creased with concentration. "I figured you might ask me that. I tried to think back."

"It's okay if you don't remember," I said.

"What was your girlfriend's name?" Nate asked.

"Marissa Minor. She was from Hanfort."

Nate nodded. "I remember that name." The creases deepened on his face while he thought. It was chilly outside, but he didn't seem to notice the cold. "The two we could positively identify were . . . Sarah Locker and . . . the other girl's last name was Shelly or something like that."

"Andrea Shelly," I said.

"That's it," Nate said. "Those were the two. Not Marissa Minor."

I looked at Laurel. She seemed to know what I was thinking.

Wasn't the whole point of the visit to Nate to put the ghosts to rest?

CHAPTER THIRTEEN

We stopped for lunch at a diner in a strip mall not far from Nate's house. Laurel ordered an egg-white omelette and wheat toast. I ordered a hamburger, but my appetite was slow to return after the thoughts of the fire, the burned and crushed bodies, the helpless 911 call. The "remains" of four people I knew. I picked at the meal, trying to ignore the odors of brewing coffee and fried food. Silverware clanged and scraped against plates, while cooks shouted in the kitchen and conversations murmured around us.

Laurel put down her fork abruptly and said, "I just can't stop wondering why that girl had your name and address in her fricking pocket."

"That dead girl," I said.

"She was alive when you saw her," she said. "She was alive with your address in her pocket, but when she saw you, she ran."

"Maybe she didn't have my address yet."

"Could be," she said.

"Maybe she had my address but didn't know what I looked like," I said.

"Possible."

Laurel was distracted. She picked up her fork and continued to eat, but I could tell she was thinking about the conversation at Nate's.

"I thought you wanted me to let all of this go," I said.

"I just don't know where to turn next," she said. "The police are looking into this dead girl, this Emily."

"Please don't call her a set of 'remains.'"

Laurel stopped chewing. She reached over and squeezed my hand. "I'm glad you said something about that. Nate didn't mean any harm, but I know it seems cold. We're talking about people. In Marissa's case, someone you loved very much. We all need to remember that."

"I wasn't a jerk to Nate, was I?" I asked.

"He's a cop," she said. "Think of how many people have treated him worse."

"Thanks. I think."

"So if the police are looking into Emily, we need to look somewhere else," Laurel said.

"We do? *We?* Does this mean you're helping me?"

"Of course," she said. "You told me Marissa said she was dropping out because of money trouble. I remember she told a few other people the same thing. But you never knew of her parents having that kind of trouble. Nobody did. Quite the opposite, right? They seemed well-off?"

"They seemed pretty comfortable," I said. "More comfortable than my parents, and we were middle class.

I took out a student loan, but Marissa never worried about that. But people can hide financial troubles. Even Heather pointed that out to me. Just because people look like they have money doesn't mean they really have it."

Laurel wasn't saying anything. She held her fork in the air.

"What is it?" I asked.

"Nothing. It would never work."

"What?" I asked again, my voice more forceful.

She set her fork aside again and folded her hands on the table. "I was just thinking that what would really help us would be getting access to Marissa's records at Eastland. Who knows if they even exist anymore and who knows if they say anything. But they might be able to tell us if she really was having money trouble, or if there was some other reason she decided to withdraw. Maybe she was expelled for something embarrassing. Maybe she got in some kind of trouble she didn't want to talk about." Laurel continued to stare at me. "If only we knew someone who had access to the highest levels of power at Eastland."

Then I understood what she was asking. I started shaking my head.

"No way," I said. "Do you want me to get arrested? For real? I'm lucky she doesn't have a restraining order against me."

"I know. And I don't want you to get arrested. For anything. Speaking of which, I bet those DNA results come back soon."

"I'm not worried about it," I said.

"Anyway, Gina's dad is a trustee," Laurel said. "She's done all that fund-raising crap for Eastland, even though she didn't go to school there. She must know some people. And her dad certainly would. Can't you ask her? Politely?"

"Wouldn't that be illegal?" I asked. "To look at someone's private records like that?"

"Well, yes."

"That's not like you, Laurel. I've never seen this side of you."

"It's not like me, and I'm a little ashamed. But I can't stop thinking about this. *All* of this. There must be something there, something we haven't seen yet."

"Do you really think there is?" I asked. "You don't think I'm crazy?"

Laurel picked up her fork and started eating again, not answering my question. "Let's just try to get our hands on those records."

CHAPTER FOURTEEN

Gina agreed to meet me in a public place. Very public. She said she absolutely didn't want me coming by her house. And she wasn't willing to come to mine. I didn't tell her what I wanted to talk to her about, and she didn't ask. But she told me she had things to say to me as well, which I was both grateful for and afraid of.

I arrived at the Irish Lion, a bar that sat between campus and downtown and attracted both students and professionals. They served Guinness on tap and fish and chips or shepherd's pie for dinner. Gina sat at the end of the bar, sending a text, while the happy-hour crowd swelled around her. Irish music—authentic or not, I couldn't say—played through the sound system, and the waitresses, college girls in white shirts and short black skirts, hustled through the masses, repeating the same words over and over: "Excuse me. Excuse me."

Gina put her phone away when she saw me. "There you are."

She sounded like she'd just discovered a tick in her bed. "Here I am."

"Do you want to get a table?" she asked. "It's more private. There's one over there." She nodded toward the back.

"It's up to you," I said. "You're the one drinking with a madman."

She ignored my comment and went to the table, where I ordered a pint of Guinness and Gina ordered wine. We'd originally met at an Eastland fund-raiser almost ten years earlier. I was there as an alum, and she was there because her dad, a local contractor, was a bigwig donor. I think she liked me because I wasn't rich like all the guys she'd known growing up and because my work with the housing authority told her I liked to fight on behalf of the underdog. Gina liked a good fight. She worked as a college counselor at a private high school, and her eyes lit up when a scholarship kid from an underprivileged background was admitted to a great university. She saw each of those small victories as a chink in the armor of the Man, whoever the Man was.

The time waiting for the drinks to arrive could only have been more awkward if we'd been naked. We both looked around the bar, letting our eyes wander to anything but the other person's face. I wished I'd had a drink before I arrived, but I'd come straight from work.

"Andrew's okay?" I asked, needing something to say.

"He's good."

"Good," I said.

"How's work?" she asked.

"It's fine. Busy. The usual. How about you?"

"It's going pretty well," she said. "We've been hearing about a lot of acceptances, which is excellent. And some really painful rejections. I hate those."

"I know. You live and die with some of those kids."

The drinks arrived. Mercifully. I took a long sip off the top.

"So what did you want to talk about?" Gina asked.

"Okay," I said. "I need your help with something, and it doesn't have anything to do with Andrew. It doesn't have anything to do with us at all. So there's that."

"I'm listening."

The music seemed to grow louder, and across the bar, a guy in a maroon turtleneck won a game of darts and started high-fiving everyone he saw. A bell rang somewhere, perhaps in honor of his great athletic feat.

"Well, I was wondering if your dad, or maybe even you, knew anyone who worked in the registrar's office at Eastland."

"Probably. Why?" she asked, a sliver of caution slipping into her voice.

"Right. You'll want to know why." I took another drink of my beer. And then I told her I wanted to get a look at Marissa's records, specifically to see if they might show a different reason why she dropped out of school right before she died. While I explained, Gina's face closed off. A curtain of anger I recognized all too well dropped across it, and she picked up her wineglass but didn't drink. She held it, swirling the liquid.

"You asked me here to use my father's influence to

look at someone's personal records. Is that it?" Gina asked.

"Yes, that's it. You can say no if you want. I understand I'm not your favorite person right now."

"You know," she said, "my dad never liked you. He didn't like your job, and he told me not to marry you. I always came to your defense with him. I defended your work. I said it was important, and it is. I believe that. Do you know what he'd say if I brought this to him? It's a huge ethical violation."

"She's dead, Gina."

"Is she?" she asked.

I sat back. "What are you talking about?"

"We were never really married, were we?"

"What do you mean?" I asked.

"I mean we went through with everything," she said, waving her hand in the air to show the fruitlessness of our time together. "We got the license, and we said the vows, and we got the gifts. But you were never really married to me. I think it's funny that everybody looks at us and thinks *I* was the one who didn't want to be married to *you*."

"You did ask me to move out," I said.

"But you were never really there. You were always hung up on Marissa."

It sounded strange to hear her name in Gina's mouth. I thought back over the time Gina and I spent together, going back as far as when we started dating. I knew I mentioned Marissa from time to time, and certainly during the inevitable litany of our previous lives and re-lationships. But I didn't think I'd *dwelled* on her.

"Did it really seem like I was hung up on her?" I asked.

"You didn't talk about her . . . too much," Gina said. "It's the *way* you talked about her." She sipped her drink. "You never talked about me that way. And I know you kept that little box of memories of her in the closet. I know that watch came from her, the one you used to take to the jeweler for a tune-up every once in a while."

"I don't see how you can hang all of our problems on a girlfriend I had in college, even if she did die."

"You're right," she said. "I can't put all our problems on her. But she didn't help."

"I'm sorry if you felt that way." A silence descended between us, if the word "silence" applied when Irish fid-dles were squealing overhead like tortured animals. I wished I'd never listened to Laurel and I wished I'd never contacted Gina. I took a couple more drinks of my beer and looked at her. "I'll just go." I started to get up and then remembered something. "Wait a minute. You said you had something to tell me. What is it?"

"It's not important," she said.

"You can't say that," I said. "You said you wanted to talk. Is it something about Andrew? Is something wrong?"

"Nothing's wrong," she said, "and Andrew's fine." She reached up and ran her hand through her thick brown hair. "I was just going to tell you . . . I was going to say I didn't blame you for any of the troubles we've been having lately. I know you're not stalking me or An-drew or doing anything weird."

"Why the sudden change of heart?" I asked.

"It's not sudden." She tapped her neatly manicured nails against the tabletop. She always did that when she was thinking of the right words to say. "I've never doubted you in any real way."

"But?"

"But I've been thinking about Andrew's future a lot. What will he think when he looks back at this time in his life? Will it just be chaos? His parents never got married. I divorced the next guy I was with. I just wanted his life to be orderly, and you got caught up in that. I see that it wasn't fair." She stopped tapping. "So is that okay?"

"It's good. Thanks." It looked like there was something more on her mind, so I asked. "What else?"

"To be honest," she said, "I was going to talk to you about figuring out a way for you to see Andrew again. To spend a little time with him."

My heart almost jumped out of my mouth. "That's great."

But Gina was shaking her head. "I don't think I can do it now. The fact that you're asking me to do this for you. I was willing to give you the benefit of the doubt on the other stuff. But this—"

"Come on, Gina. Don't be that way. You know I love Andrew. You know his happiness is all I want."

She finished her glass of wine and stood up.

"It's funny," she said. "All these years I was in competition with a dead girl. I lost back then, and I'm still losing now."

She walked out and didn't look back.

CHAPTER FIFTEEN

I spent that Friday night with the guys from my basket-ball league, including Laurel's husband, Tony. One of the guys on our team, a real estate agent, had recently become engaged, so we all met at a local bar for drinks, darts, and food. Emily Russell didn't come up once, and I was happy to have the distraction.

On Saturday, I volunteered at the shelter, making calls on behalf of their spring fund-raising campaign. Some-one brought in doughnuts, and we all cracked lame jokes about donors' silly names and bonded over the variety of rude ways people told us to get lost. That afternoon, Ri-ley and I took a long walk through the community park, and I managed to give my apartment a much-needed cleaning and vacuuming. We walked again on Sunday, and then I spent a leisurely morning lounging around, reading the paper and catching up on work e-mail. I spoke to Laurel once and told her I'd reached a dead end with Gina, and Laurel actually acted surprised that my ex-wife—who had twice called the police on me—didn't want to assist me with an unethical search of my deceased ex-girlfriend's college records.

Some people never lose their optimism.

"You haven't heard anything from the cops?" Laurel asked.

"Nothing," I said. I'd read the local paper from cover to cover that weekend, and the news about Emily's death seemed to be slowing to a trickle. What else was there to say? She'd been murdered, but they didn't know who was responsible. Her parents were preparing to bury her back home in Kentucky. Everyone was at a loss.

"Keep your chin up," Laurel said.

"Thanks, coach."

"Do you want to come over to the house tonight?" Laurel asked. "It's cold, but we're grilling out. Hamburgers and hot dogs. You and Tony can talk about basketball or beer or whatever it is you guys like to talk about."

"I'm stuck on something else here. You? Hamburgers and hot dogs?"

"Do you think I'm a total killjoy? I let the kids indulge sometimes."

"You don't mind having your single friend along for the ride?" I asked.

"Of course not." She paused. "Plus, Sally's working on a term paper for her history class. And I just happen to know you minored in history in college."

"So you're using me."

"She's writing about the Kennedy assassination. Didn't you write a paper about that once?"

"I did," I said. "I still have dreams of arresting Fidel. Didn't I help her with a paper on D-day last year?"

"She likes you. She thinks you're smart. I haven't told her otherwise. You know, sometimes the kids refer to you as Uncle Nick."

"Really?"

"Really."

Pride swelled in my chest. "That's pretty cool. Okay," I said. "I'll help the kid. *And* eat your food as payment."

"Great. And I'll keep working on this Emily Russell stuff when I have the time."

"I don't know if it's worth it," I said.

"I'll keep trying," she said. "We'll see."

After we hung up, the reason I wanted her to stop echoed in my head like a clarion call: *It's too painful. It's just too painful.*

Then I stepped out my door on Monday morning, and it all came back to me. Hoping for a quick walk with Riley before I went to work, I opened the door and someone called my name.

"There he is. Mr. Hansen?"

I spun toward the sound of the voice. The morning air felt warmer than I'd expected, and I had stepped out in a pair of gym shorts and an oversized sweatshirt. Riley was peeing near my foot when I saw a vaguely familiar blond woman approaching me with a microphone, followed closely by a guy with a huge camera mounted on his shoulder.

I froze in place. The red light on the camera glowed, meaning it was recording.

"What?" I asked. "What's this?"

"Katherine Pettis, Local Twenty news. How do you feel about being named a person of interest in the murder of Emily Russell?"

The camera moved close enough to my face to reveal every pore and twitch. I'd seen Katherine Pettis on the local news many times, and this was her forte. She liked to go out into the field, stick a microphone in someone's face, preferably someone in trouble, and ask them tough questions. If no one was in trouble, she stood outside in thunderstorms and hail and extreme heat. She once spent the night in a cell at the state prison to show what the conditions were like. Up close, her makeup looked thick, her cheeks bright red, and her eyebrows drawn on with a dark pencil.

"I don't know what you're talking about," I said.

Riley finished his work and started sniffing Katherine's high-heeled shoe. I hoped they'd get a shot of him, since he would obviously make me look more humane. *How could he have murdered someone when he loves his dog so much?*

"Sources at the police department have named you a person of interest in the murder of Emily Russell," Katherine Pettis said, undeterred. "Would you care to comment? Did you know Emily Russell? Is she a friend of yours? Was she, I mean." She frowned a little when she added that, making sure to let the viewers know she was a really sensitive reporter.

I started backing toward my apartment door. The camera tracked me, its red eye following my every movement.

"Any comment, sir?" she asked. "Anything at all?"

I went back inside, but before I closed the door I said, "Leave me alone."

Only when Riley and I were on the safe side of the door did I look down at him and realize my heart was pounding.

"What the hell was all that about?" I asked. "Do you know, boy?"

He started wagging his tail, oblivious and hungry for his breakfast.

I called Mick Brosius but reached an answering service. I tried three more times with the same result. It then took me one try to get Detective Reece on the phone, but he sounded harried and distracted, not at all interested in talking to me.

"Is something wrong, Mr. Hansen?" he asked. It sounded like he was chewing his breakfast while we spoke.

"Do you know what just happened to me?" I asked.

"I don't." *Chew-chew-chew.*

"That Katherine Pettis fool from the local news just stuck a microphone in my face outside my door. She called me a 'person of interest' in the death of Emily Russell."

"And?" he asked.

"Come on," I said. "You really think I did it?"

"You've known all along we're wondering why your name and address were in that girl's pocket." He spoke to someone else in the room, his voice distant, then came back on the line. "I guess I don't know what you want me to do for you right now. I'm sorry if the media invaded your privacy. It happens in cases like this."

"Did you send them here?" I asked.

"No. I don't talk to Katherine Pettis," he said, sounding almost offended by the question, as though Katherine Pettis were a much lower class of person than he was. "But we have an election coming up in the fall. Everyone wants to make sure they look like they're doing their due diligence. Somebody leaked your name to the media, probably out of the sheriff's office. They like to do that. It happens."

I expected him to say more, to say . . . anything. But then I understood how naive it was to think he'd have something helpful to offer me. I was a big boy in the middle of a big-boy problem. I couldn't count on soothing words from the detective investigating the crime. And even if he did have soothing words, they couldn't erase the images I carried around in my head. That girl in the grocery store, looking at me with such fear on her face. And then the image I could create only in my mind: her young body, twisted and bent on the floor of some cheap, ugly motel room. She was somebody's daughter, somebody's child. Somebody's friend.

Why?

I pulled a chair out from the table and sat down. Riley wandered into the kitchen, his leash still trailing after him. He sniffed his empty food bowl and looked back at me. I held up one finger, telling him *just a minute*. He knew what I meant.

"So do you have any idea what happened to this girl yet?" I asked. "Or why?"

"You know I can't talk to you in any great detail about this case," Reece said. "And I've already heard from your attorney, Mr. Brosius, a couple of times. He has your best interests in mind. But I can assure you of one thing— we're going to do everything we can to answer those questions about Emily Russell." He paused for a moment, his chewing completed. "Everything. We'll follow every trail we find."

His words seemed to be directed at me. But I also knew what he was really saying. *We have no idea what happened to Emily Russell.*

CHAPTER SIXTEEN

News traveled fast. Before I was even out the door again, showered and clean, my supervisor from work, Olivia Bloom, called, asking me what was going on and did I need to take some time off to figure it out.

"How did you hear?" I asked.

"Twitter," she said. She was sixty-three and happily played the role of mother hen to her younger employees. I kind of liked it. It felt good to have someone treating me that way.

"Oh, God," I said.

"Do you need anything, Nick? Help? Advice? A lawyer?"

"I have one of those already." And then I told her everything was fine, that it was all a misunderstanding and soon enough the police would be clearing me of everything. I tried to sound as confident as Detective Reece when I said, "It's just election-year politicking."

"You're probably right," Olivia said. "But since your

job requires you to interact with the public so much and go into their homes, maybe you need to take a day. . . ."

I got the point.

She was giving me a day off, whether I wanted it or not.

Then Mick Brosius called. He sounded like a man who'd woken up with a migraine.

"Did you talk to Reece?" he asked.

"Yes." I felt guilty, like I'd gone back on a solemn vow.

"What did I tell you about that?" His voice rose higher. "Let me handle Reece. You stay out of it."

"What am I supposed to do about what they're saying on the news?" I asked.

"Ignore it," Brosius said. "It doesn't mean anything."

I wasn't sure he sounded convinced.

"But everybody's going to hear that stuff. My boss already did. And then there are my friends, my clients at the housing authority."

"It was bound to be made public sooner or later," he said. "Just ignore it. When this all blows over, if you want to pursue a civil case, we can look into it."

"It's not that," I said, but he cut me off.

"Remember, not a word to the cops. Not without talking to me."

He hung up.

I waited for Laurel to check in, but she didn't. She had a job and a family. I couldn't expect her to tend to my problems twenty-four hours a day. I worked from home a little, which always felt like playing hooky to me. I made plans with one of the guys from my basketball team to meet that evening and practice our shooting. When it was time to take Riley for an afternoon walk, I peeked through the closed blinds first. The coast looked clear, and indeed it was. No reporters ambushed me that time, so Riley could take a whiz in peace. On the way back, my phone rang. I didn't recognize the number, so I decided to ignore it. Then the exchange registered in my brain. Someone from the Eastland campus was calling, so I answered.

"Is this Nick Hansen?" a man's voice asked.

"It is."

"I'm calling from the office of the registrar at Eastland concerning the information you requested," he said.

"Information I requested? What information . . . ?" Then it dawned on me. "Oh, right. The information I requested."

"Are you available to meet with me this afternoon?" he asked.

"Strangely, I am."

"Do you know where Hammond Park is, just off campus?"

"Of course," I said. "I know it well."

"I'll see you there at three," he said. "I'm wearing a blue Eastland polo shirt."

"Okay. Thanks."

But he was already off the line.

Hammond Park occupied two blocks on the west edge of campus. It wasn't much of a park. It was some green space with trampled grass and a few benches where students sometimes congregated to protest the government or big business by handing out flyers and chanting while the rest of the world went on with their lives. Most of the time the park sat empty. People passed through. Occasionally an old man stopped and fed birds or a mother with a stroller rested her feet.

I took Riley with me, and we arrived early. The day was warmer than expected, the high reaching the mid-fifties. Two students, a boy and a girl, sat on one side of the park, their thin legs in their tight jeans intertwined on a bench beneath a bare maple tree. The girl held a book of poetry by Pablo Neruda and appeared to be reading the boy passages and making overly dramatic gestures while she did so. The boy kept laughing. Then they'd stop and make out for a while, then go back to the book. Young love.

Marissa and I had spent a little time there. One semester we both had classes on that side of campus, and we'd meet in Hammond Park beforehand. We probably didn't look much different from the kids in the park that day. We were young, thin, naive, and horny. We'd hold hands on a bench and tell each other what we'd been doing with our day, which was usually nothing important. Then we'd part, each going our own way, but not before kissing and kissing some more and then kissing good-bye as though we'd never see each other again. But I never really worried about that possibility back then. I figured we had forever, years and years stretching before us until infinity. Who didn't think that at such a young age?

I looked down at Riley. His muzzle and feet were getting grayer by the day. He walked slower. He slept more. Time marched on.

The man with the Eastland polo shirt showed up five minutes after three. He looked younger than me, maybe thirty-five, and he walked with his hands in the pockets of his khaki pants in a way that made him seem not to have a care in the world. He noticed me and acted like he recognized me, nodding his head and walking over, still as nonchalant as anything. I had no idea who he was.

"How're you doing, Mr. Hansen?" he asked.

"Good. How are you?"

He sat down next to me on the park bench. "Not bad."

Our surreal conversation made me feel like we were in a spy movie, and I wanted to look around for enemy agents. But my new friend seemed unconcerned with such things. He bent down and scratched Riley's ears. Then he straightened up and crossed his leg, left ankle on right knee.

"How do you know Gina?" I asked.

"She and I . . . well, we're friends."

There seemed to be more to it. "Friends? Did you meet through Eastland?"

"We're good friends," he said, almost mumbling the words.

Suddenly I saw the light. I'd had the feeling lately there was someone new in Gina's life, someone besides her babysitters and her Zumba instructor. I studied the man in profile. His face was unlined, his hair full and neatly combed. I could imagine his blue eyes scanning the ocean waves while his yacht skimmed across the water.

He probably spent time with Andrew. More time than I did. I had no doubt he'd seen Andrew's latest trick football play.

He held out his hand, and we shook. "Dale Somners."

"Nick Hansen. But I guess you already knew that."

"Gina told me you're a good guy," he said. "She wanted me to help you."

"I'll have to thank her," I said. "It can be a tough trick to get your ex-wife to speak highly of you."

"She told me you needed to know something, and she also assured me that you could be discreet. It's not like these are the nuclear codes, but it wouldn't look good to find out that just anyone could call and get access to our records."

"Of course," I said. "I don't want to make trouble for you or put you in an awkward position."

"Thanks. So what did you want to know?" Dale asked.

"I guess Gina told you the name of the student I was interested in," I said.

Dale nodded.

"I just wanted to know if her records said anything about why she decided to leave school that year—1993."

"I checked for you," Dale said. "The file mentioned financial difficulties at home. That's what she told her advisor."

"That's what she told me back then," I said, somewhat to myself.

"A friend of yours?" he asked.

"She was," I said. "A very good friend."

"It's a shame," he said.

I figured he meant the fire. "Thanks."

He looked over at me, his face puzzled. "For what?"

"I'm sorry. What's a shame?" I asked.

"That she dropped out," he said. "Withdrew. She came from an Eastland family. That's what they call them down in the admissions and development offices. Eastland families. Legacies. Your friend's parents went to school at Eastland, and so did she."

"I remember that," I said. "If I recall correctly, her parents met here as well."

"Exactly," Dale said. "We push that tradition hard. Meet your mate here; send your kids here. . . ."

"Kiss on the Kissing Bridge at midnight; spend the rest of your life together."

"You remember," he said.

"Sure," I said. "I did it once."

"With . . . Marissa?" Dale asked, treading lightly.

"Yeah."

"I see. Gina mentioned that your friend died shortly after she withdrew from school," Dale said. "The file just says she's deceased, but it didn't give any details. I'm sorry for your loss."

"Thanks."

I wanted to tell him we didn't need to bond, and he was welcome to step into my place in Gina's life. Be her husband, be the new stepfather to her son. It happened, and like two grown men, we could just shake hands and move on, pretending that none of it bothered us.

"Did you know Marissa's sister?" Dale asked.

"Jade?"

"I think that was the name," he said. "I took a quick look at her file as well."

"Marissa did have a sister named Jade. She was three years younger, still in high school when we were at Eastland."

"And she was supposed to come to school here, too? Right?" he asked.

"Jade? Yes, she was. I remember now that you mention it," I said. "I know she came to visit and applied, and that meant a lot to their father. He used to say he bled Eastland blue. It would have been his dream to have both his girls go to school here. But it was fall when Marissa died, too early for a high school kid to know if she was getting in or not. I figured once Marissa died here, Jade and her family wanted nothing to do with the place. Too many bad memories. They moved out of state right after the funeral."

Dale leaned in closer. He acted like he didn't want Riley to hear what he was about to say. "She *did* know her admission status in the fall. The sister. Jade. She learned it early."

"How?"

"Have you ever heard of the Presidential Scholarships at Eastland?" he asked.

"No," I said. "I clearly didn't get one."

"It's a full ride," Dale said, "and I mean *full* ride. Room, board, tuition. Even books. They use them to lure the best in-state students to Eastland. And they use them preemptively, meaning they hand them out in the fall *before* the best students are hearing from more prestigious schools. It makes sense, right? Eastland can't compete with Kenyon or Oberlin or DePauw, so they start handing out the big money up front."

"Sure."

"Guess who got one of those offers in the fall of 1993?" Dale asked.

"Jade?"

Dale nodded. "And she accepted it. She was planning to go to Eastland in the fall of 'ninety-four just like her parents and her sister. But then she called the admissions office in October and informed them she *wouldn't* be coming, that she didn't need the scholarship or the offer of admission or the spot in the dorm. None of it. She walked away and left all that on the table."

"She called and told them this in October of ninety-three?" I asked.

Dale nodded. "Why turn that down if your family is having financial trouble? No other school was going to offer that sweet of a deal. She was a legacy and her sister was here."

"That's a lot to pass up," I said, "but would she want to walk by the spot where her sister died every day? Would she want to be reminded of that?"

"No, I guess she wouldn't," Dale said.

But he seemed to be holding another card, something he was just waiting for the right moment to lay down in front of me.

"What?" I asked. "There's more?"

"She made that call, the one in which she turned down a full ride and everything else, the day *before* her sister died."

CHAPTER SEVENTEEN

I wanted to talk to Laurel and tell her what I'd learned from Dale Somners, but she still wasn't answering her phone. She may have been off somewhere, forcing a minimum-wage clerk to confess to skimming from the till, so I left her another message.

Then I found myself with little to do. No work for the day, just me and my dog. Hammond Park and the area around campus had made me feel nostalgic, and I didn't like feeling that way. It hurt too much. Even though I lived in the same town where I had attended college, I avoided the campus as much as possible. Too many memories. Places I'd walked with Marissa. Places we'd made out, places we'd laughed. The parking lot we used to go to in her SUV when our roommates were around and we needed—wanted—to have sex.

And the memories weren't just of Marissa. It was everything. The passing of time, the unfulfilled dreams, a swirling vortex of nostalgia and regret that could swallow me if I let it.

Could I have ever imagined I would end up where I was? A middle-aged divorced guy, living alone? A murder suspect?

Riley and I wandered the winding paths through campus. Students streamed by at the change of class, looking so young, so happy, so much like babies I would have sworn they weren't any older than Andrew. They laughed. They shoved one another playfully. Boys and girls held hands. Some of them stopped to scratch Riley's ears. He loved it. I wondered what they thought of me, the guy gripping the leash. Did they think I was a professor? A parent? Did they assume I was an alum strolling down memory lane?

So much had changed on campus. New buildings. New landscaping. But familiar places remained. Parker Hall, where I took most of my philosophy classes, the building where I first met Laurel. Culpepper Hall, where I lived freshman year. I'd learned recently, from an alumni newsletter or someplace, that Culpepper had gone coed in the previous five years. I felt certain it made living there more pleasant.

And then I was on the far side of campus, where the university gave way to single-family houses and small apartment buildings, all of them taken over by students. Someone, maybe Laurel, had told me that six or seven years after the fire a new house was erected on the old lot, and students lived there as well. I wondered if anyone knew what had happened there on a distant fall night. Did the students exchange ghost stories about the fire? Did they claim to hear the muffled screams of four young women in the middle of the night?

College campuses were full of such lore. Culpepper Hall had a ghost story, one that said the fourth floor was haunted by a young man who committed suicide in his room in the 1940s. We used to share the story around Halloween, or during finals week when everyone was tired and on edge, joking about the poor sap who found college so stressful that he fashioned a noose out of a bedsheet and stepped into his closet. We laughed because we were young, but also because we were afraid. The laughter held off our own mortality—while we made fun of someone else's, someone we never knew.

Did anyone currently on campus even know Marissa's story?

I was sure a few old-timers did. Administrators who were still around. Some professors who never retired. But after twenty years, as Nate said, life goes on.

I hadn't been down that street since the year Marissa died. And I didn't intend to go that day.

I'd never seen the new house, the new students coming and going through its doors, free as birds, unaware perhaps of what had happened on that very ground. I'd gone back to the rubble-filled lot almost every day for a month after the fire, and then I had to tell myself no more. *No more.* Time to move on. Time to let the wound heal instead of picking at it.

Wasn't it time I took that advice again? Was that all I was doing with my visits to retired cops and sneaky administrators—trying to keep something alive that had died twenty years ago?

"Let's go, Riley," I said, giving his leash a gentle tug. He was more than ready to leave.

CHAPTER EIGHTEEN

The evening paper carried details about Emily's funeral, and while I ate my reheated Chinese food, I studied them like there was going to be an exam. The viewing would be held the next night at a funeral home in Richmond, Kentucky, where Emily grew up. Then a Catholic mass the following morning, with the burial in the family plot.

I checked my phone, trying not to dribble soy sauce on the screen. Richmond was about three hours away. I could easily go down for the viewing, stay overnight for the mass and burial, and be back the next day.

Marissa's funeral had passed in a blur. A group of us traveled to Hanfort to attend. I remembered seeing Marissa's mother, Joan, at the back of the church. She gave me a long hug and invited me to sit near the family at the front, so I did.

The coffin was closed, of course. It will sound morbid, but even back then I wondered what they had managed to find of her. Of any of them. Some charred bones. Some scraps of clothing. Did they bother to put them in a coffin and go through the charade that something meaningful was inside?

The priest eulogized Marissa. He talked of knowing her since she was a child, her kindness, her energy, her passion for travel and photography. I agreed with all of it, even though it didn't seem that personal. I wanted to stand up and say something, but I wasn't invited to do so. And I knew even then I wouldn't have been able to hold things together. I tried to speak at my father's funeral when I was thirty-five and couldn't get a coherent word out. No way I could have done that for Marissa when I was twenty.

Marissa's father, Brent, a man I never knew well despite the fact that I dated his daughter for two years, stared straight ahead during the service, his face stoic. Jade looked a lot like her dad, not just physically but in her demeanor as well. Her hair was darker, like her dad's, not the bright red color that Marissa and Joan shared. She was shorter than Marissa, more solidly and athletically built, although they were clearly sisters. Jade always seemed quieter and more reserved, and at the funeral she barely shed a tear. But Joan turned around to me during the post-Communion meditation and placed her hand on my arm.

"She really loved you, Nick."

"I know," I said. "I loved her too."

"I wish this had all been different," Joan said. "I really do."

She seemed to want to say more, but chose not to.

Did anything more need to be said?

Couldn't those words sum up so much of our lives?

I wish this had all been different.

Laurel finally called and told me she was on her way to my apartment. When she arrived, she looked a little tired, and I asked if she needed to be at home with her family.

"They're fine," she said. "I'll get there soon enough. And I'm sorry I didn't call you back earlier. I was on the road all day."

"I get it," I said.

"But you said in your message you had something to tell me?"

We sat on the couch with Riley at Laurel's feet. He acted like I never paid attention to him, reveling in her ear scratching and head rubbing.

While I told her all about my meeting with Dale Somners, she continued to stroke Riley's back. She listened to the information about Marissa's withdrawal from school, the claim of financial hardship, and then Jade's turning down the full ride before her sister died. Her face remained as hard to read as an ancient rune.

"That's the weird part for me," I said. "I'd get it if she didn't want to come to school here, if the memories were too intense after Marissa died. I'd get that completely. Hell, I thought about transferring when Marissa died. I walked past Blakemoor Street today when I was on campus. Do you know I haven't been back there in years?"

"Really?"

"I can't do it," I said. "I went there every day when it was just smoldering rubble. I guess everybody on campus did at some point."

"People were curious."

"Ghoulishly so," I said, trying not to sound like a complete prude. "And it makes sense when something like that happens. But I haven't been back since that first year. I haven't seen the new house they put up. I thought I could do it today, but I just couldn't bring myself to go down there."

"You don't have to," she said.

"Isn't that avoidance or something? Don't I need closure?" I held my hands up and made air quotes when I said the word "closure."

"Overrated," Laurel said. "And unnecessary. It suggests there's some magic way to get over something, like you get to a certain point and your feelings are wrapped up in a pretty box with a pretty bow. Life isn't like that. If you don't want to walk down that street, don't do it. You're a free man."

"Thanks."

"But you're right about something," she said. "It is weird that she would withdraw before Marissa died. If you were going to college, and you had that sweet offer, wouldn't you hold on to it for a while? Wouldn't you wait and see if anyone else offered you something and then play the other schools off each other?" She rubbed her hands together. "That's what I'd do."

"Maybe they forced her to make a decision," I said.

"Maybe they said, 'Let us know by the end of October or the offer goes away.'"

"Maybe," Laurel said, but she sounded unconvinced. "But they *wanted* her. She was a legacy or whatever this Dale guy called it." Laurel lifted her hand from Riley and scooted forward on the couch. She pulled out her phone. "Which brings me to my next question. What do you remember about Marissa's parents? Anything?"

"I knew them kind of well," I said, trying not to over-state things. "We dated for two years, and I went to their house half a dozen times. Some of the visits in the summer and over Christmas break were pretty long. They were nice people. Her dad was pretty reserved, almost uptight. Her mom was straight out of central casting, a real June Cleaver type. Warm, inviting, efficient. She always greeted me with a hug and sent me away with one. I liked her a lot."

"Do you know where they are now?" Laurel asked.

"They moved after Marissa died. Colorado, I heard. But really I have no idea where they are."

"That's interesting," Laurel said. "Because nobody else knows where they are either."

CHAPTER NINETEEN

I sat there for a few silent moments, trying to contemplate what Laurel was telling me.

"What do you mean nobody knows where they are?" I asked.

"I was away for most of the day, like I said. But before I left, I gave a little task to my assistant. I gave her the names of Marissa's parents. We've been looking into all of this stuff, but wouldn't it be easy just to go right to the source? If we talked to them, we'd be able to find out if this kid, Emily Russell, is related to them. We don't want to bother Emily's parents, of course. They're devastated. But maybe Marissa's parents could shed some light."

"Makes sense."

"It's easy to track people down these days," Laurel said. "We just run a background check. We have software for it. Everybody leaves an electronic trail." She ticked items off on her fingers. "E-mail addresses. Bills. Utilities. Schools, jobs, the whole deal. My point is, if you've lived at all in the last twenty years, you should have some kind of trail we can pick up. The system will find it."

"And what are you saying about Marissa's parents?" I asked.

"It's as though they haven't lived since 1993," Laurel said. "They fell off the radar back then and there's no trace of them."

I started to absorb what she was saying. "Maybe they're dead," I said. "They wouldn't be that old, probably around seventy. But they might have died. My parents were a little older than they were, and they're both dead."

"They might be dead, of course, but even if they were both dead, their trails would still show up." She pointed to me. "Even though your father's deceased, if we looked him up we'd see his records. Addresses, real estate purchases, criminal activity if there was any. All of it. But there's *nothing* during the last twenty years. Do you remember what they did after Marissa's funeral?"

"They moved to Colorado," I said. "I heard through friends they wanted a new start. Her dad had some business interests out west, a new job opportunity. It was too painful for them to stay in the town where Marissa grew up. Every time they drove by the school she attended or the doctor's office where she had her checkups or saw a playground where she climbed on the jungle gym, they'd be reminded of her. And it would hurt. I understand that. Look at me— I can't even walk down the street where she died."

"And you never heard from them after that?" Laurel asked.

"No." I laughed a little as something came back to me.

"What's funny?" Laurel asked.

"It's nothing, really," I said, almost too embarrassed to share. But I trusted Laurel, so I went ahead. "I guess I had this silly fantasy that we'd stay in touch. I thought we'd exchange Christmas cards over the years or something. Maybe I'd even go and see them wherever they ended up. Colorado sounded nice. I thought I could go visit, and they'd welcome me with open arms, like I was their prodigal son. I'd fill the empty space for them, and they could do the same for me. Hell, I don't even know if Marissa told them we broke up. Anyway, my fantasy faded away pretty quickly. I never even had their address once they moved." I drummed my fingers on the arm of the couch. "I sent them a card that first Christmas after Marissa died. They'd already moved, but I hoped it would get to them. It came back saying there was no forwarding address. It was a nice little dose of reality."

"How so?" Laurel asked.

"It killed that silly little fantasy I had that we'd all stay friends," I said. "They had moved on. Literally. I figured they hadn't moved on emotionally and probably never would. But that was it for me and them. I guess it seems strange they wouldn't have their mail forwarded. Wouldn't a lot of people be writing to them? Trying to be supportive, trying to stay in touch."

"What did her dad do for a living?" she asked.

"He ran a consulting firm," I said. "It was one of those vague things I didn't understand. I don't think Marissa understood it either." I shrugged a little at my lack of knowledge concerning the business world. "Her mom didn't work. She volunteered a little, that kind of thing. And her sister was in school. Pretty typical stuff."

"Did they have other relatives?" Laurel asked. "Do you remember?"

"Her dad was an only child. Marissa had a grandmother on one side, her mother's. Maybe there was an aunt and some cousins. They lived back east. Virginia, I think, but her grandmother would have to be dead. I don't even remember the other relatives' names. I only met them once, at some reunion."

"The all-American family, right?"

"I guess so."

"So then why did they fall off the map like this?" Laurel asked. "Do you know what happened to Jade?"

"She moved with her parents to Colorado. We know she didn't go to school here. I imagine she's gone on and lived her life. Married. Kids. But I don't know where she is or what her married name might be."

"I'll see if I can find her, but you're right. It might be tougher if she got married and took her husband's name." Laurel's lips puckered with concentration. "None of this adds up."

"It seems like you're reading something sinister into it," I said. "Is it hard to believe they would want to start over after their child died? You're a parent. You can understand that."

"Moving away I can understand," Laurel said. "Disappearing off the face of the earth is another matter entirely."

CHAPTER TWENTY

I was lucky to find a seat at the back of the church. The odors of burning candles and incense hung heavy in the air, and people murmured respectfully as they filed in. The pews quickly became packed, and a number of mourners ended up standing in the aisles, which didn't surprise me. People turned out when a young person died.

I had skipped the viewing the night before after driving all afternoon from Eastland—three hours down I-75—and checking into a hotel a mile from the funeral home. I'd packed a nice suit and a couple of ties and brought Riley along with me. He didn't mind car trips. He liked to sit in the backseat, his head resting against the upholstery. I snuck him past the clerk in the hotel, avoiding the pet deposit. How would they know he was there when he never barked?

I knew why I wanted to attend Emily's funeral. She and I were linked, even if I didn't know all the details about why she'd died, and since she was apparently looking for me, I felt a measure of responsibility for her death. I didn't know what she'd wanted from me, or if I could have even delivered what she'd wanted, but it felt like she'd needed or wanted something from me, so we shared that connection, real or imagined.

And I also felt sick about what had happened to her. I knew all about a young life being cut short, and I could only imagine Emily alone in that crappy motel room in Eastland. Her life ended in terror, someone's hands clutching her throat and squeezing until the breath went out of her. She deserved better, as Marissa had, and at least we could give that to her in death. I wanted to be a part of celebrating her life and saying good-bye.

If she were my daughter or sister or friend, wouldn't I want as many people as possible to celebrate her life?

But once I was in the hotel room, I reconsidered. I felt more like an outsider, an intruder, than anything else, so I passed on the viewing and resolved to go back home the next morning. I ordered a hamburger from room service and watched a basketball game on TV. While I chewed and stared at the running and dribbling men on the screen, I wondered what Andrew was doing, and if he missed watching the games with me, or if he was content to watch with Dale Somners, the comfortable, easygoing guy in the Eastland polo shirt.

In the morning, I walked Riley around the back of the parking lot, letting him sniff every lamppost and car tire he could find. When I returned to the hotel, I saw a stack of local papers in the lobby. And on the front page of every one of them was a photo of Emily Russell underneath the headline SAYING GOOD-BYE. Once I saw her face again, even just a picture, I knew I had to go to the church, and that's how I ended up squeezed into the pew, my tie pinching my freshly shaved throat, my suit jacket riding up behind me.

Here, unlike at Marissa's funeral, I remained clear-headed, noticing every detail. The somber organ music. The colored light streaming through the stained-glass windows. The devastated looks on the faces of Emily's parents, who shambled behind their daughter's coffin like shell-shocked refugees. They stared straight ahead, tears streaking their cheeks.

A lot of young people sat scattered throughout the church, classmates and friends of Emily's, and during the quiet moments, when the music and the voices stopped, sniffles echoed throughout the cavernous building. My father had died five years earlier after a long illness, and my mom died not long after. I was prepared for their deaths well in advance, and while it affected me profoundly, I also saw it as part of the natural order of things. Children outlive their parents. Older people die. That's the way the world worked.

Even at my own parents' funerals I didn't feel the same emotional pull as I did at Emily's. I didn't cry, but the sadness pushed against the inside of me, clawing to get out, and I bit back on it so no one would wonder who the strange man blubbering by himself in the back of the church was. I'd had enough attention drawn to me over the past few days. I didn't need any more. And neither did the Russells.

For the most part, the priest avoided mention of the circumstances of Emily's death. He spoke in general terms about the loss of a young life, about the promise that had been cut short by her loss. He reminded those who knew her—a statement that excluded me, of course—that Emily lived on inside all of us, that we carried her with us everywhere we went.

Only at the end of the homily did he make passing reference to the murder. He told us that while life on earth could sometimes seem terribly unfair, in God's kingdom justice was always delivered.

His words gave me a cold chill.

And for some reason I felt like everyone in the church was staring at me.

CHAPTER TWENTY-ONE

With the rest of the mourners, I trudged across the sickly brown grass to the graveside service, dodging the tombstones, watching where I stepped on the uneven ground. The weather had turned cooler as the morning progressed, and the rising wind cut through my light overcoat and poked at my body.

Again, I stayed near the back, letting people who had really known Emily have the prime spots closer to the grave. When the priest spoke, his words barely reached me, most of them carried away on the wind. I scanned the crowd, looking for . . . I didn't know what. A familiar feature? A hint that would help me understand my connection to Emily Russell's life and death?

No matter how many faces I saw, most of the heads bowed in prayer and meditation, I didn't see anything that told me what I needed to know.

When the service ended, the priest announced that everyone was invited back to the Russells' house to continue to celebrate Emily's life. I knew I wasn't going.

Riley waited in the hotel room, and I needed to get back to my life and quit lingering on the edges of someone else's. I started walking to my car.

"A hell of a thing, isn't it?" a voice asked.

I turned. A woman about ten years older than I was waited for my response. She looked a little rough around the edges—frizzy gray hair, crooked glasses—not at all like Emily's parents, and she held a balled-up tissue in her hand, which she used to take occasional swipes at her nose. She wore white sneakers and black pants. Her heavy winter coat was zipped up to just below her chin.

I didn't know what to say. Did anyone know the right words at a funeral?

"It is," I said, acknowledging the universal awfulness of Emily's death.

"She was such a beautiful girl," the woman said. She held her hand out to me, the one that wasn't holding the dirty tissue. "I'm Margie Rhineback, a cousin of Emily's mom's."

"Nick."

She stared at me expectantly. Then I understood what she wanted.

"I'm a friend of the family," I said.

Margie nodded. "I hadn't seen Emily since she was a little girl, but her mom used to send a Christmas card and letter every year. She always included a picture of the whole family, and I watched Emily grow up that way. I live over in Paducah. That's three hours away. I just can't imagine what they're going through now. Are you heading back to the house?"

"I have to get on my way," I said. "I'm from out of town."

"Well, I'm going over there," she said. "I just have to tell them all how sorry I am."

We reached the road where our cars were parked. Doors opened and engines started, everyone eager to get out of the cold wind. But Margie seemed to want to talk more, and I just wanted to get away.

"It was nice meeting you," I said. "Even though the circumstances are awful."

"You know what I keep thinking about?" she asked. "Ever since they found that poor girl dead in that filthy motel room?"

"What's that?" I asked.

"I think about what her parents went through to get her."

My hands were stuffed into the deep pockets of my coat, and I pulled it tighter around my body. "What do you mean? What did they go through to get her?"

Margie's eyes opened wider. "You must not have known them that long."

"I guess not," I said.

"Why, they tried for years to get pregnant, and they just couldn't. Believe me, they spent a lot of money on fertility treatments. They tried every trick in the book."

"And it worked eventually?" I asked. "Apparently?"

Margie shook her head. "No, it didn't. They were on a waiting list for years, and then it finally came through. That beautiful little baby girl. Emily was adopted."

CHAPTER TWENTY-TWO

"Adopted?" I asked.

"You didn't know that?" Margie asked.

"To be honest, I don't know the family that well."

Margie looked at me suspiciously, but she let it pass. We were stopped between two headstones, one of them decorated with a bouquet of cheap yellow flowers and the other unadorned.

"Did they adopt her when she was an infant?" I asked.

"They were living down in Tennessee then." She lowered her voice, as though one of the sleeping dead beneath our feet might hear what she had to say. "As I understand it, they paid quite a bit of money. And then they adopted Kate as well."

I must have worn a blank look on my face because Margie felt compelled to explain.

"Kate," she said. "Emily's sister."

"Right. Of course."

"You *don't* know them very well, do you?" Margie said.

"I bet you're in a hurry to get back to the house and see the family," I said. "I'm sure they appreciate you being here to support them."

"I try."

"Can I ask you just one more thing?" I waited for Margie to object, but she didn't. She waited patiently while the wind picked up and ruffled her hair. "Do you have any idea if Emily ever met her birth parents? Did she know who they are?"

Margie shrugged beneath the bulk of her parka. "I haven't a clue." She kicked at the ugly grass with her right foot. "But I'm not sure I would know something that intimate about the family. Like I said, it's been a number of years." She shrugged again. "Isn't it awful the way it takes things like this to bring people closer together? I mean, here we all are, and we're family, and we could get together anytime we wanted, but it takes someone's death to make it happen."

"You're right. But I think most families are like that."

"It's sad," she said. "All of it."

Above us, the clouds shifted, and the sun broke through for just a moment. Margie raised her hand to her eyes, shielding her vision from the glare. I followed her line of sight and saw a crowd of people clustered around Emily's parents and sister, hugging them and wishing them well.

"So you're not coming back to the house?" Margie asked.

"I have to get home," I said. "My dog is waiting for me in the hotel. If I stayed away another few hours, he might actually notice I was gone."

"I'm going home tomorrow," she said.

I reached out and shook Margie's cold hand. "Thanks, Margie. I'm sorry we met under these circumstances."

Margie nodded. "I know what you mean. I really know what you mean."

I sat in my car while the small crowd pressed around the Russell family. I felt certain the family was eager to get out of the cold and back to their house, where they could talk more easily with relatives and friends. I remembered how desperate and miserable I had felt at Marissa's funeral. We didn't go to the graveside for her. Instead we'd all packed into a small chapel on the cemetery grounds and stood around staring at the shroud-draped casket.

But I'd needed help believing that nightmare was real. I'd wanted to throw open the lid and see her, to somehow try to face and accept the reality of what had happened.

The cold of the car brought me back to the present just then. I leaned forward and placed both of my hands on the steering wheel, even though the car wasn't turned on yet. I needed heat and warmth, but something prevented me from moving or stirring.

Emily was adopted. And she looked exactly like Marissa.

I knew that many, many babies were given up for adoption every year. Being adopted in and of itself didn't make Emily Russell unique. But couple that with her resemblance to Marissa and her apparent desire to locate me, and . . .

As Laurel had pointed out, though, Emily was born months after Marissa died. So how did any of it add up?

How?

CHAPTER TWENTY-THREE

The crowd around the Russells was finally breaking up, so I started the car and put it in gear. I had exaggerated when I told Margie that Riley wouldn't notice I was gone. He would. He always acted happy to see me, as though he was counting the minutes until I returned home. I knew he didn't really count, that time wasn't the same for him as it was for me. But I think he really did miss me, and I felt bad about leaving him in a strange place for an extended period of time.

I started moving forward, slowly. There were people on both sides of the little road through the cemetery, talking in small groups and getting into their cars, hugging and commiserating. I knew none of them, so I rolled on by, trying not to interfere with their grief.

On my left, I saw two clusters of people. There were four mourners in one group and five in the next. Middle-aged, well-dressed. I gave them a quick look.

In the daylight between them at a short distance, I

saw a woman striding away from the service, head down, moving quickly. The way she walked, her posture . . . it struck the same chord in me as the night in the grocery store when I saw Emily. The familiarity was too much, too powerful.

She had red hair, thick and pulled back. I'd know her anywhere.

"Marissa!"

I hit the brakes. Hard.

The car stopped, and my body kept going, snapping my head forward and then back, the seat belt restraining me even though I hadn't been going more than twenty miles an hour.

I put the car in park and unbuckled, fumbling for the door handle. I looked up one more time, and I saw the woman—*Marissa?*—moving farther and farther away. As I pushed the door open, a horn honked behind me.

I turned around. A car sat right behind mine, and it wasn't just any car. It was the police cruiser that had escorted the funeral procession from the church to the cemetery. I saw the officer behind the driver's seat, the rack of lights on top. At first I thought he wanted to question me about Emily again, but then the cop pointed at me, his hand encased in a black leather glove, and he made a shooing gesture, telling me to get out of the way.

The people to my left, the ones who had originally caught my attention, were staring at me, probably wondering who the idiot was who had decided to stop his car in the middle of the tiny cemetery road.

"Shit," I said.

I pulled the door shut again and put the car in drive. I twisted the wheel to the right and quickly eased over to the side of the road, my tires crunching the already dead grass. I turned the car off and waited. The police cruiser eased past me, and as it did, the officer turned his large head in my direction, his giant aviator sunglasses making his face look like an insect's.

I pushed the door of my car open and stepped out into the road.

I hustled in the direction I had seen the woman walking, moving through the two groups standing on the side of the road. A few of the people looked at me as I passed, their heads swiveling to follow me, but I didn't care.

For a moment, I lost sight of her. The road where my car was parked, the main one through the cemetery, intersected another road just about fifty feet past where Emily's service was held, and that's where I saw the woman I was looking for. She was on that other road, a good seventy-five feet from my spot, and she was opening the door of a car and getting inside.

I started running through the tombstones, my hand raised like a child in school.

"Hey," I called. "Marissa?"

The woman didn't hear me. Or if she heard me, she didn't respond. She shut her door and started her engine. I couldn't close the gap quickly enough. By the time I made it to where she'd been, she had driven off in the opposite direction, toward a side entrance of the cemetery, out onto the street and turning right, heading away.

It looked to be an out-of-state plate, not one from Kentucky, but I hadn't managed to catch a single number.

She was gone. Simply gone.

I walked back to my car in something of a daze.

I wondered if I had really seen what I thought I had—Marissa at Emily Russell's funeral.

Or was I just doing what Heather, and to a lesser extent Laurel, had already accused me of . . . seeing things that weren't really there because of my unresolved feelings for Marissa? My twenty-year-old wound continued to warp everything I did in the present.

"You didn't get her?"

The voice snapped me out of it, and I turned around and saw one of the men from the group of people I'd seen milling around after the service. He looked to be in his sixties and had a lot of white hair and a ruddy face.

"Did any of you talk to her?" I asked.

They all looked at one another. No one said anything fast enough for me.

"Did you talk to her?" I asked again. "Do any of you know her?"

A woman who stood near the man with the white hair said, "I've never seen her before."

"We didn't talk to her," the man with the white hair said. "But I saw her in the back of the church."

"Was she alone?" I asked.

The man gave me a long look, the corners of his mouth turning down while he studied me. "You seemed to know her," he said. "You called her name. 'Marissa.' Didn't you say that?"

I looked at all of the faces. Some showed concern, and I could tell others were thinking more about getting on to the next thing and then going home.

"I thought I knew her," I said. "I thought she was an old friend, but maybe I was wrong."

I started to walk away, but the man's voice brought me back.

"You might think you were mistaken, but I don't think you were," he said. "While you were over there talking to that woman in the heavy coat, that woman whose name you called, that Marissa, she was standing over here, staring in your direction. She didn't take her eyes off you for one second."

CHAPTER TWENTY-FOUR

For his part, Riley acted happy to see me. When I walked into the room, he bounded over and sniffed at my pants leg, wagging his tail. Then he gladly accepted some ear scratching. His food bowl looked almost untouched.

"We've got somewhere to go, boy," I said. "Not home just yet."

I gathered up my things, hooked Riley to his leash, and carried my one bag out to the car, hoping no one saw the dog. Then I stopped up front and paid my bill. On my way back to the car, my phone rang. It was work.

"Nick?"

It was Olivia Bloom, and she sounded cautious and cheery. She always sounded that way, as though she wasn't sure she was as happy as she thought she was.

"How are you, Olivia?"

"I wanted to check in with you," she said. "Has anything else happened with that . . . police case or whatever it is?"

"Police case?" I asked. "You mean the murder investigation."

"Yes, that."

"I don't know anything else," I said. "They haven't solved it as far as I know. And I'm a person of interest, whatever that means."

"I see," she said, clearly thinking my situation over.

"I'm at the girl's funeral right now, down in Kentucky."

"The dead girl?" Olivia asked.

"Yes, the dead girl. Emily Russell."

"Is that a good idea, Nick?" she asked. "What if someone sees you? You know," she said, her voice lowering to a whisper, "sometimes the police look for the killer at the victim's funeral."

"I didn't kill her, Olivia," I said. "I just felt compelled to be here."

There was a long pause while Olivia processed what I had just told her. Tried to process, I guessed. It was a lot to take in, having a person of interest in a murder case working in your office.

I reached the car and slid in. Riley was in the backseat, chewing on a biscuit I had given him. He gave me a look that said, *Home, please.* I held up my index finger to him, asking him to wait. Was I on my way to that special place reserved for people who talked only to their pets?

"What did you need, Olivia?" I asked. "Are you calling to tell me to stay away longer because you think I'm a killer?"

"Nick. How could you say something like that? We're not firing you. I was actually calling to ask you back.

You'd have to work in the office for a while, until all of this is cleared up. I'm not sure we can have you out in the field yet."

"Of course."

"You can come back tomorrow morning," she said. "And we'll be happy to have you. We miss you. And, let's be honest, you're one of our very best caseworkers. We need you."

I looked at the clock. It was just after noon. If I started driving right then, I'd be home within three hours. I could get a good night's sleep and head into the office first thing in the morning, bright-eyed and ready for whatever the world threw at me.

But if I stayed away longer . . .

"I have vacation saved up, don't I?" I asked.

"Yes. Quite a bit," she said. "You haven't used it for a couple of years, even though I try to get you to. Would you like to go on a vacation? Maybe that would be good for you."

"I'm not going on a vacation," I said. "But I'm going to use the time I have saved. I'm taking the rest of the week off. And maybe next week as well."

"Next week?" she asked.

"Yes. Is that a problem?"

Olivia's concern only deepened. "Nick, level with me about this. You say you didn't kill this girl."

"Emily," I said.

"Emily. Right. You say you didn't kill her, and I believe you about that. You're so kind and compassionate. I know you'd never hurt someone. But are you in some kind of trouble? You don't really sound like yourself. You sound distracted and maybe a little down. Is there something I can do to help you with this?"

I started the car and turned the heater on. The day was turning bright and clear, but still cold. "I'm going to ask you something that may sound a little off the wall."

"Shoot," she said.

"Do you ever think there are things going on that are bigger than us and maybe beyond our comprehension?" I asked.

"Are you speaking in existential terms?" Olivia asked.

"Real terms. In the here and now."

"Nick, I work for a small government agency. I feel that way all the time."

"Then you have a sense of how I'm feeling," I said. "And I don't think there's much of anything you can do to help me with that. But thanks for understanding."

CHAPTER TWENTY-FIVE

The Russells lived in an upscale neighborhood. The houses on both sides of their street rose high above me like soaring, elegant castles, with wide, expansive lawns, and I felt lucky no one stopped me at the entrance to the subdivision and asked to see my papers.

I wound through the streets, a dwarf among the mansions. Riley made a little whining noise from the backseat. He knew we'd gone off in some different direction, one that brought us to a place rather unlike home.

I made the last turn and saw some cars in front of a house at the end of the cul-de-sac. I turned my head slightly and said to Riley, "I won't be long."

When I came closer to the group of cars, I saw two police cruisers sitting at the end of the driveway.

I slowed down and took in the scene. Three uniformed officers stood in the driveway talking to some of the well-dressed mourners. I made a slow, easing turn around the cul-de-sac. Maybe the police were there providing moral support. Or maybe they were there because someone fell and hit their head. Or because someone had chest pains, and the ambulance was on its way. Or maybe they were looking for a person of interest, someone they suspected of something more sinister.

I decided not to stay.

Except as soon as I completed my circle around the cul-de-sac and prepared to accelerate up the street and out of everybody's lives, someone in the driveway pointed at me.

It was the man with the white hair from the cemetery. He pointed at me, and then one of the police officers turned and walked toward the street. He waved his hand, asking me—ordering me—to slow down and stop.

For a brief moment—a very brief one—I considered just leaving.

But I didn't.

I stopped the car in the middle of the street and waited for the officer to reach me.

When he did, I powered down the window. The cop was young with jet-black hair slicked back against his skull. He wore short sleeves and stood next to my car with his hands on his hips. I looked behind him and saw the man with the white hair gesticulating wildly to the other two officers. Occasionally he pointed at me.

Now what?

The cop asked me for identification, which I provided. And then he asked me what I was doing at the Russells' house. An image of Mick Brosius flashed across my mind.

Should I call him? But what could he do? And I figured there was no lie I could tell, nor any reason to tell one. The man with the white hair had seen me at the cemetery. Why else would I be showing up at the Russells' house?

"I was at the funeral," I said. "I came by . . . honestly I came by because I wanted to see if someone I knew was here."

"And are they?" the cop asked.

"I don't know. I haven't been inside yet."

One side of his mouth curled up a little.

"Can you tell me who this person is you're looking for?"

Not an easy question to answer. Not an easy question at all.

"An old friend of mine. From college," I said. "Someone I haven't seen in a long, long time. It looked like her, but when I said her name at the cemetery, she didn't turn around. I think I was mistaken, but I came here just to make sure."

The cop made a noise in the back of his throat. "Hmmph."

I didn't know if it was a good noise or a bad one.

"I'm probably just going to go home," I said. "I need to get back to Ohio."

"Ohio?" He still held my license. He looked down at it again. "Eastland?"

"Yes, that's where I live."

"Isn't that where Ms. Russell was killed?" he asked.

"Yes, it is. That's how I know about her. Because I live

there. In fact . . ." It crossed my mind that I shouldn't be revealing the next part of the story to this officer, that he would almost certainly take it the wrong way. But I assumed he would find out pretty quickly anyway. "She might have been looking for me when she died."

"Really?" he asked. "Why might she have been looking for you?"

"I don't know."

I told him about the encounter in the grocery store and the address in Emily's pocket. I couldn't tell if he knew all these details or not. I assumed someone in Richmond did, a detective or someone important in the police department. The officer I was speaking to listened patiently, his face calm and encouraging. When I was finished, he looked at my license again.

"Do you mind sitting tight, Mr. Hansen?" he asked.

"I do want to get on the road."

"This won't take long." He started to move away, and then turned back to the car. "You aren't going to drive off, are you? While I'm gone?"

"You have my license," I said.

He didn't say anything.

"No," I said. "I'm not going to drive off. I'm going to sit here with my dog."

The officer flicked his eyes toward the backseat at Riley. Then he walked over to the cruisers and the other officers. The man with the white hair had wandered off, satisfied that the police were handling me.

I waited for fifteen minutes. I thought about calling Laurel and asking for advice, but what could she tell me to do? Cooperate? I did call my lawyer, Mick Brosius, but the call went to voice mail, and I decided against leaving a message. I figured the police would be letting me go on my way momentarily, so why get Brosius worked up?

While the first officer, the one with my license in his hand, spoke, the other officers surreptitiously glanced in my direction and then went back to listening. Then the first officer got in one of the cars, and I saw him using a cell phone.

I still didn't know why the police were even there. As Olivia had mentioned, I knew they sometimes came to the funerals of crime victims, hoping to see if the perpetrator showed up. But they wouldn't be so obvious if they were doing that, would they?

The officer finally came back, tapping my license against his thumbnail. He handed it back to me and said, "I spoke to Detective Reece in Eastland. He confirmed your story."

"Good."

"I also spoke to my supervisor here," he said, tilting his head toward the cruiser. "We considered bringing you in to talk some more, but in the end, we're going to let Detective Reece worry about you. He seems to have the investigation under control."

"Thanks."

"Do us all a favor, Mr. Hansen." He pointed in the direction of the Russells' house. "Please leave the Russell family alone. They've been through enough. Considering your proximity to the crime and possible involvement, you'd be better served by keeping your distance and letting them grieve in peace."

"Sounds like good advice," I said. "But I wasn't involved in the way you're implying."

"Not my problem."

"I just have one question," I said.

The officer made that low sound in his throat again. "Hmmph."

"Why are the police here in the first place?" I asked. "Is something wrong?"

The officer looked back at the Russells' house, and then he swung his head back in my direction. He leaned a little closer. "There was a disturbance earlier, just after the family returned from the cemetery."

"What kind of disturbance?" I asked.

The officer's eyes narrowed. "Did you not just hear the advice I gave to you, oh, maybe thirty seconds ago, Mr. Hansen?" He pointed up the street, telling me the direction to go.

I didn't wait. I took his advice and left.

CHAPTER TWENTY-SIX

I crossed into Ohio in the late afternoon, and thirty minutes into my home state my eyelids started to droop. It had been a long day. Emotional. Stressful. I needed gas and to fill my own tank with caffeine.

I stopped at a gas station a mile off the interstate. I didn't catch the name of the town, if it even had one. The station and its convenience store were the only things in sight besides fields and more fields and somewhere in the distance a weathered barn that was folding in on itself. I stretched while the gas pumped, and then left Riley in charge of watching the car while I went inside to pay.

An old man in a cap from a seed company was working the register. He looked like he'd seen a lot of miles, and he didn't even meet my eye when he asked if I needed anything else. I told him I didn't. I had coffee and a candy bar, enough to get me home.

It might have been my grogginess or the distractions

filling my mind, but I didn't see the car coming. I'd taken one step out of the store, my right foot just hitting the asphalt, when the silver sedan rushed by, forcing me to jump back to avoid being hit. I lost my balance and fell backward against the glass door behind me, the hot coffee spilling down my arm and pants leg.

I remained like that for a moment, frozen in place in a kind of crouch with my back against the door and my hand dripping. The car didn't stop. It rushed to the exit and out onto the narrow country road leading to the gas station. I tried, but there was no way in hell to get the license number.

Then I felt the pain in my hand. I looked down and shook the excess coffee away and went back inside, dropping the candy bar on the ground. The old-timer at the register didn't look up while I hustled into the bathroom and ran cold water over my hand.

The water was soothing. I looked at myself in the mirror. My skin was blanched, my eyes wide. My heart thumped a crazy rhythm, and a pulse beat in my neck, visible in the mirror just beneath the skin.

I felt hot. Really hot. I splashed cold water on my face, two and then three times. I wiped it with a towel.

Someone had almost run me over. I pulled out another towel and patted the rest of my face and hands dry. I thought of Emily, her life choked out of her in that hotel room. And then her body sealed in a coffin for all eternity. It all made me feel paranoid. Scared.

That car wasn't *trying* to hit me, was it? That couldn't be.

I returned to the front and cleared my throat. The old guy looked up from a hunting magazine.

"Did you see that?" I asked.

He swiveled his head around the store. "See what?"

I pointed. "Out there. That car almost ran me down when I left."

He followed the line of my finger and shook his head. "I didn't see anything." He pointed to his ear. "I can't hear so good either."

"A car came right up against me when I stepped out the door. I had to jump back. I spilled my coffee."

He looked at my stained pants. "Do you want to call the law? Or would you just like another coffee?"

What would I tell the police if I called them? That someone almost ran me over? For all I knew, it was a bad driver, a clueless person texting while driving or blabbering on a cell phone. I had no license number, no description of the driver. I did have a mind pushed to its limit by stress and shock.

Did I really think someone tried to kill me?

"I guess I'll take the coffee," I said. "And a candy bar. I dropped mine."

"Coffee's on the house," the old guy said. "But I have to charge you for another candy bar."

I dropped Riley off at home first, and then I called Mick Brosius. I gave him a quick rundown of what had happened at the funeral, especially about seeing the woman who looked like Marissa, and he told me to meet him at his office. Once I arrived, I added the part about the car almost running me down.

He listened to that part of the story patiently, but his face showed skepticism.

"Should I tell Reece about that?" I asked.

"Well," he said, "if you really want to. But it's not his jurisdiction, and you really don't have any proof this person meant to do you harm."

"But they came so close. Are you saying I'm just being paranoid?"

"There are a lot of bad drivers in the world," he said. "Let's not worry about it right now. I called Reece. He's expecting us."

So together we walked over to the police station to meet Detective Reece.

I felt a little like I was going into the lions' den, since I could only assume that they still considered me a "person of interest" in Emily's death. But my desire to tell him the things I'd learned—and seen—in Richmond overwhelmed any other concerns.

Reece sat at his desk, his tie slightly loosened. His jacket hung on the back of his chair, and his sleeves were rolled up to his elbows. On his forearm, just above his wrist, was a tattoo of a small cross.

Brosius and I sat in uncomfortable wooden chairs. Mick said, "I'm here because I want to protect my client. And I want it noted that he's voluntarily providing this information in the hopes of helping the Emily Russell case move forward."

"How was Emily's funeral?" Reece asked.

"Look, I went because I felt a connection to the girl, to her death. It's not a crime, is it?" I asked.

"Don't say that," Brosius said. "You're not guilty. You don't even look guilty."

"What did you want to talk to me about?" Reece asked. "I'm assuming it's good." A phone rang on Reece's desk, but he didn't answer it. After two rings, he pressed a button, silencing the call. "You can tell me about this disturbance at the Russells' house."

I looked at Brosius, who nodded, giving me the okay to tell the story I had told him on the phone.

"I don't know what it was about," I said. "I went to the Russells' house because I was looking for someone I thought I knew. When I arrived, the police were in the driveway. They talked to me for a while and checked me out. They obviously called you. That's all I know. When I found out something had happened, I decided to get out of there and come home. I figured if there had been some kind of disturbance, the Russells didn't need me showing up for more. Do they even know who I am? Have you told them about my address being in Emily's pocket when she died? And the grocery store?"

"They know all of it," Reece said. "They might not recognize you if you strolled into their home, but they know about it. They know everything, even things they don't want to know, I'm sure."

He let me contemplate that for a moment. I remembered sitting in the very same chair the first time I came to the station with Reece, the day I was fingerprinted and swabbed. I remembered Emily's parents walking through the room, carrying that unseen but unbearable burden. They had just identified their daughter's dead body. Yes, they most certainly knew more than they ever wanted to know.

"What was the disturbance at the Russells' house?" I asked. "Am I allowed to know?"

Reece picked up a paper clip and started twirling it between his fingers. He moved it deftly, like a magician working up to a trick.

He said, "A woman showed up at the Russells' house, right after the funeral. She claimed to be Emily's birth mother."

CHAPTER TWENTY-SEVEN

I summoned a picture in my mind of that woman—Marissa?—hurrying away from the graveside, her head down.

"What kind of disturbance did she cause?" I asked.

"She showed up as the first guests were arriving back at the Russells' house," Reece said, his voice level, almost nonchalant. "She came in the back door and announced that she was Emily's birth mother. She said she wanted to talk to the Russells and find out what really happened to her daughter. I guess she also said she had a right to be mourning alongside everybody else. Some of the guests tried to get her to quiet down and leave."

"Did they know who she was?" I asked.

"Do you mean did they know if she was really Emily's birth mother?" he asked. "No. No one had ever seen her before."

"But everyone knew Emily was adopted, right?" I asked.

Reece shifted in his chair. He pushed his sleeves farther up his arms, first one side and then the other. "Did you know Emily was adopted?" he asked.

"I just found out today," I said. "At the funeral. At the cemetery, as a matter of fact. A cousin of Emily's mother told me. Are you saying you didn't know?"

Reece rubbed his chin. "I can understand that in the grief and confusion of Emily's death certain details may not be conveyed to us in the timeliest fashion. But in a case like this, everything is clearly relevant."

"So you didn't know?" Brosius asked.

"No, but we know now. And we're curious to talk to this woman who is claiming to be Emily's birth mother. Not only did she show up making that claim, but she threatened one of the Russells' guests. Mr. Russell's brother tried to gently and calmly steer her away from the reception and back out the door. He told her this wasn't the time to be bringing things like that up. The woman threatened to come back and kill him."

"Shit," I said.

Reece's face darkened. "You have to understand that we take a claim like that very seriously when it's directed at a family member of a homicide victim."

"She probably just blurted it out in the heat of the moment," I said. "I doubt very much she'd come back and hurt someone."

"You doubt it, do you?" he asked.

"It certainly looks like you have another possible suspect on your hands," Brosius said. "One who has leveled threats against the family of the victim. And you have witnesses to the threats."

Reece raised his hand. "I hear you, Mr. Brosius."

I looked around the room and thought about what they were implying. Police business went on around us. Phones rang, and somewhere out of sight an announcement went out over a PA system, the voice tinny and rough, the message unintelligible. "I think I know who that woman is, the one who showed up at the reception."

"You do?" Reece asked. "Who is it?"

I swallowed before I spoke. I knew if I said the name I carried in my head, I was opening myself up for all kinds of ugly responses. Ridicule. Anger. Pity. But I couldn't stay quiet. If it helped Reece solve the case and exonerate me . . . and if it could possibly bring me closer to understanding whether the woman at the funeral had really been Marissa or not, I had to say it.

I looked over at Brosius, and he nodded again. We'd discussed it at his office before coming over, and he felt it wouldn't hurt my cause to share the information. "Go ahead," he said.

"I saw a woman at the cemetery," I said, trying not to sound as uncertain as I felt. "After the service, and after I was talking to Mrs. Russell's cousin, I saw a woman walking to her car. That's how the people at the reception tied us together. They saw that the woman was watching me, and then she walked away before I could talk to her."

"I'm listening," Reece said.

"I really think it was Marissa Minor."

Reece didn't laugh. He continued to study me, and

maybe his eyelids squinted shut a millimeter or so, but other than that, he showed nothing.

Then he said, "Your deceased girlfriend? The one who's been dead for twenty years?"

"Yes."

"The one you thought Emily Russell looked like when you saw her in the grocery store?" he asked.

"Exactly," I said. "That's what started all of this. And now a woman who looks a hell of a lot like Marissa shows up at Emily's funeral, claiming to be her birth mother? Doesn't that tell you it's all connected?"

Reece reached over and riffled through a stack of manila folders. He slid one out and opened it, turning a few of the loose pages until he found the one he wanted.

"You told me Marissa died in October," he said.

"I know the math," I said. "I know Emily was born seven months after Marissa died. I know none of it makes logical sense. But do you have any other way to explain it?"

"And one of the things you're basing this whole theory on is the belief that Marissa's family, the Minors, just disappeared after they moved out of Ohio in the wake of their daughter's death. Am I right?"

His question brought me up short. He knew something. "How did you know about that?" I asked.

"I talked to your friend. Mrs. Davidson. Actually, she came to talk to me."

"She did? When?" I asked.

"What is this about?" Brosius asked. He looked at me. "Did Laurel tell you about this?"

"No."

Reece looked down at the folder. "She doesn't know everything," he said. "She might know a lot, but she doesn't know everything." He removed a piece of paper and handed it to me. "Check that out."

I studied the page, with Brosius reading over my shoulder. It took a moment for me to register what it was, but then I understood. They were obituaries, printed off a website. One for Marissa's father and one for her mother. Her father had died four years earlier at the age of sixty-nine. Her mother died one year ago at the age of seventy-three. The obituaries were short on details, but they mentioned that the Minors were predeceased by a daughter, Marissa, and survived by another daughter, Jade.

I looked at the top of the page. The obituary came from a newspaper in Colorado, a town I'd never heard of, Cherokee Falls.

"You found them," I said.

"I found out they died," Reece said. "Of natural causes, and apparently at a somewhat advanced age. And didn't you tell Mrs. Davidson they moved to Colorado after the fire that killed Marissa?"

"They did. That's what I heard."

"So they were right there all along, living their lives." He made a smoothing gesture with his hand. "No mystery. No grand conspiracy. They were exactly what they appeared to be—a grieving family who moved away after their daughter died in a tragic accident."

"But what about—"

Reece took the paper back from me. "I didn't say I

had all the answers. But I think we can stop imagining this is your deceased girlfriend showing up twenty years after her death. I'm sorry, Mr. Hansen, but that girl died. In a fire. And her parents went on the best they could. And all I can really keep coming back to and wondering about is why that girl had your name and address in her pocket when we found her body. Until you have a decent explanation for that, you may want to consider not talking to me at all." He turned and looked at Brosius. "Isn't that right, counselor?"

Brosius placed his hand on my arm. "Come on," he said. "We're going."

CHAPTER TWENTY-EIGHT

I called Laurel a couple of times on my way home: once before I left the parking lot of Brosius's office, and then again when I stopped at a traffic light. She didn't answer, but I left a message both times, and in the second one I asked, "Why didn't you tell me they found those obituaries? Why were you talking to the police without me?"

But asking the question into the dead air of voice mail didn't make me feel any better. It just made me feel angrier and more confused. I pounded the steering wheel a couple of times in frustration, which only left me with sore palms.

Then I reached my apartment and found Heather Aubrey waiting for me in the parking lot.

I invited Heather in because she said she needed to talk to me about something important. I didn't ask what it was. She followed me inside and sat on the couch.

I dropped into a chair across the room. I saw the

watch Marissa had given me on the end table, its second
hands dutifully ticking off the time in two different
places. Heather looked good. She wore tight jeans and
knee-high boots and some kind of colorful scarf that
wrapped around her neck several times. She crossed her
legs, gently brushing Riley aside, and bounced her foot
in the air. As I watched her in my apartment, I remembered how I'd always thought she was out of my league.
I'd tried to figure it out in college, and I still wondered
exactly what she saw in me. There were better-looking
guys, richer guys. Why had she chosen me?

Marissa tried to explain it to me once. She said I
wasn't a typical college guy. Sure, I was good-looking—
thanks for that, I told her—but I didn't look like everyone else. I was smart and sensitive, but still something of
a guy's guy. I watched sports. I played basketball at the
rec center.

I trusted Marissa's instincts about these things. When
we met in college, she was slightly more experienced
than I was. She'd dated a lot in high school, even had one
serious boyfriend for over a year. I'd dated a little in high
school. I went to dances, groped some girls occasionally
at parties and mixers, had even had sex with a few of
them. But Marissa seemed to have lived a life. I saw the
pictures of her and her high school boyfriend, Blake, in
her dorm room and listened to the stories of their good
times and bad times together: getting drunk at dances,
sharing rides to and from school. The way Blake turned
mean when they finally broke up, showing up at her
house in the middle of the night and calling her name. It

all sounded very Stanley Kowalski, and it made me feel like Marissa lived in a different world than I did.

But Marissa was good at reassuring me. Once a girl got to know me, she said, *if* she got to know me, she'd know how charming and considerate I was. She'd know I was the keeper.

I accepted all of those compliments from Marissa—who I pointed out was completely biased by that time, since we were in love—and I figured Heather might have seen the same things in me, even though she ended up marrying a successful, golf-playing dentist.

I was always much happier, much more comfortable being myself with Marissa. I loved her.

I still did.

"Have you been waiting long?" I asked Heather.

"I was in the neighborhood," she said. "I thought I'd see if you were around."

"I was at the police station. Before that, I was at Emily Russell's funeral."

Heather didn't seem thrown by either of my admissions. She simply asked how everything was going with the case. "Do they know anything else yet?"

I told her no, that they knew nothing except that a young girl had been murdered. A young girl who I thought looked a hell of a lot like Marissa. "But I might be the only one making that connection."

"That's what I wanted to talk to you about," Heather said.

"Emily?"

"Marissa." She fiddled with her watch. "Do you have anything to drink?"

"You mean a real drink?" I asked.

"Wine? Beer?"

I went out to the kitchen, grabbing a beer for myself and a bottle of red wine that had been sitting on my counter for six months. I didn't know if it was any good or not, but I went ahead and opened it, blew the dust out of a glass, and poured. When I handed the drink to her, our hands brushed a little, and she smiled up at me.

Then she swallowed the wine. Her mouth curled like she'd sipped something that had been strained through dirty socks.

"Is it that bad?" I asked. "Do you want a beer instead?"

"It's fine," she said. "I wouldn't have bought it, but it's fine. I like good wine. I can suggest a few different kinds."

"I don't like wine at all," I said. "Somebody gave it to me. Like I said, if you don't want it, I can dump it. What did you want to tell me about Marissa?"

"Okay," Heather said. "You want to get right to it." She sipped more of the wine and made less of a face.

"It's been a long couple of days," I said. "I'm sorry to be short, but I'd love to hear what you want to tell me."

"Okay." She rested the wineglass on her knee, keeping her fingers wrapped around the stem. "We talked the other day about the night Marissa died. And that man she was seen with. I felt like you questioned my story about that man because you thought I had ulterior motives. We dated before you met Marissa. We kind of dated after Marissa, and then again after you got divorced. There was always something between us, right?"

"You don't need to worry," I said. "Someone else confirmed your account. Hell, they confirmed more than you told me. I don't have any doubt Marissa was involved with that man in some way. Some real, intense way." I stopped to take a drink of my beer. It couldn't taste as bitter as I felt. Maybe nothing tasted good anymore. "I guess I'm glad you told me the truth. I'm glad more than one person told me the truth. I needed to hear it."

Heather's shoulders slumped dramatically. "I'm so glad you feel that way." She reached up with her free hand and swiped it across her brow. "I'm relieved. I know it's tough to hear about someone you thought you knew well."

"I did know her well. Just . . . just not as well as I thought, I guess."

"Who told you this news about her?" she asked, and then started shaking her head. "You know what? Never mind. I don't need to know. If it was a good friend, then that person was just trying to help. That's all a friend should ever try to do."

"Yeah. Right," I said. "It's like eating my vegetables or something. It sucks going down, but it's for my own good." I slumped lower in my chair and drank more of my beer. I didn't care about the bitter taste. I liked what it was doing to my head.

Heather stood up and moved to the end of the couch

closest to my chair. She rearranged the cushions and sat down, wearing a sympathetic frown on her face. "I'm sorry."

"What did you want to tell me?" I asked.

She studied me for a moment. "It's not important now."

But I could see she *wanted* to tell me. And I wanted to hear. Was I supposed to just sit there and swallow my curiosity? I couldn't. And I knew that Heather knew that.

"What is it?" I asked. "Just tell me."

"Oh, boy," Heather said.

I recognized the words and the approach. It was straight out of her playbook from college. She'd act like she didn't want to say what she had to say, but I knew she did. And not only did I know she wanted to tell me, I knew it was going to be something bad. Heather used this tactic when she wanted to say something nasty about one of her friends. She liked to act as though the information was being dragged out of her. It wasn't. She wanted to share. And I wanted—*needed*—to hear it. We both knew that.

"Heather. Tell me."

"It's Marissa," she said.

"What about her? If you know something, tell me."

"I know that news about the man at Razer's knocked you for a loop. I know it came out of nowhere. But it really didn't surprise me." She took a big drink of her wine. "It didn't surprise me because Marissa cheated on you in college. She'd been unfaithful to you before that night."

CHAPTER TWENTY-NINE

I straightened up in my chair. "What are you talking about, Heather?"

"I'm only telling you this because you seemed to want to get at the truth about some things." Her voice took on a defensive tone, as though she wanted to emphasize that it was me and not her behind the secret being revealed.

"That's not the only reason you're telling me," I said. "In fact, it's not even the primary reason, but I don't care. I just want to know what you're talking about."

"Do you remember that guy named Dan Killian?" she asked. "He was a year ahead of us."

Jealousy. I felt it creeping up on me. Jealousy over someone I hadn't dated, hadn't seen, in twenty years.

"I remember him," I said. He was an acquaintance more than a friend. I didn't like him. He and Marissa were in a few classes together. She talked about him from time to time. He played in a band. A stupid band. I thought every guy who played in a band was stupid. And so were their bands.

"I think you and Marissa had been fighting," she said. "This was about three months, maybe four, before she died."

"I remember. We fought because she wanted me to come visit for a weekend. I was working back at home, and she was here for the summer. But I couldn't come. I couldn't get off work. She just didn't understand what it was like to really need to have a summer job. She didn't have to worry about that."

"I was here that summer," Heather said, sipping more of her wine. She'd grown used to it apparently. She didn't make a face when she drank it anymore. "She and I saw each other sometimes out at bars and things like that. It was a little sleepy here in the summer. Sleepy but nice. She'd complained to me earlier that week about you not coming. She said you'd fought about it, and she said she didn't understand why you just didn't do what she wanted." Heather laughed a little. "I guess that's what all girls want from their boyfriends. Anyway, that weekend I saw her somewhere. Johnny B's, I guess it was, because they had live music. And Dan's band was playing there that night. Marissa and Dan spent the whole night together in the bar. Drinking and laughing. It didn't seem right considering that she was dating you. And then they left together at the end of the night."

I gritted my teeth while she told the story. The bitterness of the beer had made my mouth dry, and I worked up some saliva before I said, "Just because they left together doesn't mean—"

"She told me, Nick. A week later we were out again, and Marissa told me. She said she felt horrible, and she wanted to tell you."

"Why didn't she?" I asked, the muscles in my face tight.

"I talked her out of it. I said . . . I knew you, and I told her you weren't the kind of guy who could handle news like that. It wouldn't just roll off you."

"*Should* it just roll off me?" I asked. "My girlfriend cheating on me?"

Heather stood up. She came over to my chair and sat on the arm, placing her hand on my shoulder. "No, it shouldn't. I'm not saying that. I'm just telling you all of this because . . . because maybe you're too hung up on the past. Maybe all of this is because you haven't let go of what happened. If you had a clear picture . . ."

"Heather, why do I get the feeling you're enjoying this?" I asked.

She drew back, breaking off contact. "That's not true."

I remembered that summer. I remembered the distance, physical and emotional, that grew between us during those weeks we were apart. When we saw each other, we fell back into our relationship with great ease, but the time apart nearly killed us. Had she cheated? Had she taken advantage of our time apart to spend a night or two with another guy?

"Thanks for telling me," I said. "I think."

"Let me get you another beer," she said.

I finished the one in my hand and put the bottle on the table. I didn't care if she cheated. We were young. People screwed up. I needed to let it go. What did it matter?

Heather breezed back into the living room with an open beer and the bottle of wine. She refilled her glass, and when she handed me the beer, our hands touched again. She looked at me, and my fingers intertwined with her fingers. I felt the coolness and condensation on her hand from the beer bottle.

It had been a long time. A long, long time.

She slid down onto my lap.

We forgot about our drinks.

CHAPTER THIRTY

A text from Laurel woke me the next morning, telling me she was on her way to my apartment. I put the phone down and rolled over. Heather was just waking up, stretching and lifting her arms high above her head. Then she brought her hand down and ruffled my hair.

"Is that work?" she asked.

"A friend's coming over," I said. "You remember Laurel Davidson, right?"

Heather made a face. She showed about the same level of disdain for Laurel as she had for the wine. "She never liked me. She always acted like she needed to protect you."

"Protect me? From what?"

"I don't know. She just seemed like a very territorial friend."

"She's loyal, if that's what you mean, and she's helping me with all of this," I said. "Emily's death . . . We're trying to make sense of it."

"So she's the one to blame."

"To blame for what?" I asked.

"Keeping all of this alive in your head." Heather was trying to sound a little playful, but I wasn't interested.

"It's not her," I said. "I want it alive."

Heather reached out again. She ran her hand over my cheek, brushing it against my stubble. "Even if it hurts?"

"Growing older usually does," I said.

I went to the bathroom and got ready, shaving and brushing my teeth and hair, while Heather dressed in the bedroom. I told her she could take a shower or make coffee, but she declined. When I came out, she was ready to go, so I walked her to the door.

"Have you ever been to a therapist?" she asked.

"No."

"You might want to think about seeing one," she said. "A good therapist can do wonders as you try to sort out your past. I can give you the name of the guy I've been working with. He helps me make sense of things." She seemed a little distracted, her voice a little wistful. "Mistakes I've made in the past. Things I'm trying to understand. They're not things I like to think about, but they're always with me."

She stared off into space.

"You mean your divorce?" I asked.

"That, of course. Everything."

"I'll think about it," I said.

"With men, that usually means no."

"Usually."

She leaned in and kissed me good-bye. It was a long

kiss. "Let's do this again sometime," she said. "I don't have the kids this week at all. They're with their dad."

"Sure."

But she didn't leave. She stood in my foyer, looking contemplative.

"Do you ever . . ." she said, but didn't finish the thought.

"Do I ever what?" I asked.

"Well, you and I met freshman year, before you met Marissa. And if we hadn't broken up, then you and Marissa would never have started dating. I know we tried later, but that was for other reasons. Do you ever wonder how things might have been different?"

"I wonder about a lot of things from the past. Sometimes I think that's all I do."

The open door revealed a bright morning. A warm breeze blew in, carrying with it a hint of the blossoming spring. A lot of birds seemed to be chirping too. And as Heather stepped outside, Laurel came up the walk. The two women greeted each other and exchanged an awkward hug. I saw the look on Laurel's face as her head rested on Heather's shoulder. She looked like she was hugging a dead animal. They exchanged the requisite compliments on how good they each looked, and then Heather gave us both a small wave and headed to her car.

When Laurel passed by me on her way into the apartment, she muttered just one word.

"Really?"

I followed her in, closing the door.

She said it again. "Really?"

"Don't start," I said, trying to cut the conversation off. "You can't judge me for my relationship choices. You're married and stable."

"Whatever gets you through the night," she said, sitting on the couch.

"Besides," I said, "I have some questions I need to ask you. For instance, what were you doing talking to Reece? I didn't know you were going to do that."

"Come on, Nick. Sit down. Let me explain."

I felt betrayed in some way. But her calm request that I sit down took a lot of the air out of my indignation.

So I sat in the chair I'd been in the previous night. I thought about what Heather had told me about Marissa—the cheating, the other man. It felt less like a sharp knife in my back and more like the slow turning of a corkscrew. Was everyone laughing at me behind my back all those years ago? How big a fool did I look like crying at her funeral?

"I know a lot of cops," Laurel said. "I don't know Reece well, but I know him. If I have information about a murder investigation, I have to share it with the police. It's a moral obligation on my part. I wouldn't feel right if I didn't. And I thought if I shared what I'd learned it might keep you off the hook. You know?"

Her logic eased my tension a bit. "Sure. But why didn't you tell me about the obituaries?"

"I didn't know about them," she said, her voice rising and growing insistent. "He tracked them down after I left his office. I didn't call you right away because I knew you went to Emily's funeral. I figured you had enough on your mind with that. And we'd talk when it was time."

"So there it is," I said. "Don't these obituaries invalidate everything you told me was going on? We'd cooked up this whole theory that something weird was happening with Marissa's family, that they'd just fallen off the face of the earth after she died. But they were right there in Colorado the whole time."

Laurel held up her hand. "Hold it. Who said they were just living right there in Colorado the whole time like everybody thought they were?"

"Reece."

Laurel dismissed Reece with a wave of her hand, and then she started digging in the messenger bag she carried with her. "It means they were *buried* in Colorado, that's all." She brought out a piece of paper. "Yes, we did that preliminary background check, and nothing turned up on them. But locating death records can be tricky. It takes time for everything to show up. If we'd dug more, we would have found the obituaries like Reece did. He's a good cop. He did his job. But it's still hard to explain how they went off the grid all those years. And none of it explains that girl with your address in her pocket." She held the paper out to me. "Here."

I took it but didn't look at it.

"What about Jade?" I asked. "You were going to try to track her down."

"Same deal," Laurel said. "She fell off the face of the earth too. Like I said, if she got married and has a different name, it would be tougher. But there's no sign of her for the last twenty years."

"Could she be dead?"

"She's mentioned in the obituaries. Both of them. Survived by a daughter. Jade. No mention of a husband for her, but maybe she's divorced. The information is scarce on her, but we'll keep looking."

"Okay, I have to tell you what happened at the funeral."

I related the whole story: the information about Emily being adopted and the appearance of the woman at the cemetery who looked so much like Marissa. Then I told her about what happened at the Russells' house.

"What am I supposed to make of all of that, Laurel?" I asked.

She didn't answer right away, so I looked down at the sheet in my hand. I recognized it instantly. It was a copy of the obituaries, the ones Detective Reece had shown me at the police station the day before.

"Why did you give me these?" I asked.

Laurel paused and looked at her hands. "It seems kind of silly now."

"What does?" I asked.

"I was hoping that seeing those obituaries and especially seeing Marissa's name listed as their late daughter would help you process things more. But it seems like we're moving in the other direction." She sounded a little exasperated, the frustration leaking out between her words.

"How can I not be? They never identified Marissa's

body. And Emily looks just like her. And then that woman is at the funeral, a woman who looks just like Marissa."

"From behind," Laurel said. "And she didn't respond to the name."

"Come on."

"Come on?" she asked. "Where are we going?"

I scooted forward in my chair. "Hanfort. Let's go to Hanfort together. We can ask around. We can find people who knew Marissa's family. Her friends from high school. You say they fell off the face of the earth. Well, let's go to where they were living right before they fell. Maybe there's something there. If not, I'll leave it alone. It's easier than going to Colorado."

"I don't believe you'll leave it alone," she said.

"Okay, I'll leave *you* alone. I won't ask for anything else."

"I don't believe that either." She gave me a look full of regret. "I don't know. I can't just up and go like you can. I have—"

She stopped herself, but I knew what was coming next.

"I get it," I said. "You have a spouse. You have a family. And I don't. It's true."

"I didn't mean it in a bad way," she said. "Sorry. I just mean I have to check and make sure."

She pulled out her phone and started scrolling through—checking her schedule, I assumed.

"I'm not alone," I said. "I have Riley."

He looked up at the mention of his name. Then he put his head right back down and closed his eyes.

"And Heather," Laurel said, her voice distracted.

"You really don't like her, do you?" I asked.

"No," she said.

"You don't have to beat around the bush. Give it to me straight."

"Sorry," Laurel said. "I just always thought she was a little bizarre, a little . . . I don't know. Untrustworthy."

"That's harsh, Laurel."

"She's always had a thing for you," she said.

"Can you blame her?" I asked.

Laurel rolled her eyes. "Just watch your back."

"I already am," I said. I told her about the gas station and the near miss with the silver sedan. "Can you believe that?" I asked.

Laurel looked genuinely concerned. "Shit, Nick. There are a lot of careless people in the world."

"Indeed." I waited a moment. "Should I be worried about it? Do you think it was intentional?"

Laurel's forehead wrinkled. "You mean you think someone might have wanted to hurt you? Maybe kill you?"

Stated out loud in that way, it sounded a little crazy. "Forget it," I said. "I don't know what I think."

"If you want to call the police in that town . . ."

"I don't even remember where I was," I said. "It's fine." I looked down at the obituaries again. Both of them contained those awful words: "Preceded in death by a daughter, Marissa."

How could words on a page make someone feel sick? They did. I could barely look at them, even after twenty years.

Then something else on the page caught my eye. I wasn't sure what it was at first, but it struck a silent chord in my memory. I scanned the obituary again. It was only listed in Joan's obituary, the most recent one. It meant something, but I wasn't sure what.

"Do me a favor?" I asked. "Right next to you on the couch is the newspaper with Emily Russell's funeral details in it. Can you hand it to me?"

Laurel did. "What?" she asked.

"Hold on."

I scanned the article all the way to the end. I saw what I was looking for and handed the paper and the obituary for Marissa's mother back to Laurel.

"Read her mother's obituary and then read the one for Emily," I said.

Laurel did, and I saw a moment of recognition spread across her face.

"Do you see it?" I asked.

"I see that the same charity is listed in Emily's obituary as is listed in Joan Minor's obituary. Something called Catholic Charities. Was Marissa's family Catholic? They were, weren't they?"

"Yes. Don't you think it's weird that they both have the same charity listed?" I asked, my voice rising along with my hope.

"Wait." Laurel pulled her phone out and started tapping away. Her brow furrowed. "It's huge, a national charity dedicated to eradicating poverty and educating the poor." She looked up at me. "Anybody could pick that, especially Catholics. It's like the United Way or something."

"You said 'eradicating poverty'? Marissa's father had no interest in that. She used to say his politics and lack of charity appalled her. He was a pull-yourself-up-by-your-own-bootstraps guy."

"But it wasn't listed in his," Laurel said, tapping one of the papers. "His asks for donations to the local Rotary club. So maybe Mom was more charitable. And how many Catholic obituaries do you think asked for donations to Catholic Charities? Thousands? It's really not anything special."

I felt a little deflated. "You're sure you don't want to go to Hanfort?" I asked.

"And do what?" she asked.

"Get closer to the source," I said. "I don't know."

Laurel came over and gave me a hug. "Let's keep our options open."

"That sounds like a dismissal."

"I have to get going," she said. "But we'll talk soon."

"That is a dismissal," I said. And she was gone.

CHAPTER THIRTY-ONE

After Laurel left, I opened my laptop and did more searching on the Catholic Charities website. I didn't know what I was looking for, but the obituary made me curious. Had Marissa's mother simply felt herself pulled more toward the Church when she knew she was dying and so wanted money donated to that cause? Or had Jade, her only surviving daughter, picked the charity?

When I knew Jade she wasn't remotely religious. She used to skip church when the rest of the family went, and when they did manage to get her to attend, she often fell asleep during the homily. So any religious feeling she had acquired had come to her long after I knew her. No surprise there. Teenagers resisted and then sometimes came around as adults.

I looked and looked. I read a lot about Catholic social justice and eradicating poverty. Charts and graphs popped up telling me what percentage of the world's children lived in poverty and how many of those children

Catholic Charities helped every year. So much information came at me as I clicked and scrolled through the site that my eyes started to glaze over, and I reached the conclusion that the Minors knew a good cause when they saw one.

Then I saw the tab on the bottom about the sanctity of life. I clicked there.

The page that opened was no longer about eradicating poverty. It was about life, as in preserving unborn life. Catholic Charities had an entire branch of their organization dedicated to counseling unwed mothers and placing the children of those mothers with "loving, forever families."

Another link took me to a list of "success stories," families who had adopted children through Catholic Charities and were so happy they couldn't contain their joy. At least according to the pictures shared on the website.

I remembered what Margie, Mrs. Russell's cousin, told me in the cemetery. Emily was adopted as an infant and so was her sister. Emily was adopted and looked so much like Marissa.

"Margie," I said out loud, stretching my brain to remember. "Margie Rhineback from Paducah."

It took a lot of explaining before Margie remembered me. First I had to remind her of our conversation in the cemetery at Emily's funeral, and then I had to explain how easy it was to find her phone number through an online database. She didn't like that at all.

"I'm going to have to get my number taken out of there," she said.

I didn't have the heart to tell her that what happens on the Internet stays on the Internet.

"I was hoping I could ask you something, Margie," I said.

"I guess so."

"When we were at the cemetery you told me that Emily was adopted by her parents when she was an infant."

A long pause. "Okay."

"Do you happen to know the name of the adoption agency they found Emily through?"

Another long pause. "Why do you want to know about this?"

I decided honesty was the best policy. "This might sound kind of crazy, but I'm trying to find out if Emily had any connection to a family I once knew. It's a long shot, I know, but I pretty much only have long shots left. Have you ever felt that way?"

"Sure. I think I know what you mean." She made a slurping noise like she was taking a drink. "But I'm afraid I don't know anything about it."

I let out a little sigh of disappointment. But what did I expect? Still, I asked. "Was Emily adopted through Catholic Charities?"

"I don't know," Margie said. "Could be. Her parents are pretty devout about their faith, as am I. All I remember is that the mother who gave Emily up was young, a college student, I think. And it was a closed adoption, completely closed. The mother gave up the baby and turned away. All adoptions used to be like that, of course, back in my day. But now things tend more toward the open. But not this one. It was free and clear. Emily's parents liked it that way, I think."

My heart jumped. "A college student? Do you know where she lived?"

"They adopted the baby in Tennessee, I think. They used to live there. They moved around a lot. Maybe it wasn't Tennessee. But it wasn't in Kentucky. I know that."

"Ohio?"

"What?"

"Did they adopt her in Ohio?" I asked.

"No, not Ohio," Margie said.

"How about Colorado?" I asked.

"Are you going to go through all fifty states?"

"No. Colorado is the last one," I said.

"They never lived in Colorado. Mostly in the Southeast. Look, I don't really feel comfortable talking about their business this way. This young girl's dead, remember? A family is grieving."

I felt appropriately chastened. And Margie was right. What did I expect to learn from chasing down cold trails?

"Thanks, Margie," I said. "You're right."

"They're a good family. A loving family."

"That's good," I said. "I'm sure they loved Emily a lot."

"They did," she said. "I'm sure somebody loves you a lot too."

"Thanks," I said.

"You know . . ."

"What?"

"Those charities . . . from what I know, you don't have to adopt a kid from the area you're living in. I mean, you could get a baby from anywhere in the country, I suppose."

My heart lifted. "Yeah, you're probably right. And you say this girl was in college when she gave the baby up?"

"I think so. A college girl. Supposed to be smart, well-balanced, and from a good family. Maybe they tell everybody that. Anyway, I hope you find what you're looking for."

"I hope so too."

I figured there was only one place to hope to find it.

I called Laurel when I was off the phone with Margie. When she answered I cut right to the chase.

"I've been asking way too much of you," I said, "and I'm sorry."

"It's okay."

"You don't have to help me anymore. This is my mess, and I'll figure it out. Okay?"

"Nick—"

"But, look, I'm going to Hanfort. I have to. It's the only way to get a little closer to the heart of things. I can't take a trip to Colorado, but Marissa's hometown is right up the road. That charity, they handle adoptions as well. And Emily was adopted and she looks just like Marissa. I'll let you know when I get back—"

"Nick?"

"What?"

"I was just about to call you. I talked to Tony. I cleared my schedule. I can go up there with you if you want."

"Really? Are you sure?"

"I'm sure. I can spare a day, maybe two."

"Thanks, Laurel."

"There's a catch, though."

"What's the catch?" I asked.

"It's pretty bad."

"How bad could it be?" I asked.

"Sally has to write a report on *The Canterbury Tales*, and I've got news for you—neither her dad nor I is going to wade through that shit with her. Guess who's elected?"

"Uncle Nick?" I said. "I'm there."

CHAPTER THIRTY-TWO

I lay in bed late that night, reading and trying to make myself tired. I could only think about the next day and our trip. I felt like a little kid before the class visit to the zoo. I'd packed, and I'd taken Laurel up on her offer to let her kids watch Riley.

Heather had texted me an hour earlier, asking what I was doing and did I want to come over? I wrote back and said I was busy. Maybe another time. She didn't respond. I didn't regret sleeping with her. I tried to remember the last time I'd spent the night with someone, and I had a hard time figuring it out. Riley was a great companion, but there was something to be said for having a woman in my bed, someone warm and soft and whose breath didn't make my eyes water. Heather and I had a long history. It wasn't exactly easy, but we knew each other well.

My phone rang. I expected it to be Laurel. Or a mistake. Apparently my number used to belong to a guy named Lonnie who had a lot of friends. They liked to call Lonnie late, and they never believed me when I told them he wasn't there.

But this was a call from Gina.

I straightened up against my pillows when I saw her name on the caller ID.

"Hey," I said.

"Am I calling too late?" she asked, her voice low and cautious.

"Not at all. Is something wrong?"

"No, nothing's wrong. We're both fine."

"That's good," I said. I laid my book aside. It wasn't grabbing my interest anyway. There was a long pause, so I filled the gap. "I want to thank you for arranging my conversation with Dale. I know it was tough, but I appreciate it."

"I hope it helped," she said.

"It did." Long pause. "He seemed like a nice guy."

"He is," she said, and chose not to offer any more details. I really didn't care if she dated someone else—we were long past the point of worrying about those things. We'd both moved on from our marriage, except for the everyday business of just trying to get along as human beings. That had its ups and downs.

"Well . . ." I said.

"I saw that stuff on the news," she said, "the stuff about you being some kind of suspect in this murder."

"Oh, crap. Did Andrew see it?"

Gina took her time answering. "He saw it."

"Shit. I knew it."

"But he doesn't fully understand it," she said. "And I explained to him that you didn't do anything wrong. I told him you'd never hurt anybody. He knows that. You don't have to worry about him. He adores you."

Sentimental fool that I was, my eyes filled a little. I reached up and brushed at them with my free hand. "Thanks. I didn't doubt that. Even after the police came to your house to haul me away, I knew you would stick up for me."

Gina laughed, a low, throaty sound. "You put on quite a show."

"I try."

"Really I'm just calling to make sure you're doing okay." She laughed again, a comment on the absurdity of my troubles. "I know you have a lot going on, and this stuff in the news just made me worry about you. Our last conversation didn't end well, and I said some things."

"It's fine." My hand rested on the book I'd laid aside. I riffled the pages, fanning them like I was shuffling a deck of cards. "You were right the other night, the things you said about Marissa. And our marriage. I wasn't aware of it at the time, not consciously anyway. But she was always there, somewhere. It wasn't fair to you."

"I survived. I'm a big girl." I heard her take a sip of something. Wine? Was that the truth serum that made her call? "You know, for a while I thought you were hung up on her just because she died young. When people die young they get kind of frozen in time. Never aging.

Never fading. It's weird. There was this guy who disappeared from my dorm when I was in college. My first year at Ohio State. I didn't know him, but I remember seeing the flyers with his picture all over the place. No one knew what happened to him, at least not back then. Maybe he just ran away. Or maybe he's long dead." I thought I heard her shudder through the phone. "But I can still see that picture, that face. He's always going to be that for me. He's frozen."

"But you said that's not the case with Marissa and me?" I asked.

"No," she said, pausing, gathering her thoughts to say more. "I used to think that, but I know it's really different now. I think you really were in love with her. I can still hear it in your voice." A rustling sound came from her end of the line, as though she were shifting her weight or sitting up. "What I'm saying is, what I think I'm trying to say is that I'm happy for you. I'm happy that you knew that at one time, even if it's in the past. That's not a small thing to have experienced."

"Okay. Thanks."

"You're welcome."

I felt obligated to say something back, something more intelligent and supportive. "So, you and Dale?"

"Oh, please." She made a raspberry noise into the phone. "We're friends who . . . you know. Mostly friends."

"I see. But you have Andrew in your life. That's pretty good unconditional love. Both ways."

"Yes, you're right." She yawned. "I need to go," she

said. "It's late, and I might start to get more sentimental or weirder than I ever intended."

"Okay. Thanks for calling."

"Nick? Good luck with all of it. Really. I hope you find what you want."

And then she was off the phone.

CHAPTER THIRTY-THREE

I did fall asleep and slept well. The alarm woke me forty-five minutes before Laurel was due to pick me up. I showered and shaved, then rushed around the apartment, throwing a few more last-minute items in an overnight bag. Laurel had thought it best if we planned to stay the night. If we ran out of leads early, we could always cancel the room and drive back.

I picked up the watch from Marissa and thought about wearing it, but that didn't seem right. I hadn't worn it since her death, so I put it back in the box in my closet.

I was just about ready to go when the phone rang. It was Mick Brosius calling. Did anyone really like to get a call from an attorney?

"Nick?"

"Is something wrong?" I asked.

"Not at all," he said. His voice sounded deeper, more

adult than ever before. "I'm calling about the Emily Russell case."

"What about it?" I asked.

"I just got off the phone with Detective Reece. The DNA results are back."

I knew I hadn't been in that room. I knew I hadn't touched the girl.

But still . . . police made mistakes. Innocent people were accused and convicted.

"It's all clear for you," he said, his voice casual. "No trace of your DNA in that room or on that girl."

I didn't know what I expected to feel. Not relief. Relief implied that something was in doubt, and it really wasn't in my mind. I knew what I had—or had not—done. And I didn't feel like there was anything to celebrate. A young girl was dead. Murdered. Just because I wasn't involved didn't mean the police were any closer to understanding what had really happened.

I felt . . . disappointed in the whole thing.

"Nick? Are you there?"

"I am. Thanks."

"You understand this doesn't mean you're entirely out of the woods," he said. "After all, you had contact with the girl right before she died. And no one, including you, can explain the address in her pocket. But it's going to be a lot harder for them to pin anything on you if they can't even place you at the scene. No eyewitnesses saw you there, and now there's no forensic evidence."

"Do they know what happened yet? Are there suspects? Anything else?"

Brosius said, "They're not going to tell me anything like that, of course, but from what I've seen I don't think they're any closer to figuring this out than they were the day Ms. Russell died. To be honest, they were probably hoping they would find your DNA there. It would have helped them say they were closer to solving the case. No one wants the murder of a young girl on their books. No one."

"I'm sorry to disappoint them," I said.

"No, you're not —oh, I see. You're being sarcastic. Well, I'll let you get on with your day. Just wanted to share the good news."

He sounded almost giddy.

"Right," I said. "Good news."

I hadn't been to Hanfort since a year after Marissa's funeral. Just before the one-year anniversary of her death, I skipped my afternoon classes at Eastland and made the hour-long drive. At that point, I knew Marissa's family was gone, so there had been no one for me to see there. But I had still headed to the cemetery and paid a visit to Marissa's grave.

I don't know what I expected to get out of the visit. Marissa's essence had burned up in the fire. But it felt like something I had to do, something that, I hoped, would complete a circle or close a door. I'd attended Emily's funeral for the same reason, to seek the elusive sense of closure that Laurel said was overrated.

Visiting Marissa's grave back then did nothing for me.

So I had found myself sitting in an empty cemetery,

the falling leaves drifting to the dying grass while I stared at a slab of granite with Marissa's name, birth date, and death date etched on it. The sight of the grave hadn't summoned any new emotions within me. Whatever emotions I'd felt the previous year were already as raw as could be and didn't need any prompting. And once I was there I felt even lonelier, more useless. I realized after I'd arrived that I'd even forgotten to bring flowers.

Laurel's voice snapped me out of my memories.

"Are you okay?" she asked.

I was staring out the passenger-side window, watching the empty fields and miles stream by. Since Laurel was a good friend who didn't mind giving me space, we hadn't spoken for twenty minutes.

"Are you worried about Riley?" she asked. "My kids and Tony will look after him."

"I'm not worried about Riley. He's indestructible. He's a wonder dog."

"I was kidding, Nick. I know you're not worried about Riley. I really just want to know if you're okay."

"I'm fine," I said. "I told you the good news. I'm not a murderer. Yay."

"You must have a lot of memories from Hanfort," Laurel said. "Memories of her."

"Of course. I used to like going there and staying at her parents' house. It felt so comfortable, so easy. They weren't my parents, so there weren't high expectations. We were just kids dating in college. It was a breeze." I paused for a moment, listening to the hum of the tires against the road, the occasional soft thump of a bump or pothole. "And it was really easy to sneak from the guest room down the hall to Marissa's bedroom. We did it every night I stayed there. Never got caught."

"How careful were the two of you?" Laurel asked.

"About getting caught?"

"About getting pregnant. You told me that you wondered if this girl might be Marissa's child. That would explain the resemblance and maybe her strange behavior before she died. Now, I'm not saying I believe any of that. I think she died in that fire, but is there any chance she could have been pregnant?"

"We tried to be careful," I said. "Most of the time. But we had a couple of scares. We gave in to our lust without protection on more than one occasion. Maybe we got more careless as time went on. There was a part of me that thought if she got pregnant, well, we loved each other. It was something we could handle together. It was risky and stupid, I guess. But we were crazy about each other. You know?" Then something awful twisted in my chest, a tangled knot of jealousy. "You saw her with that man. Maybe the baby wasn't mine."

"Young love," she said, her voice growing a little distant. The nostalgia trap could grab anyone. Even Laurel.

"Yes. What could be simpler?" I asked.

"And yet . . ."

"What?" I asked.

"Simple. And infinitely complex. Who knows what we're going to find?"

CHAPTER THIRTY-FOUR

Laurel and I went in separate directions once we reached Hanfort. She left me with the car because the things she intended to do were downtown and within easy walking distance. Hanfort was even smaller than Eastland. It was a clean, orderly, sleepy little town, best known for a watermelon festival in the summer that brought in tourists from Indiana and Michigan. Other than that, not much. Three high schools, some small businesses, a Wal-Mart. Lots of churches.

"Keep in touch," Laurel said as I dropped her off near the police station.

"Yes, Mom."

"Seriously," she said, returning to her role as the taskmaster. "Do you have the address?"

I held up my phone. "If they still live there. If they're still alive."

"That's bleak."

"It's life," I said.

Laurel walked into the building without hesitating, and I drove off on my appointed rounds. I envied the specificity of her work. She was going to talk to the police and do research at the library. Those were clear tasks, defined and concrete. My job was harder. I didn't even know if it was possible.

After all that time, twenty years, I remembered their names. Bill and Loretta Stieger. They lived two blocks away from Marissa's family. A few years older than Marissa's parents, Bill met Marissa's father through some community organization, the Optimist Club or the Lions or the Kiwanis. The families quickly became friends, and Bill and Loretta served as a kind of surrogate aunt and uncle to Marissa and her sister, Jade. The first time I came to Hanfort with Marissa, she made a point of taking me to the Stiegers' house and introducing me, as though it was important to have their approval of the boy she was dating. I saw them every time I visited and came to feel quite comfortable with them. At Marissa's funeral, I watched Bill break down and cry in front of her casket. I watched Loretta pull Jade close and kiss the younger girl on the top of the head. I figured if anyone knew anything about the Minors' lives before they moved away, it would be the Stiegers.

Except only one of them was left.

Laurel did a little digging before we left Eastland. Bill Stieger had died six years earlier. Loretta had sold the house and lived in a condominium on the edge of Hanfort, so I drove out there to find her. I'd called the day before and told her I was coming. After some initial confusion, she managed to remember me—or at least said she did—and she encouraged me to stop by and "have a visit." I felt bad about interrupting her life with a blast of questions about events that had happened twenty years earlier, but I managed to set my qualms aside. I hadn't asked for Emily Russell to come looking for me—which she appeared to have been doing. So Loretta Stieger would have to be tolerant of my intrusion.

She opened the door to me with a smile. And then she hugged me.

She looked older, that was for sure, but not so much older that I didn't know immediately who she was. Her skin was more deeply lined, her hair grayer. She supported herself with a cane, and her eyes looked bloodshot, the skin beneath them sagging with age, but it was her. I welcomed the hug. I'd spoken to Laurel about my fantasy of staying in touch with Marissa's family over the years, something I knew seemed more and more unrealistic as time went by. And maybe that was why the contact with Loretta felt like a welcome home to me, a bridge stretching across twenty years and offering a connection with Marissa.

Loretta stepped back and looked me over. She had a broad, flat face and wide hips, and her body moved through space like a block of granite. "So," she said, "you're a grown man now. An adult."

"In some ways," I said.

She waved me into her living room. I smelled coffee brewing and a sweet odor wafting from the kitchen, and

I began rooting internally for cookies or cake. Even though she seemed steady on her feet, she eased her body down into a chair as though it required a great deal of effort to land. Before I sat, Loretta asked me to bring the coffee and cookies, and I did, finding everything already spread out on a tray. Loretta declined coffee before I poured it, claiming that it was already too late in the day for her to have caffeine, but I took some.

"I'd love to hear all about your life," she said. "But I suspect you're not here to tell an old lady your biography."

"I don't mind sharing what I've been up to," I said. The cookies were delicious, and I told her so. I ate two of them so fast it was like I made them disappear using magic. We talked a little about my job, as well as my unsuccessful marriage. Loretta frowned appropriately when she heard about that.

"Any little ones?" she asked.

"None of my own," I said. "My ex-wife has a son, and I grew pretty close to him."

That news brought a smile to her face, revealing yellowed teeth that must have still been her own. I spared her the complicated details about my lack of access to Andrew as well as my run-ins with the law. Best to let one person think most of my life was swimming along merrily.

Loretta kept her thickly knuckled hand resting on the top of her cane. She wiggled it around like it was a gearshift and she was getting ready to blast off from the starting line.

"It may seem strange," she said, "but I have thought

about you from time to time over the years. I've won-dered how you were doing, how your life was going after school. After everything that happened."

"I'm sorry about Bill," I said. "I heard he passed away."

"Yes," she said. "He got bad at the end. Cancer. But he had a long life. I'll be eighty-five this summer."

"Good for you."

She shrugged. "I guess so. Being my age is like being a child. People make a big deal out of me steadily getting older. Little do they know I'm just running like a clock. I haven't wound down yet, but I will." She nodded at her own words of wisdom. "It's not a tragedy like a young woman dying in a fire, getting cut down before her life could even begin. I'm sorry you had to go through that. I'm sorry anyone did."

I resisted having another cookie. "That's kind of what I wanted to talk to you about. Marissa"—I shifted on my seat, adjusting my shirt collar and clearing my throat—"and her family."

"I figured as much. I assumed you weren't just mak-ing a social call out of the goodness of your heart." She held up her hand to stave off any half-baked excuse I might make, some claim that I really was hoping to see her and catch up. She knew the trip was about business. "Don't get me wrong. I like the company. Some days I don't hear another voice except my own. Or the TV." She nodded toward the ancient and bulky set in the corner of the room. "I don't mind being alone, but the golden years aren't always so golden. More like tarnished silver. Now, what are you here for?"

Given a wide-open invitation to ask about whatever I wanted to know, I found myself locking up. What exactly did I want to know from this woman? Where could I begin? "Was there anything unusual about the way Marissa's family left town? Anything odd about the way they behaved after Marissa died?" I asked.

Loretta shifted her weight backward, as though contemplating the question required her to lean back and adjust her orientation to the world. She tugged on her left earlobe. "Well . . . that's a lot to think about. They'd lost their daughter."

"I wouldn't bring all this up if it wasn't important," I said.

"And why exactly is it important after all these years?" she asked. "Did something happen?"

How did I explain all of that? I kept my answer vague and simple. I told her I had been thinking about the past a lot, especially Marissa, and I was trying to make sense of everything that had happened. Not exactly a lie.

"I know, honey. I've spent some time trying to process all of this myself." She scratched her head absently, and then bounced the cane against the floor a couple of times, the tip making a soft thump on the carpet. "I don't think there's a right way or a wrong way to react to a situation like that. A child dying. When Bill passed, I went back and forth between laughing and crying. None of it made any sense to me, and I was the one it was happening to."

"Of course."

"You have to understand something," she said, her

tone serious. "We weren't as good of friends with the Minors as we might have seemed to be. We knew each other well. We spent a lot of time together. But we weren't *close*. Both of them, Joan and Brent, had something of a wall up. There was an insularity to them. That's the only way I can think to describe it."

Her explanation made sense. Marissa's father had always held me at arm's length, as though there was no reason for him to get to know me in a meaningful way. He worked a lot, and I figured it had never been his dream to have his daughter bring home a philosophy major for a boyfriend. Her mother was warmer, certainly, but I knew what Loretta meant about her as well. I'd chalked Joan's behavior up to typical middle-class reserve, some reluctance on the part of a happy family to examine itself too deeply. Sure, Joan and her family welcomed me into their home, but I wasn't allowed all the way inside.

"But you were about as close to them as anyone else, right?" I asked.

Again a shrug from Loretta. "Maybe. Like I said, it could be tough to tell. Very tough." She shifted her weight again. "I'll give you an example. A week after Marissa died, I called Joan. My real goal was to check in on her, but I pretended to be reminding her of our monthly bridge game. I didn't know if she'd come or not, but I wanted to invite her. I wanted her to feel normal again, if that was at all possible. She told me she couldn't make it to bridge because she was packing. 'Packing?' I asked. I thought she was going on a trip, a getaway to clear her head. But then she said they weren't going on a trip. She said they were moving, putting the house on the market, leaving the whole thing behind. She apologized and said circumstances with their lives were changing so fast, she had no idea what to make of it all. And then she just hung up on me. She practically slammed the phone down."

"Was that the last time you talked to her?" I asked.

"I *saw* her. I called a day or so later to see how she was doing, and she didn't answer. No one answered. Bill went by Brent's office to see him and find out what was happening, but the office was closed up and shut down. They really were pulling up stakes and getting out. So I went over to the house after all the missed calls."

"And they were gone?" I asked.

"Joan was there," Loretta said. "She met me at the front door and acted like she didn't want to let me inside. It was as though I was a salesman or a Jehovah's Witness or something. I didn't like it, not at all. And there was a real distance there, a real wall. Something stronger and deeper than I'd ever seen in the past. I felt she wanted to turn me away, but at the same time, there was a sadness in her demeanor. She seemed to need something from me. I knew her well enough to see that. I thought—and maybe this is just the way women think—she was embarrassed about something inside. Maybe the house was messy, maybe she'd let it go to pot and hadn't cleaned since Marissa's death. See, I thought she needed my help. That's what friends do for each other. Though I admit some people think I'm kind of pushy and even nosy."

"It sounds like you were a good friend."

"I hope I was. I do."

I took a closer look around the room then. There were pictures of smiling children and grandchildren on almost every available surface.

"Did you ever get inside that day?" I asked.

"I did." Loretta's face broke into a mischievous smile. "I said I was nosy and pushy. I'm also determined. I wasn't going to let a friend be in need and do nothing. I talked my way in. And do you know what I saw when I got in there?"

"What?" I asked, wondering if I wanted to know the answer.

Loretta turned her face to the side, acting a little dramatic with her information. "Nothing," she said. "Nothing but boxes. Boxes and boxes. All packed. Most of the furniture was gone as well. She was ready to move. The place looked clean. She didn't need my help. Or anyone's, apparently."

"So why did she try to keep you out?" I asked.

"I don't know," she said. "I still don't. I was only there for a few minutes. Joan kept telling me she had so much to do, and I offered my help again, but she said she didn't need it. She said the things she had to do she needed to do on her own." Loretta's face grew more serious as she paused. Then she said, "We sat on some boxes and talked for a minute. Just for a minute. She acted distracted. Impatient. She thanked me for being a good friend and for being a good friend through their recent tough times. She admitted she only had one thing left to pack. Marissa's room."

I imagined it then. A grieving mother, turning her life upside down to escape the memories of her dead child, packing up everything in her life but not being able to face the impossible task of dealing with her daughter's belongings. Getting rid of them might feel cold. Attempting to pack them might be crippling.

In that moment, I knew what Loretta did. I knew before she even told me.

"I offered to pack it for her. Of course."

"But I'm guessing you didn't get to help her pack," I said.

Loretta shook her head slowly. "No. But I did excuse myself and ask to use the restroom before I left. And when I came out of the bathroom I saw the door to Marissa's room. It was just about ten feet from me, and it was closed. I couldn't help it. I went over there real quick, and I gave the knob a turn. I wanted to see how much work Joan had to do and if she could handle it all by herself."

"You really did that?" I asked, impressed by her chutzpah.

"I did."

"And what happened?" I asked.

"It was locked. The knob didn't budge."

I had inched forward in my seat while Loretta spoke. I said, "So they just had it closed off. They couldn't bear to see it. I can understand that."

"I can too," she said. "I would do the same thing if it were my child. I might never go in that room again. Ever."

It all made sense. If there was a range of normal action for someone who had lost a child, Joan Minor's behavior fell well within it.

"How awful to live with that room right there," I said. "Like an unintentional shrine to the dead child." I let out a deep breath. "So, that was the end of it?"

"Pretty much."

"Pretty much? Did you see them again?" I asked.

"No, we didn't. I left that day. I asked for their new address, and Joan promised she'd send it, but she never did." She tapped the cane a couple of times. "I just kept thinking about that locked door."

"What about it?" I asked.

"It was one of those doors they put in every house. A knob with one of those little locks that you turn. It couldn't withstand a real attempt to break in if someone was determined." More cane tapping. "But here's the thing. That day, when I went to their house, it was locked from the *inside* of Marissa's room. I tried the knob, and it didn't turn. The lock must have been on the inside. So how exactly were they going to get in there if they wanted to? It wasn't the kind of door people have a key for." She lifted her hand, palm up, as she asked the question. "Were they hiding something? What could that have been?"

"I'm trying to figure that out," I said. "That's why I'm here."

CHAPTER THIRTY-FIVE

Loretta told me she needed to take a bathroom break. I helped her out of her chair, and once she was on her feet she declined further assistance. "I can still do *that* on my own," she told me.

I ate three more cookies while she was gone, and when she came back and settled into her chair I asked her, as gently as I could, if she knew that Joan and Brent Minor had both passed away in the past five years. Loretta took the news with a stoic reserve. "That's what happens when you haven't seen people for a long time. I've lost a lot of friends over the years, but I didn't know about them."

"Did you ever hear anything from them after they moved?" I asked.

"They sent a card or two that first year after they left." Loretta tilted her head, searching through her memory banks for the information. "Maybe something came that

Christmas? They must have moved just before the holi-days, right?"

"Marissa died at the end of October," I said.

"Then it makes sense a Christmas card would have come right away. It was typical stuff, as I recall. 'We're settling in. Love to all.'"

"Where did it come from?" I asked.

"Colorado, I guess. I don't remember the town"—she gestured in the air—"and I don't have the card. I threw all that stuff away when I moved to this condo. Why keep it and make my kids throw it out after I've died?"

"Can I ask you something else?" I asked. "Something a little off the wall?"

"Why not?" she said. "It might be the most excite-ment I have all year."

"Did the Minors . . . did they have anything to do with an organization called Catholic Charities?" I asked. "Did Joan do charity work for them or anything?"

Loretta's lips pursed, and the skin on her forehead puckered. "Not that I recall. She worked on a couple of boards in town. Literacy was a big thing for her. It must have been why her girls read so well at an early age."

"And their kids weren't adopted," I said. "We know that."

"Marissa and Jade? Impossible. Those girls looked so much like their parents. They were clearly sisters. I still remember when Joan was pregnant with Jade. No, not adoption." Then Loretta's eyebrows went up like a light had just gone on somewhere deep in her brain. "Why are you asking me these things? Have you talked to Jade?"

She lifted a hand to her chest. "Please don't tell me that precious child is gone as well."

"No," I said. "We haven't been able to locate Jade. The Minors kind of fell off the map after they left Hanfort. It's as though they were trying not to be found. It's really odd."

"Like I said, they were kind of strange people. Good people. Dedicated to their children, but a little off-putting. I couldn't tell you what they were up to."

"And . . . you don't know of either of the girls' being pregnant, do you?" I asked, trying to be gentle.

Loretta's eyes widened, almost comically. "Are you kidding? Those girls? I didn't see any sign of that, believe me."

"Did they have any money trouble?" I asked.

Loretta laughed. "That's funnier than someone being pregnant. Money wasn't an issue. Never. Brent made plenty. He worked all the time. I've never seen a man so driven. When he set his mind to something, he did it. Joan used to complain about it. She said she felt like she was raising her girls alone. She worried about the effect it might have on them to not have their father around so much. But you saw all of that."

"I remember," I said. "They certainly didn't seem like the kind of people to have financial problems. I'm just trying to understand why they might have gone away and not stayed in touch with anybody."

"They must have stayed in touch with somebody in this town," Loretta said. "Somebody."

"Who? I'd be happy to try them."

"I can give you names." Loretta snapped her finger in the air. It gave off a surprisingly crisp sound for someone whose knuckles were gnarled from arthritis. "Have you talked to Roger Kirby? You must have."

"Roger Kirby . . ." I said.

The name scratched at my subconscious. I knew it, but I couldn't place him exactly in the Minors' lives. It seemed like . . .

"Was he business partners with Brent?" I asked.

"Exactly. For a while. Brent bought him out a few years before they moved on, but they were still friends. They played golf together, went fishing." She pointed to an address book on the table next to her chair. "I can give you some other names. Some of them are still alive and functioning."

Loretta let out a big yawn, and I sensed our conversation was winding down, so I took the tray and the remains of our cookies and coffee back to the kitchen. When I came back, she was scribbling a few names on a piece of paper, people in Hanfort I could look up to find out if they had any insights about the Minors. Roger Kirby's name was at the top of the list.

I thanked her and asked her not to get up. She informed me that she had no intention of doing so.

"I remember when Marissa died," she said suddenly. "Very well." Her eyes grew glassy, and she stared across the room as though a portal had opened to the past. "I know you do too." She lifted her hand in the air, index finger raised. "It's funny. The weekend before the fire, Bill drove past their house on his way home from work, and he said he saw Marissa's car in the driveway. He told me about it, and I assumed she'd just come home for a visit. We always saw her when she came to town. Even if it was just a quick chat or dessert, we *always* saw her. I called Joan and asked about Marissa being home that weekend, and she insisted Marissa wasn't there. When I mentioned the car in the driveway, Joan said it wasn't her car. And that they were getting rid of that hunk of junk anyway."

"She did go home right before she died," I said. "For the weekend."

Loretta nodded slowly. "Bill saw it. He swore it was her car." Her voice sounded a little distant. "Joan lied to me, I guess."

I knew what it felt like to be deceived. But neither one of us knew why it had happened. "I'll let you know if I learn anything," I said, standing up.

"Would you?" she said, her face growing hopeful.

"I will."

She opened her arms, and I gave her a hug. She held me tight, and it felt good to lose myself in a motherly embrace. When we let go, she wished me luck, and I left her sitting in her chair.

CHAPTER THIRTY-SIX

I checked in with Laurel after I left Loretta's condo. She told me she was doing well, having some luck, and I should go ahead and follow the leads Loretta had given me.

"Leads?" I said, laughing. "I feel like Jim Rockford."

"Just don't get your ass kicked like he always did."

It didn't take me long on my phone to find the location of Roger Kirby's office. It was in a strip mall not far from Loretta's condo, and the map led me right to the door. He worked as a management consultant, whatever that was, and I remembered that Marissa's dad had worked in some kind of consulting business as well. Roger's name was written on the glass door in gold script, and when I stepped inside, I found myself in a spare but perfectly decorated waiting area. The lights were bright, the music through the intercom system soft and soothing. If I'd chosen to sit in one of the plush chairs I probably would have fallen instantly to sleep. The only person in sight was a receptionist, an eager-looking twenty-something with perfectly straight hair. She offered to help me.

"Is Mr. Kirby in?" I asked.

But she frowned. She was so sorry to tell me whatever she was about to tell me.

"He's not in this week," she said. "He's working on a project off-site. Was he expecting you?" She bit her lip to let me know how tortured this problem made her feel.

"No. I was just hoping to catch him. I'm only in town today and maybe tomorrow. Is there a way to talk to him?"

"You can leave your name and number, and I can pass it along when he calls in. That's about all I can do."

"He must have a cell phone," I said.

Again the lip biting. "Not one he lets us give out."

"Okay. I'll leave a message."

I gave her my name and cell phone number. I started to add that I was an old friend of the Minor family, but what if there was something about Marissa's family that he was trying to avoid? Wouldn't that just give him an excuse not to call me? So I stopped short of mentioning that.

The receptionist looked up. "And what was this in regards to?"

"I'm interested in using his services for my company. We've just relocated to Columbus from Hong Kong."

I didn't know where the lie came from, but it flowed out of me like I was born to deceive. The receptionist didn't bat an eye. She wrote it all down and punctuated her note with a forceful period.

"Okay," she said, smiling at me. "I'll let him know."

"Thanks," I said. "Is he working in Hanfort today? Or somewhere else?"

The woman clicked her pen a few times. "I really don't know." *Click. Click. Click.*

"Tell him I'm looking forward to talking with him."

Loretta was right when she wondered how many of the three names she'd given me would still be "alive and functioning." The addresses were all easy enough to find. Apparently people in Hanfort, especially older people, still listed themselves in the phone book. But at my first stop, the home of a man named William Kreutzer, I encountered a nurse who told me Mr. Kreutzer was terminally ill and not able to see anybody.

I found the second person on the list—a woman named Bobbi Tilton—and she was only too happy to speak to me. She acted nervous when I first appeared at her door, but when I mentioned Loretta's name, she brightened and told me she needed to call Loretta so they could catch up. I explained what I wanted to know—anything and everything she could tell me about the Minor family—and the woman enthusiastically brought me into her home, which smelled like mothballs. But once we sat down, I found out she didn't have much to contribute. She simply repeated over and over again what a wonderful Christian family the Minors were and told me how much she missed having them as good friends.

"I need to write to them," she said, patting me on the knee. "Do you know their address?"

I didn't have the heart to tell her the truth, so I suggested she ask Loretta.

The house belonging to the third name on the list was no longer a private residence. It had been converted into a chiropractor's office, and the woman at the desk had no idea where the previous owners had moved.

"We've been here five years," she said, looking at me like I should know better.

I thanked her and left.

And then I wasn't sure what to do with myself. I checked in with Laurel again, and she said she needed another hour or so. I could have gone to the hotel room. But what would I do there besides watch TV and likely fall asleep?

I thought about the drive I took to Hanfort a year after Marissa died and my trip to the cemetery.

Then I knew where I was going next.

The cemetery was a broad, flat expanse of land on the east side of town. A black wrought-iron gate surrounded the property, and a statue of Jesus—arms open and inviting—waited to greet everyone as they drove in. The stones were mostly plaques instead of standing markers, and they were flush with the ground and easily read only by standing over them. The effect was sterile and cold, a preplanned subdivision without the houses, but I assumed it made cutting the grass easier.

I didn't remember exactly where Marissa was buried. Even if someone had asked me on the day of her funeral if I could identify the location of her grave, I wouldn't have been able to tell them. When I made my last visit, the one during college, I asked at the cemetery office, and they told me where to go. Thanks to the marvels of modern technology I could now look that information up online. Marissa was buried in section G, row 17, plot 3. Easy enough, since the letters and numbers ran in order.

When I reached her grave, I stopped the car but didn't get out. I sat and stared out the window. There was no one else around. The sky above was gray, the thick clouds moving rapidly from east to west. Colder weather seemed to be moving in, and who besides moody teenagers wanted to stand around in a cemetery on a gray, ugly day?

Marissa told me once she didn't want to be buried after she died. She said it seemed unnatural, a waste of space. "All the people in the world, and we give acres and acres and acres to dead bodies," she said. She was practical that way, always thinking of the bigger picture. When she died, and her family announced the funeral plans, I thought about telling them Marissa wouldn't have wanted any of it. The fancy casket, the flowers, the church service, the burial. But who would have listened to me? The college boyfriend? And, I assumed, the funeral brought comfort to the people who gathered to remember her that day, so I told myself Marissa would like to be remembered by her friends and family. Who wouldn't?

I looked down the row where Marissa was buried. Did

it do any good to have her there? And then . . . if her parents had been in Colorado all those years, and even chose to be buried out there, why did they leave Marissa in Hanfort? Couldn't they have relocated her to be near them? How many people even remembered that Marissa was here or bothered to visit her grave?

But when I climbed out of the car and walked down the row to plot number three, I saw that someone did remember. Someone did visit. On her grave sat a bouquet of fresh flowers. And not just any flowers. Lily of the valley—Marissa's favorite.

Someone who knew her very well had put them there—and in the last couple of days.

CHAPTER THIRTY-SEVEN

I called Laurel, and she told me to go back to the hotel alone, assuring me that one of the Hanfort police officers she had met could give her a ride if she needed one.

"Rest," she said. "Watch pay-per-view or something."

"You want me to watch porn?"

"It's not all porn," she said. "I'll see you in a little bit."

The thought of going back to the room alone made me feel a little depressed. The whole town of Hanfort made me feel depressed. It seemed small and cramped, full of fading memories and aging people. I felt like the longer I stayed, the greater the chance I would disappear into the past forever as well.

And I didn't want to sit around and wonder about those damn flowers.

But then Roger Kirby called.

I answered while I drove.

"I understand you wanted to talk to me about your company, Mr. Hansen."

I didn't want to lie anymore. Coming up with the story on the spot was lie enough for me. "Okay, that's not really true, Mr. Kirby. My interest is purely personal."

A long pause followed. I could hear his caution seeping through the phone line. "Personal?" he said, as though he were speaking a foreign word.

"I wanted to talk to you about the Minor family. I'm an old friend of theirs. A friend of Marissa's, really. She and I dated in college. Maybe you remember me? We even met a couple of times."

He didn't say if he remembered me. Instead he asked, his voice turning gruff, "What about them?"

"Can I come by your office?" I asked. "I've talked to some other people, and I just wanted your thoughts. It would be easier—"

"That was all a long time ago," he said. "I don't think I can help you with anything."

And then he hung up.

But I wasn't finished with Roger Kirby. Or he wasn't finished with me. I parked at the hotel and went back to the room, stopping for a free newspaper on the way. Before I could get my key card in the lock, my phone rang again. I recognized the number as belonging to Roger Kirby.

"You say you've talked to some other people?" he asked.

"I spoke with Loretta Stieger. I knew her pretty well when Marissa and I were dating. She recommended I speak to you."

I heard a quick breath through the line, almost like a snort.

"Do you live here?" he asked.

"I'm visiting. I can come to your office."

"Where are you? A hotel?"

"Yes," I told him, explaining which one and where.

"I know it," he said, his words coming out like shots from a nail gun. "I'll meet you there in fifteen minutes."

Roger Kirby might have been seventy-five years old, but he looked like he was ready to run a marathon. Trim. Fit. Tanned. Athletic. He shook my hand with a grip like a blacksmith's. I met him in the lobby of the hotel, and when I invited him to sit, he took a look around the space. A clerk stood at the front desk, punching things into a computer, and two businessmen sat in the corner, exchanging few words, their laptops open before them.

"Would you like to talk in my room?" I asked.

"I think that would be best."

I led him there. He was taller than me, and his clothes were neatly pressed. He didn't wear a coat of any kind despite the cooling weather, and he offered no small talk as we walked down the narrow, hushed hallway. I let us into the room. The curtains remained drawn, and I offered to get Mr. Kirby a glass of water, but he declined by making a dismissive gesture with his hand. We sat by a small round table near the door, he on one side and me on the other. He wore an impatient look, as though I was about to ask to borrow money.

He didn't speak. The first move was apparently up to me.

"I'm trying to find out some things about the Minors.

Specifically what might have led them to move away and start over in such a way that they left no trace of themselves anywhere over the years."

"Their daughter died." He looked at me like I didn't get it. "Didn't you say you dated her?"

"I know that's why they moved away. And, yes, I dated Marissa right up . . . almost right up until the time she died."

Roger Kirby studied me. His nose was long and thin, almost beaklike. He looked like an eagle examining his prey. "I think I do remember you," he said. "Weren't you studying music or something like that?"

"Philosophy."

He grunted. "You should know what a loss that was for the family." He looked away. "I went through it with them, tried to comfort them. They were wiped out. Just devastated."

"Yes, I know." I expected sympathy, but he turned back to me and held me with the same cold gaze. "Did you stay in contact with them over the years? What were they doing?"

"Not really. We lost touch. Brent and I were business partners, friends even. But they seemed to want to put this life behind them after Marissa died. I respected that."

"Marissa dropped out of school right before she died, and Jade told the school she wouldn't be coming in the fall," I said. "They both cited financial problems as the reason for not attending, but Jade had a full scholarship. If they were having financial problems, wouldn't she have taken the scholarship?" I studied him, hoping to see some understanding or help. "Do you know if they were having trouble like that?"

Roger pointed at me. "Did you say you spoke to Loretta Stieger?"

"I did."

"And who else?"

"Loretta gave me names, but they didn't help. So just Loretta. Why? Is something wrong?"

"I don't know why those girls would say those things about money," Roger said, "but I make it a point not to pry into a person's personal business. Maybe Brent grew careless with his finances, but it's not something I knew about."

"Would you find it hard to believe he would have money problems?"

"I would." He looked and sounded certain.

"So they lied? Both of them told the same lie?"

"I have three daughters. If you can figure them out for me, let me know." He adjusted his wedding band. "Maybe they wanted to embarrass their father, undermine him in some way. Kids try that stuff sometimes. Do you have children?"

"No."

He gave me more of an appraisal from the corner of his eye, judging me for my lack of offspring. That, coupled with my college major, made me suspect in his eyes. "Hanfort is a small town. People talk. They talk really easily. You may have thought you were just having a polite chat with an old lady at Loretta Stieger's house, but

I guarantee you people will hear about it. That stuff's twenty years in the past, so why bring it up now? Let the dead rest with the dead."

"So you know Joan and Brent Minor are dead?" I asked.

He nodded. "Sure, I heard."

"Did you go to the funerals? Did you—"

"I didn't go," he said. "Like I said, it's over. All over. What do you hope to accomplish by stirring all of this up again? Are you doing this to satisfy some schoolboy fantasy you have about Marissa? Haven't you grown up and moved on like everybody else?"

I shifted in my seat. He clearly wanted to play the stern father and cast me in the role of the raggedy prodigal son. But I wasn't going to let him. Twenty years had passed. I wasn't a kid anymore.

"It affects my life, so I have the right to know," I said. "It's my past. I can ask questions. If you don't want to answer them or you don't know the answers, that's fine too. But you can't tell me I don't have the right to ask. I do."

He stood up suddenly and shoved the chair back under the table. "I don't think that's a good idea. I think part of adulthood is accepting the past and moving on. Just . . ." He stood still for a moment. "Just move on like the rest of us."

"This *is* part of moving on. And I'm a suspect in a young girl's death. I need to know certain things, or I'm in trouble."

"A suspect?" He looked me over carefully, as though

I had transformed into something ugly right before his eyes. "Marissa's death, all of that, it hurt a lot of people. Don't dredge it up. Let it heal."

He didn't offer to shake my hand or say good-bye. Instead, he took two long strides to the door, and then he was gone.

I sat for a few minutes, staring at the tabletop. I told myself, *You're not just picking a scab.* There were real questions that needed to be answered, whether they had to do with Marissa or Emily Russell or both.

I could worry later about how much I'd moved on. Living in the same town where I went to school. Where I met Marissa. Where she died.

Before I could think about it anymore, someone knocked.

I was up quickly. I thought it was Roger Kirby, coming back to dispense more fatherly advice, or else to apologize, even though I suspected men like Roger Kirby didn't ever apologize. They never felt they needed to.

Instead I found Laurel outside the door, a slightly puzzled look on her face.

"What's wrong, stranger?" I asked.

She walked past me into the room. She didn't speak. She didn't sit down.

"Did something happen?" I asked.

"I just passed a man in the lobby," she said. "An older man."

"Tall?" I asked. "Gray hair? Looked like he just stepped out of an ad for a vibrant and active retirement?"

"I know him," she said.

"That's Roger Kirby," I said. "Brent Minor's former business partner."

Laurel looked at me for a long moment. She seemed to be working up to speaking.

"And?" I said.

"That's the man I saw with Marissa on the night she died."

CHAPTER THIRTY-EIGHT

I threw open the door and ran down the hallway, my feet thudding on the thin carpet.

When I reached the lobby I almost collided with one of the businessmen I had seen earlier. I skidded to a stop inches from making contact with him, and the man opened his eyes wide as though he had just come face-to-face with a crazy person.

"Sorry!" I said.

I went around him and out through the automatic doors at the front of the hotel, emerging into the cool air, turning my head from side to side, scanning and searching. One car drove off on the far side of the lot, and I turned to the left, where I saw Roger Kirby closing his door and starting his engine. I ran in that direction, but by the time I'd navigated the rows of parked cars, he had backed out of his space and was driving away. I waved my arms and called his name, but he didn't stop.

I would have gone after him right then, but I patted

my pants pockets and realized I didn't have my keys. I turned and jogged back to the room, slightly out of breath, my lungs burning a little with the burst of exertion. Laurel waited for me in the doorway of the room.

"We have to go after him," I said.

"Do you know where his office is?"

"Yes."

"And you have his number?" she asked, her voice and demeanor calm.

I was still breathing hard, so I nodded.

"What did he have to say to you?" she asked.

I grabbed a glass and filled it with water, swallowing as my breathing slowed. "He knows something," I said.

"What did he tell you?"

"Nothing, really." I gulped more water, still standing as the adrenaline subsided. "He tried to shut me up. He told me to quit asking questions and let the dead rest in peace."

"He said that?" she asked, her face wrinkling.

"Yes."

"We can talk to him soon," she said.

"Now," I said. "We're going now." I grabbed my keys.

"You need to hear what I have to say first." Laurel took my empty glass to the bathroom, refilled it, and brought it back, handing it to me. "Relax."

"How can I?"

I gulped that glass of water too, and Laurel sat, in the same chair Roger Kirby had sat in just minutes before. Nervous energy kept me standing.

"What does it mean, Laurel?" I asked as she calmly

took out her notebook and phone. "He was there with her the night she died. And you say they seemed involved. That's the word you used. *Involved*. She had an affair with Roger Kirby, right? That's why he doesn't want me asking questions."

"These are all maybes," she said, looking up, reading glasses perched on the end of her nose.

"He was with her the night she died. Right before she died. He must know what was going on." I walked around the room in a circle, my breathing almost normal by that point. "Let's go find him."

But Laurel showed no signs of budging. She had her notebook out, reading something in it with her brow furrowed. "Do you know a guy named Blake Brown?"

"No," I said. "Should I? Wait. Blake Brown. You mean Marissa's ex-boyfriend? I never met him, but she talked about him."

"Let me tell you about him."

"We have to do this now?"

"It's relevant. Listen." She studied the notebook a little bit longer. "What did Marissa ever tell you about him?"

"Too much. She lost her virginity to him. They dated for over a year, I guess, junior and senior year of high school. When they broke up, when *she* broke up with *him*, he went a little nutty. He started coming over to their house without calling. Sending flowers and gifts to try to win her back." I stretched my memory back through the fog of my young man's jealousy. "She told me that once, after they broke up, he even came over in the middle of the night and threw pebbles at her window. Apparently, he used to do that when they wanted to sneak out and fool around. But that time he stood in the yard and begged her to take him back. He said he couldn't live without her, that if she didn't get back together with him, he'd hurt himself."

"Did he?"

"I don't think so. Her family told the police. Or maybe a shrink at school. I thought it all blew over. She still had pictures of him in her dorm room freshman year."

"I remember that. He was a *really* good-looking guy."

"Thanks."

"I just mean he looked normal. Not like a stalker or a nutcase."

"Can you tell that easily?"

"With some people, yes, you can."

"Holy shit," I said. "Now I know where they came from."

"What are you talking about?"

"The flowers," I said. "I went to the cemetery today, while I was waiting for you. There were flowers on Marissa's grave, fresh flowers. Her favorite kind, too. Lily of the valley. *He* put them there. Roger Kirby. He knows her favorite flower and still visits her grave." I wanted to throw my water glass against the wall, to shatter it into a million pieces. "And then he came over here and tried to throw me off the trail."

"I need you to listen to what I have to say, Nick."

"What does it matter?" I asked. "Did you really find something important?"

"I did," she said, trying to focus me. "Just listen.

Kirby isn't going anywhere. He's been in this town for seventy years. We know where he works. I went to the library first today. I looked through the microfilm from the local paper for the dates around Marissa's death. You know, a month or so before. A few weeks after. It's a small-town paper, so it wasn't hard to wade through. I was just looking for anything that stood out as unusual. Anything."

"And?"

"People always say small towns are safe places where not much happens. That's just not true. Even a town like Hanfort had a lot going on twenty years ago. A couple of drug busts. A homicide—a brother shooting his sister over control of the TV remote. A hit-and-run accident that killed a little kid. Driver didn't stop. Miscellaneous assaults and fights. The works."

"Small towns have their problems too," I said.

"They sure do," she said. "But none of those problems had anything about Marissa."

She reached out and placed her hand on a small stack of papers to her right. It looked like she was guarding them from a strong wind.

"What's that stuff?" I asked.

"I didn't know if I was going to show them to you. Or if you'd want to see them. But they're news articles about Marissa's death, as well as the other things going on in the town at that time. I printed them off for you, but if you don't want to look, I can get rid of them. Maybe it's a bad idea."

"No," I said, truly curious. "I'll look at them. Later."

Laurel nodded. "Maybe you'll want to be alone."

"Was there anything else you uncovered?" I asked.

"Not really." She tapped her finger on the tabletop. "Except they didn't solve this hit-and-run. At least not in the couple of weeks after the accident that I looked at."

"What could that have to do with Marissa?"

"I don't know. And they probably solved it later. The cops I talked to didn't remember the case. But there was a witness back then. An elderly woman saw the whole thing happen. She said it was a dark-haired man driving the car that hit the child."

"There you go. You said you learned something, so what happened with the cops when you talked to them?" I asked. "I trust we're getting to the part about Blake Whatshisface. Meanwhile, Kirby is going on with his life, and we're just sitting here."

Laurel ignored my complaining. "The police couldn't find any problems with Marissa or anyone in her family," she said. "They all have clean records. No busts, no run-ins or arrests. Not even a parking ticket. They're as clean as the Cleavers. They almost seemed too good to be true. You know how teenagers drive, and you mean to tell me she never got a ticket? Never? Nothing?"

"It's a small town. Her dad was prominent. Maybe she talked her way out of tickets."

"Do you think the Marissa we knew would do that?" Laurel asked.

"Probably not," I said. "She'd probably tell the cop off."

"Exactly."

Someone started a vacuum cleaner in the hallway, the sound of the small motor rising and receding as the cleaning person pushed the device up and down the carpet.

"There was an officer at the station, a guy named Rich Cotton. His daughter went to high school with Marissa. Her name was Stacey or Macy, something like that. Anyway, he told me about the ex-boyfriend and all the bullshit when they broke up. So we're all sitting around, the cops and me, just talking and going over everything, and I told them all about Emily and how she looks like Marissa and how she had your address in her pocket."

"What did they say?" I asked.

"They're stumped. But Officer Cotton talked more about Blake and what a weirdo he was growing up. Apparently, he had his share of trouble when he was a kid. Busting windows, harassing animals. Then he kind of straightened out by the time he was a teenager. No real problems there, until he broke up with Marissa. Then he got a little weird again."

"Why did they tell you all of this?" I asked.

"I told you. The chief down in Eastland is buddies with the chief up here. He called for me. Cops and former cops stick together."

"How did they remember all this stuff about Blake?" I asked.

"They looked up his record," she said, as though it was the simplest thing in the world. "This Officer Cotton seemed to recall that Blake went off to college in Indiana or someplace like that. And he was wondering what ever became of him. Did he stay on the straight and narrow? Or did he get in trouble again? So just for kicks they looked him up in the system, the nationwide system."

Laurel wore a smug look, the one that said she knew something else, but she wasn't just going to hand it over to me without getting asked first. It was like the encore of a great concert. She wasn't going to go on unless I cheered.

"I'm guessing you found something out about him," I said.

"He kept his nose clean in college," she said, "but a couple of years after graduation, he found himself in a bit of trouble."

"A bit?" I asked. "What did he do, shoplift stuff?"

"He tried to kill his ex-girlfriend," she said.

"You're kidding." That news itself was disturbing enough, but then I thought about Marissa existing in close proximity to someone capable of such violence. I still held the glass, and I wanted to throw it again. "So he's in prison now?" I asked.

"Down in Florida. He won't be out for another five years or so."

"Good." But Laurel still wore a knowing look on her face. "Do I want to know how he tried to kill her?" I asked.

Laurel paused a moment before she said, "Arson. He tried to burn her house down, Nick. With her inside it."

CHAPTER THIRTY-NINE

The glass in my hands had become warm and sticky from sweat, covered with a web of my fingerprints. I didn't know what else to do, so I tapped the bottom of the glass against my open palm. My hands started to shake, and my legs felt like worn-out elastic bands.

"That's ghastly," I said, using a word I don't think I'd ever used before in my life.

"The woman escaped, thank God. A neighbor saw the flames and pounded on the door. It was lucky. She had a little smoke inhalation, but she recovered. And the police caught him and put him away."

I sat and folded my hands together on the tabletop, hoping to steady them. Hoping to steady my entire being, inside and out. Many times I'd thought of the horror of that night. The smoke rising, the flames spreading. Did Marissa even wake up? A part of me hoped for mercy, that somehow she was overcome in her sleep and never knew what killed her. But I doubted it was true.

They must have known. They must have scrambled for doors and windows, desperate and terrified, facing their own mortality. Nate's description of the 911 call had made that fact clear.

And it might have been an act of homicide, perpetrated by a jilted ex-boyfriend.

"Okay," I said, trying to keep my voice level, "that might explain the fire. But it doesn't explain everything else. What was Marissa doing with Roger Kirby that night?"

Laurel started to speak and then stopped. Then she went ahead, saying, "Marissa came home the weekend before she died, didn't she? We all knew that. If Blake was in Hanfort, or if he knew about the relationship with Roger, then maybe that drove him to a final desperate act. Maybe he tried to get Marissa back that weekend or sometime before, knowing she was involved with Roger. You know how small towns are. Everybody knows everything. It wouldn't be hard for a guy to know what his ex-girlfriend is doing."

"She never mentioned trouble with Blake to me," I said, my voice lower, distant to my own ears. "I would have—" I stopped myself. Would I have known? Would I have known any of it?

"She had secrets, Nick."

"Why didn't the cops put this together sooner?" I asked.

"This attempted murder, the arson, happened years after Marissa died. And Blake did this in another state, Florida. There was no real reason to make the connection. I'm sure the Florida authorities checked Blake out, but the fire that killed Marissa was ruled an accident. They wouldn't have connected the dots."

"But they are now?" I asked.

"They can ask Blake about it," Laurel said. "If he wants to confess, you have a closed case. But all the physical evidence from the fire that killed Marissa is gone. They bulldozed that site and put a new house up."

"And Blake has to know that," I said. "Why would he confess to a crime all these years later if they don't have anything on him?"

"People surprise us," Laurel said. "A lot of guys find Jesus in prison. Blake may have done some soul-searching and wants to get it all off his chest."

"What are the odds of that?" I asked.

"Slim. Not none, but pretty damn slim."

My mind moved forward, past Blake Brown and on to the other things that had been consuming me for the past couple of weeks. "None of this explains Emily Russell, does it? Why did she show up looking for me? Why does she look so much like Marissa?"

Laurel gave me a sympathetic look. "I agree—we don't know anything about that girl and your address. We may never know."

"But the woman at the funeral, the charity that helps with adoptions, the locked room at the Minors' house. The flowers on the grave . . ."

I couldn't sustain the energy to keep listing the details. I knew what Laurel was thinking, and I mostly agreed with her.

So what about those things? They weren't proof of anything. I remembered my high school science classes. Occam's razor. The most likely explanation was that Marissa was having a relationship with an older married man, leading her to break up with me. Her ex-boyfriend, who had a history of erratic and violent behavior, killed her, just as he tried to kill another woman later in his life.

Case closed.

Who was Emily Russell and what did she want? Laurel was right. We might not ever know, at least not until her murder was solved. *If* it was ever solved.

"I would like to have my own chat with Roger Kirby," Laurel said. "He's probably not going to talk to you again, but I thought maybe I could swing by his office and see if I can catch him. Maybe I can pick up on something."

"That he was fucking my ex-girlfriend? That he took advantage of a young girl, a family friend?"

"I get the feeling you might want to be alone for a little while and process this." Laurel looked at her watch. "It's getting late. We're here for the night. We can hang out in wild and crazy Hanfort for the evening."

"Yeah," I said. "Sure."

I gave Laurel Roger Kirby's office address and phone number. Before she left the room, she patted me on the shoulder. "The truth hurts—I know."

"It doesn't hurt," I said. "It's excruciating."

CHAPTER FORTY

Left alone, I picked up the pages Laurel had printed at the library. I remembered well the news coverage from the campus paper in the wake of the fire, the maudlin and sentimental images and words. Lots of shots of students crying and hugging other students. The obligatory photo of the makeshift shrine at the site of the fire. Cards, candles, teddy bears. I wondered then how many of those people knew Marissa or any of the other dead students and how many of them just wanted to be in the middle of something, some drama or overheated display of emotion.

The *Hanfort Times* wasn't much more restrained. The headline read, FIRE TRAGEDY KILLS BELOVED LOCAL GIRL. *Beloved*. Marissa would have rolled her eyes at that. I scanned the article and found I knew most of the facts by heart. Near the end, the fire inspector was quoted as saying that he suspected the cause of the fire was accidental: "Probably a careless smoker or faulty wiring." Several days after Marissa's death, the inspector announced that the fire had been caused by an unattended candle left burning. He added that several students were at the house earlier that night, and some of them were drinking, with candles burning throughout the place. "A deadly combination," he concluded.

The authorities never seemed to seriously consider arson as an option. Why would they? Who would want to kill four college kids?

The final printed page contained Marissa's obituary. It used her high school graduation portrait, the same photo I'd carried in my wallet for years, all the way up until I married Gina. Marissa looked beautiful, of course, slightly younger than when we dated and very much like Emily Russell. But in light of the recent revelations about Blake Brown and Roger Kirby, I looked at the photo through a different lens. I took out my phone and called up a news story about Emily Russell, one that featured a portrait of the dead girl. Then I looked at them side by side, Marissa and Emily. The forehead and hairline were different, as was the sharp point of the chin. Emily's ears protruded a little more, and her smile was wider and seemed more natural. Given Marissa's natural resistance to anything as silly as a senior portrait, I could see why her smile was forced.

Sure, they looked alike, but maybe not as much as I had imagined. What were the odds there were two pretty redheads in the world who liked to pinch their lips while they thought? Pretty high, I guessed.

I read the obituary, and I nearly choked when I saw a

quote from Roger Kirby, who was identified as a close friend of the family.

"Marissa was a special girl, a very special girl. I've watched her grow up, and I'm very sorry that we've lost her so young. We all loved her."

I crumpled the paper in my hands and threw it across the room.

When Laurel came back and knocked on the door, I was stretched out watching *Gilligan's Island*, regressing to my childhood in the face of bad news. I let her in and muted the sound, noting the disapproving look she gave my choice of programming.

"You told me to watch TV," I said.

"That junk?"

"Forget that," I said. "Did you talk to that asshole?"

"Briefly. He was on his way to another meeting."

"What did he have to say?" I asked.

"He says he wasn't in Eastland the night Marissa died or any other night around that time. He told me I was wrong to think he was in that bar with her, and he resented the implication that something 'untoward' might have been going on between the two of them. He told me he's a family man and was a close friend of the Minors who only wished them the best. About what I expected."

"Fuck him," I said.

"Indeed."

"Laurel?"

"What?"

"Are you sure it was him?" I asked. "That was twenty

years ago. Maybe you were wrong. Maybe it was some other older guy. Maybe they were just talking about . . . who knows?"

"It was him," Laurel said. "I know it. You remember what I was like back then. I wanted to be a cop. I observed everything; I remembered everything. Names, faces. Everything."

"I know."

"But it's my word against his, twenty years later," she said. "And I'm not sure that's the most important thing right now."

I knew she was right. But I didn't want to admit it.

"What have you been doing since I left?" she asked.

I bent down and picked up the crumpled copy of Marissa's obituary.

"Oh," she said. "I'm sorry, Nick."

I kept it tucked in my fist, the paper pressing against the soft skin of my palm. "What do you think happens when we die?" I asked.

"Seriously?"

"Yes. Seriously. What happens?"

"I have no idea, but I'd like to think . . . I'd like to think I'd see my kids again after I died. I'd hate to think we do all this, form these intense attachments to people, and then we just let them go when we die. But what do I know?"

"What do any of us know?"

"Exactly."

I held up the crumpled obituary again, waving the little ball in the air. "They didn't even mention me in here. They list all her family members and deceased grandparents and all of that, but there was no mention of me. I was pissed when I saw that, but then I thought maybe I'm a fool for expecting it. Why would I think they'd mention me?"

"It's tough when you date someone in college," Laurel said. "You're an adult, but you're not married or engaged. It's difficult to negotiate. But I understand why you'd feel excluded."

"Am I fooling myself?" I asked. "Maybe my feelings for Marissa weren't as real as I thought they were."

"Only you could know that, Nick."

"I don't think I can trust myself to know anything now," I said. "And you guys keep telling me that I'm imagining things, seeing resemblances and connections where they don't really exist. So tell me. Am I a fool? Did I just manufacture these feelings for Marissa? Did I do it because I'm a divorced middle-aged guy?"

"All I can tell you is what I observed when we were in school and you guys were together. I'd say the two of you were very much in love. To be honest, I was a little jealous whenever I saw you together. I didn't meet Tony until after graduation." Laurel smiled a little. "It was kind of sick how happy you were."

"Do you remember she and I always said we'd run off to New Zealand together after graduation?" I asked.

Laurel thought about it for a moment. "That does sound familiar. It sounds very much like the kind of thing Marissa would want to do."

"Exactly," I said. "We had plans. We felt like we had a future. It was going to be so full."

"I know you did," she said. "I could see it."

"Then why did she dump me like that, Laurel? Why was she with somebody else?"

"Do you really want to spend the rest of your life trying to understand the thought processes of a twenty-year-old woman who was acting irrationally? You could drive yourself crazy doing that."

I studied the crumpled ball of paper in my hand. "I feel like I'm on my way to crazy already. New Zealand? Maybe I was crazy back then too."

CHAPTER FORTY-ONE

Riley seemed to have had a good time with Laurel's kids. When I went by their house to pick him up, he looked at me like he didn't want to leave. I started to put him on his leash in the foyer of Laurel's house, but then she said, "Why don't you stay?"

I looked up at her.

"Come on, Nick," she said. "Tony will want to see you. We haven't hung out besides doing this investigation stuff."

"Are you saying that isn't helping us bond?" I asked.

"Come on," she said. "There's beer."

"I do need a drink," I said. "Maybe two."

I set Riley's leash aside and followed Laurel. Tony stood in the kitchen, holding an open beer. He was taller than me and fitter, and he laughed at nearly everything I said, which made me like him even more. He shook my hand and opened a beer for me, and then invited me to sit at the table. The beer tasted good. It felt even better to be among friends.

"Tony," I said, "I'm sorry I've kept your wife away so much."

"He doesn't mind," Laurel said. "He can do whatever he wants while I'm gone."

"Seriously, though," I said. "She's been a big help. I appreciate it."

"That's what friends are for," Tony said. "Besides, you've helped us plenty."

"I have? Not like this."

"Remember when Fiona had to do that school report on the city council," Tony asked, "and you helped her get a tour of the chamber?"

"Sure."

"And remember the time you and Gina watched the kids when my dad was sick?" Laurel asked.

"Of course," I said. "That's what—"

"That's what friends do," Tony said, finishing my sentence. He raised his beer, clinking it against mine. "Are you hungry? You can't drink all this beer on an empty stomach."

Once we were home, my head buzzing a little and my belly full of good food made by good friends, Riley settled into his bed, let out a long sigh, and fell asleep.

"See?" I said. "Being with those rowdy kids all day isn't all it's cracked up to be."

He ignored me.

I'd received a text from work. Olivia Bloom asked me if I was ready to come back on Monday and "get into the swing of things again." It was Saturday evening, and I looked at the two days of the weekend as a long trudge across a desert. What was I going to do but sit and stew and feel worse?

I told Olivia I'd be there bright and early. If I'd had a key to the office, I would have gone in right that moment. But I didn't. So I was left alone with only a sleeping dog for company.

I paced around the apartment a little. Washed my few dishes, put in a load of laundry. Then my phone was in my hand, dialing Heather.

"Do you have your kids this weekend?" I asked.

"Not tonight. They're going to a basketball game with their dad."

"Would you like to come over?"

Heather played it cool. I knew she was mad because I'd left town without seeing her and was abrupt with her in the process. She was going to make me work for her affections.

"I don't know . . ." she said finally.

"Riley misses you," I said. "And I'll tell you all about my little trip yesterday. You'll be interested."

"Hmm. Do you think I'm that easy?"

"No," I said. "But I am."

She told me she'd see me at six.

I didn't cook much. I knew how to pour dog food into Riley's bowl and boil water for my oatmeal or spaghetti. But that was as far as it went. So Heather and I went to dinner at Scotty and Maria's, a local Italian place.

Once we were seated, Heather reached out and placed her hand on top of mine. "Why don't we get a drink? Wine? Oh, wait. You don't like wine."

I ordered a beer, even though I'd already had some at Laurel's house, and once I swallowed some of it, I felt better. Heather sipped her wine and said, "Are you going to tell me about your secret trip?"

I needed to pace myself with both food and drink, and I needed to be clearheaded. I *wanted* to tell someone about my trip to Hanfort.

"Sure," I said. And I did, speaking in a low voice. While I told her about Loretta Stieger, Heather listened and asked only a few questions. When I talked about Roger Kirby and his self-righteous indignation, Heather curled her lip. She asked me how old he was.

"He must be in his seventies," I said.

"So he was in his fifties when he and Marissa . . ." She made a face like she'd swallowed a lemon. "Sorry. You probably don't want to think about all that."

"I don't." I looked around the restaurant, watching the other diners, who all looked happy and at ease. "It's tough to admit I might have lost her to a man thirty years older than me."

Heather reached her hand out again. "It's not about you. You've always been a prize. It was something about Marissa. Maybe she was hung up on her dad. That's why girls go after older men. They have daddy issues."

I pictured Brent Minor. He was distant and cold, all about business. But Marissa never doubted that her father loved and cared for her. So I gulped some more beer. Did it matter what Marissa sought in Roger Kirby?

"Is that all you learned?" Heather asked.

"Roger Kirby isn't the worst of it."

"What could be worse than that?"

I told her about Blake Brown. His breakup with Marissa and the fire in Florida. While I spoke, it felt as though everything in the restaurant grew still, telescoping down to the two of us as I shared the hideous news. Heather sat frozen, her hand resting on the stem of her wineglass. She looked away from me, while I continued to speak, and when I'd told her everything about Blake and the fire, she didn't say anything. She stared into her wine, her finger tapping the tabletop.

"They don't know for sure, of course," I said. "But circumstantially it looks like Marissa's death could be murder. I talked to that cop who investigated the fire originally, and he said he had his doubts about it being an accident back then. Something about a nine-one-one call. It was a woman who called in, and according to this detective, she sounded like she was surprised there were people in the house. I guess he was right—there might have been more to the case, but I don't know what the nine-one-one call could have to do with Blake, since it was a woman who made it."

"Shit," Heather said. She looked distracted and unnerved by the information I'd shared with her. She lifted her hand to her temple and rubbed it as if it hurt. "What are they going to do now?"

"Who knows?" I said. "It's all over. The evidence is gone, the house, the nine-one-one tapes. It's all over and gone. They'll talk to this guy, and we can all hope he'll confess."

Heather left her wineglass on the table and took a couple of long swallows of water. I remembered the way my appetite faded after talking to Nate about the fire, and I worried Heather was experiencing the same thing.

"I'm sorry," I said. "This is lousy dinner conversation. Let's talk about something else."

"It's just shocking, that's all," she said, trying to put on a brave face. "Shocking and terrible."

"And you wonder why I'm single," I said. "Talking about something this gruesome when we go out to a nice restaurant."

Heather forced a smile, but the mood was dead on the table. And we ate mostly in silence.

CHAPTER FORTY-TWO

Heather left in the morning. She had to pick her kids up from their father's house, and then they were all going to a cookout at a family friend's. She invited me half-heartedly, after telling me her ex-husband would be there, and I was more than happy to pass.

By midafternoon, I had made good progress on catching up with my work. Instead of being two weeks behind, I was only one. I slipped out for a sandwich and came back a half hour later and had just started answering more e-mails when the phone rang. I wanted to ignore it, but I figured it was Heather. When I looked at the caller ID, though, I saw it was Mick Brosius.

"Just wanted to give you a heads-up about something," he said. "I figured you'd want to know."

"What's that?" I asked.

"They've made an arrest," he said.

"An arrest?"

It didn't register with me. An arrest for what?

"Emily Russell. The murder. The cops arrested a guy this morning. They think they have their man."

It felt like I sat holding the phone for a long, long time. I wasn't even sure what I was feeling or what I was supposed to feel. I knew there were people who would have cheered or been elated over the news, but I wasn't one of them. Emily was still dead. Nothing could change that. Nothing could change any of it.

"Who is it?" I asked.

"A local scumbag. His name's . . . let me see. Lance Hillman. Apparently, they caught him breaking into a motel room last night. They checked his truck, and he had an iPod belonging to the Russell girl. Hillman admitted to breaking into her room and about twenty-five others around town."

"Did he really kill her?"

"I don't know. He clammed up. But he broke into another motel room across town and found a woman sleeping in her bed. She says he tried to strangle her too. Most burglars, if they find someone inside, they run. Not this guy. He went after this woman. He's a real maniac."

"So maybe they found their guy," I said.

"The cops think so," Brosius said. "I talked to Reece this morning. I'm sure he doesn't even remember you exist. Closing a murder case looks pretty good in a town like this. It doesn't happen every day."

I stared out the window to the parking lot. It was empty, the day quiet and overcast. Was I supposed to feel nothing when the mystery was solved?

"Are you there, Nick?"

"I'm here, yes."

"Are you okay? You got quiet on me."

"I'm okay," I said. "Thanks."

I waited for my obligatory call from Laurel. It took twenty minutes to arrive.

When I answered, she simply said, "Did you hear?"

"I did," I said. "Brosius called me."

"I've been trying to find out more, but they're being pretty tight-lipped about it all. I may sneak down there later."

"Don't worry about it," I said. "Aren't you trying to spend the day with your kids? You were gone Friday and part of Saturday."

"Sure," she said. "But I thought we'd find out as much as we could right away. To be honest, I thought you'd want to know."

"I already know what I need to know," I said, sounding very much like a Zen master. "The only thing I don't really know is how Emily knew me. Maybe you were right. Maybe she wanted to thank me for helping one of her relatives."

"Maybe," Laurel said, unconvinced.

"Maybe she ran away in the store because she's shy."

"You seem pretty calm, all things considered," she said.

"I guess I'm not a murder suspect anymore."

"I do think you're off the hook," she said.

"And I guess I've been thinking about a lot of things,"

I said. "The one thing I want I can't have. So if I can't have that, what does the rest matter?"

"And what's the one thing you want?" Laurel asked.

"I want Marissa back."

CHAPTER FORTY-THREE

They arraigned the man, Lance Hillman, a couple of days later, charging him with the string of motel burglaries as well as Emily's murder. He pleaded not guilty to all of it, despite having previously admitted to at least some of the robberies.

I watched the proceedings on the local news. Hillman wore a long, scraggly beard, and beneath his orange prison jumpsuit, his arms were covered with tattoos. Those arms had supposedly squeezed the life out of Emily Russell before she could find me and accomplish whatever mission she had set herself on, a mission neither her parents nor her friends knew anything about.

Laurel let me know that things were moving slowly in Hanfort. Yes, they intended to speak to Blake Brown about the fire that killed Marissa and her three roommates, but it wasn't a priority. I tried not to think about it. Heather's children were staying with her that week, so we saw very little of each other. We ate lunch together once and had a couple of phone calls, but that was it, even though I would have welcomed more of a distraction.

My life brightened considerably when Gina called me one evening to ask for a favor. She told me she had to run to a meeting at work, but Andrew's regular babysitter was unavailable.

"Can I just drop him off for an hour?" she asked.

"Of course," I said, trying to keep my voice steady. "I'm home."

"You're sure you don't mind?" Gina asked.

"I don't mind. We can watch the basketball game or something."

And that's exactly what we did. The Cavaliers were playing the Heat, and we watched the Cavs getting trounced in the early part of the game. Gina told me Andrew hadn't eaten much at dinner, so I made sure to give him plenty of potato chips and popcorn, all the things a nine-year-old boy and a forty-year-old man loved. I didn't know when I'd see him again. Life is short, I figured, so I encouraged him to live it up. Even Riley stirred and wagged his tail. He curled up next to Andrew on the couch and didn't move.

"Do you think LeBron will ever come back to the Cavs?" Andrew asked.

"Not a chance," I said.

"Really?"

"Really. Would you move to Cleveland from Miami?" I asked.

"I think he will," Andrew said.

"Maybe you're an optimist," I said.

"The Cavaliers are good to watch," Andrew said. "But I'm ready for baseball."

"I hear you. Just a couple of weeks. Any predictions on the Reds?"

Andrew thought this over carefully, like he worked at the State Department and was being asked for a foreign policy recommendation. I agreed with the seriousness of the question.

"I think they're a five hundred team this year," Andrew said. "Leadoff is a question mark. So is the bullpen. Five hundred."

"Impressive."

"I've been reading the blogs online," he said.

"I haven't," I said. "They depress me. I'm going to be the optimist this time and say they win ninety games and get the wild card."

Andrew looked skeptical, but he was too nice to say anything.

"You don't believe it?" I asked.

"No." He looked certain, confident, a tiny wise man.

"You're probably right," I said. "But I'd hate to think you're a cynic already."

It was the fastest hour of my life. When Gina showed up, I thought only ten minutes had passed. I expected her to complain about the potato chip remnants and the bowl with the collection of unpopped popcorn kernels in the bottom. She looked them over and smiled, ruffling Andrew's hair.

"Looks like you had fun," she said. "Both of you."

"We did," Andrew said.

"Do you mind waiting in the car, buddy?" she said. "I have to talk to Nick for a second."

"Sure," Andrew said. He came over to me and we high-fived. "Thanks, Nick."

"Sure thing." I felt lighter, happier. But I knew I couldn't tell him I'd see him soon or anything like that because I didn't know if I would. "Take care," I said.

When Andrew was gone, Gina turned to me. "Thanks," she said. "I'm sorry to dump this on you at the last minute."

"Are you kidding?" I asked. "We had a blast."

"I figured you would. I knew you'd both like it. I can't really talk sports with him, as you know. He misses that."

"Doesn't Dale talk sports?" I asked. "He looked like a healthy young lad."

Gina gave me a warning look. "He's not around much. And he's not a sports guy. Not like you two."

"I'm happy to do it," I said.

"I know," she said. "I hate all this shuttling around. When my parents split up, I vowed I'd never do it to my kid."

"I remember." I shrugged. "My parents were unhappily married, but they were always together. There's no right or wrong way to do it. And for the record, you're doing well. He's a great kid."

"Thanks," she said. I could tell she meant it. "It seems like just yesterday I brought him home from the hospital. It's all going by so fast."

"Tell me about it," I said. "I'm three years older than you. That's three years closer to the grave."

"Oh, Nick. You know, in the past, I'd laugh at you for saying something like that, but I have no room to now."

"Why's that?" I asked. "You're passing up the chance to laugh at me?"

Her face grew serious, her brow furrowing as she thought about something. "Do you remember we talked on the phone a while ago, right after you were in the news for being a murder suspect?"

"I do," I said. "Did you see I'm off the hook?"

"I did." Gina shivered about something. "That guy they arrested. Ugh. To think of what he did to that beautiful girl. I hope he didn't . . . It sounds awful to say, but I hope he *just* killed her. I hope he didn't do more to her."

"Me too."

"Anyway, I mentioned to you that some guy disappeared from my dorm when I was at Ohio State."

I tried to remember the details of the call. All I really remembered was being concerned that Andrew would see me on the news and think I was a psychopath. I'd much rather talk to him about the Reds than about what it means to be a person of interest in a homicide investigation.

"I vaguely remember."

"Well, it's not important," she said, looking down at the keys in her hand. "What's important is that it sent me into this nostalgia spiral. I started looking up old friends on Facebook. I exchanged messages with people I hadn't talked to in years. I found out what people are doing with their lives. We've all become adults with kids and jobs and houses. It's like someone hit fast-forward on everything."

"Tell me about it," I said.

"One of my friends remembered the missing guy's name. Charles Blevins. Do you know they never found him? Still. His family has a website about it." She stood with her arms folded over her chest. "I don't know. Andrew is growing up so fast. I don't want him to miss out on what he gets from you. I think about that guy being missing, being away from his family and the people he cares about all that time. I guess what I'm saying is . . . I'm open to more of this, the kind of thing that happened tonight. More time with you guys together. Let's just see how it goes."

I wanted to hug her, but I didn't. Instead I just smiled.

"Thanks," I said. "Really. I mean it, and I think it's good for both of us."

"I agree," she said.

"If they ever find Charles Blevins, I'll send him a thank-you."

"We'll talk soon." She slipped out the door into the cool night.

It felt like the start of something new.

CHAPTER FORTY-FOUR

After Gina left, I watched the end of the basketball game. I'd had my fill of junk food and intended to stare at the TV until I felt so drowsy I couldn't keep my eyes open anymore.

When I reached that point, I took Riley for his walk around the apartment complex. Since he was an older dog, it sometimes took him longer to do his business than it would with a pup. That's what happened that night, and when he struggled to make the urine flow as quickly as he wanted, I reminded him that it happened to all of us if we were lucky to live long enough. I told him I didn't care. It was a nice night, and I was in no hurry. He looked at me like he wanted me to shut up.

So I took out my phone. No texts. No important e-mails.

I thought about what Gina had said about nostalgia, all of it triggered by her vague memories of a guy she didn't really know who disappeared when we were all just kids. I couldn't fault her for feeling that way. I understood as well as anybody how both young love and young death opened the dam to a flood of memories from the past.

I slid the leash up my wrist, freeing both of my hands for typing and searching. I entered Charles Blevins's name and found the website Gina was talking about, the one still maintained after all those years by the Blevins family. I looked at the photos of a smiling young man, his clothes and hair twenty years out of date. But he looked happy and optimistic. As I stared at the photos, I wondered what could have gone wrong to make him disappear before his life had even started. A crime? An accident? A suicide? Who could tell just by looking?

Riley finally finished. He must have been relieved, because he wiped his feet with particular gusto and then walked until the slack in the leash tightened. He looked ready to go home.

"Just a minute," I said.

I clicked on the information page, the one that gave the details of the case. When I saw them, I tugged the leash harder than I intended to.

"Shit, Riley. We have to get home."

"Gina?"

"Nick?" As expected, she sounded groggy, but I needed to talk to her. "What time is it?"

"I'm sorry if I woke you," I said. "But I need to ask you something."

Riley sat at my feet, staring up at me. He seemed be telling me to wait until morning, but I ignored him.

"Is something wrong? What time is it?"

"It's midnight," I said, "and I don't think anything's wrong. But I was wondering something."

"Jesus, Nick," she said. "Call me tomorrow."

"I need to ask you something tonight. It's important."

"Is this what it's going to be like now that I've opened the door to you again?" she asked.

"Come on," I said, "that's not fair. Now just answer me. You said you talked to people who remembered this Charles Blevins guy who disappeared from Ohio State. Did any of them know him very well?"

"Charles Blevins?" She paused while she tried to place the name. "Him? You want to talk about this now?"

"Yes," I said. "I need to know."

"For God's sake, Nick, why?"

I paused. Did I want to tell her? I knew if I did, I opened myself up to all the comments and criticism I'd heard over the past couple of weeks. Not just from Gina but also from Laurel. But I had to know who might have known Charles well back then.

"It's about Marissa," I said. "This guy, Charles Blevins, he was reported missing from the OSU campus almost a week after Marissa died."

"So?" she said. "Columbus is a big city."

"He was reported missing a week after Marissa died, but his roommate hadn't seen him since Saturday. The *day* Marissa died."

"Nick, please." She sounded more awake, more agitated. "Let this go."

I pressed on. "According to the information on the

website, his roommate said Charles was supposed to be going to Eastland that weekend. He had friends there. He was going to party at Eastland. What if he went there that weekend and somehow ended up back at Marissa's house? And if he was killed in the fire that weekend . . . well, it could mean . . ."

She didn't say anything for a long time.

Finally, I said, "Gina, just do this for me."

"I get it, Nick. I do." I heard rustling around on her end of the line. "You loved her. You don't want to let go."

"It's not just that. It's the cop we talked to. He said they didn't positively identify two of the bodies in the fire. What if Marissa wasn't in there?"

"Then where would she have gone?" Gina asked.

"I don't know. I don't fucking know." I floundered around, trying to find the right words. "But things aren't adding up."

She let out a long sigh. I practically felt her breath through the phone. It was that much of a sigh. Then she said, "Hold on a minute. I'll tell you what I know."

CHAPTER FORTY-FIVE

I expected more excitement from Laurel when I told her what I'd learned. Maybe it was the early hour—I called her at six thirty a.m. and clearly woke her up—or maybe she was just fatigued by the embers of false hope I kept fanning, but she almost sounded disappointed when I told her about Charles Blevins.

Someone muttered in the background on her end of the line.

"Tell Tony I'm sorry if I woke him," I said. "I thought you guys would be up."

"We were about to be."

"Sorry."

"But that's interesting, Nick," she said. "Really interesting."

But I knew what she was saying. She was saying, *This sounds like more bullshit. Let it go.*

"This guy was supposed to go to Eastland that very

weekend, the very day of the fire. What if he'd gone there and . . ."

"And what?" she asked. "How did he end up in Marissa's house? Did he know her? Or did he know one of her roommates?"

"I don't know." I didn't say it, but I was thinking: *Apparently I have no idea who or what Marissa knew. Or who she was involved with.* "He's not familiar to me. Not the name and not his face. But he didn't have to know them. Maybe he came to Eastland to party, and he ended up hooking up with one of Marissa's roommates. That's plausible. He could have just gone home with one of them, and then he was there when Blake set the fire. He killed Charles and Marissa's three roommates, but not Marissa."

"Or maybe he died with the four of them," she said, her voice a dash of cold water. "You heard Nate. Maybe there were, pardon the expression, *five* sets of remains in there, and they only thought there were four. That's as logical as anything else."

"Okay. Maybe." Suddenly I felt a little deflated. "But what if Marissa wasn't there at all?"

"That's the key question, isn't it, Nick? The real question."

"What do you mean?"

Laurel said something to one of her kids. "Ask Dad to do it. Ask him." Then she came back on, sounding a little harried. "Let's say everything you think is true. Say Marissa didn't die in the fire that night. She's still alive somewhere despite all evidence to the contrary: the grave, the obituaries, the arsonist ex-boyfriend. Say she really is alive and has been for twenty years. Isn't it obvious she doesn't want to see you? You've been living in the same town for the last twenty years. Hell, you live ten minutes from the dorm where you lived when you met her. Fifteen minutes from the spot where she allegedly died. And not once in all that time has she tried to talk to you. Not once has she sent a card or a note or a Facebook message. And the last thing she did was break up with you. Why would you want to see someone who feels that way about you?"

If Laurel had punched me in the chest, I wouldn't have felt the force of her words any more powerfully. I took a step back where I was standing in the kitchen and lowered myself into a chair.

I didn't know what to say. I waited for my breath to come back. "How long have you been thinking this?"

"Jesus, Nick, I'm sorry. I'm not judging you. I'm just asking you . . . what is it all for? What do you hope to gain? Is it worth it?"

I had to answer her honestly. "I don't know. I've told myself all these years she couldn't have meant to break up with me, that we loved each other."

"I know. But she did. She *did* break up with you. Roger Kirby was an older man, and maybe he took advantage of her. Maybe that's obvious. Even a smart girl like Marissa could get taken in by a family friend. If she had lived, who knows what would have happened with you guys. You probably would have gotten back together and been fine."

"But we didn't," I said.

"You didn't."

"The fire ended all that," I said.

"It did," she said. "A sick man's actions put an end to all of that."

I tapped my foot against the floor. "Yeah."

"Do you want me to look into this Charles Blevins guy a little bit?" she asked. "I'm sure his family would be happy to have the tip."

"What could they do about it?" I asked.

"Only one thing I can think of. They could try to exhume whatever remains they found in the fire and test the DNA. They couldn't do it back then, but they can do it now. It's really upsetting to families, though. They don't like to think of their loved ones being dug up years later for something that might just be a hunch. But you said he has a sister. She could give permission and provide a DNA sample to match."

"There's no one to give permission on behalf of Marissa. Her parents are gone. Her sister . . . I guess you haven't been able to find any real lead about her."

"No, we haven't. They can get a court order without a family member, but would a judge do it for something this tenuous? It's unlikely. After all this time and so little evidence . . ."

"Right."

"I'm sorry, Nick," she said, and I could tell she meant it.

"No," I said. "Thanks for being honest. Maybe I needed that."

"We all do sometimes."

"I'll have to train Riley to talk to me the way you just did," I said. "Then I won't call you so early in the morning."

"I'm curious, though," she said. "This guy was reported missing after the fire?"

"A few days. He had the habit of going off and partying on weekends. His roommate was away as well, so it took a few days for anyone to really notice he was gone. When his parents tried to track him down, they found out no one had seen him for a week. They don't even know for sure that he came to Eastland that weekend. Just that he said he was going to. I guess that makes the case weaker. No one has any idea what happened to him. He wasn't in trouble with anybody, and there's no evidence of foul play, but they haven't seen or heard from him in twenty years."

"I think I'm going to go hug my kids," Laurel said.

"Hug them for me, too."

"They miss you," she said. "You're the best Wii bowler they've ever met."

"I'll put that on my résumé," I said.

"Are you sure you're okay?" she asked.

"I'm okay. Really. I didn't tell you, but I'm going to get to start seeing Andrew again. So that's good."

"Excellent. He's a good little man to concentrate on."

"He is. Thanks, Laurel." Then before I hung up I put words to what I had been feeling for days. "You're a good friend, Laurel."

CHAPTER FORTY-SIX

I made contact with Charles Blevins's family the next day.

It might have been the most difficult thing I've ever done.

I sent an e-mail through the website, trying to sound as normal as possible and stick to the facts as I knew them. I assumed they probably received their fair share of crazy and insulting comments, so I simply told them about the fire that occurred the same weekend Charles disappeared, and I added that two of the bodies were positively identified and two were not. I concluded by saying, "You might want to have the authorities look into this."

I heard back right away. The website was run by Charles's sister, Allison, and she wanted to speak to me in person. She said her family had been haunted by her brother's disappearance for the past twenty years, and if I really knew something, then she wanted to hear about it. Straight from my mouth. And even though she lived in Columbus, a full hour away, she offered to drive to Eastland to meet with me as soon as possible.

"Please," she wrote. "My family needs this."

How could I say no?

We agreed to meet the next day.

We met at a Starbucks out by the mall. It was a rainy night, and I shook water from my coat when I stepped into the warmth of the café and the comforting smell of coffee and pastries. Allison looked to be a few years older than me. She was heavy and carried a large canvas bag as a purse. Her clothes were nice, her hair neat, with not a strand out of place. The smile she offered when she saw me seemed to require a great deal of effort on her part.

We shook hands, and then I ordered a coffee from the bored college kid at the counter. Allison already had hot tea in front of her. When I sat, she told me about her day, how she worked part-time in a hospital and didn't think she'd get away on time to make the drive to Eastland. She was divorced with grown children, so she said she didn't need to rush home.

After her honest introduction, I felt I had to offer something personal, so I said, "I'm divorced too."

"It's hard," she said.

"It is."

Then she came to the point. She asked me how I put together the information I had sent her. In my e-mail and on the phone, I had purposely remained vague about my interest in Charles's story. My own story didn't really matter much to the Blevins family.

But I told Allison because she seemed to want to know, and she looked to be a sympathetic listener. And as I told her and absorbed her kind looks, I understood we were members of the same fraternity: We'd both lost someone, and neither one of us was exactly sure what had happened. If I was right about Charles, then Allison and I would see a change in our fortunes. She would receive the answers she'd spent years in search of, and I would realize I didn't know any of the things about Marissa's death I'd always thought I knew. I tried to remind myself of Laurel's words from the other night:

Why would you want to see someone who feels that way about you?

Why indeed?

Allison listened as I briefly shared my history with Marissa, the story of the fire, and then all the events of the past few weeks. Emily Russell. Roger Kirby. Blake Brown. And now Charles Blevins. It seemed like a broad, complicated web that had ensnared all of us, and I still wasn't sure if the threads hung together, or if we were like passengers on a bus—a random group of people bounced around by similar circumstances. Soon, very soon, the ride was going to stop, and we were all going to step off and get back to our lives.

When I was finished, Allison didn't pat my arm or provide any easy or false sympathy. I gave her a lot of credit for that. She'd probably been on the receiving end of her fair share of arm pats over the past twenty years.

"Wow," she said.

"Yeah," I said. "Wow."

"My mother always wanted to know where Charles was before she died. When she was in hospice, I think she believed Charles was going to open the door and come in, kneel by her bedside, and say, 'Mom, I'm here.' But of course he never did."

"A friend of mine recently told me closure is over-rated."

"I might agree," Allison said. "More likely, I would just say closure can be darn near impossible to find. Even when we think we have it, it eludes us. Right?"

I knew what she meant. For twenty years I'd thought I knew what happened to Marissa: She'd died in that fire. She was gone, a jumble of charred bones and flesh in the ground in Hanfort. But then certain things had opened the door again. Emily. Emily's adoption. Loretta's story about Joan's behavior. But those things didn't reopen an old wound. Those things simply told me that the original wound had never healed. Neither Allison nor I had fully come to grips with our losses.

"Let me ask you something," I said. "Do you really want to know if Charles died in that fire?"

Allison sipped her tea before answering. A group of teenagers at another table started laughing, their voices rising together so that for just a moment it was too loud to speak. When they quieted down, Allison said, "I don't *really* want to know. If I find out the truth, then it's the death of hope. And hope has been the fuel running my life most of the last twenty years. I have my kids, of course. But the hope that I'd see Charles again, that's been the biggest thing. I don't know what I'd use to fill that hole. I guess I'd have to find something else, wouldn't I?"

"I adopted a dog when I got divorced," I said.

"Dogs help," she said. "I have two."

"I guess I'm facing the death of hope as well."

"How so?" she asked.

"I always clung to the fantasy that Marissa and I would be together if she had lived." I swallowed my coffee. It needed more sugar, but I didn't want to get up. The rain spit against the darkened windows. "I thought the only thing keeping us from being together was a horrible accident. Now I have to face the notion she might be choosing to stay away from me, that there was someone else back then, and she has no interest in me even now."

"It's not easy, is it?" she asked. "I've lived with all of this a long time."

"Are you going to take this to the police?" I asked. "If you didn't, then I guess neither one of us would have our hopes shattered. You could believe your brother is still alive, and I could believe the love of my life is really dead." I smiled as I said it, letting her know I understood how pathetic my wish was. "We'd all be happy, right?"

Allison shared a smile with me. "I may be a fool, but I'm going to take this to the police. I guess I believe what we don't know sometimes really does hurt us."

I nodded. "What we know *and* what we don't know."

CHAPTER FORTY-SEVEN

I was at Heather's house, eating a late dinner, when the detective from Robeson County called me. Heather's kids were away for the evening, and she'd insisted on cooking an elaborate meal, most of which had been eaten when the phone rang. Pork roast, vegetables, good bread hot from the oven. Warm, comforting food. I could get used to it.

I almost ignored the call.

I didn't recognize the number, and I'd been looking forward to being with Heather. We hadn't seen each other for a few days, and the thought of a quiet evening with good food, good beer, and time alone got my blood flowing in all the right directions.

But I didn't ignore the call. I answered. And the man on the other end told me he was a retired detective from Robeson County, the county that encompassed Hanfort.

"I received your name and number from a colleague of mine in Eastland," the man said after introducing himself as Troy Cato. "You know him, right? Nate Denning? He said he talked to you recently."

"Sure. I know him."

"He and I were talking about cases we'd worked on over the years, and I thought there was something you'd want to see. Something up here in Robeson."

"Are you going to tell me what it is?" I asked.

I looked across the table. Heather was sipping her wine, but I could see the look on her face, a look that said she was quickly growing bored with me being distracted by the phone.

"I'd prefer to show you," he said. "That's better than discussing it."

I stood up from the table and walked into Heather's living room. The furniture, the carpet, the drapes—all of them were white and immaculately clean. I probably wasn't even supposed to be walking in there while wearing shoes. But I wanted to be alone, away from her while I talked.

"Okay," I said. "Show me what?"

"Again, I think in person is better. Can I explain something to you? I didn't even tell Nate about this. You're the only other person I've shared this with."

I sat in one of Heather's not-so-comfortable chairs. They had no give. It was like sitting on a rock.

"Do you want to meet tomorrow?" I asked. "I can drive up to Robeson County in the afternoon."

"No," Troy said.

For a moment, he didn't explain, his negation hanging in the ether between us.

Then he said, "I can't show you this during the day. It has to be in the evening. Or at night. In fact, it has to be tonight."

"Why tonight?"

"I may decide I don't want to do this tomorrow. I may not even be *able* to do it tomorrow."

I looked at my slightly scuffed shoes as they rested on the pristine carpet. I knew very well what waited for me if I stayed at Heather's house for the rest of the evening. After I finished my meal, I would feel stuffed and happy. I could eat a decadent dessert and drink coffee, maybe adding a shot of brandy, and then cap off the night with a round of fulfilling if not entirely unbridled sex. I could return home to Riley, sleep like the dead, wake up tomorrow with a little spring in my step, and go about my life.

Or I could go meet this guy, this Troy Cato. He claimed to be a detective, and that should be easy enough to check with Nate, even if I had no idea why he wanted to see me. But he lived near Marissa's hometown, maybe thirty minutes away. And it seemed as though the scattered fragments of her life weren't ready to let me go.

When I added it all up in my head, I didn't have much of a choice.

"How soon do you want to meet?" I asked.

"It will take you an hour or so to get here. Can you leave soon?"

It wasn't until I was off the phone that I realized my hand was covered with sweat.

Heather tried to talk me out of it.

"A stranger? He just calls you and orders you up to Robeson County and so you're going?"

"Yeah," I said. "It sounds kind of nuts when you say it like that."

"But you're going anyway?"

I thought about how to answer, but there was only one way I knew to express it.

"I have to go," I said. "I have to."

A flush rose on Heather's cheeks. She went to the counter, grabbed the bottle of wine, and sloshed more into her glass, taking a quick drink.

"I swear," she said.

"Swear what?" I asked.

"She'll never be dead. This will never be dead."

I started to say we didn't even know if the call was about Marissa. Heather shot me a look that could have peeled paint.

We both knew it was.

"Maybe you're right," I said. "Maybe it will never die. Or maybe this trip will kill it."

"Or you." She threw back more wine. "When you get back from this little trip, assuming this stranger doesn't murder you or steal your kidney up there in Robeson County, just don't bother coming back here. Don't call. Just . . . let's just move on. Well, I know I can move on. I've done it before. I've done it my whole life. I have my doubts about you."

I had to admit I shared those doubts.

CHAPTER FORTY-EIGHT

The address Troy Cato gave me turned out to be a dive bar on an isolated stretch of State Route 187. At first I thought a mistake had been made, but I checked and double-checked, and I realized I was at the right location. He had something to show me, something he could only show me at night. Something he might decide he didn't want to show me in the future. It made sense to meet me at an out-of-the-way place.

It also made sense to check with Nate Denning, but I didn't. If Troy was skittish about meeting me, he might not want Nate to know what we were doing. So I called Laurel while I drove, and I told her I was going to meet someone in Robeson County, and if she didn't hear from me in a few hours, she should assume I was lying in a bathtub full of ice with a major organ or two missing.

"Nick, don't joke. What are you doing?"

"I'm working the case, boss."

"I'm coming with you. Where are you?"

"I've dragged you into this enough. I'll be fine. But if you don't hear from me in a few hours, assume something went wrong."

"Jesus, Nick. You can't just make calls like these."

"I just did."

The bar was named Wing Ding's. It occupied a squat brick structure that may once have been a garage or gas station. The neon beer signs flashed and glowed in the evening light. The cloud cover was thick, blocking out the moon and stars, hinting at the possibility of rain or even sleet. The parking lot was covered with crushed gravel, and my four-door sedan was the only vehicle in the lot that wasn't a truck, jeep, or motorcycle. I bet they couldn't wait to see me and make me one of their regulars.

When I walked in, the twanging music overwhelmed my ears. For a Saturday night, Wing Ding's looked fairly sedate. Two guys played a game of pool against the far wall, and all heads at the bar to my right turned and examined me. Mostly men, they gave me the once-over and then turned back to staring into their beers or at a college basketball game playing on two different TVs. When I looked around the small, poorly lit room, I saw eight or ten tables, only a few of them occupied. Then I saw a man in his sixties sitting alone. He raised his hand, beckoning me to his table.

"Are you Nick?" he said. It wasn't really a question.

"I am. Troy?"

"What's your pleasure?" He raised his hand again, summoning the bartender.

"I have to drive, and I had a beer at home."

"You can have one," he said. "Besides, I'm driving."

His voice sounded rough from years of smoking, and I wasn't sure his permission made me feel any better. I didn't know how many he'd already thrown down. But when in Rome . . .

I asked for a Budweiser.

While the bartender went to get the beer, Troy and I sat in silence. He stared at the TV screen as though I wasn't there. The pool balls clacked, and one of the players let out a cry of triumph. I followed Troy's lead and watched the game. Then the beer was placed in front of me and I started drinking it.

After two more swallows, Troy said, his face still turned toward the TV, "I just want you to know some things about what we're doing tonight."

"I don't know *anything* about what we're doing tonight."

"You'll understand soon enough."

"I have to, or I'm not going."

Troy turned to look at me then. I felt his eyes on me. I turned away from the basketball game and faced him.

"I'm doing you a favor," he said.

"How do I know that?" I asked.

"I can walk out of here anytime," he said. "It's nothing to me. Nate told me you're looking for this girl you used to be in love with. The one who died in the fire."

"What do you know about her?" I asked.

"You need to listen to me first."

I nodded, hoping he'd continue.

He leaned in closer and spoke just loud enough for me to hear over the music. "What I'm doing for you tonight is a favor. It's something that if certain people found out about could lead to some trouble for me. And maybe for other people as well. I don't know what you'll end up doing with what I tell you, but you have to keep my name out of it. Nate doesn't even know about this. You didn't tell him, did you?"

"No, I didn't."

A look of exaggerated admiration passed across Troy's face. "You did good, then. That's smart." He emptied his beer and pushed the bottle toward the center of the table. "That was a test, and you passed. You can think on your feet a little. That's a good sign." He looked me over again. "What are you? Some kind of professor or something?"

"I help people find affordable housing."

Troy couldn't hide his suspicion of such a job. "The less said about that, the better, I guess. Anyway, I'm going out on a limb for you here. You have to keep me out of it. If you can't make that promise, then we're done."

"What are you getting out of this?"

Troy rubbed his hands together. He turned toward the TV again, and I saw his face in profile. The jaw was strong, the hairline receding. Something seemed to be tugging on the corners of his mouth and eyes, some weight that appeared to be aging him faster than regular time. He said, "I can tell you some of this when we get there. Some of it, my interest at least, may never be clear to you." He turned back to me. "Maybe I don't even understand it. And never will."

He turned back to me, his eyes searching mine, asking for empathy or understanding. I was willing to grant it to him in that moment for my own selfish reasons. I wanted to know whatever he knew. I wanted to see this thing his name couldn't be tied to.

He pointed to my beer. "Finish it, and then we can go."

I did. I drank it down quickly, almost guzzling, and we left.

CHAPTER FORTY-NINE

We rode in Troy's truck, a black Ford. He accelerated out of the parking lot of Wing Ding's, not even stopping to look for oncoming traffic, heading north on 187. Troy didn't wear a seat belt, but I did, and we zoomed into the darkness out where the road cut through farmland and more farmland, his headlights slicing through the night. Troy said nothing. He stared ahead, flipping on the radio, and the rantings of a talk show host filled the cab. Mercifully it went to a commercial, and Troy turned it down. We jounced over a set of railroad tracks, the crossing lights watching us like dark, unseeing eyes.

I told myself to resist the urge to look back, but I did once. Far in the distance behind us, I saw a glimmering collection of lights sprinkled in a cluster. Hanfort. And we were going the opposite way. I turned to face the front again.

"So we're not going to Hanfort?" I asked.

"I didn't say that."

I settled back against my seat. I felt the bulge of my phone in my back pocket. Laurel knew only that I had left Eastland, but she didn't know exactly where I'd gone. My car still sat at Wing Ding's, for what that was worth. They'd find it someday and wonder what I'd been doing there.

"I get the feeling you don't want me to ask you questions," I said.

"It's fine," he said.

I didn't know what that meant, but before I could say anything else, he made a sudden left turn onto a smaller county road. He turned his brights on, lighting up the underside of gnarled tree limbs and the bare outlines of barbed-wire fencing. He made two, maybe three more turns, both rights and lefts, and at some point I lost my sense of which way we were going, although I guessed we were heading south back toward Hanfort. Once we passed a small cluster of cattle, bunched together against a rail fence, their eyes flashing as we zoomed by in the dark.

I was about to insist on Troy telling me where we were going when some houses appeared in the distance, and beyond the houses the glow of the rest of Hanfort. I exhaled for the first time in five miles.

Troy looked over at me, the lights from the dashboard display catching half his face. "See. Almost there."

"Why the detour?" I asked. "Did you need to inspect the livestock?"

He smiled without showing his teeth. "Just being cautious."

We entered the town and made a couple more turns. We rumbled across another set of railroad tracks, the truck vibrating like a plane over a pocket of turbulence, and then we came abreast of a fenced-in lot. A couple of school buses and road maintenance trucks sat around several rows of low, utilitarian sheds and garages. When the entrance gate came into view, I saw the sign designating it a Robeson County vehicle storage facility. Troy eased in, the headlights brightening the darkened corners of the lot and letting us see that nothing stirred. Troy jumped out as soon as we reached the gate, carrying a set of keys. He unlocked it, pushed it open, then came back and drove through. He carefully closed the gate and locked it behind us. When he climbed back into the cab, he said, "We're looking for number two," as though I knew what was going on.

He turned down the last row of storage units, moving slowly. The tires crunched over gravel and bits of debris, the engine making a low hum in the quiet night.

"There's number two," I said, pointing to the right.

Troy nodded and eased us to a stop. He turned the engine off but didn't get out of the cab. He took a deep breath but didn't say anything.

"Are we there?" I asked.

"This is a county facility. Maintenance vehicles mostly. Sometimes it gets used as an impound lot. The police store vehicles here when they run out of room in other places."

It was quiet around us, the wind calm. Far too early in the year for the chirping of bugs and the croaking of frogs.

"Are you going to tell me now what we came to see?" I asked.

"I'm about to." He ran his hand through his thinning hair. "About a year ago, a county crew went to do some maintenance on a little pond out in the sticks. Maybe six or seven miles from here. This is mostly a rural county, and there are a lot of those kinds of ponds and creeks. Sometimes they have names. Sometimes not. Sometimes you can tell no one's been near the thing for years. But they were putting in a new gas line, and it just happened to run right along this pond. A new subdivision was going in out there, all in the name of progress. Some farmer sold his land to an asshole developer. You know the drill. Land that had been in the family for generations sold to some asshat who wants to build more houses."

"Sure."

"It was dry last spring, and lo and behold, the water in the pond had come down a foot or so. And what do they see? The top of a car sticking out of the water."

My anxiety grew. My hand, which had been resting on the door handle, tightened into a fist.

"Naturally those boys knew they had something unusual there. Why else would a car end up in a pond like that? And it looked like it had been there for a long time. A long, long time. I'm going to take you in there and show you that car."

I started to open the door. "Okay."

"Now, wait." He held his hand out. It hovered a foot in front of my chest. "Remember what I told you back in the bar. I could get in trouble for this. I'm not on the force anymore."

"But you still have a key?"

"I borrowed the key. For tonight. From someone who owed me a favor. Neither one of us needs any headaches over this. You hear me?"

"You're saying I can't tell anyone what I see inside there."

"No, you can't. The truth is I don't even know what it means. I think it might mean more to you than to just about anyone else."

I started to ask another question, but he lowered his hand and pushed his own door open. The dome light came on, causing me to squint.

I slipped out my door, following him.

He used the keys again, this time to undo the lock on storage unit number two. I stepped up beside him, the night air getting steadily colder till we could see our breath. I rubbed my hands together. The door was beat-up and dented, the paint chipped and peeling. When the lock was undone, Troy bent down with a grunt and threw the door open.

The unit was dark. I couldn't make out anything on the inside. As my eyes adjusted, I saw a large, vague shape. A car. Troy fumbled for a switch on the wall. He hit it, and the room filled with light from a single bulb.

Troy watched me, waiting for my reaction.

"What do you think?" he asked.

I had no doubts about what I was looking at. Despite the grime and scum from the pond, the flattened tires, the rust, I knew immediately what it was.

"That's Marissa's," I said. "That's her car."

CHAPTER FIFTY

I stepped toward the vehicle, standing a few feet away. I held my right hand out but didn't touch it, as though I expected to feel some tangible emanation from the car that would pass into me.

Troy moved behind me and closed the door to the unit, presumably to prevent the light from leaking out into the night and possibly calling unwanted attention to us. Then he was standing next to me.

"If you found this in a pond, submerged . . . did you find a body inside?" I asked.

"Nope. That's what those gas crew boys were worried about when they found it. They started thinking up all sorts of juicy scenarios, like some Mafia guy put out a hit and hid the body in a Robeson County pond. The Mafia stuff is far-fetched, but people do drown in ponds and creeks like that a good deal. They drive off the road, maybe they're drunk or tired, and they end up in a body of water they can't get out of. The family reports them missing, and it can take years to find the vehicle, if ever. Like I said, there are a lot of remote little bodies of water in a rural county in Ohio. If the water doesn't recede and give up its secrets, we may never see what's in there."

"Right," I said, my mind distracted. If there was no body in the car, why had it ended up in a pond one county away?

"Are you sure it's her car?" Troy asked. "It's been a long time."

"I'm sure."

I remembered it well. She drove it the whole time I knew her. When she graduated from high school, her father had bought her a brand-new 1991 GMC Jimmy. Black. He told her the SUV would be safer in an accident than a small car. We drove the thing all over: road trips to Columbus, trips home for the holidays, late-night runs to White Castle or Taco Bell. And we parked in it a lot. The backseat was spacious. Marissa kept a couple of blankets and a pillow in the car at all times, removing them only when she knew she would see her parents, and we made liberal use of them during our nocturnal visits to local parks or the football stadium, any place we could find a little bit of privacy.

Some nights we fell asleep in the back of the SUV, our heads together, our bodies intertwined. We'd come awake at one or two in the morning, meet each other's eyes in the darkness, and laugh at the absurdity of ending up passed out in a postsex coma in the middle of a Tuesday night. And then we'd drive back to the dorm, exchanging sleepy good nights, our clothes and hair rumpled.

Believe it, I knew the car.

"Same color, same make," I said. "I recognize that dent in the rear bumper. Marissa backed into a fire hydrant once. Her dad was furious. She always had a frame around the license plate that said *Hanfort High, Class of '91*. I don't see that, but I'm sure it's hers." I started walking around the car, moving toward the passenger side and examining it from another angle. "She loved this car. She really did. She even named it. 'Betty,' after the salesperson at the dealership. Her parents probably sold it after she died."

"I don't know who," Troy said, "but somebody ran this vehicle into the pond up here."

"Is that all you know about it?" I asked.

"When the police find a car like this, they figure one of a few things. One is what I told you before: Someone's been in a wreck and might be dead in the car. But we figured out quickly that wasn't the case. No body. There's also the possibility of insurance fraud. Someone runs their car into a remote pond, claims it was stolen, and then they get a new car out of the deal. Risky, of course. Insurance companies don't look too kindly on fraud."

"Those aren't the only two options, are they?"

"The third and most likely option is that the car really was stolen. You know, kids take it joyriding, realize they might be in the soup with the cops, so they ditch it somewhere. Or someone's stolen it and tried to sell it or use it for parts. Those cars come back stripped of anything valuable." Troy patted the back of the car. "This car was worth a lot back in 1994 or so. Not everybody had an SUV in those days. They could have sold it, or they could have used it for parts."

"Was it stolen?" I asked.

"We looked into that. Whoever put it in the pond emptied the thing of any personal effects. No papers, no CDs. No license plates. Like you said, not even the license plate frame. They wanted it hidden, and then they hoped if it did get found, no one would be able to identify it. Of course, they couldn't remove the VIN number. And that's how we traced the car back to the Minor family. That didn't take long at all."

"And what happened?"

"We found out they weren't in the area anymore. And no one had ever filed a stolen-car report. It was strange. A car that was probably pretty nice and relatively new when it went missing was just allowed to go without anyone filing a report? You'd think they'd want the insurance money no matter how rich they were, right?"

"They had some money, but they weren't super-wealthy. Upper middle class."

"And those people want the money more than anyone else, right? They're still hungry for more. But if they didn't file a report, there wasn't much we could do. We couldn't locate them, and it's not really a crime to leave a car in a pond out in the middle of nowhere. Illegal dumping, I guess. Unless . . ."

I looked over the side of the car. I saw something near the front right bumper.

"Unless?" I said, the wheels turning in my mind. "Unless you were covering up a crime?"

"Exactly."

I moved up to the front of the car and bent down for a closer look. The right front bumper had a small dent, a slight inward crumpling, and the headlight was shattered. I thought hard, and felt certain the damage hadn't been there when Marissa drove the car at Eastland.

"This dent," I said. "I don't think it was here before."

Troy came over and studied it, standing behind me and looking over my shoulder.

"Who knows?" he said. "The car went headfirst into the pond. It's possible it hit a rock or something on the bottom. Or those boys who dragged it out could have banged it up. They're not exactly brain surgeons with that wrecker."

"Was there anything else inside? Anything that might make you think a crime had been committed?"

Troy laughed. "After all that time? Nothing. Mother Nature has wiped it all away. If anything had ever been there in the first place." He patted the car again. "What we have here is a mystery. A family suffers the loss of their daughter, they move away, but they leave the car behind in a pond in another county. And they don't report it stolen or make an insurance claim on the vehicle. It seems suspicious as shit, doesn't it?"

"Maybe they junked the car because it was too painful to see."

"You can give a car to charity," Troy said. "And they moved away. They could have left it here. They'd never have to see it again."

"I still don't understand something," I said.

"What?"

"What is your interest in all of this?" I asked. "You talk to Nate, and Marissa's death comes up. But you don't tell him you're coming here. Apparently you didn't tell him about the car. You didn't want me to tell anyone, even though I had to guess that on my own. And you borrowed these keys for one night only. We're doing all this cloak-and-dagger stuff out here on government property. Why? Why do you care about Marissa or this car?"

Troy walked past me just then. He bent down and looked at the dent in the fender, the one I had been examining. As he stared at it, I tried to place something in my mind, something Laurel had said when we were in Hanfort. But it didn't come back to me.

"I don't know," he said. "Something isn't right here. And I guess I feel like I should have seen it when we found the car. But that was just as I was retiring, and I didn't press it. I was a little burned out, I guess. One foot out the door. When Nate told me about you, I thought it was an invitation from the universe to hand this off to someone who might really pursue it and find out what happened. I figured that guy might be you." He turned back to me. "Some cops retire, and they never think twice about cases they worked. They never think again about the job. Other cops stay up at night worrying about things they might have missed. I guess I'm a stay-up-at-night kind of old cop. This stuck in my brain for some reason. Something's not right about it."

"But you said I couldn't tell anyone about it."

"I said you can't mention my involvement. You can't

tell anyone I brought you here. But since you were already looking, I thought this might connect some dots for you."

"Maybe. But why is it still here?" I asked. "Why hasn't it been disposed of or auctioned?"

"They keep them for a year or so. They'll be getting rid of it soon. They'll junk it since it's so trashed. I doubt it would run or do anybody any good."

"They'll just get rid of it, huh?" I said, staring at the car.

"That's the way it goes. But we need to get out of here now. We've been here too long."

"Wait," I said. "Can I just have a minute? Just one minute?"

"No, we need to—"

"Just one minute."

Troy looked at me like I was nuts. And then he looked at his watch.

"One minute," he said.

I expected him to leave me alone, but he didn't. He stood over by the garage door and waited, his hand resting on the handle.

I walked away from him toward the driver's side of the car. Over the previous two weeks, I'd realized I didn't possess many tangible things that tied me directly to Marissa. Some letters and cards. A few gifts she'd given me that I'd carried with me from place to place. But that was about it. No clothes. No lock of hair. Nothing I could hold in my hand and say, "This is a piece of her." The car was the closest thing, an object I closely, intensely associated with her. A physical place we occupied together when we were happiest and most in love.

I tugged on the door handle, but it didn't budge. I wished I could take the whole car with me. Possess it. Have it. But I knew there was no way.

I heard Troy tapping his foot.

I reached out and touched the car one more time, and then we left.

CHAPTER FIFTY-ONE

The noise woke me just after midnight.

I'd fallen asleep with the newspaper articles from Hanfort scattered across the bed. I'd pored over them and stared at them again, expecting something to jump out and tell me what I needed to know. I felt the same way I'd felt in high school, studying for a math exam. Symbols and numbers danced before my eyes then, a messy jumble refusing to cohere.

Connect the dots, Troy said.

But the dots I saw didn't make sense. Something was missing.

I didn't know what *really* drove Marissa away, both from her life and from me.

These thoughts cycled through my brain as I came awake. I'd been dreaming of Marissa, seeing her face again. The two of us in a park, holding hands, walking together.

Even though the dream was heartbreakingly real and painful, I wanted it to go on forever.

But then something thumped in the other room.

I sat up and waited, blinking sleep away. I looked down at the floor. Riley lifted his head, one ear cocked. He'd heard the noise as well, and it was enough of a concern that he actually rose to his feet and stared in the direction of the other room.

"What is it, boy?" I asked. "Was that in the parking lot?"

He remained frozen for a long moment, and then he turned to look at me.

I let my head fall back against the pillow. As soon as I did, the noise came again.

"Shit." I sat up.

Someone was in the other room. I felt certain.

I reached for my phone, prepared to dial 911.

Then whoever was out there called my name.

"Nick? Are you there?"

Did I know the voice? I stood up and moved.

"Who's there?" I asked, standing at the door of my bedroom.

The lights were still out all over the apartment, but when I looked toward the living room, I saw one of my windows open, the curtains lifting and falling in the cold night breeze. When I'd come home from seeing Troy, snow flurries were blowing across the road, cutting through the beams of my headlights. I felt the chill entering the apartment.

I looked around, trying to find whoever had called my name. I held the phone in my right hand, ready to dial.

"I'm calling the police," I said. "Where are you?"

Riley came and stood by my side. He made a low whining sound in his throat.

"Heather? Is that you?"

Then the person emerged from the darkness by the front door. She stepped into a shaft of light that spilled across the living room from the parking lot. The slender body, the long legs. The graceful movements. As she revealed more of herself, I felt my body going into overdrive. Heart pumping. Sweat flowing. A ridge of bumps up my arms and down my back.

"Nick?" she said. "It's me."

I leaned against the doorjamb for support. I nearly dropped the phone on Riley's head.

"Marissa?" I asked. "Oh, Jesus, Marissa, it's you."

She bent down near the couch and flipped on a lamp.

When the light hit her, illuminating her, I knew it was true.

Marissa. She was there, right in front of me. Like a dream.

"Oh, God, honey, it's you," I said, stepping forward. Rushing forward.

And then she held up her hand, took two steps backward.

"No, Nick," she said. "I'm not Marissa."

I froze, studying her. I saw the subtle differences. She was shorter. Her face rounder. The hair not quite as fiery red.

"It's me, Nick. You remember me, don't you? It's been a lot of years, but you must remember me. We were practically family back then."

And then I understood. I knew who she was.

"Wow," I said, standing in the middle of the room frozen in place like a man made of stone, every system in my body still in overdrive. "Yes, I do recognize you, Jade."

CHAPTER FIFTY-TWO

I looked over at the open window. The curtains settled back against the wall as the cold breeze died.

"Jade, why did you come in that way?"

She followed my gaze, her face unperturbed. "I had to be careful. I didn't know what I was coming into."

"Careful? I almost called the police."

She turned her head back toward me. "That's not really what I'm afraid of. Do you mind if I sit?"

Before I answered, she was moving. She wore jeans, running shoes, and a zip-up Windbreaker with a logo I didn't recognize. While she settled onto the couch, I walked over and closed the window, locking out the cold air.

"Why are you here?" I asked.

Riley sniffed her hand, and then Jade started petting him. He gave in right away. His ears went back and his tail thumped against the floor. The poor sucker trusted everybody.

"Why don't you sit, Nick?" she said.

I came closer to the couch but didn't sit. "Why don't you tell me what's going on? All of it."

"I do want to tell you all of it. That's why I want you to sit. It's not a short story."

"Have you been following me?"

"No."

"But you've been around, close to me. You were at the funeral down in Richmond, right? You came to the cemetery and then to the Russells' house?"

Jade leaned forward, resting her elbows on her knees. Something passed across the surface of her face, a small change that gradually grew. Her chin puckered, and her eyes filled with tears.

"What is it?" I asked, but I already knew.

The physical similarities. Her appearance at the cemetery and the house.

Someone claiming to be Emily's birth mother.

Emily Russell.

"Your daughter?" I asked.

Jade nodded her head, and then buried her face in her hands. Her body shook with sobs. Riley looked at me, encouraging me to do something. I took a step forward, but Jade deserved more, so I sat on the couch next to her, pulled her to me, letting her cry on my shoulder. She smelled vaguely of cigarette smoke, and the sobs continued to shake her body with great force.

After a few moments, she calmed a bit, and between deep breaths she said to me, "My baby, Nick. They killed my sweet baby girl."

* * *

We sat that way for a good long while until Jade slowly gathered more and more of herself. I went to the bathroom and found a box of tissues and brought them back. She accepted them and wiped at her face, smearing her eye makeup across her cheeks. I felt as helpless as every man feels in the presence of a crying woman, so I did the only other thing I could think to do. I went to the kitchen and poured her a glass of water.

As I did, I sifted through my memories of Jade. She had just told me we were like family, but I wasn't entirely sure that was true. A kind of family, I guessed. She was three years younger than Marissa and me, and the two of them always had the kind of love-hate relationship common to most siblings. To be honest, I didn't think about Jade a great deal when Marissa and I dated. I didn't pay much attention to anyone else besides Marissa. Jade was the somewhat annoying and very precocious younger sister of my college girlfriend. I saw her life in broad strokes. She studied a lot and, according to Marissa, partied a lot. She visited Eastland a couple of times, sleeping in Marissa's dorm room or house, acting a little wide-eyed at the flurry of activity and craziness on a college campus. But our own relationship was limited to snarky asides and teasing jokes, an unspoken acknowledgment that in some ways we were competing for Marissa's attention.

I brought the water back to her, and she gulped it down.

"More?"

"Yes, please. I feel dehydrated. Too much crying."

I brought back another glass, which she also gulped down, and I sat down at the far end of the couch from her, ready to hear her explanation.

"Emily Russell is your daughter," I said.

"Was." Her face looked strained, on the point of shattering.

"You don't have to say it that way. She's still your daughter. She always will be."

"Thanks." She sniffled. "She wasn't mine in a lot of ways. I understand that."

"You gave her up for adoption? Is that why you're saying she wasn't yours in a lot of ways?"

She nodded. "I let go of her a long time ago. I didn't expect to get her back, but I did. Just for a short time, she was kind of mine again." She raised her hands and let them fall into her lap. "And then all of this."

"Why was she here in Eastland? Why did she have my name and address in her pocket when she died?"

Jade started crying, more calmly than before, but the tears were coming again.

"I had to protect her, Nick. I had to protect her from the people who wanted to kill her."

CHAPTER FIFTY-THREE

"Who would want to kill that girl?" I asked. "What on earth could she have been mixed up in that would make that happen?"

"It wasn't her fault," Jade said. "It was mine. It all goes back to me."

"And this is why you're in danger now? This is why you broke into my house in the middle of the night?"

"I don't know how much danger I'm in anymore. Maybe none. I'm not sure."

"Danger from what? Ordinarily I'm a live-and-let-live kind of guy, but this whole thing has turned my life upside down. You have to understand that. I won't say my life was perfect, but it was at least quiet. So I'd like to know."

Jade changed the subject. "I saw you with your girlfriend, the skinny one."

"Heather?"

"I don't know her name. The one who looks like a soccer mom."

"You watched me?"

"I had to know I could trust you. I couldn't just come in here when you were with your girlfriend. I couldn't have other people know all of this. I had to be cautious. I saw you come home alone tonight. I knew the dog didn't like to bark. Or at least he wouldn't bite. He seems pretty placid, so I figured the window was safe."

"Tell me what this is about, Jade. And when you're finished, I'm going to have a lot of questions."

She hesitated. I heard the tone in my own voice, the edge of anger beneath my words, the way my body had shifted, rising up on the couch as though to intimidate. I didn't know what Jade had been through beyond the loss of her daughter, but I lowered myself back onto the couch and scooted away from her.

"Okay," I said, "if you don't want to talk about it yet . . ."

"I do. I need to." She lifted her eyes to mine. "You're probably one of the few people I can really tell all of this to. And I know you'll understand. You know all about losing someone very close to you and having it change the course of your life. Right?"

I nodded. I knew all too well. And I wouldn't wish it on anyone.

"Okay," I said. "What happened? How did Emily get put in this kind of danger?"

"It's silly, but it's still hard for me to think of her as Emily. I named her before I had her. I told myself the baby was going to be a girl, and I called her Meredith the whole time I was pregnant. Sometimes I still think of her as Meredith, even though I met her and knew her as Emily. It's a trick my brain is playing on me, telling myself that those are two different girls. There's Meredith who I gave birth to and let go of, and she's just out there in the world doing fine. And there's Emily, the girl who died. I wish I could make that reality somehow."

"It can be dangerous to contemplate all the different roads your life could have traveled."

"Indeed. Well. I got pregnant with *Emily* in high school. My senior year. You and Marissa were juniors at Eastland then."

"Was it that guy you dated back then? What was his name? Patrick or something?"

"Patrick." Jade laughed. "He was a little fool, wasn't he? I wish it had been Patrick—I really do. He was kind. A fool, but a kind fool. No, it wasn't him. It's not important who the guy was. I got involved with someone I shouldn't have been involved with. He's out of the picture. He never really was in the picture. What mattered then and now is that I got pregnant, and I had to do something about it. Can you imagine being seventeen years old and having to tell your parents you're pregnant? You know what my dad was like. Imagine telling him."

"I couldn't imagine it. No."

"Exactly. He didn't think his little girls did more than hold hands with boys, let alone sleep with them."

"So you didn't have anyone to turn to at home. You couldn't talk to your parents, and you didn't want to talk to the boy. Let me guess. . . . You ended up reaching out to your big sister."

"Who else could I call? I knew she'd come. I knew she'd be there for me. She always was the most loyal person I knew."

Loyalty. I would have thought the same thing about Marissa. Back then and for the previous twenty years. I wasn't sure anymore.

"She dropped everything and came home for the weekend," Jade said. "When she showed up, we acted like everything was normal. She told Mom and Dad she needed to get away from school and be mellow for the weekend. I played along. Of course, nothing was normal at all. I'd been in my room crying all week, hiding it from Mom and Dad. Mom asked if something was wrong, and I told her I just had my period. The exact opposite, of course. But Marissa came home that Friday, and she took me to a clinic to take care of it."

I could picture Marissa stepping into that crisis. She would have been firm and calm, supportive and loving. She would have guided Jade through whatever she needed. Marissa often spoke affectionately of Jade, remembering times from their childhood. The things Marissa taught her little sister or helped her with—deciphering math problems or the mysteries of boys, selecting a dress for a freshman dance or dealing with mean girls. Jade couldn't have made a better choice if she needed someone to be her rock.

"I thought I was ready to do it," Jade said. "I was going to end the pregnancy and be done with it. I had the scholarship to Eastland already. I couldn't tell my parents and disappoint them. I didn't want anything to do with the guy. I had a future, and it didn't include a baby. Not at that point in my life. I knew my own mind."

"And Marissa was okay with that?"

"She said she'd support me in whatever I wanted to do. I just needed to go to the clinic and talk to the people about it. I know now what she was doing. She wanted to make sure I really knew what I was getting into. And it worked. Once I got there and started talking to the counselor, the doubts began to creep in. Maybe I was wrong. Maybe I *could* take care of a baby. Maybe I *should* tell Mom and Dad. They loved me. They'd help me. All of that raced through my brain until I just had to stop it all. I had to get out of there and think. So we left."

"I'm glad you didn't rush," I said.

"I think, all the time, that if we'd stayed that day, if I'd gone through with it the way I was supposed to, then everything that came after wouldn't have happened the way it did. That Meredith, Emily, wouldn't have ended up dead in that motel room."

"But she wouldn't have had any life at all. It was brave of you to give her up."

But Jade didn't seem to have heard me. She stared straight ahead as she said, "And that other boy, the one we killed, he would still be alive today."

CHAPTER FIFTY-FOUR

Jade continued to stare straight ahead. I wanted to ask questions, a lot of questions. But some things were coming together in my own mind as I watched her and waited.

She asked me for more water, so I went and filled the glass again. While the water ran out of the tap, I thought about my trip to the storage garage and the abandoned car. And something Laurel mentioned in Hanfort still hovered just below the surface.

I brought the water back and handed it to her. While she took another long gulp, I asked, "This boy you say you killed, was he hurt by a car?"

Her eyes widened as she turned to me. "How did you know?"

"They found Marissa's car in a pond about a year ago. A work crew pulled it out. Some retired cop heard I was asking questions and showed it to me. The car was never reported stolen by your family, so why else would it be sitting in a pond in the middle of nowhere unless there was a crime involved? And you just answered that question. What exactly happened?"

Jade didn't answer. She was hiding something.

"What happened, Jade? Just tell me. It's been years. I'm not here to judge you."

"I don't want you to think bad . . . of either one of us."

"Either one of you?" Then it became clearer to me. "*You* didn't kill him, did you?"

"I did. It might as well have been me. I wasn't driving the car, but it was all because of me. We wouldn't have been there in the first place if it wasn't for me."

"Marissa was driving?" I asked.

Jade nodded. "I couldn't have driven that day. I was too upset. Way too upset. I bawled the whole way as we left the clinic and drove home. Marissa had to take care of me. I was a mess. I was practically hyperventilating. I really did think my life was over, that I had no options or anything that could save me."

"It's easy to see the world collapsing on us when we're young."

"Sometimes it really is, though," she said.

I remembered the way I felt after Marissa's death. The agony. The long hours I spent locked away, crying and mourning. "Sometimes, yes."

"We didn't see the stop sign. We didn't see it because of me. Marissa was trying to hand me a tissue, she was trying to talk to me, and she was trying to drive at the same time. She reached over. She looked at me. We were in a part of town we didn't know as well. She ran the stop sign, and we heard the thumping sound against the front of the car." Jade stared off at a distant point in the room. "I can still hear it today. It's a memory that will never leave me. That awful thump."

"So she stopped the car and got out, right?"

"She stopped the car." Jade drank some more water. "We looked back, but I could barely see because my eyes were so puffy and watery. I didn't know exactly what was going on. I remember thinking, *It's just a dog. Marissa just ran over a dog, that's all.* But she was looking back. She turned her head all the way around, moving her body in the seat so she could look. She froze that way, Marissa. She raised her hand to her mouth and just froze. I've never seen such a look of terror on someone's face. I knew. I knew she'd hit a person."

"What did you do?" I asked.

Jade sighed. It seemed to come from deep within her. "We left," she said. "Marissa drove away."

"Why?"

"I don't know. She panicked. She didn't know what to do. Someone came out of one of the houses, I remember. An old woman. She lifted her hands to her face like she knew the kid. Marissa saw that. So she just drove off, and I didn't even tell her to stop. I didn't say anything. And when I looked back . . ." Her eyes filled with tears again, just as I knew they had on that long ago day that changed their lives. Everyone's lives. "I saw the boy lying in the street. His arms above his head. His leg bent . . . the wrong way. And that woman, that old woman approaching him, the one who came out of the house. His grandmother, we later found out. I saw them, and she looked up at the car. But we didn't stop. We just drove home. I'd stopped crying then. It was the quietest, most . . . somber car ride we'd ever taken."

I stood up and took a walk around the living room, Riley and Jade tracking me with their eyes. The accident itself was one thing, and it explained a great deal. But Marissa's behavior . . . that was the part I couldn't reconcile. The Marissa I knew—*thought I knew*—was honest to a fault. I had to accept her infidelity as well as her complicity in an accident she left the scene of, an accident that killed a child.

"What happened when you made it home?" I asked, still standing. My legs felt weak, the floor beneath me uncertain.

"We pulled into the garage. We weren't supposed to park our cars in there, but we did that day. Marissa looked over at me and she said, 'I'm going to tell Dad. And then we can tell the police.' She was crying. She leaned her head down against the steering wheel and sobbed. She kept saying over and over, 'I killed that boy. I killed him.' I tried to comfort her. It was total role reversal. I told her that it was an accident, that she hit the boy because she was tending to me. I also told her the boy might be okay. We knew a kid in grade school who got hit by a car. The car went right over him, knocked him out. He just had a concussion and a bunch of scrapes."

"But not this time," I said.

"Do you know how sometimes you can just feel something, especially things that have to do with death? I just felt it when we drove away from that boy. He was dead. I knew it. I felt it. Marissa must have felt it too."

"She clearly didn't tell anyone, right? She didn't go to the police or we'd all have known about it."

Jade held up a finger as though asking me to be patient. "Marissa did decide to tell. We waited for Mom and Dad to come home. When they did, the four of us sat down in the living room, and we told them everything. I remember Dad came in pissed because we'd parked in the garage. That quickly became the least of his worries."

"You told them about the pregnancy too?"

"All of it. I look back on that conversation and think that must have been one of the single worst moments in the history of parenting. Finding out in one fell swoop that your oldest daughter ran over a kid with her car because your other daughter got knocked up." She laughed a little, a low, faint sound. "I watched my father while we told him. I think he aged ten years during the conversation. You remember him. He could be such a . . ."

"Hard-ass?"

"A prick. A real prick. Mom once said, 'You know your father. He can be as understanding as Hitler.' Nice, right? But I sure felt sorry for the old man during that conversation. Mom held up well. She hugged me. She hugged Marissa. She told us she loved us. She told us we'd get through it no matter what. It's blurry, the whole thing, but I remember those moments with Mom."

"Didn't your parents *make* her tell?" I asked. "Didn't

they say they were going to call the police? It *was* an accident. Marissa wanted to tell. Did they make her go?"

Jade leaned forward, staring at the floor. I waited. And waited.

She started shaking her head.

"Dad stood up. He said, 'I've made a decision. We're going to take care of this, and we're going to take care of this the right way.' I thought he meant he was going to call the cops and march Marissa down there to face the music. Instead, he asked if anyone had seen us hit the boy. And then he said he wanted to look at the car."

"What was he doing?" I asked.

"I knew immediately what he was up to. I'd seen him get that way before. He was working up some kind of a plan."

CHAPTER FIFTY-FIVE

"Dad went out and looked at the car. Marissa couldn't look at it, she couldn't bear to, but I went with him. I saw the blood and a little bit of hair on the bumper and the headlight. I actually puked when I saw it. I went outside the garage and puked. Mom was inside with Marissa, and Dad came out where I was puking and took me by the arm. He said, 'Jade, what are the odds that old woman got the license number?' I said she didn't seem to be looking at us. She was looking at the kid. And he asked me how old the woman was. I said, 'She looked pretty old. Maybe eighty.' Back then, of course, everybody looked old to me. I was a teenager. The wheels were turning in his head. He asked me if anybody knew about the baby, and I said no." Jade shook her head. "You know what's funny? In the middle of all that, neither one of them asked who the father was."

I went out to the kitchen. I kept a bottle of bourbon in the cabinet, something I only took out on rare occasions: after a long day at work or on the off chance I received a raise or a promotion. It seemed like a good time for it, although not a celebration. I grabbed the bottle and two glasses and brought them to the living room. I poured each of us a shot. Jade threw hers back without hesitation, and I followed suit. I poured another, and we both did the same thing.

"So your dad wanted to cover the whole thing up?" I asked, the liquor burning on its way through my system.

"He *did* cover the whole thing up. He said we both had bright futures, and it was his job as a father to do anything in his power to see we lived them to the fullest. He said he'd put his money, his job, his reputation on the line to protect us." Jade poured herself another shot but only sipped it. "It's funny." She grimaced a little from the liquor. "I know it was his way of saying he loved us. He saw himself that way. The protector. The big man. That's who he was."

"And you all just went along with it?" I asked.

"Hell, no. Mom pitched a fit. She said there was no way we were just going to make it go away. She said they'd raised us to accept responsibility for our actions, no matter what they were, and we both had to face the music. She'd love us and support us always, but we had to be responsible." Jade swirled the glass of bourbon in her hand. The amber liquid caught the light from the lamp and glowed through her fingers. "Mom always gave in to Dad, but that night she showed a lot of steel. She bowed her back and stood up to him. And they reached a compromise. They said we'd all wait until the next day to see the news. If the boy lived, maybe it wouldn't be so bad for Marissa. If he died . . . well, nobody really admitted that as a possibility. Even though Marissa and I both suspected the truth."

"I bet that made for a long night," I said.

"I'd forgotten all about me and my problems. I didn't think of the baby. I listened to Marissa cry all night. I even went into her room and lay with her, holding her close to me. I half expected she'd leave during the night."

"You mean run down to the police by herself?"

Jade nodded. "But she didn't. She was scared because Dad filled her head with so much noise. She thought she might go to jail. And Dad said over and over again that just having an arrest like that on your record could ruin you. No job. No credit. Her education would be set back. Maybe she'd never finish college. You know how concerned with appearances they were."

"Why didn't she call me?" I asked.

I tried to remember how I'd passed the time that weekend when Marissa was at home. I remembered going to a party off campus and working up a good buzz, and then stumbling home with my friends, trying to distract myself until she came back.

"I told her to. Dad said not to tell anybody what was going on, but I told her to call you or another friend. Anyone. Just to say hi. But Marissa wouldn't listen. She said the same thing over and over."

"Did she say she wasn't worthy?" I asked.

Jade pointed at me. "How did you know?"

"I heard a variation of that right after she came back

to Eastland. After your dad clearly won the argument. Right?"

Jade stared into her glass. "When the paper came out the next day, it said the boy had died." She lifted her hand to her chest. "Samuel Maberry. He was nine. Just a little boy."

"So your dad wouldn't let Marissa go confess?"

"The paper had a report from the only witness, Samuel's grandmother, the woman we saw in the street. She got the color of the car wrong. And the make. She said it was a blue van and not a black SUV. And she said it looked like a dark-haired man was driving the car. She didn't get any of the license number. Apparently, she really was too old to see that well, and I remember Dad staring at the paper and saying, 'That's about as good as the news could get.'"

"That's harsh. What about the dead boy?"

"He didn't mean about him, I'm sure."

"Are you?" I asked.

"This is my father, Nick. I loved him. He did act out of love, even if it's hard to see."

"So what did he do next?" I asked. "What was the loving plan he came up with?"

Jade finished her drink. "He started pulling strings. He wanted to get rid of the car. He wanted to move. He wanted us to go somewhere no one could ever find us. He wanted to go away so we could still have our lives, Marissa and I. Mom and Dad didn't have a lot of close friends. They knew a lot of people, but they weren't tied to things. We had some cousins back east, but that's about it. He wanted to pull up stakes and run, but he couldn't put it all together right away. He had to look into some things and make some calls. So he sat Marissa and me down and told us that, for the time being, maybe for the next week or so, we had to act like everything was perfectly normal. That meant I had to go back to my senior year of high school and hang out with my friends and do all the things I would normally do."

"And Marissa had to come back to Eastland," I said.

"Exactly. She didn't want to go, but she did." Jade looked over at me. "I guess she didn't really act normal, did she?"

She came back from that trip home, a trip I didn't expect her to take or understand why she took at the time, and was immediately distant. She wouldn't tell me why she'd gone to see her parents or what she'd done back in Hanfort. She'd never acted that way before.

And then she broke up with me, repeating the line I'd heard Jade say.

"I'm not worthy of being in a relationship with you," Marissa told me, her voice and eyes distant. "I just can't do it."

I begged and pleaded with her to explain, to just tell me anything at all that would help me understand how we went from being blissfully in love and happy to her dumping me as the result of one trip home.

Thanks to Jade, I finally understood.

At least I understood some of it.

CHAPTER FIFTY-SIX

"I need to ask you something, Jade," I said, "and I need to know the answer." I tried to contain my emotions, holding them back like thrashing wild horses. "And you can't lie to me. You just can't. What happened to Marissa? Did she die in that fire?"

Jade looked away from me. She still held the glass in her hand, but it was empty. I couldn't see her face or read the thoughts racing through her mind.

"Jade? Is Marissa alive?"

"It's so hard for me to talk about her," she said. "It's my fault, like I said. I ended her life. None of this, none of the things we all lost, would have happened if it hadn't been for me."

I moved closer, close enough to touch her arm though I didn't. "Just answer my question."

"I want to talk about that fire. That may help you understand some things."

"Tell me, then. Fast."

She turned back around, and her eyes were clear, the tears gone. She said, "That fire . . . it saved us all in a way."

"How?"

"Marissa withdrew from school. She went back to Eastland and severed all of her ties. Including with you. I told Eastland I wasn't going to school there either. I made something up about financial trouble, and I gave up the whole scholarship. What was I going to do? Show up for college with a baby? Dad was hatching his plan to leave town. We had enough money to go. He was looking into getting us all new identities. They'd sell the house when they could. They thought we'd be fine." She shuddered. "But something else was happening with the accident."

"What?"

"The father of the boy we killed, Bill Maberry. He was all over the news. He was kind of well-known in Hanfort. He owned a few restaurants and a used-car lot. He was a small-town big shot. He used to do TV ads for the restaurants, and he always seemed like a jerk. In the wake of the accident he talked to everyone in the media he could. He talked to every cop. He put up a reward for information. He said he wanted justice."

"That's not really surprising, is it?" I asked. "He lost his son, suddenly and awfully." I felt a shard of grief in my own heart for the Maberrys, people I didn't even know. "Imagine that . . ."

"I know, I know," she said. "I've thought about it many times. I know what it's like to lose a child now. I've never had so much empathy for the Maberrys."

"Yeah."

"But the way Maberry talked about it back then—he said it over and over again. *Justice*. He gave that word an edge, a sharp edge. What he really seemed to be saying was he wanted revenge. He may as well have just said an eye for an eye. And then the police started expanding their search. They said maybe it wasn't a blue SUV. Maybe it was any dark-colored vehicle. And maybe it wasn't a dark-haired man driving. So it felt like the net was widening." She shuddered again. "And that fucking car was sitting in our garage, just waiting for someone to find it. Finally, that's when Dad started to lose it."

"I can't imagine your dad really losing his cool," I said. "He always seemed so in control. Almost like a robot."

"I'd never seen him that way either," she said. "He got really paranoid. It scared the hell out of us. He bought a gun, this huge, ugly black thing. He had the locks reinforced on the house."

"If he was that scared, why did he send Marissa back to school?"

"He thought she'd be safer there, away from the family. He wanted to send me away too, but I refused to go. And Mom wouldn't let me out of her sight."

"What did he think was going to happen?"

"That guy, Bill Maberry. Dad had heard about him. He had a reputation. He'd been arrested a couple of times for assault. People said he had ties to criminals, that the cars he sold were stolen. I always thought it was just small-town gossip. You know how that can be. But

Dad believed it all. He thought we were in danger, and he wanted to get out of town as fast as possible. He had just a few loose ends to tie up when the fire happened."

"Tell me, Jade. About Marissa. Tell me."

She took a deep breath. "She called us the night of the fire, Marissa did. She had been upset earlier in the evening. She felt bad about breaking up with you, about leaving her whole life behind. Dad's friend, Roger Kirby . . ." She looked over at me. "Do you remember him?"

"I do."

Jade placed her hand on her stomach as though she might be sick. "He's a jerk. Anyway, he had gone to Eastland to see her, to make sure she knew the plan and was ready to go."

I felt the familiar stab in my heart. "People saw them together that night."

"I guess he didn't want to talk to Marissa in front of her roommates."

"Why did Kirby go and not your mom or dad?"

"It was Dad's cloak-and-dagger stuff. He thought he might get followed. He wouldn't let us go, Mom or me. He saw everything spinning out of his control, and he couldn't stand that. So he sent Roger. Roger was the only other person who knew what had happened. Dad told him everything."

"I have to ask you."

"What?"

"Were he and Marissa . . . was there something between them? Something romantic?"

Jade whipped her head around to stare at me. "Roger

and Marissa? Are you kidding?" She laughed a little. "Marissa was too smart for that. Far too smart. She loved you, Nick. She really did."

Jade must have seen how unconvinced I was. She reached out and squeezed my hand.

"She loved you, Nick. I know she did. I mean it. She didn't want any of this to go the way it went. None of us did. If I could take back those few minutes in the car . . ." Her eyes looked hollow, and a flush rose on her cheeks. "How I wish I could."

"If I'd known about it I would have helped her," I said. "I would have fought for her. Hell, I would have run away with her."

"I know." She squeezed again. "She was young. We both were. Dad controlled everything. We were children. Remember that. We were old enough to live as adults, but we were still children. Dad treated us that way."

"The fire. What happened? Did she die? You said she called you."

"She called us, Nick. She called to tell us that when she came home that night her house was burning down. She called to say she thought her roommates were dying. She called *after* the fire. She was alive, Nick. She wasn't in the house when it burned."

CHAPTER FIFTY-SEVEN

The feeling that passed through my body and mind in that moment was unlike anything I had ever experienced. I felt a release of some kind, the slacking of some tension that had been infusing every fiber of my being for the previous twenty years. My body went limp. I slid forward on the couch, almost flopping all the way onto the floor. I lifted my hand to my head, covering my eyes.

Marissa didn't die in the fire. Marissa had not died twenty years ago.

The words cycled through my head with centrifugal force, knocking around the inside of my skull. I was overwhelmed.

Jade moved next to me. "Are you okay, Nick?"

"She's alive," I said, repeating the words like a prayer. "Marissa's alive."

"She didn't die in the fire," Jade said. "No."

The clarification hit me with force. I lifted my head.

"What do you mean by that?" I asked. "Where is she?"

"Let me finish the story," Jade said.

"Where is she? Is she dead?"

"Nick, I told you it's hard for me to talk about my sister."

"Just answer the question."

"Nick, wait. Listen to me." She held her hands out to calm me down. I pushed myself back into place on the couch, but my mind still raced. The tension, the questions flowed through me like a wild river. I wanted to know. I *needed* to know.

Jade said, "The fire ended up playing right into Dad's hands. At first, he panicked even more. He went crazy. He thought it was the Maberrys, that they'd found out about the accident and Marissa's involvement and they went to Eastland to kill her. He ordered Marissa home right away. He told her to get back to Hanfort as soon as possible, and he started packing things immediately. He wanted us to drive off as soon as Marissa walked in the door, even though it was the middle of the night. But by the time Marissa got home, he'd calmed down a little."

"That's all he could think of?" I asked. "His plan?"

"The police showed up about an hour later. Detectives from Hanfort. They must have been dispatched by the Eastland police. When they knocked on the door, Dad thought they were there to arrest Marissa, that they knew about the accident. He made her hide in her room. I don't know what he was going to do if they really did want to arrest her. He had that gun."

"Jesus."

"But they weren't there for that."

"No," I said. "They were there to tell you that Marissa had died in the fire in Eastland."

Jade nodded. "They said they were working to identify the bodies, but they asked if we knew if Marissa had been home that night. Dad said he assumed she was. Where else would she be? And the next day it was official. Four people lived in the house. Four sets of remains found in the rubble. That was that. As far as the world was concerned, Marissa was dead. And Dad intended to take full advantage of it. Here was her new start without the threat of the police or the Maberrys ever coming after her. She was released to a new life completely. A clean slate, Dad kept calling it."

"A clean slate?" I asked. "Meanwhile he was content to let some other family not know their child had died in that fire? He didn't care what happened to anyone else so long as his family was together and protected. Jesus, Jade. Your dad sounds like a psychopath."

"He was protecting us."

"One child was left dead in the street. Another family had to wonder for twenty years if their son died in that fire. I met them, Jade. They're still wondering where their loved one went. And all because your dad wanted Marissa to have the future he dreamed for her."

Jade shifted in her seat. She looked agitated, nervous. "I don't like the way you're looking at this. He was a parent. His child was in trouble. A parent should do anything when their child is in trouble." She looked around the apartment. "Maybe you don't understand that."

"I understand that." And I knew it was true. Would I do anything to protect Andrew? Of course. Would I break the law to do it? I might. I really just might. "But other people were affected. Other families." I felt my argument losing a little steam the more I thought of Andrew.

"We had a funeral for Marissa," Jade said. "We bought the coffin and the plot and the stone and everything. They buried . . . whatever they found in the house."

"Charles Blevins. His name was Charles Blevins. That's who they put in that grave."

Jade looked at me, curious. But she didn't ask how I knew.

"We let everyone believe Marissa was gone," Jade said. "Her friends. The town. Our relatives. We let them let her go. And a week after the funeral we left. New identities, new town. New lives."

"Colorado?" I asked.

"How did you know?"

"Your parents died there," I said. "But why were they buried under their real names?"

"They wanted it that way, especially Mom. They'd been living as other people for so long, they didn't want to spend eternity under an assumed name. Who could hurt them then?"

"Weren't they worried about you? Couldn't these people track you down through the obituaries?"

"I was living under another name. I wasn't living in

Colorado. It was a long shot, a risk we were all willing to take."

"Okay," I said. "So they got away with it. And you got away with it."

"I didn't get away with it," she said, her tone sharpening. "None of us did. You don't know what it's like to uproot your life, to give up everything you know. To live in fear."

"I lived with grief," I said. I rubbed my hands together, trying to ease the tension I felt. "For twenty years. Where is she, Jade?"

She didn't respond, and something about her lack of response pushed my buttons harder than it should have. She'd taken on the countenance of a stubborn child: lips pursed tight, chin thrust forward defiantly. She owed me one piece of information. *One.* I moved a foot closer and raised my hand, palm out, calmly but in a way that was meant to signal that I meant business.

Jade shrank back from me. "It's not my place to talk about Marissa. Her life has been so difficult."

"She's alive?"

"Nick. I can't—"

I reached out and clamped my hand on her wrist. "Jade, goddamn it!"

She tried to jerk away. "Nick. No!"

I didn't see the blow coming. She swung her free hand, the left one, while she still held the small glass. It struck me against the side of the head, and while the glass didn't shatter, I found myself watching swirling firework patterns before my eyes.

I let go, slumping back against the far end of the couch.

I reached up, feeling the growing lump above my ear. "Where is she, Jade?"

She didn't answer. The door slammed, and everything went black.

CHAPTER FIFTY-EIGHT

Laurel insisted on bringing me an ice pack from the kitchen. Except I didn't own an ice pack, so she brought me a bag of frozen corn wrapped in a towel and placed it against the side of my head.

"I still think you should see a doctor."

"I'm fine."

"You could be concussed," she said.

"Cursed is more like it."

I sat on the couch with the bag of corn pressed against my head. It brought some relief, so I didn't mind looking ridiculous.

"So Marissa and this Jade ran over a little boy in Hanfort, and the family chose to run away rather than have the girls face the music?" Detective Reece sat in a chair to my left. He wore a coat and no tie. It was early in the morning, just before seven, and he held a small notebook in his hand. "And all of this happened because Jade got pregnant in high school?"

/ "That's right." I shifted the bag a little and winced at the pain. "And it explains Emily Russell."

"How does it explain Emily Russell?" Reece asked.

"She's Jade's daughter," I said. "Jade gave her up for adoption, and Emily looks just like Marissa, even more than she looks like her mother. That happens. I look more like my uncle Stan than my dad, which is kind of a blessing. Uncle Stan aged better. I'm still thinking about that obituary. Jade must have given her baby up to Catholic Charities. Giving Emily up obviously made a huge impact on her."

"Exactly," Laurel said. "I work with a woman who gave a baby up for adoption when she was in high school. She spent her whole life worried that something awful had happened to that child, that the kid would be homeless or abused. But she met the kid later in life and saw that she was okay. My friend, she never forgot what that adoption agency did for her daughter."

"And that's how Jade felt," I said. "That adoption agency gave Jade's daughter the chance at a great life. Of course they would remember the agency when their parents died."

"I really only have one interest in this, unless you want to press charges for the smack on your head." Reece pointed at my bag of corn. "Do you?"

"No. It's fine."

"Then I still want to know who killed Emily Russell. Right now I have a suspect in jail who has a history of breaking into hotel rooms and assaulting guests and was carrying something that belonged to Emily Russell among his effects. I've got a real nice case there, and I don't want to turn away from that based on the speculations of someone who doesn't even seem that trustworthy. Did Jade say anything about who might have wanted to kill her child?"

The sun started to light up the drawn curtains, and the chirping of the birds rose in volume. "She didn't exactly. She just said the family of the dead kid has always wanted justice. Since Marissa and Jade ran away, they have never received it. As far as we know."

"Are you suggesting they killed Emily?" Laurel asked.

"I'm speculating," I said. "I'm just trying to make sense of all this and the death of this young girl."

"But after twenty years? And why the girl? Why not Jade herself? Or Marissa?"

"How long would you burn for vengeance if your child was killed?" I asked. "Would there ever be a point when it was made right in your mind?"

Reece looked less skeptical, but he gave me his standard police answer. "I'd feel satisfied when the justice system took care of things. And that's what we're trying to do with the man we have in jail. That does it for me."

"Does it?" I asked. "What if it were your kid? They ran over a child and drove off."

"They were kids themselves," Laurel said. "Don't forget how young twenty is."

"You're right," I said. "They were kids. But their parents weren't. Can you justify them not taking those girls to the police and telling the truth? Would you do that with your kids?"

"They should have gone to the police," Reece said. "You're right."

"What would have happened to them?" I asked.

He scratched his head. "The driver could have faced some jail time. A little. Accidents happen, but we get punished for accidents as well. I tell you this: They made it all a hell of a lot worse by leaving the scene. And so did their parents. They dug the hole a lot deeper. Obstruction. Conspiracy. Not good."

"But the parents are dead. Their father masterminded the whole thing, and he's gone, so no one can touch him. He was always such a smug bastard. So pious. Sitting there in church at Marissa's funeral knowing the whole thing was a lie." I looked at Laurel. "Can you believe that? You went to the funeral. You cried for Marissa. It was all a fraud. Everything about them looked so perfect and good from the outside. Inside, it was a lie."

"Most things fall apart when you look that closely," she said, seeming distracted.

"What's the matter?" I asked. "Is all of this catching up with you?"

It took her a moment to answer. "I'm thinking about the things you said before, about Marissa and Jade's parents. I'm not sure I can go all the way with you on that."

"What do you mean?" Reece asked.

"With all due respect for the law," Laurel said, nodding at Reece, "I'm not unsympathetic to the Minors. I have kids. I hope I'd never cover up a crime they commit, but I understand the temptation. They were staring down the barrel of their daughters' lives being seriously damaged. I can see that those things would cross my mind."

"Cross your mind," I said. "Lots of things cross my mind. But I don't act on them."

"It's tough," Reece said, lifting his eyes to meet mine. "I hope I'm never in their shoes."

A silence settled over us. The corn was starting to defrost, and water dribbled down the side of my face. Riley looked up at me. During Jade's attack and escape, he'd sat on the floor placidly, watching the whole thing unfold as though he were staring at a distant event.

"I have to return to being a cop now," Reece said. "Jade didn't tell you where her sister is?"

"She refused. That's why she hit me. I tried to grab her. I don't know what I was doing, but I wanted to shake her and make her tell me."

"Did she say if she's alive?" Reece asked.

The question made me sick. A nauseous churning started in my stomach. *No way,* I thought to myself. *No way.* I hadn't pined all these years only to find out Marissa had survived the fire, but died somewhere else.

"She didn't say. But I got the sense Marissa is alive."

I also knew a lot could happen in twenty years. Accidents. Illness.

"Is that wishful thinking on your part?" Reece asked.

"No. Not just that. She knew something, Jade did. She just wouldn't tell. She's protecting Marissa, I guess. Wouldn't Marissa still face charges if she showed up?"

Reece looked doubtful. "Not really. It's a felony, vehicular homicide. The statute of limitations would have been up a long time ago. She's not exempt from civil charges if the victim's family pursued it. And there'd be the embarrassment that it all might become public. Friends, coworkers, family would find out. That might be worse in some ways."

"Kill a kid and face no charges," Laurel said. "Shit."

"It's treated different from conventional murder charges," Reece said. "These girls didn't intend to kill the kid. They were just negligent. They could always run into trouble if a prosecutor really wanted to be a jerk. They could say the statute of limitations was suspended if she left the state. They could try to say the conspiracy was ongoing. That's all above my pay grade. I'm just curious if Marissa tells the same story her sister does. It seems awfully convenient for this woman to show up and say her sister was the one behind the wheel of the car when the kid was killed. How did the two of them get along? How do we know she doesn't have it in for her sister?"

They both looked at me. I shrugged. "They got along like most sisters. They fought. They loved each other. Do you really think Jade is trying to stick it to Marissa?"

"How do we know what she's up to?" Reece said. "You've got a person who's been living under an assumed identity for the last twenty years showing up, breaking into your home, and telling a heck of a story. She crashed the funeral and caused a disturbance there. She threatened a member of the Russell family. She hasn't told you much of anything about herself. Are we going to accept every word she says as gospel?"

* * *

Laurel stayed after Reece left. I took my soggy bag of corn to the kitchen, tossing it back in the freezer, and when I returned to the living room, Laurel was studying me.

"What is it?" I asked. "Why do you look like that?"

"Have a seat."

I sat. My head felt better. Cold but better. Laurel was already dressed for work, looking beyond capable and put together. I hadn't really dressed yet and was sitting in my living room in a T-shirt and loose-fitting gym shorts I wore around the apartment when I wasn't expecting company.

"Do you think it's true?" I asked. "The accident, the cover-up. All of it."

"It sounds true. Other pieces we know lock in with the pieces Jade gave you."

"I guess they do."

"Reece is right to ask what Jade would gain from lying to you about all of this," she said. "If she spins this wild story, what does she get out of it?"

"She shifts all of the blame to her parents and sister."

"Why? You heard Reece. There's no real legal jeopardy."

"Then why was she here? I wanted to find that out, to understand what she hoped to get out of showing up and laying this whole story on me, but she bashed me in the head before we got to that."

"What is there to wonder about?" Laurel checked her watch and seemed satisfied with what she saw. "I know

I'm as bad as anybody at assigning base motives to people's actions. It's part of the job. I've dealt with so many petty thieves and liars that it's second nature to assume everyone is hiding something. I'm sure Reece feels the same way."

"I understand. I deal with landlords all day."

"Exactly. But think about what Jade's been through. If Emily is really her daughter, then she just lost her. Violently. And if Emily was adopted, Jade probably didn't know her very well. Or she was just getting to know her well. Maybe Jade came here because she wanted to connect with someone. Someone who knew her sister and her past."

"And the last friendly face to see her daughter alive, right?"

"Sure."

For twenty years I'd known none of the things Jade had told me. Had she just decided enough was enough with the deep, dark secrets? Had she just wanted to close a circle that had been broken for twenty years?

"But if that's the case, why didn't she just tell me where Marissa is?"

"Maybe she doesn't know. Or maybe she's still protecting her."

"Or maybe she can't be found?"

Laurel didn't say anything to that.

CHAPTER FIFTY-NINE

Late on Sunday afternoon, while I sat in my cubicle catching up on a variety of end-of-the-month reports at work, Detective Reece called. When I answered, he asked me how I was doing and seemed genuinely concerned for my well-being. Something shifted in his voice for just a moment, and he no longer sounded like a cop. He sounded like a real person.

"I'm fine," I said. "Tired." I paused. "Do you mean this for real? You really want to know how I'm doing?"

"I asked," he said, some of the steel coming back into his voice.

"Right. Okay. I'm hanging in there. I'm confused, I guess. A little overwhelmed."

"That's understandable. I wanted to give you an update on some of the things we talked about this morning."

"That would be great," I said.

"We've been trying to learn more about Jade Minor, and there isn't much to find. Just like Laurel struck out on the parents, we're striking out on her. I have no doubt that given enough time and resources we could find out what she's been doing and what name she may have been using, but . . ."

"But what?"

"It's really not going to be a high priority for us. She's committed no crimes we know of, unless you want to press charges."

"I don't."

"Even then, it's a small break-in and a bump on the head. Not really worth getting worked up over."

"But she might know more about Emily's death," I said.

"If the investigation leads us back to Jade Minor, we'll certainly go there. For now, that's not where we're putting our energies."

"Where are you putting your energies?" I asked.

"Lance Hillman. He's our guy. He's going to end up at trial unless he changes his plea."

"Right."

"And in case you were wondering, that guy who used to date your ex-girlfriend? The firebug? He's denying setting the fire that might have killed her. He's maintaining that he's innocent. I guess there's a lot of that going around."

"Aren't you at all interested in finding out whether Marissa is alive or not? She was living in Eastland when she supposedly died. Wouldn't it matter to you that there's a case everybody got wrong in the past?"

"A case they *allegedly* got wrong. And we take cold

cases very seriously . . . as soon as there is sufficient evidence to reopen them."

"So you're calling me for what reason?" I asked. "To remind me that nothing has really changed?"

"I'm calling you to be nice," he said, his voice flat. "I don't do this for just anyone. I know you've been through a lot, so I'm trying to reach out. And because I did learn something that might be of note to you. Something that helps shore up the story this Jade Minor told you last night before she smacked you."

"What is it?" I asked.

"Bill Maberry, the father of the kid your girlfriend allegedly ran over?"

"Yeah, what about him?" I asked.

"The Hanfort police went and spoke to him today. They wanted to see if he had an alibi for the night Emily Russell was killed."

"What did they find out?"

"The police were already pretty familiar with him, as far back as the original accident. He rode the cops pretty hard to find out who was at the wheel of that car."

"Makes sense," I said. "You can understand he'd want to know who did it. I'd want to know if something happened to my kid."

"Of course," Reece said. "We all get it."

I waited for him to say more. His words carried with them the implication of more to come.

"But?" I said, trying to prompt him.

"Mr. Maberry has been a little . . . zealous in his pursuit of justice. At least in the first ten years or so after the accident. He made veiled threats at the officers investigating the case back then. He hinted strongly that he was carrying on his own investigation. He filed lawsuits seeking access to documents and then more documents. He was pretty relentless back in the day. Even ruthless."

"How so?"

"You said there was a witness to the accident, right? Mr. Maberry's mother, the boy's grandmother. She saw the whole thing, and somehow she said to police that she thought the driver of the car was a dark-haired man. The Hanfort police actually questioned a suspect shortly after the accident, probably a week or two after the Minors would have pulled up stakes and left town. A guy fitting the description who happened to own a dark SUV and who regularly drove through that neighborhood. The police cleared him, but somehow word got to Maberry that this guy was being questioned by the police."

"How would that happen?" I asked.

"Small town," Reece said simply. "Maybe Maberry has a friend on the force. Maybe he paid the right person. It doesn't always take much. Long story short, the suspect, the *cleared* suspect, ends up taking a beating one night. Broken leg. Fractured jaw. Busted teeth. When the police found out about it, the guy says nobody jumped him. He says he fell down the stairs at his house."

"How do they know he didn't?" I asked.

"The injuries," Reece said, as though it should be obvious to me. "The emergency room doc says no way it was a fall. Unless the guy fell down over and over again. And landed on someone's fist."

I wondered how I had ended up in a place where I was even having a conversation about someone like Bill Maberry. I wasn't supposed to be connected to people like that, even tangentially. I'd seen and heard of people like that at work, but that was work. Yet somehow Bill Maberry had possibly moved into the circle of my personal life.

"So what happened today? What did he say to the police?" I asked.

"He denied any involvement, of course. And not only that—he has a pretty good alibi that the police were able to verify. The night of Emily Russell's death he was with his second wife and a few other friends. They've backed his story."

"Friends can lie," I said.

"They can. And sometimes do."

"I know you're hung up on this Hillman guy, but isn't it still possible Maberry is the one who killed Emily Russell?" I asked.

"Based on what?" Reece asked.

"I don't know. She's Jade's daughter. Maybe . . ." It sounded good when I started to say it, but in the cold light of day, I couldn't weave the two strands together. "I don't know."

"Believe me, I thought of it. I've thought of everything. From what I understand, the family had a rough go of it after their son died."

"You'd kind of expect that, wouldn't you?"

"Of course, but it's still worth noting," he said. "Their marriage broke up. The wife, Kendra Maberry, she never fully recovered from the shock of losing her child. She's had some mental health and substance abuse issues. Mr. Maberry seemed to have moved on. Mrs. Maberry didn't really." There was a pause. "But I'm trying to think of a way Maberry would know Emily was Jade's kid. How would he learn that?"

"I don't know," I said. "How did he know to beat the crap out of the poor guy who just happened to drive the wrong-colored SUV?"

CHAPTER SIXTY

When I walked in the door of the apartment, Riley danced a little and licked my hand, and we enjoyed a short walk around the complex. The evening felt warmer; the sky was clear after the previous night's flurries. We had almost reached April, which felt like a milestone. Most of the cold weather was past, and nothing but budding flowers and green leaves and baseball stretched ahead. Even Riley seemed to feel it. Several times we stopped on the walk, and he lifted his head in the air, eyes half closed, as though he just wanted to soak in the warming breeze.

But I was hungry, and I assumed he was as well. So we went back, and I fed him, and then I put something on the stove to feed myself. Spaghetti. The very meal I had intended to have but never ate the night I saw Emily at the grocery store. While I watched the pot boil, I tried to comprehend how much time had passed since that night. On a calendar, not much. A couple of weeks. The blink of an eye if I was talking about my entire life span. But where had that night led me? Far into the past—twenty years. How could such a brief, accidental encounter lead to so much?

Then the phone rang, and it was Gina calling. I felt pleasantly surprised to see her name pop up on the caller ID screen. I hoped—again, I always hoped—she was looking for a way for Andrew and me to spend time together. Baseball was about to start, and he and I occasionally watched the Reds' opening-day game together. Maybe she would let that tradition stand. . . .

"Nick?" she said.

"Yeah?"

The steam from the pot rose past my face. Gina sounded breathless, rushed.

"I was worried you wouldn't be home," she said.

"Is something the matter?"

I heard the hesitation. Something was going on.

"Gina?" I asked.

"Everything's fine," she said. "Andrew's fine. We're both fine. I wasn't going to call you about this. It didn't seem like a big deal, and I didn't want you to worry."

I put down the wooden spoon I was holding. "I'm worried now. What is it, Gina?"

"Okay. Andrew had a little incident today."

"What kind of incident?" I asked. "Did he fall?"

"I know you're crazy about that boy, so I need you to remain cool about this. It might be nothing. It's *probably* nothing." She took a deep breath. "He was coming home from his friend Jay's house. You know Jay?"

"Sure."

"It's only a few blocks, so he was walking back. And,

look, Nick . . . Jesus, it scares me just to say it. But some-one pulled up in a car and tried to get Andrew to get in."

Steam continued to rise from the boiling pot on the stove, and the water rolled and cascaded, a few drops sloshing over the edge and sizzling on the hot burner. I placed my hand on the counter to steady myself.

"A man?" I asked. "He tried to get Andrew?"

"The person was wearing a hat and sunglasses. He offered Andrew a ride. He said Andrew needed to go with him, and if he did, everything would be fine."

I tried to listen. It sounded like Gina might have been crying. Gina never cried. Not when we got married, not when we split up, not when Andrew got shots at the doctor. She never cried. She was a rock. But she sounded like she was sniffling. "The man in the car said the most aw-ful thing, Nick. Oh, shit, I really don't want to tell you."

"Tell me."

"Please don't be hurt by this. Don't take it personally or anything."

"What did he say?"

"The man said that he was a friend of yours. He said you had sent him to get Andrew, and if he got in the car, he'd take him to you."

I held the phone against my ear while I eased my body down to the floor. When I was finally on the ground, I sat with my back against the cabinet under the sink, my free hand resting on my forehead. Riley came along and nosed against my side. The pot continued to boil and spit on the stove.

"Andrew got away, Nick. He's a smart boy. He knew

you wouldn't do that, so he ran. He ran right back here and came tearing through the door. He's fine. I locked all the doors and called the police. They just left."

"Are you alone?" I asked.

"I'm . . . Dale's coming over. He's going to spend the night."

"Good," I said.

"And the police are going to up their patrols or whatever," she said, sounding confident. "Nick, the police are also on their way over to see you. I'm not supposed to call, but I had to tell you. I didn't want them to be the ones to break this to you."

"That's fine," I said, feeling shaky.

"They're going to ask you questions."

"I'm not worried about it," I said. "I'm worried about you and Andrew."

"Nick . . . we're okay. Really. I'm trying to remember that this guy might just be a weirdo who wants to scare kids. Or he's . . . I don't know. I just know Andrew is home now. He's safe. That's all that matters."

Someone rang the front doorbell.

"Okay," I said. "They're here. The police."

"Then I'm getting off the phone," she said.

"I'm going to check back with you later."

"That's fine."

I stood up and turned off the burner. Riley followed me to the front of the apartment to answer the bell.

When I pulled the door open, I came face-to-face with Detective Reece. Again.

I told him up front what my intentions were.

"I'm going to my family," I said.

He held up his hand. "Not yet."

"You have to let me."

"I don't have to do anything, except ask you a few questions." He pointed into the apartment. "Can we sit? Please?"

But I refused to move.

"You know what this is about," I said. "It's not about me. It's those people, that Maberry guy."

Reece gently placed his hand on my shoulders, guiding me into the apartment and then closing the door. "You think this was Maberry who tried to pick your kid up?"

"Don't tell me you didn't think it either. Don't tell me it didn't cross your mind for the tiniest little second."

Reece didn't act the least bit in a hurry. He sat on the sofa and didn't say anything until I sat down as well. He looked as calm as a man waiting for a bus that wasn't scheduled to come for another two hours.

"Where were you this afternoon?" he asked.

"Oh, no," I said. "No, not this."

"Where were you?" he asked.

"Work. You can check. You called me there."

"On a Sunday?" he asked.

"Yes," I said. "It happens sometimes. I'm getting caught up. Do I need to call my lawyer?"

I reached for my phone. I had Brosius programmed. I could reach him in a minute.

"Have things been okay with your ex-wife and son?" he asked.

"She told you they have. Right? She couldn't have said anything else."

"And you don't know anyone who would attempt to pick Andrew up this way?" he asked. "No friends? Relatives?"

"I don't have any relatives here. And Andrew knows my friends. No. I'm telling you, it's Maberry. We just talked about it."

"And what interest would he have in your son?" Reece asked. He sounded curious and not dismissive. "He doesn't know you. He doesn't know the kid. He doesn't even know you exist."

I wanted to burst. I stood up. I raised my hands to my head. I nearly screamed.

"I don't know," I said, managing to keep my voice somewhat level. "What else could it be?"

"This person in the car—your stepson gave us a description. Andrew wasn't sure if it was a man or a woman. The suspect wore a hat and sunglasses and spoke in a soft voice. He said the person seemed older, and they were driving an expensive car, some kind of dark luxury sedan. Does it ring any bells?"

I almost said it. Roger Kirby? I didn't really know any other older well-off people. But Roger Kirby? Why? Just to scare me?

So I reminded Reece of him. Kirby's name had come up the night before when I was telling him about Jade.

"This is the guy you thought was having an affair with Marissa?" Reece asked.

"Yes. That's the one."

I expected Reece to dismiss my wild connection, but he wrote something down in his notebook.

"And that's it?" he asked. "No one else? Troubles at work?"

"Haven't we been over this enough?"

"What about this new boyfriend your ex-wife has?" Reece asked.

"What about him?"

"Have you met him?" he asked.

"Yes, and I'm thrilled he's spending the night with Gina and Andrew tonight. So can I go?"

Reece gave me a long look. "Why are you going over there?"

"I want to see Andrew," I said. "I want to know he's safe. Sometimes we can only do that with our own eyes."

Reece looked down at his notebook again. He nodded to himself and tucked it back into his pocket. He didn't say anything to me, but he stood up, and I had the sense our conversation was over.

I grabbed my keys, wallet, and phone.

At the door, Reece stopped and looked over at me.

"This is three times I'm here in the last two months, Mr. Hansen. Normally when that happens with some-one . . ."

"They're really in the soup," I said.

"I hope I'm not wrong about you," Reece said, and then he walked out ahead of me.

* * *

I didn't stay long inside Gina's house. Dale was there, and Andrew was already getting ready for bed, but I was able to have a few minutes alone with him in his room.

The kid was unruffled. He acted as though the incident with the stranger was no big deal, the kind of thing that happened to kids all the time. He said his mother taught him never to get into a car with a stranger no matter what they said. And he followed her instructions.

"I ran fast," he said. "No one could have caught me."

"I bet."

"Maybe I'll go out for track someday."

"Maybe you will." I looked at the clock on his bedside table. "Okay, time for bed. You've had an adventurous day."

Before I left the room, he said, "You look tired, Nick. You should sleep too."

"I'm on my way," I said.

But I didn't return home. I went through a drive-through and bought the biggest coffee they had and a couple of greasy burgers. I drove back to Gina's street and parked across from her house.

I stayed there all night, watching.

I wouldn't leave them alone. No chance in hell.

CHAPTER SIXTY-ONE

Someone tapped on the window. I jumped.

It took a moment for my circumstances to come back to me.

The street. Gina's house. Andrew. I'd fallen asleep.

I looked out the window.

Gina waved at me. I rolled down the window. My neck ached, and I was cold despite wrapping myself in a coat. A sour, stale taste filled my mouth. I needed to brush my teeth.

"Hey," I said.

"Were you out here all night?" she asked, her voice wavering between disapproval and admiration. "Never mind. I know the answer to that. Of course you were."

"I shouldn't have fallen asleep."

"You're lucky the police didn't arrest you," she said.

"They didn't drive by as much as I thought they would." I turned my neck one way and then the other, trying to work out the kinks. Cool air blew in through the window. "I almost called Reece and asked for more cops, but it was the middle of the night."

"We were fine," Gina said. "I think it's all fine."

I wasn't convinced, but I didn't want to alarm her more than she already was, so I just asked, "Did Andrew sleep okay? Was he scared or anything?"

"He did fine." She looked over my wrinkled clothes and the empty coffee cups and fast-food wrappers. "I think he was more at ease than you were."

"I just took a nap at the very end there," I said.

"Are you planning on doing this every night?" Gina asked.

"I haven't thought that far yet."

"Well," she said. "I have to get to work and get the kid to school. You probably need to be moving on too."

"Does the school know about last night?" I asked. "Are they going to keep a closer eye on him?"

"I wasn't even going to let him go to school today. I really wasn't. But I spoke to the principal, and she assured me they'd keep a careful eye on him. She made me feel better, and I guess it makes sense for his life to be normal. I don't want him to sit at home with me locked in the house."

I couldn't think of any other angles to cover. I felt like there should be, but I couldn't summon them in my groggy, overly tired state.

Gina bent down closer to the open window. She placed her hand on my arm. "You need to take care of yourself, Nick. Go home and clean up."

"Yeah. Okay. I know my breath stinks."

"And, Nick?" She squeezed my arm tighter. "Thanks. You're really a champ."

"I just . . . well, you know I care about Andrew." I waited, not sure if it seemed right. "And you," I said. "We may not make a good married couple, but I do like you."

"I know. On both counts. And we care about you. Both of us."

She squeezed my arm one more time and walked off toward the house.

The time at work dragged. When lunch rolled around, I fought to keep my eyes open. I walked downtown to try to get my blood flowing and then ate a sandwich in a diner on the square and swallowed several more cups of coffee but still remained groggy. A nervous, jittery groggy. Not an improvement.

I decided to walk it off. The day was warm, the sun bright. Everywhere I looked, it was spring. I saw couples paired off, pregnant women pushing strollers. The planters around downtown, the ones maintained by the city, overflowed with budding flowers. I ambled with no purpose in mind, or so I told myself, but I quickly saw where my legs were taking me. I crossed the edge of the campus and walked toward the street where Marissa lived.

More students were out, thanks to the warm weather. They threw Frisbees around the Hightower Meadow, the guys with their shirts off, the women catching the sun on their bare arms and legs. Music played and people laughed, and it wasn't hard to get caught up in the energy of their youth. I wished I could step into one of their bodies or extract some of the life from them. But I also wanted to issue a warning. *You never know,* I wanted to say. *You just never know where your life will take you.*

But I wouldn't have listened to a middle-aged guy when I was twenty, and I assumed they wouldn't listen to me. And I didn't want to stop because if I did, even for a moment, I might not go ahead and do what I intended to do.

It took just a few minutes to reach the end of Blakemoor Street. Marissa's street. I'd passed by there many times over the years without making the turn. But on that day I made it. I turned right and started walking up Blakemoor. Marissa's house had sat on the left side, halfway up the block. The houses all looked the same as they had twenty years earlier. A new coat of paint here, some improved landscaping there, but otherwise the same. The recycling bins on the porches were filled with beer cans and wine bottles. The furniture looked grubby, telling me students still lived there. And then, when I reached the spot—number 784—I stopped.

Marissa's house had been limestone with a wide front porch and three dormer windows across the top. The house built in its place was made of red brick. The porch was smaller, the second floor larger. I glanced at the sides of the house and around the yard. Nothing to indicate a fire had ever taken place there. No rubble or charred remnants of the former house. No candles or makeshift memorials. Why should there be? The kids who lived in the house may not have been born when four people died on that spot. It meant nothing to them.

The door of the house opened just then. A young guy with long hair came bounding out and down the steps. I wasn't sure if he'd even noticed me as he approached. He whistled while he walked and carried a small stack of books under his arm.

"How's it going?" he asked, only mildly curious about me.

"Nice house," I said.

He looked back like he'd never seen it before. "Yeah, it is."

"I'm an alum," I said, as if he cared.

"Right on." He pointed at the house. "Did you used to live here?"

"No," I said. "Some friends did."

"Cool. You must have good memories to be coming back like this."

I started to explain but decided against it. I settled for simple agreement.

"You're right," I said. "Lots of good memories."

Then I walked from Blakemoor back to campus and behind Beech Hall. A small creek ran through campus over there, and in the 1920s, a group of alums had pooled their money and had the Beech Bridge constructed. Except no one ever called it the Beech Bridge. Everyone called it the Kissing Bridge. Campus lore said if two students kissed just as the clock tower in the quad chimed midnight, then they were destined to spend eternity together. I had no idea what the success rate of the Kissing Bridge might be. I suspected the university really didn't want to know. It made the campus brochures and tours so much more appealing to simply tell prospective students they might find true love on a small wooden bridge over a trickle of a creek than to discuss love's fleeting nature.

As I told Dale, Marissa and I kissed there. We waited until our one-year anniversary, and then we went out there one night and managed to get the bridge all to ourselves. We waited, shivering in the autumn cold, until the bell tolled, and we started making out like we wanted to swallow each other's face. We never talked in any real terms about getting married someday. A concept like that seemed too big, too far away. We clung to our plans for New Zealand, though, and in a way that made it feel like forever for me, with or without the silly Kissing Bridge. I couldn't imagine forever feeling like anything else but being with her.

I stood on the bridge and stared down into the water. The little creek grew deeper as it passed under me, and I watched the shifting layers of silt and the occasional appearance of a small, darting fish. Overhead, the trees were just starting to fill out with green, so enough light filtered through to keep me warm. Classes must have been changing, because a stream of students passed me in both directions, their footfalls rocking the tiny bridge ever so slightly. A few of them bumped against me, but most of them went on, talking and laughing, without making contact of any kind with me.

I stood and stared a long time, long after the student traffic had slowed to nothing. I knew I had to get back to work, but I didn't want to go. I felt tired, wrung-out. The rest of the day would be a slog. But being an adult meant slogging through when no other option presented itself.

I was just about to return to real life when I thought I heard someone say my name.

One word. My name.

But who there would know my name?

Then she said it again.

And I knew who it was even before I turned around.

She'd come back.

She'd found me.

Marissa.

CHAPTER SIXTY-TWO

We were alone on the bridge again, just like that kiss twenty years earlier.

We stood on opposite sides, separated by about eight feet of wooden planks.

It was her. A little older, of course. A few streaks of gray in her red hair. A few more lines on the face. But it was Marissa. Alive. In the flesh.

Marissa.

But neither one of us made a move for the other. I felt paralyzed. Stunned. I feared that if I moved I would break the spell, end the dream, and she'd be gone.

Again. Maybe forever.

She finally shrugged. "It's really me, Nick. It is."

"I know," I said.

To that point, I had been inadequate to the moment. And I knew the moment ticked away faster and faster.

Was I going to let it speed by me like a runaway train? Like the previous twenty years?

I moved toward her then. And she moved toward me too. And we were in each other's arms, hugging, holding each other tight.

"My God," I said. "It's real. It's really and truly you."

We held each other a long time. I absorbed the sensations: the vanilla scent of her hair, the soft brush of my skin against hers, the tangle of her hair against my face. I didn't want to let go.

"I'm sorry about all this," she said finally.

"How did you find me?" I asked.

"Jade. She told me she'd talked to you."

"But here . . . the bridge?" I asked.

"I didn't want to just show up at your house," she said. "I didn't want to ambush you. Jade looked up where you worked, so I drove by there. It's lunchtime. I looked around downtown and around campus. I found myself coming this way, and, of course, I remembered the bridge. To be honest, I drove by your office a few times this morning, hoping I'd see you. It sounds crazy, but I wanted to lay eyes on you again."

"I don't care. I don't care at all."

I released my grip on her a little. I held her at arm's length and studied her face. It was the same. She was there. The same girl.

"I'm worried about Jade," I said. "I scared her. I wanted her to tell me where you were." For a moment, I couldn't speak, and then I asked, "Where have you been? What have you been doing? My God, Marissa, how did all of this happen? Is what Jade told me true?"

"Whoa," she said. She appeared guarded, nervous,

looking around, averting her eyes from mine. "I'll tell you. I promise."

"Right. Sorry."

"I do want you to know something right away," she said, returning her eyes to mine.

"What? Anything."

We still held hands, our arms extended.

"I've looked you up over the years. People-finder programs on the Internet. Facebook. I knew you were here. I saw things happening in your life. I wanted so much to make contact, but I couldn't. I just couldn't. Too much was at stake."

"I heard. And I'd want you to be safe."

"But that doesn't mean I didn't want to reach out to you. I wanted to tell you everything twenty years ago." She closed her eyes as though she'd been stricken with a sharp pain. "If only I had. If only I had told everyone the truth about everything back then."

"You were young. You were under your father's control."

Marissa was shaking her head. "I can't use that as an excuse anymore. The expiration date on that one is up. Dad is dead. So's Mom. It's us now, we're the adults, and maybe it's time to clean all of this up."

"We can take our time figuring that out."

Marissa looked away. The breeze picked up, blowing a strand of hair across her face. A couple of students came walking by, and we stayed silent while they passed, her body pressing closer against mine, a surge of energy speeding through me, illuminating every cell. Filling me.

When the students were gone, Marissa said, "I dreaded you ever knowing those things. About the accident. Honestly, a part of me didn't want to see you because I didn't want you to hear about all of that. I worried—"

I placed my hand on her shoulder. "There's nothing to worry about. It was an accident. You were helping Jade."

She didn't look at me, but said, "Thanks." And then she did it. She lifted her hand to her mouth, pinching her lips between her thumb and index finger. Just like Emily in the grocery store. "I'm glad to hear you say that."

"I want to talk to you. Can we go somewhere?"

"We should." She nodded. "We're out in the open here."

"Do you want to go to a coffee shop or something?"

"No." Her voice carried surprising force. "I want to go someplace private, someplace safe. I don't even like being out here this way. Campus always felt safe to me, but it doesn't now." She turned to face me. "Can we go to your place? I don't have much time."

"My car's downtown," I said.

"Mine's right here."

She took me by the hand, and we left the bridge.

CHAPTER SIXTY-THREE

When we reached her car, a red hybrid, Marissa held the keys out to me.

"I want to look around at the campus and the town," she said. "Do you mind driving? I haven't been here in twenty years."

"I don't mind."

When I took the keys, she held on to my hand for a moment. "I used to think I'd never drive again, after the accident. But I did. I had to." She let go and we got in.

Once we were moving, I asked, "Would you like to see anything in particular?"

"Not really."

She stared out the window and seemed to have settled into a moody silence. I didn't want to push her, but I said, "I went somewhere today, right before I saw you."

"The house?"

"Yes. It's weird. It's like it never existed."

"I went by there too. It wasn't easy to see. I was so close to those girls. They were my best friends." She swallowed. "And I know someone else died in there as well."

"Charles Blevins is his name."

She turned to look at me, her face expectant and nervous.

"Long story," I said. "His family knows. We'll see what they do with the information."

We fell back into silence, twenty years hanging between us. Not exactly my vision of our reunion, but what could I really expect? We drove through the center of campus and then out on the north side, heading toward my apartment. Marissa made a couple of comments about buildings that had been torn down or put up. She said, "The whole place seems bigger than it used to be. I thought it would seem smaller, more cozy."

"The town and the campus keep growing," I said.

"I guess so."

I looked at her, and she was looking out the window. I said, "I know you don't want to be bombarded with questions, but there are so many."

"One at a time," she said.

"Fair enough. Did you call nine-one-one that night?" I asked.

"No, it wasn't me," she said. "I remember the police tried to find the caller, but I have no idea who it was." She swallowed hard again. "When I came home . . . that night, the police and fire engines were already there. It was obvious what was happening."

"I'm sorry I brought it up."

"It's okay," she said. "Maybe we'll talk about it all more. I'm prepared for that. Why did you even ask about the nine-one-one call? Did you remember they tried to find out who made it?"

"I didn't remember that," I said, "but I talked to one of the cops who investigated the fire. He said they never found out who made the call, so I thought maybe you had."

"Not me. Probably some other drunk kid stumbling home who came upon the scene and freaked out."

"Probably."

When we pulled up to my building, Marissa tensed up. She looked around the lot, one way and then the other. "Can we get inside quickly? I don't like being exposed this way."

"Sure," I said. "I'll get the door. And I have a dog, but he doesn't bite."

"Just go, Nick. Please."

She sounded desperate, so I hustled to the door and pushed it open. I turned to summon Marissa, but she was already moving, brushing past me and inside the apartment like a Special Forces operative.

Riley came out from the kitchen. I could have sworn his eyebrows went up when he saw Marissa. After living with me during a couple of years of near celibacy, he was seeing the fourth woman cross my threshold in the past few weeks.

Marissa asked me to lock the door, and I did, going so far as to put the chain on. I wanted to do anything I could to reassure her, even though the only break-in I'd ever had was perpetrated by her sister.

But then I remembered Andrew and the attempt to get him into the car.

I understood her fear. Very well.

"Jade said you live alone."

"I do. Me and Riley."

I saw the apartment through her eyes, and it seemed small and bland.

"But you have a son?"

"A stepson. Did I mention that to Jade?"

Marissa sat down on the couch, in the same spot where her sister had sat. "No, I spied on you on Face-book. I saw some pictures of you with a boy, a really cute little boy."

"I'm divorced. And he's Gina's, my ex-wife's, son. But I got pretty close to him when we were married. I've been trying to see him more lately."

Marissa smiled up at me. I was still standing. I didn't want to sit. Too much energy, and I didn't know where to direct it.

"I can tell you're crazy about him," she said. "I can see the way your eyes light up when you talk about him. And you used to say in college you couldn't imagine yourself being a dad. Remember?"

"I certainly couldn't imagine it back then. I guess I still can't now. Being a kind of dad just fell into my lap when I met Gina. Maybe it was easier that way. I had less of a choice." I needed to ask the next question. I couldn't follow Marissa's life on Facebook, so I had to ask her out loud. "And you? Kids? Married?"

"It's easy to forget how little we know about each other."

"Not for me, I guess. I *know* how little we know about each other. I've been thinking about it a lot."

She reached up and pushed a loose strand of hair back off her face. "I struck out in the marriage department like you. I got divorced three years ago. Two kids, though. Two daughters. They're twelve and fourteen. It's about to really become an adventure. I'd show you pictures . . . but it seems silly to be thinking about that. I'm sure you have some bigger things you want to talk about."

"I'd love to see the pictures," I said. "But I agree, we have bigger things to talk about. Except I'd like to know where you live. Are you so close to Eastland that you could just show up today? Have you been right here the whole time?"

"Wisconsin," she said. "I live with my kids in Wisconsin."

"Wisconsin. I've never even been there."

"It's cold in the winter. But I've liked living there. It's been good . . . until lately."

I looked at the clock. "I need to call work."

"Am I keeping you? Do you need to go back?"

"Are you kidding?" I said. "It's been twenty years. They can fire me if they want."

I stepped out of the room to call. I told Olivia something had come up and I needed to take the rest of the day off. She acted unconcerned, but then asked me if I would be in the next day since my caseload was getting backed up.

I answered her honestly. "Tomorrow? I have no idea what tomorrow holds."

"Well, that's mysterious," Olivia said.

"It *is* a mystery. I agree."

When I walked back to the living room I found Marissa looking over the things in my apartment. Books I'd both read and never read. A few pictures of Andrew. Old magazines.

"It's not as clean as it should be," I said.

"I don't mind. It's not like you were ever a neat freak."

"I've gotten a little better since I was twenty."

I asked myself a question then: What happens when the thing I've always wanted finally happens? Does that moment automatically erase all of my fears and anxieties? Should I have felt a sudden lightness, as though a heavy burden had been removed from my shoulders?

I couldn't answer my own question. I felt as though I was still walking in a dream, which had been the only way I could approach Marissa for the previous twenty years. If anything, I felt further away from her than I had before, when I thought she was dead. During that time, she had no history. Those twenty years simply didn't exist for her. But facing her in reality, I had to reckon with someone who had lived and loved and lost, someone who had been buffeted by things I could only imagine. Things I realized I might always have to imagine.

"I'm not sure what I'm supposed to do now," I said.

"I don't think there's a playbook for meeting your first love after twenty years of thinking she was dead."

"First love," I said, echoing what she said.

She studied me. "First and truest," she said.

I was shaking then, inside and out. "Yes, Marissa. The truest for sure."

She came over and took me by the hand, and then she guided me to the couch where we sat down next to each other. Our knees touched, and the familiar but long forgotten surge of electricity that had always passed between us returned. It raced up my leg with a jolting quickness, hitting me in the center of my body and speeding on to my brain. I remembered the sensation well. It was ingrained like a primal instinct, and it felt so good to experience it again.

"I have to be honest with you," she said. "I can't stay. My children are with my ex-husband right now, visiting their grandparents. It's spring break for the schools up there. But I have to get back to them. I'm scared thinking about them being there without me."

"What are you afraid of? These people, the Maberrys?"

"Partially. They killed Emily. I know it."

"How did they know who she was?" I asked. "Jade didn't raise her. She looked like you more than Jade. But they couldn't just go on that. How did they know?"

I saw disappointment on Marissa's face. Either she didn't want to be asked these questions or she simply didn't want to answer them. But I didn't see how we could move forward in any way without covering that ground. Whether she wanted to talk about it all or not, I had been swept up in everything.

She backed away from me just a few inches, breaking off the contact between our knees. She said, "I can't say anything for certain. I only have guesses." She looked over at me, and I nodded for her to go on. "Jade and Emily connected when Emily turned eighteen. That was the earliest age they could reach out to each other, and Jade initiated the contact. She found Emily through the adoption agency. And they started getting to know each other. *They* only had eighteen years to get caught up on. But they hit it off pretty well. Sometimes adoption reunions don't go very well. I've known people who've been through it. But Jade and Emily did very well. They connected. They liked each other. Emily loved her parents, but she was curious about her birth mother. It seems natural to wonder about something that big. And it worked. It really worked."

"That's great for both of them," I said. "They found exactly what they were looking for."

"And Emily wanted to meet me, so she came to visit once up in Wisconsin. Jade pushed her to do it. She wanted us to get to know each other. She wanted Emily to have a sense of her family, especially since Mom and Dad are gone. Jade has lived a lot of different places over the years. Her life hasn't always been easy since we moved away from Hanfort. Anyway, Emily came up for just a couple of days, and when I met her I couldn't believe it. I'd always wondered what happened to that baby after Jade gave her up. You know, Jade didn't want to go through with it after the accident. She wanted to keep her. But Mom and Dad said no way. They made all that effort to get us out of Hanfort and give us new lives, and they weren't going to have a baby slowing Jade's life down. They made her give Emily up. It ripped Jade's heart out." Marissa paused, looking at the floor and rubbing her hands together. "You know, she never had kids again after that. Emily is her only child."

"That's one of the saddest things I've ever heard," I said.

"We'd started to hear the Maberrys suspected us. It was the car, really. Roger was the one who dumped it out in that pond. He did Dad's bidding for him. Once they pulled the car out, the Maberrys must have heard about it. I think Bill Maberry has friends on the police force. He was prominent in the community. He knew everybody around there. He put it together somehow. We moved so suddenly after the accident. We owned a dark SUV. And that SUV ends up dumped in a pond. The pieces fit together, at least enough to prompt the Maberrys to look further into things. They tried to see if they could find me. Or Jade. Any of us, I suspect, but we were the only two left."

"But you were off the map," I said. "You were dead, as far as anyone knew. Weren't you living under another name?"

"I was. Shae McKee. My married name was Shae Hancock."

"Shae's your middle name."

"I knew you'd remember." She smiled at me, reaching

out and squeezing my hand. "Everyone in Wisconsin calls me Shae."

"Even your ex-husband?"

"Even him. I was Shae when he met me. He knows the whole story, by the way. He and Roger Kirby are the only people outside of the family who know it all, and Dad didn't talk to Roger too much after we moved. And you now." She steepled her fingers in front of her mouth for a moment before going on. "The Maberrys tracked me down. Maybe they used an investigator or something. I know they had money. And I hadn't gone so far off the grid that I couldn't be found. I wasn't in witness protection. I was a suburban mom with two kids and a deep, dark secret." She sighed. "Some weird things started to happen right before Emily visited. I felt like I was being followed. To be honest, I'd started to feel normal again over the previous five years. I'd quit looking over my shoulder all the time. We put Mom and Dad's real names in the obituaries since Jade and I didn't live in Colorado. I just wasn't thinking every minute that someone was going to find out what I'd done when I was twenty. But this sensation felt real. I saw the same car behind me every time I went out. Then my daughter Liza saw the same car when she went to school one day. Bill Maberry found me. I knew it, and it scared the hell out of me. I kept thinking he'd tell the police, that one day an officer would knock on the door and arrest me in front of my kids. That was my real fear."

"And clearly that didn't happen," I said.

"No. Worse. The Maberrys took matters into their

own hands. Emily came to visit about two months ago. I don't know what happened after that, but as near as I can guess, he saw me with Emily. He tracked her down to her home and then to here. Maybe he thought killing her was greater punishment for me than anything else." She reached up and wiped her eyes. "Maybe he thought she was my daughter instead of Jade's."

I didn't know what to say.

Marissa closed her eyes and looked very much like someone who wanted to disappear, to wish her surroundings and problems away and never see them again. She sat that way for a long moment, eyes closed. Silent.

Then she opened her eyes. "When I broke up with you after the accident, I told you I wasn't worthy of you. That's how I felt."

"No," I said. "It's an awful thing to say or think."

"It's true. It was true then, and it's true now. Everyone who follows me, everyone who gets dragged into my orbit ends up getting hurt." She sprang off the couch and grabbed her purse. "I have to go."

"No."

She moved quickly across the room.

I was up and after her, taking two long strides so we met at the door.

"No," I said. And I remembered the lesson from Jade. Marissa had been through as much. More. She wouldn't want to be grabbed or manhandled. I held out my hand. Gentle. Easy. "Where are you going to go now?"

"Home. My girls. My life. That's my life."

"No," I said. "Just stay. It's too far to drive tonight."

"You're in danger. We're both in danger."

"We can handle it together," I said. "I know the police. A detective. Tell *him* the story. They can protect you. They can stop the Maberrys."

"I told them about it, but what good would it do?" she said. "I told them I thought someone was following me, but unless I tell them the whole story, they really aren't going to listen to me. That's why I belong at home, protecting my kids." She shook her head. "I have to go."

"You can't do it alone," I said. "Nobody could."

She held out her hand, lifting her index finger and placing it against my lips. "When my kids are eighteen, I'm telling the truth. I'm going to the police in Hanfort. Everyone will know what I did. Jade and I agreed. When they're eighteen, I'll take whatever punishment is coming my way."

"And for now?" I asked. "What are you doing now?"

She stood on tiptoes, and we kissed. Long and passionately. My hands slid down her back, below her waist. I gave in to it, lost myself. I pulled her back toward the bedroom. She resisted for a moment, and then finally came with me.

CHAPTER SIXTY-FOUR

I slept deeply and soundly, like a child. I couldn't say when the last time I'd slept that well was.

I was dimly aware of Marissa through the night. Our lips brushed each other's. We nestled close together. I didn't dream.

Before the sun was even up, Marissa stood over me, her hand resting gently on my shoulder.

"What is it?" I asked, coming up from my deep slumber.

"I have to go."

"No," I said. "You can't."

"I do," she said. "You can stay in bed."

"I'm not going back to sleep."

I threw the covers off me and stood up. She was already dressed and held her purse in her hand. She hadn't showered and she wore her hair pulled back off her face.

She smiled at me, a little exasperated. She reached up for a moment and pinched her bright red lips between her thumb and forefinger. Exactly like Emily in the store. Her niece. The young woman whose murder started everything.

"I told you this was only for a short time," Marissa said. "I have to get back to my family. Today. It's a long drive."

"I'll go with you," I said. "You can't go alone. It's dangerous, and you're tired and upset. I'll come along."

"You have a life here."

"Not enough of one," I said as I went to my dresser and grabbed fistfuls of clothes—underwear, T-shirts, socks. I looked around for a bag. "I can get another job. I can—"

Then I remembered Andrew. Could I just walk away from him when they needed me the most? No. But I could work something out. Weekend visits. Summer trips. Holidays.

"I'm not letting you walk away again," I said. "Jesus, after twenty years, to get another chance."

"Stop, Nick. Just stop." She placed her hands on my arms, interrupting my attempts at packing. She gently guided my hands back over to the open dresser drawer and nodded at me. I released the clothing, letting it drop where I'd found it. "You can't come with me."

"I don't understand." I turned from the dresser and took Marissa in my arms. I pulled her closer to me. "Is it your ex-husband? Are you dating someone else? Why can't I come?"

"It's not about a man," she said, almost laughing. She moved back. "Why do men always think it's about another man? Jade told me you thought all of this was about me and Roger Kirby. And now . . . you still think it's about a man."

"I never . . . People told me those things," I said. "I didn't know what else to think. How else could I explain your behavior to myself?"

"I'd never do that to you."

"So what *is* it about?" I asked.

She looked up at me, her eyes clear and determined. "I told you last night. It's all just too much right now." She let go of me, her hands slipping out of mine. "I can't bring anyone else into this. I have to concentrate on my family and keeping them safe."

"I *am* in this. I didn't ask for it, but I am. Ever since that girl, your niece, showed up with my name in her pocket, I've been in it. And other people are too."

"Don't try to follow me," she said.

I took a step toward her.

"Don't," she said. "Stay here. Take care of your life. Your stepson, your job, all of it. It's good. Trust me, it's very good here."

"Not without you, it isn't," I said.

She stared at me for a moment, and I could see her wavering.

I turned and went to the closet. I dug into the box and brought out the watch, holding it in the air between us.

"Oh, Nick," she said. "You kept that?"

"I kept it running. And the time's still set to two different countries. I'm sure you know which ones."

"Of course. Did you ever get to New Zealand?" she asked.

"No," I said. "I told you I've never even been to Wisconsin." I locked eyes with her, holding the gaze. "After the fire, I told myself I'd never go to New Zealand. I couldn't imagine it. Not that it was likely to happen."

She looked down. She lifted her hand and brushed her eye.

"Marissa . . ."

I waited, expecting at any moment she'd come back into my arms, hold me and embrace me and never let me go.

But she didn't.

She turned and walked to the front of the apartment, unfastening the chain and lock.

I followed her. I called her name.

I wasn't even dressed, but I went out the door as she slid into her car, starting the engine and turning on the lights. They caught me in their glow, blinding me.

"Marissa, wait!"

But she backed out, away from me. She swung around and drove off, giving me one last wave as she disappeared.

I didn't even have my car. I couldn't catch her.

CHAPTER SIXTY-FIVE

When it was time for work, I called one of my friends from the basketball team for a ride, but he was in a meeting. So then I called Laurel. I hoped to leave her out of it so I wouldn't be tempted to talk about Marissa, but I needed to get to work. Laurel came and picked me up, and then asked why my car was downtown. I said I'd stopped for a drink after work and had too many.

"I took a cab back home," I said. I felt bad for lying after all she'd done for me.

"I'm glad you had fun," she said.

"Yeah."

But she had to know something was wrong. We didn't talk much. I felt empty and defeated, like a black cloud infused my soul. I stared out the window at the sunshine, watching all the happy people go about their business. We arrived at my car, and I thanked her, reaching for the door handle.

"Did you hear about Lance Hillman?" she asked before I could get out.

"No, what about him?"

"You really didn't hear?" she asked. "It was on the news last night."

"I went to bed early."

"He tried to kill himself in jail. He got ahold of a bedsheet or something and tried to hang himself."

My body went cold. I dropped my hand from the door, and it fell against my lap like a deadweight. "Tried to? Is he okay?"

"He's at the hospital. I guess he's going to pull through. It's a big deal when a prisoner tries something like this. Lawsuits, investigations. Everybody's in an uproar."

"But he's innocent," I said.

"He's what?"

Laurel stared at me, her eyes narrowed.

"What if he's innocent?" I asked. "He hasn't even had a trial."

"Maybe," she said. "The suicide attempt . . . you could certainly see it as an admission of guilt. Nobody knows. He's a disturbed guy."

"Clearly."

I checked out of the conversation. I replayed Jade's words and then Marissa's in my mind. If everything they'd said was true, then Lance Hillman was probably an innocent guy who almost ended his life over a false murder charge.

"Laurel, what would it take for Reece or the cops in Hanfort to investigate Bill Maberry further?"

"He has an alibi. Remember what Reece said? He has a suspect in jail, a guy who possessed something that belonged to Emily Russell. A guy who liked to break into motel rooms and once attacked a woman. It's a lot stronger than hearsay."

"True." I stared out the window at the increasing bustle as Eastland woke up. "And those people . . . the Maberrys. I can't imagine what they've been through. They saw their child run down in the street right in front of their house. I can't even comprehend that."

"I don't want to comprehend it," Laurel said. "Let's face it, there are no winners here. Everybody's taken a few body blows, the Maberrys most of all." She tapped her fingers against the steering wheel. "My assistant looked into them a little. Kendra Maberry, the wife . . . she never did recover from that blow."

"What happened to her?" I asked, although I wasn't sure I wanted to hear.

"Substance abuse problems mostly. It's a small town, and everyone knew about her downward spiral. I don't know if that contributed to the end of her marriage, but I have to think it did. You know the stats on marriages breaking up after a couple loses a child."

"I suspect the stats are worse for people whose child gets run over right in front of their house. I bet it's worse for people who don't find any real justice in the courts or anywhere else."

"I suspect you're right." She stopped tapping. "Kendra Maberry seemed to be doing better for a while. She cleaned up. She went to work again. She looked to be moving on in a productive way, but she started to spiral again about a year ago. She started drinking again and who knows what else. She lost her job. Her friends, the ones she has left, are worried about her. They say she started talking more and more about her son, the one who died in that accident all those years ago."

A year ago. Around the time the car was found in that pond.

How did she even know?

I felt sick to my stomach. A dull nausea ate away at my insides. I so wanted to exonerate Marissa, to excuse what she and Jade did and grant them the second chance everyone deserved. *They were young. They were guided—poorly—by their father.*

But a child died. A child. And the Maberrys lived with that in a much more intense and tragic way than any of the rest of us.

"Is something else on your mind?" Laurel asked.

"I was just thinking, and it seems shallow now. But what if someone like Jade told her story to the cops?"

"It would help. What is this about? You seem really distraught over this guy's suicide attempt. Don't you want to see him brought to justice?"

"Not if he's innocent." I lifted my hand again and opened the door. "Thanks, Laurel. Talk to you soon."

"Nick?" she said.

But I was gone.

* * *

Fresh flowers sat on Emily's grave in Richmond. The earth over her plot had started to settle, but no grass grew yet. They hadn't placed the headstone either.

I took the flowers as a bad sign. Maybe she had already come once that day or the day before and didn't intend to return. Maybe she was so far away I'd never find her again.

But I was prepared to wait.

I parked my car down the road a little ways and played the radio low. I hoped the chatter of talk or the jagged notes of jazz on the local public station would keep me alert. I'd stopped for coffee and a sandwich on the way down, but I didn't think I'd need the fuel. My body felt energized, alive. I sensed I was coming to the end of something.

Around five fifteen my spirits started to flag. I tried to tell myself the trip hadn't been a waste, that just trying to get some answers made the trip worthwhile. But I didn't know what I'd do if I struck out. The way we'd all been living—in fear, in confusion, an apparently innocent man in jail and then the hospital—was no way to go on.

Something needed to change.

And then around five forty-five I saw her approaching from the same direction she had walked on the day of Emily's funeral. She wore large round sunglasses and a belted raincoat and carried a bouquet of flowers. She stepped purposefully among the headstones until she reached the grave she sought.

She stood there for long minutes, and I waited. I didn't want to rob her of the chance to say whatever she had come to say. After a while, she lifted her hand to her mouth, covering the lower half of her face. Her shoulders shook while she cried. I felt like an intruder. A spy.

She bent down and laid the flowers on the dirt-covered plot and then straightened up again.

I pushed the car door open and made the slow, careful walk to the grave.

When I was about ten feet away, I stopped.

Jade must have heard me. She spun around, but didn't seem scared or nervous.

"It's you," she said. "Why are you here of all places? Do you want to wrestle me to the ground or something?"

"I'm sorry I startled you at my house," I said. "I just needed to know where she was." Jade stared at me, her eyes still obscured. "And I wanted to thank you. You told Marissa how to find me, and she did."

"I'm glad," she said.

"It was short," I said.

"That's life on the run," she said. "I'm on my way out of here now." She turned away from me and back toward her daughter's grave.

"Jade?" I said. "You can't go."

"Why can't I?" she asked, her back still toward me.

"Because an innocent man is in jail for killing Emily. And he tried to hang himself last night." She lifted her head a little, as though she'd heard something that caught her attention. "Jade, there are a lot of things going on here. Emily was killed. Someone tried to kidnap my stepson. Don't you think it's possible that it's all related? Those people . . . the people who lost their son in that accident . . . they're responsible for these things as well."

"Based on what?" she asked.

"What else could it be?"

"And you want me to throw myself on the mercy of the cops on a hunch?" she asked.

"Andrew, my stepson, he's only nine. He shouldn't be paying any kind of price for this."

"What happened to your stepson?" she asked.

"Someone tried to kidnap him, to hurt him."

Her shoulders slumped a little, but she still didn't turn around. "I've paid a higher price. The proof is right here. Hell, even Marissa didn't pay that kind of toll. And she was driving the car that day. She's on her way back to Wisconsin now, you know? Her kids. Her house. She still has all those things. I don't."

"I know. And it's really not fair."

"You bet it's not." She sniffled a little.

"But think of that family. The Maberrys. Their child was killed. They need answers too. Everybody deserves answers. Everybody needs to try to move on."

"Dad *said* we'd all get a fresh start once we moved. Marissa got it. She always got everything she wanted. But what happened to me? I gave up my baby. I never had another kid, Nick. Is that fair? Is that justice?"

"It's not. I'm sorry. You've been screwed over by all of this as well. But you're here now. We both are. And there is *something* you can do about it."

She turned toward me and lifted the sunglasses. I saw the tears, the red-rimmed eyes and red nose. "Really? There's something I can do that will bring Meredith back to me?"

I took a step toward her, my hands out, signaling peace. "No, not that. But you can try to bring the people responsible to justice. And you can get an innocent man off the hook."

"Why don't you ask Marissa, my sister, to do it?"

"Because I don't know where she is," I said. "She didn't tell me. You can just come back to Eastland and confirm the story I told the police. They'll track Maberry down with this new evidence. Who knows? Maybe they're innocent and we can all cross them off the list. Just come back and see if you can end all of this."

Jade reached into her pocket and brought out a crumpled tissue. She wiped at her nose and eyes, making loud sniffling noises as she did so.

"Do you know why Meredith—Emily or whatever—died with your name and address in her pocket?" she asked.

"I don't. But I'd like to."

"*I* gave it to her. It's my handwriting on that note. When all of this started coming to a head, and I worried that Mer—Emily might be in real trouble, I knew she needed someplace safe to go. Someplace that couldn't be directly traced to either one of us, Marissa or me." She rolled her eyes. "The McKee sisters or whoever we'd become."

"What on earth happened to Emily that she would be so spooked?" I asked.

"First it looked like someone tried to break into her apartment. The lock was bent out of shape and scraped up. It freaked her out, and she called the cops. But what could they do? There are college kids all around, and people try to break into student apartments all the time. She got a new lock and a can of Mace and life went on."

"When was this?"

"A few weeks ago. She called me and told me about it. It scared me, but I wasn't certain it was the Maberrys. Then . . . then, right before she died, someone tried to get her into their car. She was walking home alone, near dusk. She shouldn't have been alone, but she was. You can't tell kids anything. I guess I regret that I didn't really and truly emphasize how dangerous the situation was. Maybe we'd relaxed over the years, let our guard down."

"Get her into their car? You need to tell me more about this."

"Meredith was walking home and someone pulled over right next to her. This person . . . they wore a hat and sunglasses. She couldn't even tell if it was a man or a woman for certain, but she thought it was a woman. The person opened the passenger door and asked for directions. It seemed innocent enough. But this person, this lunatic, said they couldn't hear well, and when Emily leaned in to give the directions, they made a grab for her. They got ahold of her arm, but Emily pulled away. She was strong. She was a fighter, I promise. She ran. No license number. Nothing."

I felt weak all over, like my bones and organs were made of glass. They tried to get Emily before they killed her. If they had managed to get Andrew into that car . . .

"And she told the police?"

"Of course. They put out an alert all over campus. It got a lot of attention, but they couldn't do much with her limited description." Jade studied me. "You don't look so hot."

"I'm having some things confirmed. Some disturbing things. So . . . why didn't she go to you for help?"

"She did. She called me right away. She was scared. I'd warned her, and she'd promised to let me know if anything weird ever happened to her. When it did, she called. I put the two things together, and so did she. The attempted break-in. The attempted kidnapping or whatever it was. Someone meant to do her harm. *Her*. Meredith. It wasn't random. And I told her what to do."

"She should have gone to her parents," I said.

"No. Then they'd be in danger."

"So you sent Emily to me?" I asked. "For God's sake, why?"

She looked off into the distance. "I remembered you. How nice you were to me when you and Marissa dated. How you talked to me like I was an adult and not just a pesty little sister when you came to visit. I remember how much Marissa cried when she knew she had to go back to school after the accident and break it off with you. She cried all night. I know she was crying for that boy she killed, but she was also crying because she had to go back to school and break your heart. I've never known a man I felt that way about."

"I'm sorry, Jade."

"I'm sorry too. I threw a grenade into your lap. Honestly, Nick, I didn't know it would all go this way. But I needed someone I could trust, someone the Maberrys couldn't immediately connect to us. Meredith . . . Emily needed a safe house. I thought if she could hole up with you for just a few days or whatever was needed . . ." She sniffled some more. "I went up to Hanfort the other day. I put flowers on Marissa's grave. Lilies of the valley, her favorite."

"You did that?" I asked.

"Sure."

"Why?"

Jade looked away, her gaze trailing up to the sky where a flock of birds, frantic black dots, swept across the clouds. "It seemed fitting. I did it for whoever is buried there. Just so they aren't alone."

I reached out to her, but I didn't grab.

"Come with me," I said. "Let's try to put an end to this. For Meredith."

She stepped toward me and took my hand.

CHAPTER SIXTY-SIX

While Jade spoke to the police, I waited in the lobby, sitting on a hard plastic chair that made my back cry. A middle-aged man in a polo shirt and khaki pants sat nearby. Every five minutes he made a phone call and spoke to someone in an exasperated tone.

"No," he kept saying, "I haven't seen him yet."

The room smelled like burned coffee and disinfectant.

I texted Laurel and gave her an update. I didn't hear back, but I knew I couldn't expect her to *always* be there. She had a job. She had a life.

I called Brosius and got him caught up. He offered to come to the station, practically insisted, but I told him not to worry about it. I promised to call if I needed anything.

At one point, Reece came out and called me back. When he opened the door, the man with the phone looked up expectantly, but then his face fell in an expression of utter disappointment. Reece wasn't the person he was hoping to see.

The detective led me back to his desk, and when we sat down, I asked if I could see Jade.

"Not yet. She's talking to my colleagues."

"Is all of this helping?" I asked.

Reece looked at me like I was an especially slow child. "Do you think I'm going to discuss these matters with you, Mr. Hansen? I can't."

"It was worth a try."

He shuffled some papers around on his desk, and then lifted something but didn't show it to me.

"Do you know this William Maberry she's talking about?" he asked.

"I don't know him personally. I've only heard what Jade has told me about him."

Reece nodded. He slid a photograph over to the edge of the desk where I could see it. "Do you know this man?" he asked.

I studied the photo. It showed a man about ten years older than me, a man with a head that looked too small for the broad shoulders it rested on. His hair was yellowish blond and thinning, and he wore a goatee that had some streaks of gray. His eyes were small and blue, the lids narrowed as though caught in a flash. It might have been a driver's license photo or a mug shot. I wasn't sure, but something lurked beneath the surface of his placid face, some coiled violence that might spring off the flat page at a moment's notice.

"Is this him?" I asked.

"Do you know this man?" Reece asked.

"I've never seen him before."

He nodded. "That's William Maberry, the father of the boy those girls apparently ran over twenty years ago."

"You believe Jade, then?"

"We want to talk to Mr. Maberry again, so if you see him, call us. Don't try to talk to him on your own."

"He's dangerous?" I asked.

"He has a record from a while ago. But he's been a model citizen the last decade or so."

"So you think he might have killed Emily? And he might have tried to lure Andrew into that car? You think all of this might be some act of revenge?"

Reece slid the picture into a manila folder. He held it against his chest but didn't stand up. His rolling, reclining chair allowed him to tilt back, the springs squeaking, and he considered me from that position, his chin nearly resting on his chest.

"All of these things are yet to be decided, Mr. Hansen. It's all just a theory now."

"Can I talk to Jade?" I asked again.

"Not a good idea. We're going to be with her for a while, maybe late into the night. You should head home, get something to eat. She can call you when she's finished. *If* we get finished and are able to let her go."

He didn't let me ask any more questions. Instead he stood up and ushered me to the front of the station.

CHAPTER SIXTY-SEVEN

As I cruised through the darkening streets, lights came on in the houses, and the sky turned purple. I felt tired and anxious at the same time, drumming my fingers against the dashboard the whole way. I looked forward to seeing Riley, who had been in the house alone all day.

On the way, I called Gina. When she answered, I asked her how things were going.

"Everything's fine," she said. "Andrew is perfectly safe. We drove him to school this morning and dropped him off right at the door. Shit, Nick, I drove by the school on my lunch break. I just had to . . . look at the building and see that it was safe. Like that really did any good."

"Did it make you feel better?" I asked.

"Yeah, I guess. I picked him up at the end of the day. He was never out of an adult's sight."

"Good." The relief coursed through me like a healing

drug. I felt it hit every atom in my body. "What about now? How is he?"

"He's here. He has a friend over. And all the doors and windows are locked. Look, it's quiet. Where are you? Are you driving?"

"I'm on my way home. It's a long story."

"I'd rather you got off the phone and watched the road."

"I'll tell you all about it someday. I promise." As I spoke, the idea of sharing the story with someone made me feel better, like going to confession or therapy. Gina would listen, and so would Laurel. "But I just want you to know that the things I've been saying are true. Andrew may very well be in danger. All of you might be. This guy who may have tried to get Andrew into that car is bad news." Then I thought of something, and I pounded the steering wheel. "Shit. I meant to get you his picture in case he showed up at the door or something."

"It's fine." But she didn't sound fine. I heard the fear, the uneasiness in her voice, the slight tremor of nerves that Gina almost never displayed. "Maybe I'm better off not seeing a picture. I'll just be on alert for everything until this is over."

"Can you go to your mom's house? Or Dale's?" I asked with the hope I'd hit on the right solution. "Somewhere off the beaten path a little."

"Yeah, maybe we should," she said, her voice full of agreement.

"You should. Or I can come by and watch again."

"No, don't do that. Jesus, Nick, you need to have a normal life. We all do. I'll go to Dale's. Okay? We can spend the night there."

"Excellent. And I want you to know something." I stopped at a light a mile from my apartment. The traffic streamed in front of me in both directions, headlights and taillights glowing in the dark. A car pulled up close behind me, its brights filling the rearview and making me squint. "I want you to go to Dale's house so you're safe. But I also don't mind you going there because I'm not jealous or anything. I'm happy for you. I think it's good for you to date and have a new relationship. As long as the guy is good to Andrew. That's my concern."

She laughed. "But no concern for me?"

"I don't mean it that way." But I liked hearing her laughter. It broke the tension, eased my mind. The light changed, and I pulled through the intersection, the car behind me still too close, its lights still too bright. "You can take care of yourself. Andrew's just a kid."

"I knew what you meant," she said. "And I appreciate you telling me how little romantic interest you have in me."

"It's true," I said, squinting more against the brights. "Go around."

"What?"

"The asshole behind me. Anyway, we both should be moving on."

"Aren't you still in love with the dead girl?" she asked, her voice light and joking.

"I guess I am," I said. "Except . . . well, surprise, she's not dead. I love her and she's not dead. But it looks like we won't be together."

A long pause settled over the call. I was a half mile from home, anticipating seeing my old friend Riley and taking him for a walk.

"Wait, Nick, you sound serious."

"I am. That's the short version of the long story I promised. She's alive. But for now, just get to Dale's house."

"Really, Nick? Are you telling me the truth? After all those things I said to you about moving on and how you always loved her more than me. I feel like an asshole. She's alive? Where was she? Are you getting back together?"

"No, it's over. Don't worry. Just take care of Andrew—"

Then the headlights behind me grew even larger in the rearview mirror. And they didn't stop. They grew and grew until with a bone-rattling jolt and a grinding smash of metal and glass, the car plowed into my rear bumper, pushing me off the road and into a drainage culvert. The force of the landing rocked my head back and forth and threw the phone from my hand.

The air bag popped and smacked me in the face, clouding my vision.

I hovered for a moment, trying to make sense of it all. Gina's voice reached me from somewhere in the car, calling my name. Fainter and fainter I heard my name being called until I slipped away into blackness.

CHAPTER SIXTY-EIGHT

I blinked my eyes open. My nose felt like I'd taken a punch from King Kong, so I reached up and felt the center of my face. Everything was numb, smacked into feeling nothing, and my hand came away covered with blood.

My neck ached. I squeezed my hands into fists, hoping they functioned the way they were supposed to. Then I moved my legs, which also worked. My left knee screamed with pain. I'd banged it against the steering column, but I could move it. Stiffly, roughly, I could move it.

The car sat at a forty-five-degree angle, tilting with the driver's side higher than the passenger's. Only the seat belt kept me from sliding out of my seat and down to the other door, which was pressed against the bottom of the culvert. I knew from driving by it daily that a thin trickle of water usually flowed through the bottom, and I saw some of it leaking in through the cracked window below me. The phone sat down there as well, getting soaked.

It lit up, ringing. Gina? She heard the accident. But I couldn't reach it, not strapped in as I was.

"Shit," I said.

I pushed the crumpled, deflating air bag out of my way and tried to make a move.

Whoever had smashed into me must have been calling the police. Unless they were worse off than me.

Or—

Unless they wanted to hurt me.

Fragments of the accident came back. The headlights filling the rearview, the car behind me not stopping at all.

How could that happen? It wasn't a blown stop sign or a missed turn. They'd rammed me.

"Shit," I said. "Shit, shit, shit."

Bill Maberry. He'd followed Jade. He'd watched me.

Shit.

My hands shook as I unbuckled myself. My body slumped to the right when the harness was released, and I exerted enough pressure and will to hold myself in place and avoid flopping over to the increasingly soaked passenger side. I pushed against the driver's-side door, working against the gravity of the tilted car to swing it open. It took two heaves, two big heaves I felt in my back and arms, before it swung far enough open that I could swing my feet around and plant them on the ground. I pushed myself to a standing position, my head brushing against the doorframe as I stood up.

The headlights of the other car glowed to my left. It

sat on the berm safely away from the culvert, the engine still running and making a low humming sound in the night.

And just then a figure, just a shadow, a dark stain in the bright cone of the lights, came toward me.

A voice spoke.

"Mr. Hansen? Don't leave. We have something to talk about."

I froze. The glowing lights burned my eyes, but I heard the voice. It wasn't what I expected, and my guard dropped for a moment.

"Who are you?" I asked.

"Mr. Hansen, I think you know who I am and what I want."

A woman's voice. A little husky, but a woman. And the figure approaching me was that of a woman as well. Thin, dressed in black, wearing a cap pulled low on her forehead and sunglasses.

The same look as the driver who had tried to lure Andrew into the car.

She approached . . . thirty feet away, then twenty.

I looked to my right. No other cars. No help, no phone.

"What do you want from me?" I asked.

My knee stung, my neck burned. A woman? Kendra Maberry?

She raised her hand in the darkness, leveling it before her body.

The shot she fired whizzed past my ear with a stinging crack.

I grabbed my phone and ran. Like a wounded animal fueled by fear and adrenaline, I ran.

I ran for my apartment complex. I hoped someone—a passing car, a friendly face—could offer help or shelter. But I saw no one.

And I couldn't stop running.

I couldn't let her catch up to me.

My feet pounded the pavement, my legs moving seemingly of their own free will, as though disconnected from my brain and fueled purely by fear for my life.

I huffed and puffed as I ran. My lungs burned.

Another shot came, and I tensed, lifting my arms over my head. But I felt nothing. No impact, no pain, not even the whistling sensation of it passing by.

Would it hurt to be shot? Would it hurt to die?

I turned into the complex. A car came toward me, its headlights filling my vision. I waved my arms, seeking help, but the car didn't slow. It zipped past me, the face of the driver, an older woman, looking out at me like I was a madman. Which I was.

And I had a madwoman breathing down my neck.

I cut across the landscaped lawn at the center of the complex and headed for my building. I tried to look back but feared I'd fall, so I kept running. Running and running, until the building and my door came into sight. I pulled up when I made it there, hoping against hope that my pursuer would be gone, would have given up the chase.

Then it hit me. *The keys.* My keys were still in the car.

I needed to keep running but didn't know if I could. I was out of breath. Way out of breath. My legs felt rubbery and loose. They could barely support my body.

The woman approached, a dark shadow in the night. She still held her hand out before her, getting a bead on me. I expected another shot. I expected to die on my stoop.

Marissa.

Andrew.

I wanted to sit down. To fall to the ground and let my body go limp. I bent over, my hands on my knees as the woman came closer and closer. She was a little shorter than me, slender like a runner. She breathed a little heavier than normal, but more like she'd just taken a quick run up a flight of stairs. She possessed the advantage. Completely.

Should I scream? Would I get shot?

She came closer, walking slowly, catlike, her shoes making no sound in the night. Her face was disguised by the sunglasses and the hat, but I saw the feminine shape of the mouth, the lipstick.

"Inside, Mr. Hansen," she said in the husky voice.

"I can't. No keys."

"It's unlocked. I was here earlier."

"The police will be coming. The accident. My ex-wife was on the phone when it happened."

"Inside."

Her voice sounded cool and indifferent, like a winter

wind. She spoke like someone who expected her orders to be followed, someone who knew her prey lacked options. I was trapped. Truly.

"What do you want from me?" I asked. I held my hands up, indicating I meant no harm. No tricks up my sleeve. No weapons or mischief.

"Go ahead," she said. "Inside. We'll talk."

I turned and twisted the knob. The door was unlocked and gave. Nothing but darkness waited inside. Darkness and Riley.

"I have a dog," I said. "He doesn't bite."

"I know. I met him."

A cold pain clutched my heart. *No.* She didn't do something to Riley, did she?

I stepped across the threshold and looked around. Riley didn't appear. I didn't call him either. If he was hiding or scared, then so be it. I wanted him out of the way. If only he hadn't already been harmed by this woman.

"Who are you?" I asked.

She followed me in, her presence looming at my back like an enormous dark shadow. She reached over and flicked on a lamp, filling the front of the apartment with light.

"Don't you know who I am?" she asked.

"Kendra Maberry?"

"Good guess."

"What do you want me to do?" I asked.

"Sit on the couch. We'll talk."

For a smaller woman, she gave me a hard shove from behind, sending me stumbling toward the coffee table. I caught myself before I fell, and then regained my balance. I followed orders and sat on the couch, relieved to be off my feet after my wreck and my insane run. I lifted my hand to my face. The trickle of blood from my nose seemed to have slowed, as I found a smaller smear of red across the back of my hand. Feeling crept into the center of my face again, a jagged tingling as the nerves woke up, and I started to believe my nose hadn't been broken.

Kendra Maberry stood over me, her feet set as wide apart as her shoulders. She looked coolly confident as she took off her hat and sunglasses, a woman without a care in the world. And that scared the hell out of me.

"She came here and told you the whole story, didn't she?" she asked.

"She's telling the police right now."

For a moment, a ripple of uncertainty passed across her face. Then the composure returned, a solid mask of unfeeling.

"So she told you the whole thing?" she asked. "She must have."

"She did. And let me say, I'm sorry about your son. I can't imagine—"

"No, you can't," she said.

"I can't. Right. But why would you want to do that to someone else? Kill or kidnap their child?"

"You're one of those people who wants everything to be simple, aren't you? Have a problem, call the police. You get wronged, you get justice. Do you really think the world is going to work that way?"

"Most of the time it does."

"You're a fool if you think that."

"Then I'm a fool," I said. "Look, just go. Whatever you do to me, the police are already looking for you. Get out of here and run away."

"Running away won't change anything. That's what your girlfriend tried to do all those years ago. Run away. Pretend that the accident never happened, that she never killed my baby boy."

"She never forgot."

"I did *more* than never forget. I lived and relived that moment every day for twenty years. Picking up his broken body in the street, having his blood on my hands. Burying him. And everything that came after." In the glow of the lamp, her eyes shimmered brown, and I saw the pain there. "I couldn't have another baby. My husband drifted away. We got divorced. I lost it all, everything from the life we once had. Do you know what that's like?"

"I've had a taste."

"I wish I could forget," she said. For a moment, her face showed the emotion, the wear and tear of years of grinding grief. "I wish I could."

"Your fight's not with me. Or with the Minors, really. Take it to the courts, let the police sort it out."

"I know there's no fight with you," she said, some sympathy creeping into her voice. "Not really. But like my son's death taught me, sometimes there are innocent bystanders."

"Like my stepson, Andrew. You tried to kidnap him."

"You were getting too involved, nosing into too much

of what was going on. I had to scare you, to brush you back a little. You were falling for their lies."

"And terrify a young boy? And his mother?"

"He got away. It could have been worse."

Her words carried a chilling logic. "Like it was for Emily Russell?" I asked.

"Yes."

"Who killed her?" I asked. "You or your husband?"

"My husband lost his taste for the fight many years ago," she said. "Even when they found that car, the car that proved we were right all along, he didn't have the stomach for it anymore. He'd gotten remarried. He moved on. He forgot."

"But he knew about the car?" I asked. "He could have—"

"He told me about the car," she said. "*He* told me." She pursed her lips, and her chin quivered. "I was fine. Better. Off the booze. Off the pills. Working. And then Bill told me about that car. About the Minors' car. He had spent years looking for answers, and he never found anything useful. Just dead ends. Until they found that car in the pond. And then he told me those girls, those Minor girls, were living their lives happily with their children. He said one of them was living in Wisconsin under another name . . . with her kids and her wonderful life." The hurt showed in her eyes, twenty years of grief. "I lost it. I fell completely apart."

"And you went after them? You went after the Minors because of what your husband told you? You could have gone to the police."

"Bill told me not to. He told me . . . he convinced me the police wouldn't listen, that after all those years they wouldn't do anything. I felt like I had no choice, like I had to take matters into my own hands."

"He wound you up like a top," I said. "He turned you loose."

"I tried to bury it, but I never forgot. Once I knew about the car and who was driving it, I couldn't bury it anymore."

"And he just handed it off to you, to let you do his dirty work."

"It was my dirty work as well. And he had his new wife and his new life. He couldn't risk that."

I put my head in my hands. "I'm trying to understand this. You went all the way to Wisconsin, where Marissa lived? And then you went down to Lexington and back here to find Emily?"

Kendra looked confused. "I didn't go to Wisconsin. I've never been there."

"Did your husband go there?" I asked.

"*Ex*-husband."

"Ex-husband," I said. "Did he go there and see Emily visiting her aunt?"

I believed Kendra when she said, "I wouldn't put it past him. More than likely he hired someone to do it. He has money. He gets people to do things for him by throwing that money around. He's one of those people who doesn't like to get his own hands dirty. He prefers that other people do it for him. All I know is he told me about the car being found. And then he told me that the one Minor girl had a daughter, and she was going to college in Lexington. He told me her name and where she lived. I tried to get to her down there but couldn't. And shortly after that . . . Bill told me she was coming up here to Eastland, looking for you, I guess." She paused. "He knew where she was . . . and he kept telling me where she was. I knew what he hoped I would do. Bill had always talked about revenge. He used to be obsessed with it. He got me obsessed with it. We used to fuel each other. He never said murder, but I knew he was thinking it. When they found that car, and he told me where to find that girl, I couldn't stop myself. I wasn't married to Bill anymore, but it felt like something we did together."

"So you killed Emily in that hotel?" I asked. "Strangled her. And all because you *thought* she was Marissa's daughter? And all because you couldn't resist the sick impulses of your ex-husband?"

Kendra lifted her shoulder, a slight shrug. "Sometimes innocent people get hurt."

"That girl, Emily, didn't kill your son," I said. "She had nothing to do with it."

"But now that family has a tiny glimpse of what it's been like to be me all these years." She pulled her left hand out of her pocket and held it in the air, the thumb and forefinger less than an inch apart. "A tiny glimpse."

"That girl was adopted," I said. "That other family raised her, the Russells. You've put them through hell, and they have nothing to do with this."

She blinked her eyes a few times, and I felt, just for a moment, that I may have gotten through. It was a foolish, vain wish, but it rose within me, some last vestige of hope for a human connection.

"It's unfortunate for them," she said, her voice flat. "What matters is those Minor brats getting a taste of it. That's what counts for me."

"All these years, you've harbored such hate for people you didn't even know."

"Not hate," she said, her tone becoming lecturing. "Never hate. Love. I loved my son. I loved my husband. Still do, as a matter of fact, even though he hasn't returned the feeling for a long time. *That's* what I've nurtured all these years. Do you know what it's like to have someone you love taken from you through no fault of your own? And to live with that for two decades?"

"I do know," I said. "Not the same, of course, but I know. I lost someone very important to me, someone I love very much. Someone who was also involved in this situation."

Kendra Maberry studied me for a moment, her head cocked to one side as though she had just discovered me sitting on the couch. Every nerve ending in my body felt tight. Stretched to the limit and sizzling with energy.

"The girl?" she said. "You were in love with one of those awful girls? Is that why you're in this mess?"

"Marissa," I said.

"*Don't* say her name. It makes me sick."

"Yes," I said. "That's her."

"Then you're right," she said. "It's not the same. She's alive . . . for now. And you can try to get her back."

"I doubt it," I said.

"No, I know the difference. As long as someone is alive, there's hope."

"Then let's keep everyone alive."

She laughed a little. "It's too late for that. For me."

"No one's forgotten what you've been through. You lost a child. It's incomprehensible. I get it."

"I doubt it. I really doubt it."

The hand holding the gun rose.

At the same time, something moved to my right, something sleek and low to the ground.

Kendra heard it at the same time I did, and she spun as Riley leapt, throwing his old body against hers with as much force as he could muster. Kendra stumbled to the side, leaning over like a stack of falling blocks, and as she fell she swung her gun hand in the direction of Riley, making solid contact with Riley's head, causing him to yelp.

But I was up by then, diving off the couch for Kendra. I ended up on top of her, as she grabbed me around the neck. I felt the surprising power in her grip, the same power that had choked the life out of Emily Russell. I tried to pull away but couldn't. My air was cut off, my neck about to burst.

Then Riley was back. He snapped at Kendra's arm, taking a quick bite above the wrist, just enough to loosen her grip for a moment. Kendra swung at Riley again, missing, but when her head was turned I swung my fist, once and then again against the side of her head. She turned back to me and reached for me, but I twisted out of the way.

The gun sat on the floor next to us. I picked it up. It felt heavy and awkward in my hand. I started to swing it at her head, but she dodged out of the way, and I ended up smashing the floor, feeling the shock of the contact all the way up my arm. Then Kendra backhanded the gun away from me, and it thudded against the carpet.

She managed to jerk her knee up in the confined space between our bodies, taking aim between my legs. I twisted my body to avoid the contact, and while she missed her target, the movement threw me off-balance, allowing her to break loose, and she scrambled across the floor.

I grabbed for her from behind, and then climbed over her, both of us clutching at the gun. My hand landed on top of hers, and beneath it I felt the heavy steel of the weapon. We both squeezed at it, trying to get a grip. She jerked her free arm back, using her elbow against my side. She couldn't get a clear strike in, and while she tried that, I shifted my weight on her back. I leveraged my body up, moving along her back, until I placed my knee against her spine. I leaned in, applying pressure, and then more pressure. She grunted beneath me, her breaths coming in shorter and more labored bursts, and I felt her hand loosen until I was able to knock the gun away.

Then sirens.

I heard sirens.

I didn't let up on the pressure. I held it steady, keeping her against the floor.

And then people were coming through the door.

Hands grabbed me from behind, tossing me to the

side. Several cops in dark uniforms, their voices loud and efficient.

"Are you okay, sir?"

"Are you Nick Hansen?"

"Do you need medical attention?"

I couldn't answer any of them.

They grabbed Kendra Maberry, pulled her hands behind her, and cuffed her, and then asked her if she needed medical attention.

I held my breath. Had I hurt her? Even though she had tried to kill me, I was suddenly worried I had injured her.

Then she said, "I'm fine, dammit. I'm fine."

I tried to breathe evenly, to return to normal.

And I did—at last—feel like I was okay.

CHAPTER SIXTY-NINE

The police led Kendra Maberry out of the apartment, informing her of her rights, and then after they hovered over me for a few more minutes, asking again if I needed medical attention, which I told them I didn't, I shifted my attention to Riley.

He turned in circles a couple of times, his belly low to the floor, his ears pinned back. When I got close enough to examine him, he made a whimpering sound and stopped moving, settling onto the carpet ungracefully, letting his legs give way as his body weight took over.

"What is it, boy? What's the matter?"

I looked at his head. A knot had already risen where Kendra struck him during the struggle, and I knew Riley had taken one or two other blows in my defense.

"Mr. Hansen?" one of the cops asked behind me. "Do you need help?"

"I'm checking on my dog."

"We need to ask you some questions."

"Can't it wait?"

"Not really."

I stood up. Two cops waited by the front door, and outside I saw the swirling blue lights and figures moving about in the darkness. "You're going to have to. This dog saved my life tonight. I have to get him to a vet."

I returned to the floor, and Riley moved his eyes in my direction. He looked tired and pathetic, as though he'd just given everything he had.

"Detective Reece is on his way—"

"That's great," I said. "He knows me. He knows I'm not going anywhere. And he knows I didn't do anything wrong. I'm going to take my dog to the animal hospital, and I'll meet Reece at the station or wherever he wants me."

I gently eased my arms under Riley's body and lifted him up.

He whimpered a little more but didn't resist as I carried him to the parking lot. The neighbors had gathered, gawking. I recognized a few.

"Shit," I said, more to myself. "No car."

A woman stepped forward, someone I recognized from seeing her walk her own dogs. She came over and stroked Riley's head. "Poor guy," she said. "Is he okay?"

"I need to get him to the vet. I don't have a car. Mine got smashed out on the road."

"Come on," she said. She led me to a Volvo wagon and lifted the hatch. "Put him in there." I did. "I'll drive you."

"Are you sure?"

"Yes. He needs help. And I love dogs. Let's go."

"Thank you."

I climbed in, while she started the car. As we backed out, I looked, and I couldn't see Riley. His head was down.

"All those years, you didn't make a sound," I said. "You were saving it up for when I really needed you."

They took Riley back as soon as I got to the animal hospital and for a short time I paced around the waiting room, wishing there was more I could do. My neighbor— who said her name was Alicia—offered to stay with me, but I told her to go home. She did, but only when I promised to tell her how Riley was doing as soon as I heard, a promise I was more than happy to make. While I resumed my pacing, Reece called and asked me how soon I could make it to the station to, as he put it, tie up all the loose ends. I told him I didn't know when I'd get away. He tried his best to show patience and understanding, but then gently reminded me that the things he was dealing with were kind of urgent as well.

"This woman here tried to kill you," he said.

I promised to hurry up.

Not long after the call, I was liberated. A technician came out and told me Riley was going to be there all night. When I pressed for more information, she told me what she knew.

"He's an old dog, and he's been through a lot. We're going to do everything we can."

* * *

I walked the four blocks to the station. I called Brosius on the way, waking him up and letting him know all the events of the evening. He said he'd be there soon, but I told him to hold off. He warned me to be careful, but I assured him I felt pretty safe from prosecution or suspicion given everything that had happened.

I ended up at Reece's desk, telling him the whole story. The drive home, Kendra Maberry's car ramming into mine and pushing me into the culvert, the chase through the complex and to my apartment door.

"She admitted to everything," I said. "Killing Emily. Trying to kidnap Andrew. She was the one doing all of it. We were assuming it was the dad. *I* assumed it was the dad."

"And all of it because of that car accident in Hanfort, the one that killed her kid?"

"Yes," I said. "All because Marissa drove away. And her dad convinced her not to go back."

Reece sat there tapping a pencil against the top of the desk. "She's an ambitious person, I'll give her that. Ambitious when it comes to vengeance."

"Relentless."

"Until she ran into your wonder dog."

"Right. Never underestimate Riley," I said.

"I'm going to get back to talking to Mrs. Maberry now that we have your side of things. She's in for a long night, and so are we."

"What about her ex-husband?" I asked. "She told me—"

"We're paying him a visit right now. We'll see what role he played in getting Mrs. Maberry on the revenge trail. He's not off the hook."

"Good. I was also going to ask you about Jade. Is she ready to go?"

"She can't go yet either," he said. "But she did ask to talk to you, and, out of the kindness of my heart, I agreed to give you a few minutes together."

"Now?"

"Now."

Reece stood up, and so did I, but before we left the area of his desk, he held his hand out to me. I took it in mine, and we shook.

"Thanks, Mr. Hansen," he said. "It's been a long, strange trip, hasn't it?"

"The most complicated trip to the grocery store I've ever taken."

Reece opened the door of the small room, and I saw Jade sitting inside at a functional table with a Formica top. There were two chairs in addition to the one she sat in, and when she looked up and saw me, she smiled, relief playing across her face.

"I'll be back pretty soon," Reece said, and then he stepped away, closing the door as he left.

I looked around the room. It contained none of the things I was used to seeing on cop shows. No two-way mirror, no recording equipment or cameras. No rubber hoses or brass knuckles. I walked over and took a seat next to Jade.

"I'm glad you're here," Jade said.

"You heard about what happened?" I asked.

"I heard that they got her. A mother. A mother doing all of that."

"How far would you go to avenge your child's death?"

"I wouldn't kill another mother's child," she said, her voice bitter. "I wouldn't do that to anyone." She looked at the tabletop and picked at a chip in the finish. "She's here somewhere, isn't she?"

"She is." I folded my hands on top of the table and studied Jade's face. She looked tired, as tired as when I'd found her in the cemetery, but she didn't appear to have been crying. "I was thinking . . . I'm an only child. You might be the closest thing I've ever had to a baby sister."

She smiled, reaching out her hand to where mine were folded. "That's sweet," she said. "And I wanted to tell you something. I wanted to thank you for bringing me here to the police. It was the right decision."

"I'm glad you feel that way. And you've been mostly right about everything. You thought it was the Maberrys, and it was."

Jade wore an unsettled look on her face. Something brewed inside her, something she wanted to tell me.

"What?" I asked.

She lowered her voice. "You know how you said that if I told this story it would be a way to end all of this once and for all?"

"I said that, yes." I wondered what she was driving at.

She seemed to be suggesting something deeper, more permanent. "What do you have in mind, Jade?"

"I'm really going to end it all, right here." She leaned closer, although I doubted anyone was listening to our conversation. "I'm going to tell them *I* was driving the car that day. I'm going to tell them I'm the one who ran over that little boy, little Samuel Maberry. That will get Marissa off the hook. It really will all end right here."

"No, Jade, I wasn't asking you to do that."

"I know you weren't. But it makes sense now that I'm here."

"How does it make sense?" I asked.

"Don't you see?" she asked. "This will set Marissa free. She can live her life without fear of this coming back to haunt her someday. She keeps saying she's going to admit to everything when her kids are old enough, but do her kids need her any less just because they turn eighteen?" Jade looked at me, but she seemed to be seeing past me, to something only she could envision. "I don't have any children. I never did, really, but I certainly don't have any now with Meredith gone." Her focus sharpened, her eyes fixing on me. "I started all of this, remember? I got involved with an older man and got pregnant. I called Marissa home. I distracted her in the car that day. It was all me. She can be done with it. And so can you."

"Jade—"

But she wasn't listening. She turned away and bent down to the floor, where she rummaged through her purse. She came back up, holding a piece of paper. "Take this," she said, pressing it into the palm of my hand. "Read it later. You'll thank me for it."

"Marissa doesn't want you to do this, and neither do I. I can just tell Reece you're lying. We already told him Marissa was driving—"

"Your word against mine," she said. "And I was *there*. I'm the only one besides Marissa who was there, and I don't see her around." She placed her hand over my closed fist, the one that held the piece of paper. She squeezed my hand tight, as though she wanted to mash the paper into pulp. "Later."

Reece opened the door and stuck his head into the room. "Time's up, Nick."

I looked up at him, starting to say something. Jade squeezed my hand even tighter, so that my nails dug into my own palm.

I met her look and saw the earnestness there, the plea for me to shut up and let her say what she wanted to say. And I'll admit I was selfish about it. I wanted Marissa off the hook as much as Jade did. More. Even if I wasn't going to be with her again, I didn't want to think of her living under the cloud of legal jeopardy for the rest of her life. The guilt she carried would be enough.

"Good-bye, Jade," I said.

"Thanks, Nick. For everything."

Reece held the door for me, and I walked out.

CHAPTER SEVENTY

I stepped out into the parking lot, intending to go back to the animal hospital and wait. I checked my watch. Three thirty in the morning. I didn't feel tired at all. Sore, yes, but not tired.

I didn't have a car, and I thought about going back inside and arranging a ride home with the police. The sodium vapor lights glowed above, making the asphalt lot feel like the moon.

I held the crumpled paper in my hand and was about to open it when something Jade said came back to me.

I got involved with an older man and got pregnant.

"Holy shit," I said.

I needed a car. I had a drive to make.

I was the first customer at the rental car agency in Eastland, and by six fifteen I was driving out of town. I arrived in Hanfort with a little time to kill, but I didn't mind. I was wired, anxious. I waited in the parking lot, my eyes glued to the door of the office.

When Roger Kirby finally arrived just before seven thirty, he locked his car and walked across the blacktop, attaché case swinging by his side, looking like a man without a care. I pushed open the door of my rented Toyota and took a few quick strides, intercepting him before he reached the door.

When he saw me, his head jerked back in surprise, as though my very presence before him was some kind of slap.

"Mr. Hansen?" he said. He looked around the lot. "What are you doing here so early? I don't think we had an appointment."

"No, we didn't. I figured you'd want to talk about this here rather than at your house. With your wife around."

"My wife? What does she have to do with anything?"

"I'm a fool, Mr. Kirby. You *were* with Marissa the night of the fire. My friend saw you. I assumed the worst, that you and she were involved in some way. Romantically involved. I guess I was just a jealous and insecure little college boy back then who couldn't handle that his girlfriend had dumped him without explanation."

Roger Kirby set his briefcase on the ground and crossed his arms over his chest. "I'm glad you realized that."

"I know you went to Eastland because Marissa's dad asked you, to smooth the transition as the family ran away from that accident. Right?"

"What are you driving at, Mr. Hansen?" he asked. "As usual, I find your questions pretty tiring, and the day just started."

"You weren't fooling around with Marissa. But you were more than happy to help the family rush to get out of town and away from Hanfort. It made your life a lot better, didn't it?"

"Brent Minor was my best friend," he said.

"And Jade Minor was carrying your baby. You *were* involved with one of those girls, just not Marissa."

Kirby lowered his hands. For one second, a shock passed across his eyes, a flare of exposure like the flash of a camera as my words sank in, penetrating the veil of propriety he had erected over the rest of his life. But just as quickly, the defenses were up again. The wall still stood.

"You're an aggravating little shit, aren't you?" he said. "You were never good enough for that girl anyway— Marissa. The family let you hang around like a little puppy. They didn't want to leave town, of course, but it sure made it easier to give you the brush-off once and for all." He let out a short, condescending laugh. "They used to joke about you, Brent and Joan, when the kids weren't around. 'What are we going to do if Marissa wants to marry that pathetic Hansen boy?'"

"Your own flesh-and-blood daughter died," I said. "She was murdered. Do you even care?"

"What do you want from me, Hansen? Yes, it was a horrible mistake to get involved with that immature girl. Maybe I did sweat bullets some nights thinking she'd tell her parents the truth, but she never did. I think . . . events were moving awfully fast back then. For all of us. Besides, I didn't break any laws by being with the girl."

"Wasn't she only seventeen?" I asked. "Isn't that breaking the law?"

He ignored the question.

"And you also broke laws by covering up their crimes," I said. "And Jade is with the police right now, telling them the whole story."

He bent down and picked up the briefcase. "Statute of limitations. Conspiracy or something like that." He waved me off dismissively. "Keep tilting at windmills, boy. It might be the one thing you're good at."

He bumped against me as he walked past, his shoulder knocking into mine, sending me stumbling back a couple of steps.

"You could have helped them," I said. "If you were their friend, you could have been the voice of reason. You could have sat Brent Minor down and told him to do the right thing, to let Marissa tell the truth. We all could have been spared the last twenty years. That girl, your daughter, would be alive. Her name's Emily."

He stopped and looked back at me. "I was nothing but a good friend. All the way. That night I was in Eastland, the night of the fire, I helped Marissa out of a jam that you caused."

"Me? What are you talking about?"

He took two steps toward me and spoke with his index finger raised. "Some crazy girl, some bimbo who wanted to go out with you . . . She confronted us outside of Marissa's house when I picked her up that night. The other kids were supposed to be gone, but this girl just popped up. She screamed at Marissa, saying *you* wouldn't go out with her because you were still hung up on Marissa. It was so fucking childish. So . . . embarrassing for all of us. That emotional girl just ranting and raving. She looked like a lunatic. So I stepped in. Marissa was very upset, and she was already distraught because of the accident, but I got the girl to leave us alone." He jabbed with his finger more. "I told her you weren't worth being upset about. And she never could or should touch or come near Marissa again." He straightened up, acting very proud of himself, pulling his jacket into place with both hands. "I knew how to defuse the situation. I *always* did that for them. I always pulled Brent's nuts out of the fire, in life and in business. And that's all I was doing in the wake of that accident. Nothing else matters."

He turned to go, spinning with military-like precision.

But his words lingered in the cool morning air.

There was only one woman who could have been saying those things on that night, begging to be with me and harassing Marissa.

"What did she look like?" I asked, my voice rising to carry over a sudden gust of wind. "This girl."

Roger Kirby stopped and looked back. "How the hell do I know? Some blond wreck. Some stupid little girl hung up on you." He studied me for a moment. "I should have sent her to your house. You could have been together all these years, and maybe you wouldn't still be chasing after Marissa." He smirked at me, dismissing me. "Good-bye, Mr. Hansen. And good luck."

He left me standing in the parking lot, contemplating the unthinkable.

CHAPTER SEVENTY-ONE

Heather didn't answer the door when I rang the bell. I pressed my face to the glass and cupped my hand against the side of my head, cutting down on glare. Her house was open, airy, and I could see all the way through the kitchen to the deck off the back. A still, solitary figure sat there.

I started around the right side of the house, down the slightly sloping lawn until I came to the rear, stopping at the side of the deck. Heather sat at a circular umbrella table, the umbrella closed despite the bright, early-morning light. She wore sunglasses and held a small glass full of an amber-colored liquid. She wasn't reading or listening to music or talking on the phone. She stared straight ahead, the object of her gaze not apparent to me or perhaps to anyone. I came all the way around to the bottom of the steps leading up to the deck, and even though I stood just ten feet from Heather, she made no acknowledgment of me.

I cleared my throat.

She tilted her head a fraction of an inch in my direction, the sunglasses still obscuring her eyes.

"Oh, it's you," she said.

"What are you doing out here?" I asked.

"I could ask you the same question."

I went up the three steps so I stood on her level. She drained the rest of her drink and pushed herself out of the chair.

"I'm going inside for a refill. When I come out, you can be gone."

She was at the sliding glass door when I spoke.

"You called nine-one-one that night, didn't you?" I said.

Her hand rested on the handle of the door. She looked back at me.

"I don't know what you mean."

"The night of the fire. You called nine-one-one. Right?"

I still couldn't see her eyes, but her cheeks and the tips of her ears reddened in the morning sun. A flush rose along her hairline and spread beneath the loose, long-sleeved T-shirt she wore. With her free hand she maintained her grip on the glass tumbler, her knuckles turning white.

"You didn't think anyone would be home," I said. "That's why you said what you said in the nine-one-one call. '*They're* in there.' That's what you said because you thought they were out at that party. It was around one thirty, and you didn't think they'd be home until much later. But someone got sick. They left the party early to take care of her."

For a moment, all was silent. A car horn honked somewhere in the distance, its bleat urgent and aggressive in the still air. Heather turned her head away from me slightly, and her breathing quickened. Then she took one deep, huffing breath, something close to a sob, and her chin puckered. But she didn't break down. She held herself in check, hiding whatever deeper emotion revved beneath the surface.

"Was it really because of *me*?" I asked. "Were you following her that night? Stalking her? You were outside the house earlier in the evening. I know that."

"I have children, Nick."

"Is that what you were doing? You wanted me, and I rejected you, so you tried to kill Marissa?"

"I didn't try to *kill* anybody," she said. "I wanted to scare her. I wanted to . . ."

"To what?"

"I wanted to do something to her. Just do something. Anything." Some of the tension went out of Heather's body. Her shoulders slumped. She threw the empty glass out into the yard, where it made a dull thump in the grass. "She always seemed untouchable. Above me. Above everyone. I just wanted to strike back. I wanted to make a mark on her."

"By killing four people?"

"That was never the intent. You're right. I did see her earlier in the night outside the house. She was with that older guy. And then later, when I went back to the house . . . I didn't know they were home. After the fire and everything, somebody told me about Andrea getting sick at the party. They left early and came home."

"It was still late. There were four people in there, four college students, and you didn't hear them? You didn't even think about it?"

"The house was quiet when I went in." She shuddered, reliving the memory. "Everyone had been drinking at that party. It was a blowout. It always was on Halloween. They must have all just gone to sleep after they put Andrea to bed. Maybe they all passed out. I expected to hear music or talking, something that would tell me they were home, but there wasn't anything. You know what we were all like back in college. We were never quiet. If the house was quiet, I figured they weren't home."

I shuddered as well, her words sending a deep chill through my body.

"They always left that back door unlocked. We all knew it. We used to warn them about it. Four girls living in a house with a back door that's never locked." She rubbed her hands together. "I didn't want to kill anyone. I was angry, irrational. I found a candle they left burning in the kitchen. I touched it to the curtain above the sink. The curtains were old, some gross polyester blend or something. They smoked a little, but they didn't catch right away. And then . . . *whoosh*. They went up. The flames were going so quickly I couldn't believe it. I thought about tearing the curtains down, throwing them in the sink, but I couldn't grab them, they were burning so fast." She looked up at me, my face reflected in the lenses of the sunglasses. "So I left."

"You left a fire going?"

"I watched from the outside. I was confused, and I thought I'd get in trouble. How could I explain any of it? And then . . . when I heard . . . when I heard someone scream from inside the house." She took a deep breath. "When I saw someone come to the window once the flames grew, someone who was inside and trying to get out, I made that call. I wanted to get them help, but it was too late. It was over." She scuffed her foot across the sealed wood of the deck. "I can still hear those voices, calling for help. I've lived with that, Nick. I've gone to therapy for it. Therapy can't erase things."

"My God, Heather." I had to walk away from her. I moved across the deck, my back to her. When I turned around, she remained in the same spot, her arms folded across her chest. "We *dated* after that. Back then . . . and now. We laid in bed together. We had sex, and all that time you knew what you had done. You knew what it did to me when Marissa died."

"I couldn't change the past. None of us could."

"You could have accepted responsibility."

Heather came forward and returned to her seat. She slumped into it, her shoulders drooping forward. "I was a mess back then. I was angry. I was jealous. You remember how I was. How I could be." She looked up at me and removed the sunglasses. I saw her eyes for the first time that day. They were clear and piercing. "I'm not like that anymore. That's not me, that person who set that fire."

"None of us are who we used to be," I said. "Or who we seemed to be."

And I thought of Marissa, who had also committed a crime when she was in college and failed to take responsibility for it. But one was an accident and one was murder. No, Heather hadn't intended to kill anyone. But she acted out of anger and jealousy. Four innocent people got in her way.

"I'm telling the police," I said.

She was out of the chair, reaching for me, placing her hands over mine so I couldn't move. "No," she said. "You don't have any real evidence, Nick. And I have children."

"Those four kids probably wanted to have children too."

Heather took a step back, letting go of my hands, and then with a sudden movement, she slapped me across the face. The blow surprised me, leaving a stinging sensation across my cheek and awakening the pain from my accident. I touched my nose, making sure it wasn't bleeding again.

Heather backed away from me, heading toward the door of her house, but she stopped before she lifted her hand to go inside.

"You're so good, Nick. Aren't you? You . . . Sir Galahad. Sitting on the sideline judging everyone else. Pining over Marissa these last twenty years while the rest of us lived. That's why I have kids. That's why I have *something* to live for. Don't tell the police, Nick. It won't help anyone."

Her eyes looked open and pleading. I saw through them for perhaps the first time to the person beneath. Someone scared. Someone who loved her children. Someone who in some strange and twisted way had always cared about me. Someone who killed and went on with life, passing as the most normal of people.

"Don't tell them, Nick," she said.

I turned and walked off the deck.

I sat in the car a long time. Thinking.

Thinking.

And then I drove to the police station.

CHAPTER SEVENTY-TWO

I spent an hour explaining everything to Reece, while he dispatched a car to Heather's house to take her in to the station. I told him about all of it: Nate's suspicions about the origin of the fire, the 911 call, Roger Kirby's admission that someone confronted Marissa on the night of the fire, and my long, unusual history with Heather.

When we were finished, he said he'd look into it. All of it. But he didn't sound that hopeful.

"That fire was a long time ago, Nick. Without a confession . . . it's tough to see how anyone gets convicted."

His words were a splash of cold water. I told myself I'd done all I could do.

Then I asked him how Jade was doing.

"She's already on her way to Hanfort," he said. "That's where the crime was committed. That's where she'll face the music."

"Will it be bad for her?" I asked.

He paused for a second. "As bad as having your son

run over and killed in the street? As bad as having your child killed in a fire? Not even close."

We shook hands. Again. I needed to get my dog.

I parked my rental car and prepared myself for the worst. The woman at the front desk didn't make me feel any better. When I gave her my name and the name of my dog, her face remained impassive. She held up an index finger and asked me to wait while she went to the back.

It couldn't be good. Not if she needed to go to the back.

It was never good when they went to the back.

He's just a dog, I told myself. Not like the people who died. Not like the children who were killed. *Just a dog. Just a dog.*

But I didn't believe it, not for a minute.

And when she led Riley out by a leash, I dropped down onto my knees.

"Oh, Riley," I said. "Are you really okay, boy?"

He looked at me impassively, his expression asking where I'd been and why I'd left him overnight among strangers. But when I reached out and rubbed his back and ears, he started licking my face.

"Is he really okay?" I asked.

"He's fine," the technician said. "We kept him over-night and checked him out. The doctor says no broken bones, no internal injuries. He slept well and ate this morning."

"What was wrong with him, then?" I asked.

"He's an old dog. He probably just got overexcited.

And he has a little lump on his head. Keep an eye on him for a couple of days, but chances are he's going to be fine."

I took Riley right home, and when we went inside I fed him his favorite food and gave him a treat from the cabinet. He ate more than normal and gulped the treat down like he'd never tasted anything so good before. We were both tired, and when the food was gone, he curled up in his bed and let out a long, contented sigh.

I needed to shower and change my clothes.

I needed to get my car fixed, even though I suspected it was totaled.

I needed to get back to work. I needed life to be normal again.

I emptied my pockets.

I found the piece of paper Jade had handed me in the police station the night before.

"Oh," I said.

Riley raised his head.

I unfolded it. In Jade's handwriting, the same handwriting on the note in Emily Russell's pocket, was written another address.

This one in Wisconsin.

Would I let the love of a lifetime pass me by again?

The watch sat on my nightstand. I picked it up, fastened it to my wrist.

"Riley?" I said. "Are you well enough for a road trip?"

ACKNOWLEDGMENTS

Thanks to all my friends and family for their love and support, especially Kristie Lowry and Kara Thurmond.

Thanks to all the readers, bloggers, reviewers, librarians, and booksellers who keep books and the love of reading alive.

Big thanks to Loren Jaggers and the entire NAL publicity team for getting the word out about my books. Special thanks to Jan McInroy for the thorough copyediting.

Huge thanks to my editor, Danielle Perez, for her ability to gently push me—and the book—in all the right directions.

Huge thanks to my agent, Laney Katz Becker, for her loyalty, drive, and friendship.

And special thanks to Molly McCaffrey for everything else.

SOMEBODY I USED TO KNOW

DAVID BELL

QUESTIONS FOR DISCUSSION

1. Nick is hung up on Marissa twenty years after her presumed death. Do you believe that someone could still have feelings for a college love after so much time? Do we ever forget our first real loves? Do you think part of the reason Nick hasn't been able to move past his relationship with Marissa is that he has idealized her and/or their relationship since she supposedly died?

2. Nick gets a great deal of happiness from his relationship with his stepson, Andrew. Do you think Nick has a significant role to play in Andrew's life?

3. Nick relies a great deal on Laurel. Do you think they have an equitable relationship in which they both benefit? Or is Nick taking advantage of Laurel?

4. Do you think the police handled the initial investigation of Marissa's death appropriately? Or did they make assumptions and overlook obvious clues?

5. Why do you think Nick and Heather maintain their on-again, off-again relationship? What is each of them getting from the other? Do you trust Heather's motives for being with Nick?

6. What do you think of the reason for Marissa's family disappearing? Do you think her parents did the right thing? How far would you go to protect your child from legal jeopardy?

7. The Maberrys lost a child and never really received justice for it. Do you empathize with them? Do you understand why they behave the way they do?

8. Jade has been through a great deal: the pregnancy, the accident, and then the adoption of her child. Do you think she can ever move on from these things and have a normal life?

9. Roger Kirby plays a pivotal role as a friend of the Minor family. Did you know or suspect he was covering up for them the whole time?

10. Were you surprised that Marissa was still alive? Do you think she's gotten off easy over the years, since she was able to have a normal life and raise her own children?

11. What do you think of Riley, Nick's dog? Were you surprised that he played such a heroic role at the end of the story?

12. What do you think is going to happen when Nick travels to see Marissa? Will they be able to resume their relationship after twenty years? What challenges will they face as they try to pick up where they left off?

Read on for an excerpt from David Bell's
latest novel of suspense,

SOMEBODY'S DAUGHTER

Available now from Berkley

CHAPTER ONE

Tuesday, 8:16 p.m.

The doorbell rang shortly after eight o'clock.

The doorbell almost never rang. Certainly not so late in the evening.

From the kitchen, Michael heard the scrape of silverware against plates, the opening and closing of the refrigerator as Angela put the leftovers away in preparation for Michael doing the dishes. It was their usual, long-agreed-upon routine for nights when she cooked.

Then the doorbell rang. At first the sound was so small, so distant and surprising, that Michael decided he'd imagined it. An auditory hallucination. Maybe two glasses clanked against each other in the kitchen, and he just thought it was the doorbell.

But then the bell rang again. Two times in a row. An

insistent ringing, a sound that said someone outside meant business about getting their attention.

Angela appeared in the kitchen doorway. Her hair was pulled back off her face, and she held her hands away from her body as though they were wet or dirty.

"Who is that?" she asked.

"I'm not expecting anyone."

"Can you get it? My hands are dirty."

"I've got it," Michael said. He looked at his watch. Eight sixteen. "Probably a kid selling something."

"A determined kid, apparently," Angela said as the bell chimed again. She smiled. "They must know who they're dealing with."

"What's that supposed to mean?" Michael held back a laugh as he said it. He knew exactly what Angela meant.

"They know you're an easy mark," she said. "You always buy from them. Candy bars, magazines. They love you."

"Should you go answer, then?" he asked. "You can be the bad cop, and I'll watch baseball."

"I don't mind what you do," she said, smiling wider. "I like that these kids know how to push your buttons."

"Admit it. You don't mind eating the chocolate I buy."

"Touché."

Michael started for the door.

"Hey," Angela said, stopping him. "Did you call your sister yet?"

"Not yet."

"Don't forget, okay? This is a big deal. Lynn's coming up on five years cancer free."

"I know, I know. You sent flowers, right?"

"Yes. But you still need to call. It will mean a lot to her."

"I will. I promise."

Michael felt light as he walked to the front of the house. He looked forward to watching some of a baseball game or maybe reading a book. He felt encouraged as he reflected on the continued good news about Lynn's health. Next week, he and Angela were going away, a trip to St. Simons Island, just the two of them. Summer was good. Languid. Less work. If they relaxed more, if they got the time away, maybe they'd finally have luck in their ongoing struggle to have a child.

If not, he wasn't sure how things would play out. He and Angela were both feeling the strain, the weight it was adding to their marriage. He hated that sex had become a chore, a duty to be performed with the specific goal of producing a baby. Michael so wanted to get back to normal.

Michael entered the foyer and opened the front door. The sun was dropping, the horizon orange and hazy with the heat that brushed across his face. Someone was grilling, the rich odor of sizzling meat reaching his nostrils.

It took him a moment to comprehend the reality of the figure on his porch. She paced from one side to the other, a cigarette in her mouth, arms crossed.

He couldn't find the words. He didn't know the words.

So he just said, "What the hell?"

She stopped pacing, removed the cigarette. She looked scared, haunted. Her eyes wide and flaring. "I need you, Michael. I need your help."

"I don't understand. Why are you even here?"

She took a step toward him, gesturing with the hand that held the burning cigarette. Michael caught a whiff of the smoke, leaned back as the cigarette came closer to his body.

She dropped it on the porch. The ash sparked as it hit the ground.

"I just need your help, Michael."

"You need to back up, Erica. You need to—you need to leave."

"Michael. My daughter. Someone kidnapped my daughter this morning."

CHAPTER TWO

"What is it, Michael?" Angela called from the kitchen. "Chocolate? Magazines?"

"I've got it," Michael said, his voice hollow and barely audible.

Michael moved onto the porch, pulling the door shut behind him. Erica stepped back, allowing Michael room. She started digging in the pocket of her jeans, which were dark and fitted, and brought out more cigarettes. While she shook one loose from the pack and flicked her thumb against the lighter, Michael took her in, observing the changes ten years had etched on his ex-wife. Some lines had formed around her eyes, some skin hung looser beneath her chin, but her shoulder-length hair showed no gray, and the cut looked more stylish and professional than the messy ponytail she had preferred in college. Michael noticed the gray Apple Watch on her wrist, the smartphone tucked in her pocket.

She looked like a grown-up. An adult. And the difference was striking.

She took a long drag on the cigarette and blew the smoke away from Michael. "You never liked this habit. I'd given it up until about twelve hours ago."

"What do you mean, your daughter?" Michael asked. "You have a daughter? How old is she?"

Erica's hand shook as she held the cigarette between her index and middle fingers. "Felicity. That's her name. Felicity."

"Your favorite show," Michael said, remembering. Erica coming to his dorm room after class, sprawling across his bed, her shoes kicked off, catching reruns of *Felicity*. She loved to analyze and debate the character's choices of men, wailed in distress when an episode played in which Keri Russell's hair was cut short.

Michael remembered it all. The late nights with friends in college. The drinking and the partying. Their histrionic fighting and the ensuing make-up sex.

The day of their wedding. And also the day a year later when he left.

All of it so long ago. When he looked back on that time, he thought they had both acted like children.

"None of this makes sense, Erica. I haven't seen you in ten years. I'm married."

"I know."

"You know? You can't just show up at my door like this."

"There's a man." She started pacing again, lifting the cigarette to her mouth, the tip glowing the same color as the sky while she dragged. "He's a music teacher at her school. He's odd. I think he liked her. Felicity. In an un-healthy way—you know? This man knows something."

Her words became more and more clipped, her gestures more frantic as she spoke. Ash fell off the cigarette and hit the concrete porch. Even when things had been at their best between them—many days in college, the early months of their marriage—Erica tended toward ex-aggeration. She had always managed to turn even the smallest misunderstanding—either with him or with someone else—into an operatic blowup.

Michael reached out, placed a hand on her arm. "Stop, Erica. Just stop and slow down."

She did. She looked at his hand where it held her arm near the crook of the elbow, his skin touching her skin for the first time in a decade.

Michael let go. But he said, "If someone you know is in trouble, you need to call the police. They can figure it out. I have to work tomorrow."

Erica paused for a moment. She dropped the ciga-rette, ground it under her sneaker, a new running shoe, and scuffed her foot, leaving a smear of dark ash across the concrete. Erica had run cross-country in high school, jogged three to five miles a day in college, even on morn-ings after late nights of partying. She'd always been ener-getic, almost frantic when she did anything—walking, studying, talking, having sex. She looked at Michael as if he didn't understand something fundamental. "The po-lice *are* looking. They've been looking all day. Do you know what happens if they don't find someone right away? Do you know what happens to the missing person? The child?"

"Erica—"

"I've been talking to the police constantly, answering questions about me and my finances and my personal life and everyone I've ever known. Including you."

"Me?"

"Everyone. Everything about my life. They look into everything when a child disappears. I've had to answer the most embarrassing questions. The most personal questions."

Michael took a step back. He reached behind him, his hand fumbling for the doorknob. *Baseball,* he thought. *A good book.* Michael craved those things. And needed to get back to them.

To his real life. Not somebody else's.

He saw a wasp's nest in the corner of the porch, where a support post met the roof. He had been supposed to knock the nest down the weekend before, but he hadn't, even though a wasp had managed to get inside and zip around the kitchen, throwing itself against the window above the sink until Angela swatted it with a magazine. The nest was bigger now. More wasps stirred, floated above their honeycombed dwelling. The odor of the cooking meat grew stronger as the wind shifted. The sky was transitioning from the day's blue to the evening's purple.

"You should go talk to them," he said. "The police. Go back to them. Listen to them. Tell them whatever they want to know. You were never one to keep secrets, so tell them anything that might help. I'm just a guy you don't know anymore. I can't help you."

Erica stared him down. While she did, her eyes filled with tears. She bowed her head, an exaggerated gesture like she was praying. The movement took him right back to their college days, to times she was upset and times they fought. In both the past and the present, the gesture reached something in Michael, summoning empathy and concern for the person before him. Erica could look so vulnerable at times, she seemed always to feel more deeply than anyone else. It hurt to look at her when she was in pain or distress.

And then she glanced up again, the tear-filled eyes meeting his. Her chin quivered.

"You have to help me, Michael. You have no real choice."

Her tone of voice had shifted. Gone was the manic edge, the revved-up energy. Erica sounded shaken, scared.

She spoke again, her voice just above a whisper.

"She's yours, Michael. Felicity is your daughter, and I need your help getting her back."

Ready to find
your next great read?

Let us help.

Visit prh.com/nextread

Penguin
Random
House